SENTINALS RISING

BOOK TWO OF THE SENTINAL SERIES

HELEN GARRAWAY

Published by Jerven Publishing

Cover by Jeff Brown Graphics

This is a work of fiction. Names, characters, organizations, places, events, and incidents are either products of the author's imagination or are used it. Any resemblance to actual events or persons, living or dead, is entirely coincidental.

eBook ISBN: 978-1-8381559-3-3

Print ISBN: 978-1-8381559-4-0

Sign up to my mailing list to join my magical world and for further information about forthcoming books and latest news at: www.helengarraway.com

First Edition

Created with Vellum

For Jennifer

I love you

HAPPY BIRTHDAY

Love Mum

CONTENTS

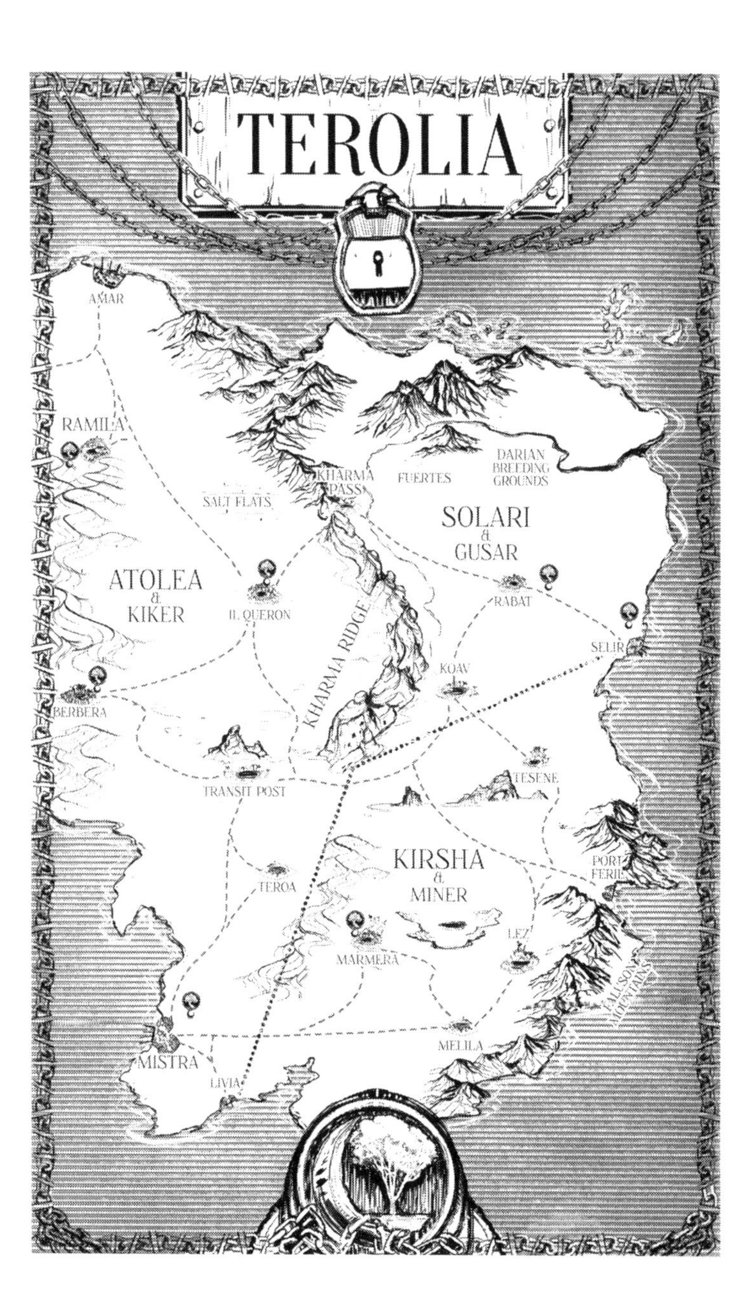
TEROLIA
AMAR
RAMILA
SALT FLATS
KHARMA PASS
FUERTES
DARIAN BREEDING GROUNDS
SOLARI & GUSAR
ATOLEA & KIKER
IL QUERON
RABAT
SELIR
KHARMA RIDGE
KOAV
BERBERA
TESENE
TRANSIT POST
KIRSHA & MINER
PORT FERIE
TEROA
MARMERA
LEZ
MOUNTAINS
MISTRA
MELILA
LIVIA

1

CHAPTERHOUSE, OLD VESPERS

Darkness crept over the chamber walls as the wax candle guttered in the lantern. Long fingers of shadow absorbed what little light illuminated the parchment Jerrol was skimming. Unable to read any more, he straightened up and stretched his aching back, his bones cracking in time with the creaking of his chair. That was his last candle, and he was getting nowhere; there were too many false trails and misleading references. But then, if he was trying to hide something, he would have done the same.

The stone walls of the musty room pressed down on him, and he flipped the manuscript shut and rubbed his eyes. How the scholars spent hours at a time buried underground amazed him. He had always preferred to work in the open cloisters. Though he supposed, if he were a true scholar, he wouldn't notice, but then he wasn't a scholar.

Rising, he straightened out the silver robes of the Lady's Order of Remargaren, which he wore over his silvery-green uniform of the Lady's Captain, picked up the lantern, and grimaced at the shimmer of the material poking out from the sleeves. He wore the same uniform the Sentinals wore, which was an unexpected side effect of his encounter with the Lady Leyandrii, who had claimed him as her Captain.

What that meant was yet to be determined. Still, Jerrol thought that it didn't bode well if the deity who protected their world believed she needed a new Captain, especially as the last Captain had so spectacularly disappeared with her when she had sundered the Bloodstone all those years ago.

At the same time, she had encased the men and women of her personal guard in a protective sleep within their sentinal trees for over three thousand years. Jerrol had accidentally woken one, a young man called Birlerion. At his behest, Jerrol had figured out how to wake more Sentinals, all of whom now reported to him as Leyandrii's Captain. One of which, Tagerill, stood guard at the top of the stairs.

The Sentinals were adamant that he should be guarded at all times; a duty Birlerion and Tagerill had taken upon themselves. Not that he was complaining; they were a reassuring presence behind his shoulder. He was only just beginning to discover who the Lady's Sentinals were as he watched them adapt to a strange world, coping with unimaginable losses. It was surprising how well they were adjusting, but then their last memories had been of war, so maybe just waking up was a miracle in itself.

He shivered.

The fact that there were men and women still protected by their trees, waiting for him to awaken them, terrified him.

Raising the lantern, Jerrol checked he had everything. As he turned to leave, the dying candle revealed a symbol over the door to the chamber that he had never noticed before; an engraving of a sentinal tree with the crescent moon curving underneath. It was a complete image; the tree's roots and branches reaching for the moon. A sentinal and the Lady, as one.

Instead of climbing the steps, he swung around and

descended to the next level of chambers below. The stone corridor wended its way into the shadows and he lifted his lantern to inspect the walls. Peering above the doors, he found the same symbol. A thought struck him, and he continued walking through the long corridor to the dead-end that had been stumping the scholars. He raised the lantern and there it was.

He reached for the ceiling, but he was too short. Casting about for something to stand on, he remembered seeing a stool in one of the upper rooms. Returning with the stool, he leant against the wall and touched the engraving. The walls around him immediately began to shake.

A low rumble grew, echoing in the narrow corridor, which culminated in the floor collapsing, taking Jerrol and his lantern down into the gaping darkness below. The high-pitched splintering of glass amongst the deep thudding of the stone slabs descending around him, marked the demise of his only source of light.

The fall took his breath away as he tumbled down a steep staircase, his shoulder taking the brunt of his landing. He slammed against a wall and came to an abrupt halt, gasping for breath. Tagerill, the Sentinal guarding him, called out in alarm from above as falling rubble blocked the narrow staircase, as well as all light and sound.

Heart racing, Jerrol untangled himself and choked on the dust as the ground settled. He rotated his shoulder, wincing at the twinge; at least it wasn't broken, though he knew it would be stiff later.

Cautiously, he felt around him; the darkness was absolute. He closed his eyes instead of straining them when there was nothing to see. He concentrated on his other senses as his friend Taelia always told him to do. She always said he depended too much on sight. He guessed she should know, seeing as she had been blind from birth. Well, here was a chance to test himself.

Jerrol listened, but all was silent except for the occasional shifting of debris. He shuffled around on his knees. If the steps were behind him, then the wall must be in front of him. He extended a trembling hand and bumped into the wall. Running his fingers over the smooth stone, he realised he wasn't facing a wall; it was a stone table.

The sides of the table were engraved, and his hesitant fingers explored the indentations, but he couldn't make sense of the patterns; Taelia was the expert on engravings. He levered himself up and ran his hands over the rough surface of the table, which was at waist height for him and much lower for a Sentinal.

Jerrol explored the table but couldn't discover anything except that it was stone and engraved. He fumbled for the wall and continued his tactile search, but his fingers weren't sensitive enough to tell him what he felt. Frustration ended his search and he groped his way back to the table. Placing both hands flat on the surface, he brushed the grit and debris off, sneezing as rising dust drifted in the air.

A flash of light blinded him for a moment, and then a vision of a black-haired warrior kneeling before the Lady filled his mind. They were surrounded by a grove of ancient trees, gilded by the full moon overhead. The Lady wore a long green gown, and her gilt-edged blonde hair curled around bare shoulders. Her emerald green eyes were focused on the man as she bestowed a sword on him, it looked ornate and heavy. The blade gleamed in the moonlight, and when the man stood and first took the weight, he adjusted his stance as he brought the sword up in front of his face in salute.

The light of the blade illuminated the distinctive curves of the man's face. A striking mix of angles and strength, with dark winged eyebrows that met above a straight nose. The expression of awe on his face morphed into one of acceptance. He reminded Jerrol of Birlerion, though he wasn't sure why. The man's deep green eyes met Jerrol's, and as their gaze locked Jerrol knew it was Guerlaire, the Lady's Captain before him. Guerlaire saluted Jerrol before handing the sword out toward him, hilt first.

Jerrol's hand rose of its own accord, and he braced to take the weight as Guerlaire had done, but it wasn't heavy. The blade shone, its edge promising a crystal sharpness that Jerrol knew would cut anything. The hilt of twisted silver fit his palm, and engraved just below the cross-guard was the symbol of the sentinal and the moon—the mark of the Lady.

His awareness of the chamber flooded back into his senses as the grove faded, and the velvety darkness engulfed him. Muffled voices called his name. They sounded rather anxious. As he turned back towards the stairs, the sword faded from his view, and a familiar weight pulled on his belt. He wondered if it would be visible when he returned to the light.

Ari popped into view; a shimmer of silver in the darkness. Chittering in excitement, he hovered above Jerrol's head; a small, furry cat-like creature with the reptilian features of a scaly tail and wings. Jerrol coaxed him down to his shoulder. "You heard the Lady, huh?"

Ari chittered and rubbed his face against Jerrol's cheek, making him grin. The muffled voices of his rescuers were getting more anxious.

"I'm fine," he shouted. His lips quirked at his definition of fine, considering he was trapped in a dark cell underground and on his own. He jumped back as more stone and gravel descended as his rescuers began to shift some of the rubble.

"Jerrol? Do you have room to move back? Some of these

slabs are rather large." Torsion's voice penetrated the rubble, edged with concern.

"Yes, I'm fine. I'm in a chamber down here. Carry on." Jerrol wasn't surprised that his friend and mentor was one of the first on the scene. Torsion had been watching over Jerrol for years, ever since Jerrol was a raw child grasping at life's choices. If it hadn't been for Torsion introducing him to the scholars and a fortuitous meeting with a King's Ranger showing him a taste of ranger life, he would never have considered leaving Stoneford and pursuing the opportunities in Old Vespers. Torsion had only been passing through, but he had taken Jerrol under his wing and set his feet on the path he now trod. He had much to thank him for.

Jerrol frowned. Now he came to think of it, the first time he had met Torsion, he had been chasing someone. He had ridden straight into an ambush, even some of the Stoneford guards had been injured. He pursed his lips; if he remembered right, his friends, Jennery and Bryce, had been involved. He'd have to ask them what they remembered. Had the Ascendants been searching for the means to overthrow Leyandrii and the king's rule even back then?

"Stay in that chamber, Jerrol. Don't explore any further." Scholar Deane Liliian sounded stern; she knew him well. Jerrol winced. As the head of the Remargaren Scholars, he was sure she had more important things to do than dig him out of a hole.

"It's pitch black down here, and I can't see a thing. I'm not going anywhere!" Jerrol shouted.

"Once we make a hole, we'll lower a lantern. This could take a while," Liliian warned.

"Yes, ma'am," Jerrol called back. He stroked Ari. "Tell Tagerill I'm fine."

Ari meeped and disappeared.

Jerrol sat with his back against the table and set to wait as patiently as he could. His mind drifted over recent events, and he rubbed the silver scar on his left palm, remembering the crystal he had found beneath the ancient Watch Towers. The Lady had led him to the first piece of the crystal, which had greedily drunk his blood before sinking into his hand. Maybe she would help him find the others.

He was an idiot! He had forgotten the benefit from absorbing the piece of crystal was that he could now hold light in his hand. He opened his left palm and a silvery glow hovered in the air above it. Twisting around, he inspected the table by the soft light. The engraving could be words, but not in a language he recognised.

Shifting to his knees, he massaged his aching thigh, a reminder of the injury he had taken rescuing King Benedict from an Ascendant plot to overthrow him. Since then, he had been wading through old manuscripts in the Chapter-house archives, recuperating and waiting for the king to return to Old Vespers and grant him an audience.

Tagerill distracted him as he called his name, and a dim glow marked the top of the mound of rubble. "Captain, we're going to lower a lantern."

"I'm ready," Jerrol shouted, positioning himself at the foot of where he thought the stairs were. He reached for the lantern and unhooked it. The rope slithered back up the rubble.

"We're lowering some water," another voice called. Jerrol thought they could have supplied something a bit stronger but called back an acknowledgement and waited for the bag to descend. He untied the bundle and retreated to the table. Climbing up onto the surface, he placed the lantern beside him as he unwrapped his package, revealing a flask of water and a meat-stuffed bread twist. He took a swig of water to clear his dust-clogged throat and started on the bread; he was starving.

Inspecting the sword in the lamplight, he admired its sharp edge, the fine workmanship and how well the hilt fitted his hand as if it had been created just for him. At least the sword was real and not just a dream. Though how he would explain how he'd come by it and whether they would let him keep it was another matter. The sword vibrated in his hand, and a sense of possessiveness pervaded his thoughts. Maybe the sword had other ideas.

Lifting the lantern, he peered around the chamber. Lines carved in the stone ceiling crisscrossed above him. They appeared to be the same gridlines he had seen in the ceilings at the Watch Towers, and he almost overbalanced as he tilted his head back. The reclining chairs in the towers suddenly made sense. He jumped down from the stone table, re-sheathing the sword, and moved towards the wall.

The symbol on the ceiling in the far corner beckoned in the lamplight. Until he had a search party on hand, that symbol would remain untouched. He turned back towards the steps, as more rubble clattered down. They had a way to go yet before he would be getting out.

Placing the lantern at the head of the table, Jerrol climbed up and lay down. He stared at the ceiling, conscious of the sword at his waist and the cold stone beneath his back. The chill faded from his awareness as he focused on the lines crossing the ceiling; the junctions glowed in his mind.

And then he tensed as an overwhelming expanse of space and twinkling stars surrounded him; an unending vista of night-black darkness dotted with bright sparkles, flickering in the distance. Only it wasn't empty. A swathe of light comprised of glowing, questing strands stretched out above him. The Veil, wrapping their world in a protective sheath, preventing harmful magic from returning.

He was drawn towards the swaying tendrils, drifting seductively above him. He relaxed as the Lady whispered his name, sensing other minds tinged with age and weariness; guardians watching through the millennia.

"My Captain, follow the trail. Find those who have lost the way. Help them," the Lady beseeched him.

"Who must be found?" Jerrol asked, frowning in confusion.

"*You will know. There are others here; it is not safe to speak.*" Her voice faded along with the vast emptiness, and Jerrol returned to the sound of voices and light and someone shaking his arm. He opened his eyes to be blinded by a lantern held over his face.

"I suppose it makes sense to sleep if it is dark, but you'd think he would notice his rescuers have arrived," Torsion's voice said from above him.

Jerrol sat up and swung his legs over the side of the table. His body dragged at him; a familiar heaviness after the unexpected vastness of the beyond.

"Took your time, didn't you?" He grinned at his rescuers, relieved they had arrived. Led by his friend Torsion; tall and muscular, his broad shoulders draped in scholar's robes.

Torsion's grip tightened on his arm; his fingers digging deep. "I wish you wouldn't make it so difficult for us to help you."

"It wasn't deliberate," Jerrol protested, "and anyway, I wasn't sleeping. I was studying the grid lines in the ceiling." He pointed upwards.

"In the dark, with your eyes closed," Torsion said, curling his lip as he raised his lamp to look up above him and indicating that Jerrol's lantern had gone out. He sighed. "Jerrol, are you sure you didn't hit your head? There are no grid lines in the ceiling."

Jerrol glanced up to where he could clearly see the lines in the light of the lamp, but he held his tongue. "Honestly, I'm fine, just a few bruises. I'll be glad to get out of here and have a bath."

Torsion peered around him, inspecting the room, and Jerrol watched amused as he crouched by the stone table and ran his fingers over the engravings. Torsion started muttering under his breath. "Look! Look at this text. We've never found enough to be able to translate it. But now, this will give us the key."

"Glad to have been of assistance," Jerrol replied as Tagerill arrived at his side.

Torsion ignored him, engrossed in his inspection.

"Captain, are you alright?" Tagerill asked, gripping his arm.

"Fine, be glad to get out of here and leave the exploration to the scholars."

"I should think so. You must be starving. It took all day to clear the rubble, and there is still much excavation to be done," Tagerill said.

"Well, let's get out of here then and leave it to the others," Jerrol suggested, sudden exhaustion overwhelming him. He didn't think Torsion noticed them leave as he accepted Tagerill's assistance to climb over the rubble to the steps they had cleared, and allowing eager hands to pull him up. Liliian gave him a keen inspection before she led him back to a guest room and sent him off to the baths.

No one commented on his new sword, though Tagerill opened his mouth to say something before closing it when he met Jerrol's glare, so Jerrol left it out of his report.

2

CHAPTERHOUSE, OLD VESPERS

The next morning, Jerrol entered the main hall and squinted at the shafts of sunlight that shone through the tall windows down the east wall. Scholars sat at long wooden tables set up throughout the room. Some sat singly, engrossed in ancient parchments, and others in groups deep in some vital discussion.

He spotted his friend, Torsion, seated at the end of a table, talking to a slight young woman opposite him. As he watched, Torsion waved his hands in the air to punctuate his point, and Jerrol headed towards him.

The young woman lifted her head, flicking her cloudy brown hair out of her face in a well-practised motion and smiled as Jerrol approached. She always seemed to know when he was in the vicinity. His heart thumped.

"Jerrol, join us." She patted the seat next to her, interrupting Torsion's flow. Her voice had a tinge of desperation to it, and Jerrol wondered how long Torsion had been pontificating. "How are you feeling this morning?"

"I'm fine. Thank you." Jerrol slid along the bench next to

her. "Taelia, my dear, good morning. Torsion, what bee is in your bonnet this fine morning?"

"Bees? There are no bees in here," Torsion replied, scowling at the interruption. "I said that the king should appoint a new minister, since there has been no news of Chancellor Isseran. The king should replace him and move on. Trade is suffering, and the merchants are nervous. We need a chancellor to release the docks and get us back in business."

"I'm sure the king will sort everything out soon enough. Give him time. He has a lot to deal with," Jerrol soothed as he snagged a mug of coffee off a passing tray.

Taelia leaned over, and his chest clenched as her curls drifted in front of his nose; he inhaled the scent of apples and warm spice.

"I hope you are having more for breakfast than a mug of coffee," she said as the aroma of fresh coffee permeated the air. "You should be more careful, Jerrol; you could have been hurt yesterday."

"How did you manage to get through that wall?" Torsion asked, scowling at him. "We've been trying for weeks."

"I took a leaf out of Taelia's book." Jerrol's voice warmed and his eyes twinkled as he watched her. Petite and slender, she had beautiful, expressive turquoise eyes that made him catch his breath; eyes, which, unfortunately, could not see anything. "I found an engraving and touched it."

"You did what?" Taelia asked.

Jerrol leaned forward. "I've never noticed it before, but there is an engraving over each door; an image of a sentinal tree and the Lady's moon. So, I went to check the dead end, and there it was again."

"An image," Torsion repeated. "Like the ones at the Watch Towers?"

"I don't know. What did you find up there?"

"Come to my rooms and I'll show you," Torsion said, beginning to rise.

"Not until he's eaten something," Taelia said.

Jerrol laughed as Taelia grasped his sleeve to keep him seated. "That's rich, from you! When discoveries are looming, I believe you are the tenacious one, are you not? The one who forgets to eat when a knotty problem presents itself?"

"That was only once," she responded, her voice clipped.

Jerrol chuckled and glanced at Torsion. "It has been more than once we've dragged her away from those tablets, hasn't it, Torsion?"

Torsion scowled at them both. "Too right, and how come you haven't said two words to me all the time we've sat here but as soon as Jerrol turns up, you have lots to say?"

"But Torsion." Taelia widened her eyes at him. "You were in full flow; I couldn't get a word in edgeways!"

Jerrol reached over to punch his friend's arm. "You do realise that no one in their right mind would interrupt you once you start speechifying?"

Torsion straightened, offended. "What about those Sentinals of yours? Are you still allowing them to run about freely? You know nothing about them, yet you have them guarding the king."

"They are the Lady's, Torsion. Why wouldn't I trust them with the king?"

"You need to be more careful, Jerrol. I'm telling you there is something strange about them."

Taelia laughed. "Of course, they are strange. They're over three thousand years old; they come from a different time. I would have thought you'd be all over them; firsthand knowledge of the Lady at your fingertips."

Torsion physically growled. "If they would tell us, yes. That Birlerion is as slippery as a bathhouse soap. He knows a lot more than he is sharing. When are you going to force him to tell us, Jerrol?"

"Give them time, Torsion. They have much to adjust to. The Lady trusts them and so should you. Anyway, I wanted to ask you something. Do you remember when we first met in Stoneford? You were chasing a group of people who had stolen something. Do you remember what they stole?"

Torsion gaped at him. "What?"

Jerrol grimaced. "I know it was a while ago, but it was that time when you were injured, along with Bryce."

"Jerrol, that was years ago. How am I supposed to remember that? And what does that have to do with the Sentinals?"

"Nothing. Only I wondered what they stole to make you chase them clear across Vespiri. It must have been important. They escaped as well, if I remember right."

Torsion shook his head. "The things you come out with. I have no idea. And why are you still here pretending to be a scholar? Don't the rangers need you?"

"Why, Torsion, anyone would think you don't want my company," Jerrol said, fluttering his eyelashes outrageously.

"Stop messing about and come and tell me about these symbols, and I'll show you what I've found so far."

"I will tell you," Jerrol said with an air of someone bestowing a favour, "if you grant me the chance to finish my coffee and enjoy a stroll in the gardens with my favourite scholar here." Taelia's face reflected her pleasure, though Jerrol knew she didn't realise how much her face showed her thoughts.

"I will accept your kind invitation if you eat something first," Taelia said.

Torsion's scowl deepened as he stood. "Fine. It's obvious my presence is not required. I will see you both later." He stalked off, his back rigid and his robes flapping around him as he left the hall.

"Oh dear, I do hope we haven't offended him," Taelia said, her face reflecting her concern.

Jerrol laughed again and sipped his coffee and then, at Taelia's urging, went to choose something off the buffet at the head of the room.

Later that morning, Jerrol knocked on Torsion's office door. He waited, listening to the muffled movements inside before Torsion called out for him to enter. He took a deep breath and opened the door.

"Torsion, here I am, as requested. It seems ages since we were last in the same place at the same time," Jerrol said as he closed the door behind him.

"Well, if you will gallivant all over the place causing havoc, it's not surprising," Torsion replied. His rooms were full of the usual clutter; books and scrolls overflowed from an overloaded desk and were piled on chairs and even the floor.

"I was only gallivanting, as you put it, because I was searching for you."

Torsion raised his eyebrows in surprise. "Oh? Why were you searching for me? You know where I live," he said, indicating his rooms.

"Yes, and you are in them as often as I am in mine."

"More often, I think. You need to speak with your boss about having some time off. You're looking a bit peaky, lad."

"Oh, it's nothing, been on the road a while." Jerrol waved away his concern. "I wanted to speak to you about the councils and ask if you'd noticed any changes."

"The councils?" Torsion asked, turning away from Jerrol and picking up a piece of paper.

"Yes. I know you often sit on the council at Velmouth

when you are at the towers. Jason said you had been gone for months. They were getting concerned because they hadn't heard from you. Did anything happen? Were you alright?" Jerrol watched Torsion's reaction. Birlerion was adamant that he had seen Torsion at the Watch Towers, though at the time, he had called him Clary. Birlerion had suffered a severe beating, and Tagerill thought he'd had a concussion and had dismissed his claim. Jerrol wasn't so sure.

Torsion laughed at him and began rolling up the paper. "Like what? As you can see, I'm fine. I spent some time up at the towers before returning here. I told Jason I wouldn't return via Stoneford. He worries over nothing. I find the Watch Towers fascinating. I don't know why scholars don't visit more often."

"Liliian said you referred to it as a care home for old men and there was no point in scholars visiting," Jerrol said, watching him fiddle with the papers.

"Nonsense. Yes, the Watchers are ancient, but the buildings have a lot to tell us. It is as important as the catacombs here, from a historical sense. They are an important part of our history."

"I agree. I went up there searching for you."

"You did?" Torsion stilled. "And what did you find?"

"What would you expect me to find?"

"A tired and forgotten outpost of history, filled with dying old men."

"And Ain'uncer?"

"Ain'uncer?" Torsion repeated, his grip tightening on the scroll of paper in his hand.

"Surely you've met the man running the towers?"

Torsion shook his head. "No, you mistake me. I've met the warden, but I didn't know he was called Ain'uncer. But then, I don't tend to speak with the staff. I spend my time in the towers. Each room is slightly different and they are all steeped in history. I am gradually recording all the features. Look," Torsion tossed the paper aside and began unrolling an unwieldy scroll across his desk, weighting the corners to keep it from rolling back up.

"What did you make of the grid in the ceiling?" Jerrol asked.

"Grid? I haven't seen a grid. But I did find this image. Look, these are the images I've captured so far from the West Tower. All the rooms are occupied, but the Watchers never wake up, let alone speak."

Leaning forward, Jerrol examined the drawings. They were different from the rooms he had visited, except for the symbol of the tree and the moon. Jerrol pointed to it. "That's the one I touched. What do you think it means?"

"Some representation of the Lady, I suppose. That image is present in every room. But as you can see, there are no grids in these rooms. Where did you see them?"

"In the South Tower there are lines across and down the ceiling, forming a grid. It was sectioned out, and the Watcher was talking about co-ordinates."

"The Watcher spoke?" Torsion straightened.

"Yes. He was quite peeved that I wasn't writing down his report," Jerrol said, remembering the notebook in his room.

"Do you remember the co-ordinates?" Torsion picked up the letter opener he had used to weight the corner and the scroll began to curl back up.

"Goodness, no, you know what my head is like for numbers."

"Better than you would have most believe."

Jerrol grinned. "You know me so well! I don't remember. I made a note of them on a pad. It's in my room."

"Maybe you can show me later?" Torsion said, rolling the scroll up.

"Of course. I'm supposed to be down in the archives,

now," Jerrol agreed as he turned to leave the room. He paused at the door. "Torsion, momentous things are happening; the Watches are under siege, the Guardians are failing. Are you sure you haven't seen anything at the towers?"

Torsion looked up from the scroll and shrugged. "I'm not sure what you expected me to see. The Watchers never speak. The tower staff do their best to look after them, but it is a dusty, forgotten place, and nothing exciting happens there."

Jerrol nodded slowly in acceptance. "Very well. Meet you later for dinner?" he suggested as he pulled the door shut behind him.

Torsion stood staring at the door for a long time after Jerrol had left.

3

KING BENEDICT'S PALACE, OLD VESPERS

The summons for Jerrol to attend King Benedict arrived later that day. Jerrol dressed, selecting a clean uniform. He had purchased a ranger's uniform in the king's colours, but as soon as he touched them, they transformed back into the Lady's silver-green. He gave up. The Lady was determined. He buckled on his belt and sheathed Guerlaire's sword, wondering whether he would ever find out what Prince Kharel had done with his sword. He had lost his sword when the prince had him arrested for treason. He grimaced at the irony. Now the prince was incarcerated for treason, having tried to overthrow his father, the king.

Birlerion, a lean and capable Sentinal, stood guard outside Jerrol's room. High cheekbones curved down to a stubborn chin, which was softened by a dimple. His black hair had grown since he had been awoken and now touched his collar and accentuated his striking features. He had been waiting to escort Jerrol from the Chapterhouse back to the barracks. The Sentinals were taking their Captain's safety seriously, and Jerrol had to admit it was reassuring having

Birlerion behind his shoulder. His predatory grace was a silent comfort. Calm and assured, he was as different to his irrepressible brother, Tagerill, as he could be.

Arriving at the king's private chambers, having passed Fonorion's inspection, the Sentinal Jerrol had assigned as personal bodyguard to the king, Jerrol now paced the antechamber.

When Darris, the king's steward, finally called Jerrol, he was considering trying out his supposed new powers over the king. The king had invoked the Oath when his life was in peril. He had made Jerrol his Oath Keeper in an attempt to use an ancient protection to help defeat the Ascendants. Maybe he should remind the king he was his Oath Keeper, and could request the king's presence at any time, just as the king could call on Jerrol.

He entered the chamber and paused as he saw the image of the tree and moon engraved in the wood panel of the door. His fingers traced the depression; he had never noticed it before. As King Benedict said his name, he turned and stepped over the threshold, closely followed by Darris.

He dropped to his knee and bent his head.

"Rise," Benedict said.

Jerrol inspected the king keenly. He was much improved from their last meeting. He had regained some weight, though he was still thinner than he had been. At least he looked healthier, though his dark hair now glinted with streaks of grey. His blue eyes were alert; the intelligent wit apparent behind his clear gaze.

They stood assessing each other for a moment before King Benedict spoke. "I don't believe I've released you from my service," he said, inspecting Jerrol's uniform.

Jerrol grimaced. "Ah, about that, sire. I'm afraid the Lady has other ideas. As she has claimed me as her Captain, she has decided I should wear her colours. I have tried to change them, sire, but no matter what I put on, she changes the colours to this. She seems to be very stubborn."

"And what happened to your sword? I seem to remember you had a fine sword, which I am sure I presented to you last year?"

"I lost it, sire, that morning in the throne room when you attempted to invoke the Oath and Prince Kharel interrupted us."

"Shame. That was a good sword; expensive, too. I suppose you expect me to replace it?"

"Not at all, sire. The Lady has provisioned me, and I am sure the prince will return it in due course," Jerrol replied. His king seemed in a whimsical mood. He wasn't sure where this conversation was going, but he had a feeling he was going to suffer for the way he had treated the king the last time they had met. To combat the influence of a drug the Ascendants had forced on the king, Jerrol had given him alcohol. Unfortunately, the side effect was that it had made the king violently sick.

"You had to use the best brandy, didn't you?" Benedict said, pressing his lips together.

"Sire?" Jerrol blinked.

"You do realise I can no longer stand the smell of brandy; it makes me want to heave," Benedict said. "I can't enjoy my favourite drink, and it's your fault," he finished, pointing his finger at Jerrol, which Jerrol thought was a bit unfair.

Darris, the third member of their private meeting, snorted. He was grey-haired and slightly stooped, but his gaze was sharp and observant. Darris had been at the king's side for the entirety of his reign and was a constant presence.

Jerrol's lips twitched. "Forgive me, sire. I used the only antidote to hand at the time."

Benedict glared at both at them. "You think it's funny?" he snapped.

Darris wiped the smile off his face. "No, sire," he replied, though his eyes still twinkled.

"Your first task, my Oath Keeper, is to find me a new drink. I expect you to find a replacement."

"Yes, sire," Jerrol replied.

Benedict narrowed his eyes. "Jerrol," he paused. "Thank you," he said, his face grave. "If you hadn't arrived when you did, we wouldn't be here today. Our world would be in a very precarious position, indeed."

"Sire, I only did what anyone would have done," Jerrol argued.

"No; no one else came close. The Lady picked well."

Jerrol silently disagreed, but considering the dire circumstances in which the king had invoked the King's Oath, an ancient legend that many people no longer believed in (or had even forgotten), Jerrol had assumed he had just been the only person available at the time. The words of the Oath ran through his head:

'Do your Duty, Never Falter, Never Fail.

Lady, Land, and Liege obey.

All are one, Entwined ascending

Keeper's Oath Never Ending.'

The words were carved in the wall above the king's throne. The king had spoken the words and Jerrol had been bound by the Oath.

"Sire, I don't fully understand what being the Oath Keeper means," Jerrol said with caution, not expecting to like what the king was going to say.

"I'm not surprised. I am not aware of the Oath Keeper's duties being written down anywhere. The information is restricted to the reigning monarch and is only passed down through the reigning line. Both of you sit." The king gestured to the chairs in front of his desk.

Jerrol sat.

"I'd offer you a drink," the king said with an edge to his voice, "but seeing as I am abstaining, so can you."

"Yes, my liege." Jerrol could see the king was going to milk this for as long as possible. "At least it will save your treasury some money," Jerrol offered. "That brandy was extortionately over-priced."

King Benedict choked. "You go too far!" he said, his voice shaking. "That brandy was worth every penny." He tried to glare at Jerrol but failed miserably as he began to chuckle.

Jerrol grinned in return.

"Oh dear," the king said as he wiped his eyes, "that certainly feels better. I haven't laughed in a long time. But to business." He nodded his thanks as Darris poured out a glass of water for each of them. "The King's Oath is the bond between my crown and the Lady and the Land. It is a final defence against that which threatens us, and once invoked empowers an individual to act in the king's name should the king not be able to. You can see why the decision to invoke the oath is not taken lightly.

"I invoked the Oath, the only time I am aware that it has ever been used, because my son had managed to isolate me, and my voice was no longer being heard. There should be at least one person who could always gain access to me and if necessary, speak in my voice; no one should be able to prevent it. The Oath Keeper has that right. You are my representative. You'll be able to make your way into my presence at any time of day or night. I trust that you will use that power appropriately." The king stared at Jerrol until Jerrol nodded in agreement.

"Of course, sire."

"We'll have to test it later. I've always wanted to see how it works. You are responsible for making me keep *my* oath. Should you believe I am not honouring my oath to my people or the Lady, is it your job to intervene, as you did in New Vespers. The Oath will not be broken until one of us dies."

Jerrol stared at him, aghast. "Sire?"

"The Guardians don't do oaths by half; that's why it has never been used before, I expect. No one trusted anyone enough to bind themselves for a lifetime."

A lifetime bound by an oath. Jerrol shuddered at the thought. Though he had restored the king to his throne, and defeated the Ascendants plot to overthrow him, they still had much of his kingdom to reclaim. Maybe having the king's voice would be useful.

"The Ascendants are not finished yet. They still control Deepwater and the Watch Towers."

Benedict nodded in agreement. "We have much work to do, and I am afraid it is only just beginning."

Jerrol grimaced. "I agree, sire. The purpose of the Watch Towers and the Watchers has been forgotten. We should be stimulating the Watchers to report their sightings, not letting them vegetate.

"I would like to suggest that you ask Scholar Deane Liliian to reassess who should run the towers. They should be under the king's jurisdiction. I asked Lord Jason to send a unit to take over from the warder currently in situ, but he doesn't have the manpower. Many of his men were incapacitated by the Ascendants spells. It will take time to undo their work. He is already understaffed, coping with the border patrols and the smugglers; he needs reinforcements. The Watchers are at risk, and we have left them at the mercy of whoever is behind this uprising, unprotected and forgotten."

King Benedict nodded as Jerrol continued. "There is also

the Veil. I left Sentinal Saerille up at the towers repairing it, which is only a temporary measure. I need to get back up there and seal her repairs."

"Is there anyone else who can help with the repairs for now? I need you here while we assess the Watches."

"I'll have to check with the Sentinals, sire. I ought to go and awaken the East Watch and Marchwood Sentinals, at a minimum. We need to find out where the others are. They should all be awake."

"How are the Sentinals taking their awakening? It can't be easy to find that all you knew and loved is lost. We must have changed significantly in three thousand years."

"They're taking it better than expected, though they are still a little disoriented. Liliian is in her element; living history in her hands. She will be able to fill in many gaps in our records."

King Benedict pursed his lips. "Still, we need to focus on current events, not just the past."

"I agree, sire. At least Simeon now holds the Guardianship in Greenswatch. Versillion's report that the Guardianship had transferred safely was a relief. If only we could retrieve Deepwater as easily. But at least we have one Watch regained and back under the protection of the Lady."

There was so much to do, Jerrol wasn't sure where to start. "I have spent the last week in the archives searching for any mention of the Oath Keeper and the Guardians, but there is nothing that the scholars don't already know, sire. We still have a Watch without its Guardian; we have to find out how to reinstate it. The Land is suffering, and the Lady grieves."

The king sighed deeply. "I fear you are correct. A Lady's Captain and an Oath Keeper at the same time are landmark portents. The loss of one Watch guardian, not to mention many others, is unheard of. I will consider what is best for the

Watches and the Watchers. We must protect them and the Veil. I will speak to Liliian about reinstating a chapterhouse at the towers."

"And sire," Jerrol paused as he contemplated the king. "I believe there are broader issues afoot. We need to confirm where Prince Kharel fits into all this. Was he using the Ascendants' rebellion as a front for his personal ambitions or were they using him? He wasn't listed in that notebook I found when I was following Chancellor Isseran. Commander Nikols said he gave it to Prince Kharel. We need to retrieve it, sire, as it listed all those affected by the Ascendant's spells and their keywords; we need it to unspell those we can."

"Get Nikols searching for it. We need to know who we can trust in Old Vespers."

"Yes, sire. I gave Healer Francis the list of those I could remember and explained how to unspell them with the keywords, but I don't think your son was enspelled, sire."

Benedict nodded; his face inscrutable at the mention of his traitorous son. Jerrol knew the king had been coldly furious when the extent of his son's treachery had been exposed. Icily rigid in his dealings with his son, Benedict had focused his pent up anger on regaining control of his kingdom.

He had demonstrated his grip by appointing a new Commander of the King's Justice, the man responsible for the internal security of Vespiri. Jerrol now reported to Commander Fenton as the Captain of the Sentinals. And yet he was sure Commander Nikols believed Jerrol still reported to him as a Captain of the King's Rangers. Jerrol felt a headache brewing.

He ploughed on. "I can confirm Chancellor Isseran is one of those Ascendants. He demonstrated some of the Ascendant's abilities, more than once, including his escape. Momentum is building behind the Ascendants for their own purposes. They were attacking the Guardians, with the Lady as the ultimate target. Sire, I am sure they are searching for something that they believe will help them take power from you and the Lady. I don't think this is over."

Benedict frowned in thought. "I will speak to Liliian. She will know the best way to help us search for whatever it is the Ascendants are looking for. We need to find out what our enemies know that we don't. For now, let the scholars focus on the archives. You need to awaken the Sentinals and find out what they know about the Ascendants. I think we need to keep you under wraps for as long as possible." The king's eyes glinted. "You ought to know one of the other, ah, shall we say, peculiarities of being the Oath Keeper."

"Yes, sire?" Jerrol asked with some suspicion.

"The words of the Oath carved into the wall of my throne room… they will start to glow whenever you are in the room."

"What?" Jerrol gasped.

"Yes, it's supposed to get a little excited whenever an Oath Keeper is present. I've never seen it," the king said, clasping his hands before him. His face brightened again. "That's another thing we can test."

Jerrol held his head in his hands. How many more things was the king going to find for him to test? The fact that there was an Oath Keeper wouldn't be secret for very long.

King Benedict stood, signalling that the meeting was at an end, and Jerrol leapt to his feet.

"You have your orders. We'll meet again next week. Oh, and Jerrol," the king had one last parting shot. "I expect Liliian knows that there is an Oath Keeper, because when you accepted the Oath, your acceptance was felt and heard in every corner of the world. People may not know who the Oath Keeper is, but those who know the legends know that the Oath was invoked and that it was accepted."

4

OLD VESPERS

Was home still home even if he didn't recognise it?

Tagerill stared down at the sprawling city of Old Vespers. It had been called Vespers in his day; there was only one city with the name then. His brow furrowed as he traced the unfamiliar streets and buildings. The whole shape and feel of the city felt wrong. Even the sounds and smells were different.

He missed the soft-toned quarter bells from the Chapterhouse bell tower. Gone was the gentle scent of the Lady's roses, which had perfumed the air and uplifted everyone's spirits. Gone was the delicate bridge that had gracefully arched over the city; its fragile structure sparkling like gossamer threads in the evening sunlight.

Instead, a bustling practical city with the sound of a different bell, much higher in pitch than he remembered, in the single golden tower of the Chapterhouse, chiming the passing of the day. A new palace, with admittedly delicate spires, sat above the town, somehow aloof without the link to the Chapterhouse. The tang of the sea mingled with the aromas of a working city; hard-earned sweat and coal fires.

He smiled ruefully. Maybe his memory was a bit selective, but still, he missed his home and his family. They had teased Captain Guerlaire something rotten when he had built that bridge. But the Captain had persisted, and what he had built had exceeded all expectations and silenced his harshest critics. Tagerill was still unclear what its purpose had been, but its physical presence linking the Chapterhouse to the palace had been jaw-droppingly beautiful. Such a delicate structure from an intensely physical and practical man. All lost now.

No one living knew what had happened, but the Captain and many Sentinals had been lost with the Lady when she destroyed the Bloodstone, causing a Veil to descend around their world, banishing all magic; a physical protection against the undisciplined use of magic and its destructive forces.

Tagerill had spent the last three thousand years cocooned in a sentinal; a tall silver-trunked tree that guarded the Lady's memory and her Guardians, until the new Captain had awoken him and returned him to duty in this time of need. He had recently reaffirmed his commitment to the Lady and King Benedict of Vespiri, and today he had a 'day off', though he wasn't quite sure what he was supposed to do with it.

His friend, Jennery, had tried to convince him to spend the day in the tavern, find a wench, and have some fun. Fun. Tagerill chewed thoughtfully on a blade of grass as he lay back on the tufted turf and stared up at the blue sky above him. Oh, he liked a drink now and then, and this lighter ale they drank today—he was starting to acquire quite a taste for it. He missed the warmth that good company provided, but he felt adrift. He'd rather be guarding the Captain, who seemed to be a magnet for trouble.

Captain Haven, the new Lady's Captain, was a worthy captain. Astute, decisive, and a skilled fighter. A mite smaller than the previous incumbent, but no less powerful because of it. The Captain listened and took advice, which Tagerill found refreshing, and he was considerate of those around him. Take today, for example. Tagerill had a day off. The Captain had said, *Take a break, find your bearings.* He was observant; he had noticed Tagerill's discomfort in Old Vespers.

Tagerill pondered the king's decision to appoint a new Commander of the King's Justice. The King's Justice was responsible for domestic security and the safety of the king. The Sentinals reported to the Commander via the Captain. Tagerill hadn't warmed to the new man who now controlled their lives. Such an aloof and coldly controlling man, who was as different to the Captain as possible.

He breathed in the balmy autumn air and wondered why he hadn't followed Jennery's advice. He didn't want to be on his own. Tensing, he thought of his sister, Marianille, who was still missing, presumed dead, along with many other Sentinals. He was luckier than most, considering the Captain had only woken a total of ten Sentinals out of over one hundred. Tagerill shuddered. At least his brothers, Birlerion and Versillion, were alive and awake.

The city may not be the one he remembered, but the Lady was still present, and she expected her Sentinals to guard it. Tagerill watched the fluffy white clouds slowly drift across the sky, morphing from one shape into another as the winds up above drove them. They changed shape as a result of unseen forces, but they were still clouds. So be it. He would spend his day off learning this new city as well as, if not better than, he had known the old.

Decision made, he rolled to his feet and began walking back down the hill towards the city. He raised his hand to shade his eyes, glinting silver in the brilliant sunlight, as he heard a horse galloping recklessly behind him. A woman was trying to rein the horse in and keep her seat whilst trying to keep her hat on. She lost both as the horse swerved away from Tagerill and jinked her out of her saddle. She landed with a breath-stealing thump on the grass, and she lay winded for a moment before beginning to gasp as her horse shook itself and galloped off, no doubt back to its nice, comfortable stable.

Tagerill knelt by the woman and offered a hand. "Are you alright, my lady?" he asked as he helped her sit up. She waved a hand as she leaned into him, gasping, her hand holding her side.

"Try to relax, take deep breaths. Count to three as you breathe in and out," Tagerill soothed. The lady threw him a disgusted glance as she tried to bring her breathing under control.

Tagerill's lips twitched as he took in her dishevelled state. Her blonde hair straggled around her face, escaping the confines of the knot she had tied it in, her hat long gone with the horse. She wasn't young. The fine lines at the corner of her eyes and mouth indicated that she had experienced life. Tugging her grass-stained habit, she revealed more of her creamy skin hidden beneath, instead of covering it. Shuddering, she caught her breath and stiffened as she realised that she lay in the arms of a stranger and sat up out of his embrace.

Her rueful blue eyes flicked up to his face. "I thank you for your concern." Her voice was deep and rich and her eyes widened as she stared at him. His silver eyes gave him away.

"Are you hurt?"

"Just my pride and a few bruises. If you would be so kind as to help me up?"

Tagerill lent her a strong arm and, holding her waist,

helped her stand. She wavered and he tightened his grip. She looked up and blushed as she met his concerned gaze.

"Oh, please, I can stand," she murmured, pushing against his chest, and Tagerill released her immediately, keeping a hand ready should she need it. She patted her hair in horror as she realised her disarray. "Oh!" She lifted her chin as she moved further away.

Tagerill grinned. "May I say, you look enchanting and not at all as if you fell off a horse."

A reluctant chuckle escaped her lips as she glanced around for her steed, or maybe her hat. "It was my own fault. I should have been paying more attention. She got away from me. That will teach me. Was she alright?"

"She seemed fine and has probably reached her stable by now. May I offer you an escort back to the city?"

The woman held her hand to her face. "And caused a panic, no doubt. I'll never live this down." She smiled her thanks. "Your escort to the palace would be appreciated. I assume you are billeted there, too?"

"Indeed, Tagerillion of the Captain's Guard at your service, my lady," he said with a slight bow.

The woman held out her hand. "A pleasure to meet you, Sentinal Tagerillion. I am Lady Miranda of Greenswatch."

Tagerill bent over her hand. Greenswatch? He wondered if she was related to the newly confirmed lord of the Watch, Simeon and his sister Lady Alyssa. "A pleasure, my lady. I would offer you my horse except I didn't ride him today. I'm afraid we will have to walk." He tucked her hand in the crook of his arm before she could protest and steered her down the hill.

"Do you prefer to walk?" she asked as they began the descent towards the palace.

"I had the 'day off' today," he said, emphasizing the words, "so I thought my horse should, too." Tagerill grinned.

"I was considering what to do with my day. I thought I might explore the city. It is very different from what I remember."

"Are days off so unusual then?"

"It is my first in many years."

Lady Miranda glanced at his face. "I do thank you for your help. If you would like, and please do not feel obligated, I could guide you around the city. I know it quite well," she offered, as a delicate blush rose across her face.

Tagerill considered her. "If you have the time, and you are sure you are up to it, then I would enjoy your company."

"I'm fine." She waved off the fall. "I have a day off, too. If we could go in by the stables and make sure Magya is alright, and if you could give me time to change my clothes, I'll join you shortly."

Tagerill nodded in agreement as they reached the outskirts of the palace grounds. They entered through the northern gate and cut across the terraced gardens and rounded the corner into the stable block. The palace guards observed their progress through the flower beds, though they didn't challenge them. She submitted to the resultant interrogation from the stable master and Tagerill recruited himself to wait as Lady Miranda dashed off into the palace corridors.

To Tagerill's surprise, she appeared no more than half a chime later. A change of dress, a snug jacket gathered at her slim waist, and a new hat sitting primly on top of her reordered hair. She laughed at his expression as she approached, pulling on her gloves. "Not all ladies take hours to get ready," she said, tucking her hand under his arm. "Anyway, I didn't want you to waste any more of your day than you had to. A day off is precious and we need to make the most of it."

"But you said this was your day off, too. Are you sure you want to spend it walking around the city?"

"But what could be more fun than showing off my favourite city? You can tell me what it used to be like. A fair trade."

"Sounds fair to me," Tagerill agreed. "Lead on, then, my lady. Where do you suggest we begin?"

"Why don't we walk down to the temple, then return via the Chapterhouse and back through the markets?"

Tagerill happily followed her down the switchback, listening to her explain the theory behind the city plan. They passed the garrison and the courthouses to the north of the city. They would admire the architecture on the way back, so said Lady Miranda as they skirted the lowland fields, surprisingly not yet built on, so her narrative went, until they entered the Lady's Gardens.

"The gardens are said to be the remnants of the Lady's actual gardens, though we have no proof. She apparently loved her flowers," Lady Miranda said as they strolled under the leafy trees.

"Roses," Tagerill said. "Leyandrii loved roses. You could smell their perfume across the city. It is one of the things I miss most; the scent of her roses."

"I can't get over the fact that you knew the Lady. Was she as amazing as they say she was?" Lady Miranda asked as she led him down a side path, damp and chilly in the shade.

Tagerill's face lit up. "There are not the words to describe her; she was amazing and loving and special. It was and still is an honour to serve her in any way possible."

"Well, you should like this, then," she said as she waved her hands towards a small arbour opening before them, as if she had conjured it herself.

Tagerill strolled under the wooden archways, staring about him in wonder at the rose bushes being trained up the woodwork. A small smile hovered over her mouth as she watched him, pleased at being able to show him something he would like. "These have just been pruned, but once they have grown and begin to bloom next spring, maybe you can tell me if these are the same roses?"

Tagerill laughed. "It would be my pleasure, though I highly doubt they are the same. Her Palace and gardens would have been over where the garrison is now. This area would all have been arable fields right up to the temple, which is in about the same place as before, I think," Tagerill said, rotating to get his bearings.

They continued through the gardens, Lady Miranda pointing out the infirmary and the foundling hall, both nestled in the soft greenery and under the watchful eye of the temple. Lady Miranda paused as they approached the temple and settled on a stone bench beside the tall sentinal tree arched over the white marble building. A small dome crested the top. "I'll wait for you here," she said, stretching out her legs and crossing her ankles. Grass stained boots peeked out from under her skirts.

Tagerill hesitated. "Don't you want to come in too?"

"No, this time is for you. I can come another day. Don't rush. I will be happy sitting here under the trees. I always find it so peaceful here."

Tagerill nodded his thanks, paused to greet his brother Birlerion's sentinal tree, smiling at the soft caress he received in return, and entered the white stone arch, which led into the temple.

The air was cool and the light subdued. Voices echoed softly in the domed ceiling as visitors walked around the walls; their words muted and indecipherable.

Tagerill walked up the central aisle and knelt before the altar. Bending his head, he emptied his mind and waited. The white marble warmed beneath his knees and his tension and uncertainty bled away as She gave him her blessing. He stirred as he heard the words: "*Don't forget the forgotten.*" He glanced around in surprise, but the temple was quiet and still. Dust motes sparkled in the shafts of light coming through the circular window above.

Reluctantly, he stood. Usually, he would have stayed a lot longer. He hoped the Lady would forgive him for his rude haste, but with Lady Miranda waiting for him, he felt obliged to cut his visit short. As he rose, a sense of approval permeated the air, or maybe it was his imagination.

Lady Miranda was still sitting on the bench, her face raised to the sentinal above her. He studied her. Was she Lady Alyssa's mother? She didn't look old enough, but he was only aware of one Lady Miranda at court and she was closely linked to Princess Selvia, the wife of Crown Prince Kharel, who was currently under house arrest, having been caught plotting the downfall of his father, the king.

5

KING'S PALACE, OLD VESPERS

Jerrol left the king's chambers with his mind reeling. As if he didn't have enough people trying to kill him already, he had another responsibility to deal with. Keeping the king in order in his current mood was likely to be difficult, especially as King Benedict was simmering over the fact that his son had tried to depose him, had drugged him, and had colluded with the chancellor so that he could be declared Regent in the king's place.

King Benedict was busy cleaning house. His inquisitors were checking the loyalties and behaviours of all the chancellor's men and those holding office. The justice buildings were quiet as men and women alike tried to keep out of the king's line of sight. Jerrol was sure the king wondered if his eldest son and heir would have gone as far as to kill him to gain the throne.

The court reflected the caution and uncertainty that was rife in the administration; the usual high jinks and pranks in abeyance as a subdued air pervaded the palace, especially as the mysterious Sentinals became more visible, patrolling the corridors and grounds, whispers of tall tales and conjecture following them. Jerrol hoped the imminent return of the king's youngest son, Prince Anders, from his sojourn in the army, would lighten the king's mood.

Deep in thought, Jerrol didn't notice Birlerion arrive as he strode through the corridors. His musings took him out of the palace, down the wide stone steps, and around to the barracks. It was much easier to skirt around the building than to try to traverse the warren of corridors. He stopped at the bottom of the steps and Birlerion skittered around him.

"What is it?"

"Nothing, sorry. I forgot you were there," Jerrol said in apology, as the Sentinal relaxed.

Birlerion was the first Sentinal Jerrol had ever met, though he thought he had imagined him at the time. Jerrol often forgot his young age, as he was always so calm and self-assured. Alert silver eyes missed nothing. His wore his bow strapped across his back, a sword at his waist, and he had already proved he knew how to use them both. At one point, Birlerion had been Jerrol's only defence against persistent assassination attempts.

"Where is everyone?" Jerrol asked.

"The excavations at the Landgard progress well. Serillion is in charge and has an army of eager scholars assisting him."

"Excellent news. I'll leave that in his capable hands. I look forward to his report."

"Tagerill has the day off. Fonorion is with King Benedict and Darllion is with Deane-Scholar Liliian, undergoing an interrogation, I think he called it."

"He's the best person for it," Jerrol agreed. "Where is Jennery?"

"I think he was trying to instruct Tagerill on what a 'day off' meant. I'm not sure he succeeded."

"And do you know what a day off means?" Jerrol asked

with a smile as they walked around the barracks to the stables. Zin'talia, his pure white Darian mare, crooned in his head. Their telepathic link a comforting presence. She liked the palace stables because she got spoilt. The king had found out she had a love of Baliweed, a sweetgrass she was partial too, and was keeping her in supply. The king was a fan. Jerrol had an inkling that he was coveting her for himself, but although Zin'talia allowed him to give her treats, she had no intention of swapping Jerrol for anyone.

Zin'talia nudged Jerrol's shoulder affectionately as the stable lad bustled about, preparing her. "*Where are we going?*"

"Down to the Chapterhouse."

"To see Taelia?"

Jerrol grinned. Zin'talia had taken a strong liking to Scholar Taelia, maybe a reflection of his own feelings, he had to admit.

He swung up into the saddle and led Birlerion out of the stable courtyard.

Birlerion was answering his question. "It has been so long; I think we've all forgotten. Just being outside, breathing fresh air, is a novelty. Having a whole day to do with as I wish?" He shrugged as they rode down the hill towards the outskirts of the town of Old Vespers, side by side.

"As I said, breathing the air is enough for me. Adjusting to how much has changed is the main challenge. I think staying within the Watch eases you into the present day more gently, but coming here and seeing Vespers, with a different name and none of the landmarks remaining—it doesn't feel real."

"What was it like being trapped in the sentinal all those years? Could you talk to each other?"

"I wouldn't say we were trapped; more like we were wrapped in Leyandrii's protection, and I don't think we experienced time in the same way. It was more awareness of company, but not existence, if that makes sense."

"A bit of a shock to find yourself here, then," Jerrol said with a wry smile as they rode down the switchback towards the city.

"Yes, it takes some adjusting to, but Lady willing, we will. She still has work for us to do. What I want to know is what happened to the Vespers Sentinals; there should be more Sentinals here. I don't remember where they were at the end. The palace was in chaos, though Leyandrii had sent as many of the staff home as she could."

He stopped speaking as they concentrated on wending their way through the morning crowd of people, hurrying from one place to another. Their horse's hooves echoed on the stone paving lining the city streets. "Niallerion and my sister, Marianille, should be here, as well as others," he mused, lifting his gaze to the rooftops as the grey walls of the government buildings passed by and wood clad structures took their place. "I remember terrible winds and being battered by the gusts. The Ascendants caused violent storms..." Birlerion tensed. "'ware archers!" he shouted, barging Zin'talia towards the side of the road. Sliding off his horse, he grabbed his bow, cursing as he got tangled with his quiver.

Jerrol slid off Zin'talia, daggers in hand. People were screaming in shock as the body of a man dressed all in black fell into the road with a dull thud. He gaped at Birlerion: was he using a sling?

The road cleared fast as people ran, and Jerrol pushed Zin'talia into the mouth of an alley, scanning the rooftops for their assailants. Birlerion untangled himself and dived across the street to the shelter of a doorway. Balancing on Zin'talia's back, Jerrol levered himself up to an overhanging balcony and climbed up on the roof, scanning the scene.

Birlerion drew all the fire. Arrows peppered the woodwork around him, though in return, a body slumped on a roof and another had fallen into the now-empty street.

Jerrol muttered a soft command as he traversed the roof to the next building, keeping out of Birlerion's line of sight. The sound of a door splintering preceded Birlerion diving into the closest building, avoiding a return volley of arrows, which thumped into the remains of the wooden door swinging behind him. Jerrol spotted one of the archers positioned on the roof next to him and he ducked behind the chimney and slithered down the tiles to the ridge that joined it to the next building.

He crept up behind the archer and hit him behind his ear. The man collapsed, and Jerrol grabbed the bow and broke it across his knee. Picking up the man's quiver, he looped it over his shoulder in case Birlerion needed the arrows; he was going through his own at a ferocious rate. Jerrol crouched, scanning the rooftops.

A bright flash caught his eye and he squinted at a man who peered through an eyeglass and seemed to be talking to his hand. Jerrol stealthily worked his way towards him, pausing as Ari popped into view in front of him. The cat-like creature hovered in front him, his scaly wings extended like a bat, sunlight gilding the scales. Jerrol instructed the little Arifel to bring help, and as he disappeared, Jerrol resumed his journey across the rooftop.

A low whistle attracted his attention. Birlerion had reached the roof opposite and he indicated where the archers were located. Jerrol threw the quiver across the narrow street, where it clattered on the tiles. A volley of arrows thumped into the roof where Jerrol had just been, and Birlerion grabbed the quiver as Jerrol disappeared.

Birlerion kept the archers occupied as Jerrol scaled the rooftops, veering towards the last location he had seen the man with the eyeglass. A sharp curse below made him backtrack and peer over the edge of the roof. Birlerion had hit another target, and the body slumped over the side of the building.

A man crouched on the balcony below him, and he muttered into his hand as he stared across the street at Birlerion, who still drew most of the fire.

Jerrol dropped straight down on top of the man who collapsed beneath him. He held his dagger against the man's throat. "I suggest you drop it," Jerrol said in the man's ear, pressing the knifepoint deeper. A line of bright blood sprung up along its edge. The man froze, his eyes widening in shock. His hand jerked open, releasing a clear crystal, which clouded over as it struck the floor.

"Who are you?" the man whispered, his voice cracking on the words.

"More to the point, who are you? And why did you attack us?" Jerrol replied as he pocketed the crystal.

The man stilled.

"Don't make me repeat the question," Jerrol said, twisting his knife.

Jerrol spun as Birlerion shouted a warning. The man cried out as he pulled him up in front of him and an arrow thunked meatily into the man's stomach. The clatter of galloping horses echoed down the street behind them. Jerrol dropped to his knees, keeping the man as a barrier as another arrow thudded into him. "Who were you sent to kill?" he asked.

The man gasped for air. "It doesn't matter now. If I'd known what you are, I would have charged more! They are after your head." He grinned, blood bubbling in his teeth as he wheezed. He coughed out a spray of blood over Jerrol, who flinched back.

"The assassins? You mean the Kirshans?" Jerrol asked,

but the man's eyes had glazed over and Jerrol let him slump against the wall. At shouts in the street, he peered over the balcony. The king's soldiers had arrived and were beginning a sweep of the roofs. He searched the man, sucking in his breath as he found a Kirshan blade, proof that the Terolian assassins were still hunting him. Inspecting the ornate carving on the hilt, he admired the remarkable workmanship and pondered on the Terolian involvement. Why would the Terolian Families get involved in Vespirian politics? They never had before. It was like an unspoken agreement to not get involved. He slid the knife into his belt, straddled the balcony, and climbed over. He let go and landed lightly on the ground.

Birlerion rushed to his side. "Captain, you take too many risks," he said, his face hardening as he assessed Jerrol's blood-spattered appearance.

Jerrol gestured at the Sentinal, relief that he was unharmed flashing through him. "Look who's talking. I'm amazed you didn't get skewered. It's not my blood," he said, trying to reassure as Birlerion's frown deepened. "I saw a man talking into this." Jerrol held out the cloudy crystal. "Do you know what it is?"

Birlerion took the faceted crystal and studied it, a crease between his brows. "It looks like a voice crystal."

"A voice crystal? Where would they have got that from?"

"The Telusions, probably. That was the main source of crystal mining."

"Telusions? Where were they?"

Birlerion raised his eyebrows and then grimaced. "I suppose they are no more? The Telusion mountains ran down the southern coastline of Terolia. A string of fire mountains. The last time I was there, they were running hot, so I'm not surprised they blew."

Jerrol stared at him. "You went near an active volcano?"

"Volcano? I suppose I must have, if that's what you call them. Not by choice, I can assure you," he said, his voice fading as he stared down the street. Jerrol was sure he wasn't seeing the empty street as his mouth tightened.

Terolia again.

"How do they work?" Jerrol asked.

"Someone with the knowledge would have had to charge it for a specific person's use. When the crystal is clear, that person can send messages to whoever they want within a certain radius. When it turns cloudy, it is depleted."

"Who can create them?" Jerrol stared at the crystal.

"One who knows the old ways. There must be someone who understands how to harness its power within Vespers."

"Could you do it?"

"Me? No. Niallerion or Parsillion, maybe."

"Is there any way of finding the people at the other end?" Jerrol asked as he took Zin'talia's reins from the soldier leading her up the road. Her concern bombarded him, and he squinted at Birlerion, trying to tune her out.

"Jerrol! Are you alright? You are covered in blood. Are you hurt?"

"I'm fine," he reassured her as he focused on the Sentinal beside him.

"I doubt it. The recipients would have to be in the local vicinity for the crystal to work; they don't work over great distances, but that would still be most of Vespers." Birlerion heaved a dejected sigh as he glanced around him. "Tagerill is not going to be happy when he hears about this."

"Well, let's see if we can sneak into the Chapterhouse and get a bath before anyone sees us."

Birlerion shook his head and mounted up. "Wouldn't the garrison be better?" he suggested as one of the soldiers assisting with the clearing up handed him a few of his arrows. Most had been lost, shattering on impact. Twisting, he slotted them into his quiver. Birlerion indicated for the guards to close around them and led the way down the street. People peered out of their doors, watching wide-eyed as the troop of soldiers passed.

"How many got away do you think?" Jerrol asked as he gazed up at the passing roofs, wondering if he would ever again be able to walk safely down a street in Vespiri.

"Only a couple. The inquisitors will have their hands full with the bodies. It will be interesting to see if they can tell us anything."

"Unlikely," Jerrol said as they passed through the garrison gates. As he dismounted, Jerrol nodded dismissal to the lieutenant at the head of the guard. His friend Leander Jennery strode across the courtyard. Once a lieutenant in the King's Guard and now a reluctant Lady's Guard, though the Lady had not turned him full Sentinal for some reason. His eyes remained a bright blue instead of the usual silver of the Lady's Guards.

Jennery was his oldest friend, both of them having grown up in Stoneford under the eye of Lord Jason and their foster mother, Hannah. He was currently courting Lady Alyssa of Greenswatch, and Jerrol inwardly chuckled as he remembered when she had found out his first name and insisted on using it. Not that he would have gotten away with it, Jennery only answered to Jennery.

"Jerrol, are you alright? What has happened? Are you hurt?" Jennery grabbed Jerrol's shoulders in concern.

"I'm fine. I just need a bath," Jerrol replied. "It's nothing."

"Nothing?" Jennery said, shaking his shoulder. "You arrive covered in blood and surrounded by guards. I think that's a little more than nothing."

"I need a bath before Nikols sees me," Jerrol muttered, trying to slide out of Jennery's grip.

"I think it's too late for that," Birlerion murmured as he braced himself for the inevitable onslaught of questions.

"Maybe we should have gone back to the palace." Jerrol scowled as he turned towards the commander who crossed the courtyard, closely followed by Darllion, who glared at Birlerion as if it was all his fault. Birlerion straightened up and glared back.

Birlerion groaned out loud as Tagerill sauntered into the courtyard, assessing Jerrol keenly before turning to his brother.

"Busy day?" Tagerill inquired.

"We dealt with it. What are you doing here?" Birlerion asked with some bitterness.

Tagerill grinned. "Enjoying a tour of Old Vespers. We were passing the garrison when we saw you arrive and, considering your appearance, I wanted to check that the Captain was in one piece."

Jerrol started laughing as Birlerion took umbrage. "Tagerill, please, enjoy your time off. Tomorrow will be early enough for you to return. Birlerion is quite capable of keeping me in one piece."

"He'd better," Tagerill growled, the threat clear as he sauntered back out of the courtyard and joined a woman hovering outside the gates.

Jerrol's eyes widened as he recognised Lady Miranda. He drew everyone's attention back inside the courtyard as he suggested they move inside and allow both Birlerion and himself to clean up before giving an update on what had happened.

Outside the garrison gates, Tagerill paused beside Lady Miranda. "How are you feeling? Had enough? Or can I tempt you to have dinner with me?"

"Haven't you had enough of me? Was everything alright? Wasn't that Captain Haven? He looked a bit worse for wear."

"He does seem to attract trouble, but they are fine. I have enjoyed today. Thank you for taking the time to share your city with me. Hopefully, I will learn to love it as much as you do."

"That was my downfall. I misjudged how much I liked the city when I moved to Greenswatch. I thought I could adapt to life in the country, but I couldn't, I hated it. Oh, don't get me wrong, I like the gardens and the peace and calm of the temple, but I don't want to live in it."

Tagerill watched her. "I wasn't sure, but I met Lady Alyssa and your son, Simeon, in Greenswatch. I think Lady Alyssa intends on joining you here, now that Simeon is confirmed." He hesitated. "I am sorry for your loss. Lord Hugh will be greatly missed."

"I was the wrong wife for him. He tried—he really did. I was just too young when I got joined. I don't regret leaving; Hugh was quite capable of bringing up the children to revere the Watch." Lady Miranda sighed, her face pinching. "Hugh didn't deserve to die the way he did."

"You said you had the day off today. Are you still waiting on Princess Selvia?"

"Yes, the princess sponsored me when the queen passed away. The princess is the daughter of the Grand Duke of Elothia. I knew her before she joined with Prince Kharel. It was a difficult time at court, and she made it possible for me to stay. It was quite natural to move into her employ. I've waited on her for the last ten years or so."

"How does she go on? Did she support Prince Kharel's bid for the throne?"

"Let's not get into politics. We'll only end up disagreeing." Lady Miranda turned away. "I think it's time for me to return to the palace."

"I appreciate you showing me the city. I hope you will not suffer for it. You ought to have a hot bath, just to make sure you are not too stiff tomorrow."

"I'm not as fragile as you think." Lady Miranda said and clamped her lips shut as she strode through the narrow streets of the government quarter. The tall stone buildings rose around them, casting long shadows in the early evening torchlight.

"My apologies," Tagerill murmured, wondering what he had said to offend.

Lady Miranda gave a gentle sigh. "No, I'm sorry. I'm not used to having someone looking out for me. Thank you for today and for lunch. I enjoyed it."

"As did I," Tagerill replied, falling silent as they walked up the switchback towards the palace. "Thank you for making my first day off memorable," Tagerill said, bending to kiss her hand as they paused at the palace entrance.

Lady Miranda's eyes twinkled. "It was a pleasure. Thank you for sharing your memories with me."

"I hope we have the opportunity to repeat the experience when we next have a day off," he said with sincerity as she withdrew her hand.

"Thank you," she said as she mounted the steps, leaving Tagerill to walk around to the barracks and mull over the day and the mystery that was Lady Miranda.

6

MISTRA, TEROLIA

Var'geris was brooding. He knew he was, but he couldn't help it. Everything had been so clear when they had started. The steps they had taken were well thought through and well planned. They had been extending their influence unnoticed throughout Vespiri; where had they gone wrong?

The Ascendants' plans were unravelling. But there was a force moving around Vespiri that seemed to see through their subterfuge and strike it down instantly. He had sent people forth to investigate; they would soon find out who it was.

How had they lost their grip on the king? It was untenable. They'd had the chancellor and the Crown Prince, the two most influential people in Vespiri, after the king, and still they had let control slip through their fingers. Not only had they lost the king, but the prince was now out of reach under house arrest and closely guarded.

The chancellor was lucky to have escaped, and he hoped Iss'aren had a good explanation. He'd better have good news of the situation in Elothia.

The Grand Duke of Elothia was preparing a document

protesting against the treatment of Princess Selvia, though Var'geris didn't think it would make any difference. King Benedict was taking the attack on his throne personally. They wouldn't be able to catch him unawares again.

There had been no word from Mer'iteras in Greenswatch either, which was worrying. At least they still had Deepwater in their grip. For'teras and Pev'eril between them could re-entrench them in the watches. Stoneford was also susceptible, being out on the borders and far from the king's watchful eye. It could still be a distraction as they continued their infiltration in Terolia. Terolia was nearly ripe and ready to fall into his hands. The Families were disintegrating; his next speech in Mistra should tip the scales and finish the Families forever.

His deliberations were interrupted by the Veil, coaxing him to return. He had thought the Veil was a myth; a story told by those who should know better. He had been wrong. The stories were true. The Lady had brought down a Veil of protection around the world of Remargaren and banished all magic and she had taken his ancestors with her. He had been shocked when he had first experienced the Veil. What an amazing sight. It would consume him if he let it. He had expanded his mind as his father had taught him, extended his awareness up and out of his body, and he had heard its call.

Its wondrous beauty had drawn him closer; the twisted strands caressed his skin and murmured sweet promises if he would stay, and as he hesitated, he had heard them; his ancestors calling from beyond. It was down to him and his brothers to open the way.

Relaxing into the cushions, he closed his eyes, feeling his way out to the Veil. Ignoring the sparkling beauty beyond, he sensed the weakness in the weave; yes, there! Someone had tried to patch it, but they hadn't been able to seal the edges properly. He focused his mind and sent a burst of energy, which forced the seam apart and unravelled the fix. He tried to sense the location of the person who was fixing it. A taste; a woman. Where was she?

Expanding his mind, he searched the perimeter. She was elusive, but he had her scent now. He knew what to look for. Concentrating on the tear, he tried to widen it. It resisted. He released the strands and folded his awareness back into his body and opened his eyes.

He trembled with exhaustion. Communing with the Veil was draining. It sucked the life out of him, craving more each time he visited, yet he could no longer resist.

Returning to his brooding, he scowled. The Vespirians hadn't seen anything yet. He would find them, and they would regret interfering with his plans.

7

PALACE BARRACKS, OLD VESPERS

The day after the attack, Birlerion was off duty, having handed the Captain over to Tagerill.

He rose with the dawn and met his friend Serillion on the training field. Along with Tagerill, the three of them had been inseparable at the academy, until they had graduated and been posted all over Remargaren. It felt good to go through the movements of Apeiron with his friend, stretching and preparing for what he knew would be vigorous workout. Both Serillion and Tagerill had always bested him with the sword; he had never quite reached their standard. After all, Tagerill had been born with a sword in his hand.

Memories of his days at the academy flooded his mind as he flowed through the movements, stirring memories that he didn't want to revisit, and he clamped down on them as he drew to a halt and breathed deeply.

He caught Serillion's flick of a glance, and he turned away as he shed his shirt and picked up his sword, throwing the sheath over with his canteen. They were both stripped to the waist, their pale skin gleaming with sweat, sleek muscles rippling as they moved. They were of a similar height and build, though Serillion was fair to his dark hair. Well matched in theory. Blue sparks of energy crackled around Serillion and his sword; it was obvious Serillion needed this sparring session, and Birlerion had better make it a good one so he could work off his excess energy.

Without warning, he launched at Serillion, his sword a curving arc in the pale grey dawn and the clash of steel reverberated across the training ground. They pumelled each other for a good chime, gradually drawing an audience as the other guards on the training ground stopped their own training and watched the display.

Once the crackles of energy dissipated, Birlerion drew the session to a close by twisting into his friend and forcing him down on the ground with a thump. Birlerion grinned down at him, sweat dripping off his brow. "Good workout."

Serillion grunted from beneath him. "When did you become so good, Birlerion? I barely held you off most of the time."

"You're just out of practice." Birlerion rose and offered his hand.

Grasping it, Serillion hauled himself to his feet and went to grab his shirt, using it to mop his face. Dirt and grime smeared his back, sticking to his sweaty skin. Birlerion followed, glancing around at their unexpected audience. "Well, we had to give a good show," he murmured, gesturing towards the guards who were slowly turning back to their own training. Birlerion shrugged into his shirt observing the guards, who were now training with a bit more enthusiasm.

"That was not just a show." Serillion groaned as he stretched.

"You needed it. I'm sure Tage will need it too, maybe you should make sure you train with him tomorrow."

"Not me, let him beat you to a pulp. You can show him how much you've improved."

As they began walking back to the barracks, their shirts flapping in the growing breeze, Birlerion said, "Maybe I'll suggest Darllion; I am sure he must need a workout."

Serillion chuckled as they entered the bathing room. "I wish Tianer was here, she would soon put him in his place."

Birlerion grimaced in agreement. She would have flattened him as well.

Showered and clean once more, they returned to the barracks. Birlerion dressed in shirt and trousers; the linen soft against his skin, reminding him that he lived again. Yes, in a different time, but was it really so different? He buckled on his sword belt, and caressing the ornate hilt, he remembered the day Tagerill's father had given it to him. Repressing the memory, he picked up his jacket and slid home his daggers.

Leaving the barracks, they went to the stables, both heading down to the city. Serillion veered off to the Chapterhouse with a wave and Birlerion stopped outside the temple, promising to meet him later. Greeting his tree as he passed, Birlerion smiled at the frisson of welcome and he entered the Lady's temple. The white marble gleamed in the morning sun, and it shimmered as Birlerion knelt at her altar. For some reason, the temple had always reacted to his presence. Once again, he prayed for her forgiveness as he opened his mind, searching for the deity who controlled his destiny. Emptiness echoed around him; she wasn't there. His heart clenched as he wavered. But no, she had given him his orders; protect the Captain. Until she said otherwise, that was his purpose.

Rising, he bowed to her altar and left. He planned to do some research in the Chapterhouse, if he could avoid Scholar Torsion. Maybe if he tucked himself away in a corner, they wouldn't find him.

A shadowy alcove hid him from prying eyes as he found a book on the histories of Vespiri. He began working his way through the last century, trying to learn the vagaries of the country he now lived in. He read about the politics and spheres of influence of the current administration, with the intent of identifying any internal threats against the Captain. As if there weren't enough external threats already.

He had gone from having a pulse on the political landscape to knowing nothing, and he didn't like the feeling. He sat working his way through a weighty tome about the current administration of Vespiri when the presence of another Sentinal impinged on his senses.

"I thought we were going to meet for lunch? I might have known I'd find you here. You always did like Leyandrii's library," Serillion said.

Birlerion looked up at his friend and grinned. "I have a lot of reading to catch up on. You all had a head start on me."

"Through no fault of your own, you didn't have access to any books until you joined the rangers," Serillion said, sitting next to him. He peered at the book. "What are you reading?"

Birlerion held up the cover: *A History of Vespirian Administration, 4005 - 4105*. "Thought I'd see what's been happening in the last century or so, according to the scholars, anyway."

Serillion laughed. "I wouldn't believe all that you read. I've just had an interesting session with Scholar Torsion, and if his interview techniques are indicative of how they collate history, then it will be far off the mark."

Birlerion leaned back in his chair. "Oh, yes?"

"I'm quite glad I had such a vigorous workout this morning, it helped keep me calm. As you said, he's very interested in you. In fact, I would say he is rather fixated. He was desperate to find out what you did at the end."

"And you said?"

"That I had no idea, which is true. I was there and yet I have no idea what you did. What did happen at the end?"

Birlerion stilled, his heart fluttering in his chest as his brain shut down. He closed his eyes as he unconsciously withdrew behind his considerable reserve, and Serillion reached over to grip his shoulder. "Stop blaming yourself for something that wasn't your fault."

Birlerion stared down at his book, the text blurring. He had to clear his throat to make his voice work. "She'll never forgive me."

"For what?" Serillion asked as he eased the now crumpled book out of Birlerion's fingers.

"I saw Leyandrii and Guerlaire fall. I couldn't help them."

"Why couldn't you help them?" Serillion asked.

"I wasn't with them, and I should have been. I couldn't reach them in time." Birlerion cleared his throat again. His chest constricted as Leyandrii's final moments spooled past his eyes.

"You said it was Leyandrii's choice; you were following her orders. Do you think you could have stopped her?"

Birlerion shook his head, unable to speak.

"You couldn't. So, stop thinking you could." Serillion gentled his voice as if aware how tenuous their connection was. "Where were you?"

"The Ascendants built a communication array in the Justice building. It was huge; rings of crystals. Leyandrii sent me destroy it. Marguerite sent Taurillion to protect me. It didn't quite go to plan." Birlerion twisted his lips. "She rescued Taurillion. He was hurt. Who knows if he made it, or Marianille and the others." Birlerion gripped Serillion's arm, his eyes gleaming, and Serillion returned the embrace.

"Marguerite wouldn't have sent Taurillion after you if it hadn't been important. If you hadn't taken out that array, it would have been much worse for everyone. You know that, Birlerion."

Birlerion eased his shoulders. "I should have been with her."

"No, that was Guerlaire's job. Yours was to follow Leyandrii's orders." Serillion's grip tightened on his arm. "You hear me? None of this was your fault."

Out of the three of them, Serillion always saw things so clearly. Birlerion nodded. "I'm so glad you are here," he whispered.

"I'm glad you are here, too," Serillion replied, pulling his friend into a rough embrace. He blinked furiously as he cleared his throat. "I'm sorry. I didn't mean to drag up old memories."

"They are not that old; it seems like only yesterday we were at the academy and you were teaching me to read."

Serillion laughed. "I only started you off. The scholars taught you the rest."

Birlerion gave him a tentative smile. "No, it was those late-night sessions."

"What do you think Torsion wants?" Serillion asked.

Birlerion sighed. "He reminds me of Clary. The same arrogant sneer; the anger simmering under the surface as if he's owed. He doesn't like me."

"You don't say." Serillion frowned. "It's not just dislike. Torsion is determined to turn everyone against you, much like Clary did, come to think of it." He tilted his head inspecting his friend. "What is it about you that they fear?"

Birlerion snorted. "Don't be ridiculous. I am nobody. You said it yourself; I was dying on the streets of Vespers until Guerlaire found me."

"Not Guerlaire. Leyandrii. She was the one searching for you. She relied on you, trusted you. She always turned to you after Guerlaire."

"I'd prefer you didn't tell anyone that."

"Not even the Captain?"

Birlerion shrugged. "Focus on where I came from, not where I went. It will drive Torsion crazy."

"Think of all the things you achieved in Terolia and Elothia. We *should* be speaking of it, if only to show that Torsion is stirring trouble. If we don't tell the king or the Captain, how will they know?"

"I don't trust Torsion; no matter what you say, he'll only twist the truth. Don't give him any more fodder to chew."

"Leyandrii always rode your shoulder," Serillion said, and Birlerion flinched, her loss an ache deep in his gut. He felt incomplete, her absence a gaping hole in his soul.

"That's probably because I was rougher around the edges than the rest of you; she didn't trust me to be diplomatic."

Serillion laughed. "Rubbish. You were the best of us all and you know it. She trusted you, and you always managed to find what she needed, along with the trouble." He smiled fondly and patted Birlerion's shoulder. "I always said you would be the one to achieve the most out of all of us."

"Yeah, right." Birlerion leaned forward. "What else was Torsion interested in?"

"You. What powers we Sentinals have. What power the Lady had. What we knew about the Bloodstone. How many of us there were and where I think they might be. And then back to you again."

"Is that all?"

"Oh, he was also interested in our sentinals. He wants to visit one. Yours being the closest, he was angling for me to get you to invite him in."

"Maybe we should let him visit and then not let him out again," Birlerion said with a vicious grin.

"Now, now, stop showing your teeth. He is only a scholar, and the Captain trusts him."

"He shouldn't. But I suppose he will have to find that out for himself." Birlerion frowned at his book and began smoothing the crumpled pages. "Do you think you'll find the palace?" he asked, changing the subject.

Serillion relaxed in his chair as if aware that confidences were over. He began describing the progress, or rather the lack of progress, that they had made up at the Landgard. "I'm going up to the palace to search the king's library if you want to come? He gave us permission to search for any records of the old palace."

Birlerion closed his book. "Got to be more interesting than this," he said as he rose.

King's Palace, Old Vespers

That same morning, Jerrol returned to the palace archives. He was the first to start work. Tagerill stood on guard outside his room in the palace barracks as he opened the door that morning.

"How was your day off?" Jerrol asked, smiling as Tagerill's face lit up. He looked relaxed; his day off had done him some good.

"We explored the gardens and the temple. Some parts aren't so different from the old Vespers."

"How did you manage to meet Lady Miranda?"

"She had a day off as well. She offered to show me the city, which was very kind of her."

"So, you got on all right?"

"Very well. Though she was a bit sensitive about the prince; we avoided politics, to be honest."

"Probably safest," Jerrol agreed. "It would be interesting to know how much she knew of the prince's plans."

"I'm sure she would already have spoken to the inquisitors," Tagerill replied. "I did get the impression that she felt alone, isolated."

Jerrol descended the stairs, Tagerill close behind. The archives were very similar to the Chapterhouse records rooms; dark, secluded chambers lit by carefully placed oil lanterns. The risk of fire was high, and the custodians were strict on the rules. The air was just as dry and musty.

He frowned at the notes he'd written. The families who had supported the Ascendants were no more, yet he didn't recognise any of the family names, except Clary, and that was only because Birlerion had mentioned them. They were not prominent today, no matter how important they had been previously. So, what had happened to them?

It was much later when Jerrol glanced up as Tagerill shifted in his chair. "I'm starving," Tagerill said, "let's get something to eat. It will all still be here tomorrow."

Jerrol grinned at his guard's presumption, but now that he mentioned it, he had a headache from the lantern's fumes and hunger pangs were cramping his stomach. Stretching, he stood and tucked his notes into his jacket. "Alright then, let's find some food," he said, following Tagerill out of the archives.

They approached the open hatch where the kitchen staff were serving, and selecting their lunch, moved off to an empty table. Glancing around the room, it looked like they had the place to themselves. A few King's Guards lingered over their coffees, but most people had already eaten.

"You found the Captain's sword," Tagerill said, wrinkling his nose as he pushed the turnip to the side of his plate. He stabbed the pie crust to let the steam escape and Jerrol inhaled the tantalizing aroma of stewed meat.

"Yes, Guerlaire handed it to me the other day down in

the chamber. It doesn't seem as though anyone but you and I could see it."

"It's taking steps to conceal itself. People will register that you are wearing a sword but won't realise it is that particular sword. Captain Guerlaire wore that sword the last time I saw him."

"What can you tell me about it?"

Tagerill shrugged, scanning the room. "It was forged by the Guardians, and it is thought to be indestructible. The Lady bestowed it on Guerlaire when she made him her Captain. There were many rumours about it being sentient, though Guerlaire never confirmed them one way or another."

"Sentient?"

"Yes, it's rumoured that it can communicate with the Captain and channel the Lady's power. You should be able to create waystones, or at least find those that still exist."

"Waystones? Serillion mentioned them before."

"There was one up near the Lady's Palace, but it's lost. We've found no sign of it. You'll have to create a new one."

"I don't know how."

Tagerill grimaced. "However Guerlaire did it, he was extremely discreet, but Birlerion or Niallerion knew, I'm sure."

"Your brother seems to be at the centre of everything. I think he knows more than he is letting on. Why would he keep anything to himself?"

Tagerill pursed his lips. "My brother learnt to defend himself the hard way. But don't you ever doubt him; he is the Lady's. He always kept his thoughts close; he never was much of a talker. He was always good at attracting trouble. Sometimes, I think Guerlaire used him as a distraction. Dominant Clary couldn't resist an opportunity to put

Birlerion down. He never succeeded, though he tried hard." Tagerill smiled sadly. "He really tried."

"That doesn't help me much," Jerrol said.

Tagerill grinned. "I'm sure the sword will tell you what you need to know."

"That's what I'm worried about."

Tagerill watched more off-duty guards enter the hall. "The only thing I can tell you is that any deception the sword is projecting will stop if it is not attached to you. So, don't let it go."

Jerrol leaned forward. "Tagerill, what can you tell me about the Ascendants?"

"What do you want to know?"

"Well, what were the Ascendants like in your time? I've traced their descendants, but all their families have disappeared. Didn't they hold land in Vespiri?"

"Of course. Most of them were from the old families with large estates. From what I can tell, the Administrative structure you have today is much the same. The Administrators ran the country on behalf of the Lady. They tended to be the wealthier families, and their children had access to the academy and the chapterhouse.

"It all started to change when a few of them joined the scholars and showed a bent for diplomacy; they were appointed to the Lady's council. Those who were able to perform magic and evinced special skills began to believe that they were better than everyone else. They called themselves Ascendants and began using the title 'Dominant' instead of Councillor or Administrator. The power of a name," Tagerill said, rolling his eyes.

"Then they began to argue that they were the elite and should be in power, that they were pure of blood, and if you didn't have an old family name with the wealth behind it, you should bow down before them. We had quite a few run-ins with Clary. He was the main instigator of the trouble. He had the power and knew how to use it."

"Birlerion said he saw Clary at the towers."

"Birlerion hates him. He gets a bit unreasonable if you mention him. You can't blame him. Clary couldn't stand the fact that Birlerion came from nowhere and graduated as a Lady's Ranger and that Leyandrii supported him. They had a bit of a feud. Clary tried to discredit him, if not downright kill him, in the end.

"Well, as you can imagine, that didn't go down well with Leyandrii, especially when they started throwing their magic around with little regard for the rest of us or the land itself. The last few months before Leyandrii sundered the stone, we were all running around the country trying to protect the people from their wild magic."

Tagerill paused, collecting his thoughts. "Captain, that is what I don't understand. Where are the rest of the Sentinals? There should have been far more than just us."

"Well, I haven't woken everyone yet, and we don't know how many still survive across the other kingdoms, but I did get a message from the Lady. She said: 'Heal the wounded, restore the forgotten.' I wondered if the missing Sentinals are the wounded and the Ascendants are the forgotten." Jerrol pushed his empty plate away.

"Or the other way around. I could have sworn that the Lady spoke to me in the temple the other day. I heard the words: 'Don't forget the forgotten'. It could be the missing Sentinals who are the forgotten. I mean, you found those you could see, but what about the rest; there are many still missing."

"That would mean they didn't go across the Veil with the Lady as we all assumed. They must still be here somewhere, even without a sentinal tree. Which would also mean," Jerrol said slowly, feeling his way, "that the Ascendants or maybe their descendants are here as well. The wounded or possibly the lost. But where are they? We only hear about the top of the tree, those out preaching and casting their mind spells. Where are all their dependents?"

A comfortable silence fell as Jerrol finished his coffee. Jerrol started when Ari appeared in front of him, chittering in distress as he bombarded him with a jumble of images. "Saerille? Is Saerille in trouble?"

Tagerill held his arm out, encouraging the Arifel to land, and gently stroked his soft white chest. "Shhh, we can't understand you, calm down," he soothed as the little creature wrapped his tail around his wrist. The Arifel flapped his wings and glared at Tagerill, who grinned back, unrepentant.

"Saerille. What about her?" Jerrol tapped the Arifel, drawing Ari's attention back to himself.

Jerrol got a short burst of images showing Saerille getting tangled in the Veil. There were areas of damage, and he got the impression that someone was searching for her. She couldn't hold the Veil much longer on her own; she needed help.

"Can anyone else patch the Veil or do we need to go now?" Jerrol frowned at Tagerill. "Could another Sentinal provide Saerille with relief? The king wants me here. I really need to follow the trail and find out more about the Ascendants."

Tagerill scrunched his face up as he thought. "Serillion, maybe, but he ought to get the Landgard excavated. That would assist you in travelling these long distances. The Captain always popped up when we least expected it. Kept us on our toes, I can tell you."

"The Scholars can do the digging. It sounds like they've barely started. We could spare him for a month or so to help Saerille. He might have something to work with by the time he gets back. Within the month, I should be able to travel up to the towers and seal the Veil properly."

They rose from the table, aware of the men casting them strange glances. Jerrol tightened his lips as they returned the trays and hurried out of the mess hall, Ari gliding above them. Quickening their pace, they entered the palace and went in search of Serillion. They found him in the king's library amongst the polished wooden shelves of leather bound books. A slender blonde-haired Sentinal poring over an old map of the Lady's palace with Birlerion.

"Where did you find that?" Jerrol asked, momentarily diverted.

Serillion grinned. "Birlerion found it at the back of the king's shelves. I think Leyandrii left it out for him to find."

"As if," Birlerion said with a fond smile. "Leyandrii was never organised." He extended his arm to let the Arifel land, and Ari chittered at him as he settled.

"Well, I don't think she would have wanted you to find this. Look, there is a hidden passage leading outside of the palace grounds. She had a hard enough time keeping track of us all as it was." Serillion said as he leaned back over the map. "Though I think if we can find the boundary, we should be able to locate the palace. It would take years to excavate, but it would be nice to know where it was."

Birlerion smoothed his free hand over the parchment. "At least we'd know where they fell."

Serillion straightened up, clearing his throat. "Anyway, Captain. Do you need us?" he asked.

"Yes. You, in particular. Saerille needs some help up at the Watch Towers. I was hoping you could go and help until I can get up there to seal it properly."

"As you command, Captain. There's nothing happening here. It'll be months before they dig down far enough to find any evidence of the palace, and the Veil is key." Serillion cast a glance at the map. "The palace would be down deep, as well. Marguerite would have kept it safe. I doubt we would find it."

Marguerite, Leyandrii's sister. The casual mention of the goddess still shocked Jerrol. He tried to concentrate on the matter at hand.

"Report immediately and call me if the situation is dire and you need me. Do not risk the Veil, Serillion."

"No, Captain. I won't." He glanced at Birlerion and punched him on the shoulder. "Come and help me pack." He embraced Tagerill before departing to prepare for his journey.

Jerrol sent Ari to advise Saerille to hunker down and hide until help arrived. If he hadn't been sure that he was on the tip of a discovery about the Ascendants, he would have dropped everything and gone himself, but he was tantalizingly close to something significant and he couldn't afford to lose the trail.

8

KING'S PALACE, OLD VESPERS

"We ought to go and wake the others. Denirion is stirring, as is Anterion in Marchwood," Birlerion said the next morning as he stood stiffly, holding Zin'talia's reins.

Jerrol jerked upright, his hands busy with Zin'talia's saddle. "Do you know where everyone is?"

"I wish I did. Then I could tell you how many we are, but they are the only ones I can sense." Birlerion tightened his grip on the reins as Zin'talia stirred, pulling against him.

"He doesn't like me. Make him let go of the reins," Zin'talia said.

"Don't be silly, of course he likes you. Though if you skin his hand, he may change his mind."

"We don't have time to travel across the Watches, not now. The king wants me here, he expects me to focus on researching the Ascendants," Jerrol said.

"I get the feeling the more of us you have, the better off we'll be."

Jerrol scowled. "If I knew how to make these waystones you keep mentioning, it would be much easier."

"If you want, we could try to make one down by the

Chapterhouse. I did close down a waystone once. We could see if we can create one."

"I knew it. I was sure you knew more than you were saying," Jerrol said with a laugh.

"Leyandrii was upset with me. I wasn't supposed to know how. If we could find Niallerion, he could explain it better. Who knows where we'll end up with one of my making?"

"It's worth a shot. It would make it easier to traverse Vespiri. I get the feeling we are running out of time."

They mounted and rode down the switchback with a unit of the King's Guards around them. Jerrol screwed up his face; the thought that he needed a twelve-man guard was ridiculous. But he kept silent. The king wouldn't let him stir without one.

Arriving at the Chapterhouse, the guards dispersed around the perimeter and Birlerion strode out of the courtyard, searching the surrounding area. "I think it would be better to position the waystone outside the Chapterhouse; they might get upset with the constant traffic. What about behind that copse of trees? It's secluded enough that it's unlikely to draw attention."

Jerrol shrugged. "I have no idea. You choose."

"You are very trusting, my Captain."

"Why wouldn't I be?" Jerrol followed Birlerion over to the trees, shadowed by one of the guards.

"Guerlaire would be expecting gotchas, paybacks, and goodness knows what by now."

"So, life wasn't so peaceful back then, as history would have us believe?"

Birlerion's eyes crinkled as he crouched in the dust. "It was never peaceful for me, anyway." He stacked some stones into a small pile. "Ok, this is the marker. Now you need to use the sword to concentrate the… the…" Birlerion trailed off, frowning. "I know what you need to do. I'm just not sure how to explain it. I wish Niallerion was here."

"So you keep saying," Jerrol said, watching him closely. "Do you want to try?" He offered Birlerion his sword.

Birlerion reached for it and hesitated as if it might bite him. His hand shook as he took the sword, and he let his breath out in a hiss as he held it. "The last time I used this, Leyandrii nearly killed me."

"Well, be assured, I won't."

Birlerion's lips quirked. "Are you sure? She said I could have obliterated the palace."

Jerrol stiffened. Was Birlerion serious? "If it's dangerous, then no, I forbid you. Don't risk your life for a waystone."

Waving the sword above his head, Birlerion drove it into the pile of stones before Jerrol could protest further and a soft chime resonated through them. "Well, look at that," Birlerion said in surprise. His face relaxed as if he felt the contented hum of the sword vibrating through the air.

"What did you do?"

"We have a new waystone. Now we just need to find an active one at the other end to go to."

"Active? To go where?"

"Wherever we want to go." He moved closer to the echoing chime and stepped forward. He vanished, sword and all, and Jerrol gasped in shock. He waved his arm across the space in which Birlerion had just been standing in. Nothing. He had disappeared. Before Jerrol could raise the alarm, Birlerion reappeared, his silver eyes sparkling.

"The Grove is open," he said, a huge grin on his face. "Come on. Just think of the Grove and step with me." Birlerion grabbed Jerrol's arm and tugged him forward.

The next moment, they stepped out in the Grove in Greenswatch.

"What?" Jerrol spun, disoriented, grappling with the fact

that he was suddenly in the Grove, surrounded by tall sentinal trees. "How is that possible?" He patted his body down as his stomach settled. It may have been one step, but the swirl of the changing landscape was unnerving.

"Waystones," Birlerion laughed. "They make life so much easier. For Sentinals, anyway. Other folks don't tend to travel so well."

"I'm not surprised. How do we get back?"

"Think of the Chapterhouse and step forward." Birlerion handed Jerrol his sword back.

"And there is a waystone in every Watch?"

"Should be. We just need to find them. The Land is much changed, and they may have been buried, which is why I can't sense them." Birlerion surveyed the avenue of sentinal trees. "We ought to tell Parsillion we're visiting so he doesn't get concerned."

Jerrol turned towards the elegant trees. They were all empty now, bar one; the Sentinals awake and scattered around Vespiri at his bidding. They were interrupted by the jingle of a harness, and they both dived behind the tall monoliths surrounding the Lady's altar.

Jerrol peered around the rough stone and watched a posse of men dismount. They were dressed in unfamiliar brown uniforms; all matching. So they belonged somewhere.

"Spread out. Make sure it's clear, then we'll begin." A large man strode into the glade, an axe in his hand. Jerrol's glance, before he ducked out of sight, caught a hooked-nose and a hard face. He didn't recognise him, unsurprisingly.

"Captain, I'll cause a diversion and you return to Vespers," Birlerion whispered.

As if he would leave Birlerion to defend his retreat. Who did Birlerion think he was? "I'm not leaving you here on your own, so don't even suggest it."

"It's my fault. I should never have brought you here. I didn't think."

"It was pure chance, and anyway, this is our opportunity to find out what is going on."

Birlerion called an Arifel.

"We can't stay here. They'll find us," Birlerion whispered.

"We have every right to be here," Jerrol replied, his silver eyes glittering.

"I don't think these are pilgrims, Captain."

"Then we need to find out who they are."

"Captain, we have to leave." Birlerion's voice died as a light voice spoke from the clearing.

"Can I help you?"

Jerrol recognised the voice; Parsillion, the Sentinal he had left here to guard the Grove. A sharp voice replied, accompanied by the menacing rasp of unsheathing swords.

"Grab him, quick. He's one of them."

Jerrol tensed at the sound of the scuffle and then gasped in dismay as Birlerion took a deep breath and stepped out from behind the monolith.

"Release him." Birlerion's voice cracked across the grove.

"There's another one, and which one are you?" the man asked, his gaze skittering around the glade, searching for more Sentinals.

"Does it matter?" Birlerion asked, nocking an arrow in his bow.

"I suppose not. But I know you, you're the archer."

Birlerion laughed. "Sorry to say, I don't know you."

"You're outnumbered. Put down your bow and we'll make it quick."

"The Lady would be most displeased, so I think I'll have to refuse."

The man roared a command, Parsillion twitched, and Birlerion loosed his arrow, followed by another. Parsillion wrenched himself out of his falling captor's grasp and grabbed the nearest sword. He spun, slicing the throat of the man reaching for him, flinching back from the spurt of blood.

Jerrol rushed up beside Birlerion, his sword glowing in the dim light, and Birlerion discarded his bow and stepped towards him in support. Jerrol grimaced as Birlerion cursed under his breath and swung his sword, forcing the hook-nosed man back, the clash of swords loud in the soft air.

"Get Versillion," Birlerion gasped as the black and white Arifel, Lin, appeared and disappeared in a blink. His distraction cost him as his knuckles took a skinning. He changed hands and counterattacked, shaking out his hand.

Jerrol cut in front of him and efficiently dispatched his opponent, and Birlerion paused, gasping for breath as he checked the glade. Parsillion was holding his own, though it looked like they were regrouping for another attack.

"Captain, Parsillion, centre," Birlerion barked, turning his back so that the three of them faced outwards with swords raised. They met the oncoming rush as the glade was suddenly filled with many men and horses, led by a large, red-headed Sentinal. The attack collapsed.

Birlerion exhaled. "Versillion, I am so glad to see you."

Versillion strode over and hugged his brother close. "Birlerion, what are you doing here?" His eyes widened as he realised Jerrol was also present, turning over the bodies. "Captain, what is going on?"

"That's what we would like to know. These men were here to attack the Grove and its sentinals. If we hadn't been here, they would have succeeded."

Parsillion returned from reassuring his tree and frowned at the carnage. "But who are they?"

Jerrol looked up from riffling through the clothes of one of the bodies. "It seems they are for hire to the highest bidder. The question is, who hired them?" He frowned as he watched Birlerion struggle to sheath his sword. "Birlerion, are you alright?"

"Yes, fine. I'm fine. We should get you back to Vespers, Captain. Before the guards miss you."

"I suppose. Versillion, can we leave you to clear up here?"

"Parsillion and I will escort you back to Vespers, and then I will return and clear up here. I assume you travelled by waystone? You were fortunate I had found the Greens waystone, else the outcome might have been different."

"Yes, we found one in Vespers and here," Birlerion said. "Good news, eh?"

"For some," Versillion said, watching his brother closely.

9

OLD VESPERS

As they stepped back into Old Vespers, Tagerill strode out of the Chapterhouse, accompanied by Jerrol's guard. He took one look at them and exploded into recriminations.

Birlerion held up a bloody hand. "Tage, for Lady's sake, enough. Do you think I deliberately led the Captain into trouble? We were just trying out the waystone."

"I never thought I'd say it, but you just don't think. You know the Captain's a target; you should have known better."

"That's rich coming from you. You're not exactly the world's greatest thinker."

Tagerill loomed in front of Birlerion and Birlerion glared back at him. A tiny crease appeared between Tagerill's brows. "At least I would have thought twice before dragging the Captain between a new waystone."

"Really? When did you become so restrained?"

"When did you become so irresponsible? I thought better of you."

Birlerion stiffened, and Versillion stepped between them

before Birlerion could respond. "I think you both need to cool down."

Birlerion backed away as Torsion rushed up. "Jerrol, I just heard. Are you alright?"

Jerrol rolled his eyes. "Yes, fine, thank you."

Torsion spun on Birlerion. "It was you, wasn't it? I knew you weren't to be trusted."

Birlerion twisted his lips, but Parsillion beat him to it. "What nonsense. The Lady called him. I needed help."

"That's convenient. Just Jerrol and him; that's a great defence."

"You'd be surprised how much damage they can do," Versillion said, squeezing Tagerill's arm in warning.

"Don't you think it's funny that every time Jerrol's life is put at risk, Birlerion is the one supposedly defending him?"

Tagerill glared at Torsion. "That's why the Captain is still here: because Birlerion was defending him."

"Only because he put him at risk first."

"Torsion, you know that's not true," Jerrol said, frowning at his friend.

"Of course, it is. You're blinded by the fact that the Lady made them Sentinals, but they are still men, easily swayed. It's been three thousand years, for Lady's sake. He's probably given up on her."

"No, he hasn't." Jerrol's quiet voice was drowned by Tagerill's angry reply defending his brother. Jerrol flicked a concerned glance at Birlerion. He was concentrating on wrapping his handkerchief around his bleeding knuckles. As he watched, Birlerion straightened and focused on the conversation. He stepped towards Torsion; his face tight. "Enough!" His voice was unexpectedly sharp. "We were supposed to be in the Grove; the Lady needed our help. Men were attacking the sentinals and Parsillion needed support."

Torsion sneered. "He *would* say that. He leads Jerrol into

danger and then says it's alright, the Lady was expecting them. You expect us to believe that? He's lying through his teeth. Who does he think he is? The Lady's Captain?"

Birlerion met Torsion's derisive glare, and Torsion fell silent.

Jerrol spoke firmly. "This is not the place for this discussion. It was not Birlerion's fault. It was lucky we were there or we could have lost Parsillion. As it is, we prevented an attack on the sentinals. Versillion, you need to place a guard on the Grove. We can't leave the trees unprotected."

"They are not that easily cut down," Versillion replied, "but we'll keep a closer eye on them. I'll advise Lord Simeon."

"Jerrol, you are not going to let him get away with it. He deliberately led you into an ambush. You can't trust him. Even his brother said that." Torsion was back on the attack.

"I never said any such thing. Birlerion would never deliberately put Jerrol in danger," Tagerill growled.

"That's not what you said earlier," Torsion said, jutting his chin out.

"No more," Jerrol commanded. "It's done." Jerrol moved to stand between Birlerion and Torsion. He frowned as he saw the blood staining Birlerion's rough bandage. "Birlerion? Do you need a healer?"

"It's nothing. My sentinal will sort it."

"Tagerill, help Birlerion to the infirmary. Birlerion, don't argue. Versillion, you ought to return to Greens. Parsillion here can escort me up to the palace. No, I said enough, Torsion. We'll bid you a good day."

Jerrol herded his Sentinals out under the watchful eye of the lieutenant, aware of Torsion's scowl following him. He didn't understand why Torsion hated Birlerion so much.

Birlerion resisted Tagerill's entreaties to see the healer and led his brother back to his tree.

Taelia appeared beside Jerrol, making him start. She hadn't been there a moment ago. How did she keep appearing out of nowhere?

Taelia gripped his arm, her turquoise eyes wide.

"Taelia, I wish you'd stop doing that; whatever it is you are doing," Jerrol said with a huff of breath as he scanned her face. "You turn up when I least expect it."

"I can't help it. When there is need, I respond. Jerrol, there is trouble in the Watches, but I can't tell which. One is affecting the other, and it's confusing."

Jerrol sighed. "There is always trouble in the Watches. You'll have to be a bit more specific if you want me to do something about it."

"I can't see. It hasn't happened yet."

"Then, unfortunately, we will have to wait until it does."

Taelia screwed up her face.

"Hey, it's not your fault. Don't worry. We'll deal with it when we know more. At least we know something is brewing." Jerrol looked around. "I need to return to the palace. I think I've caused enough trouble for one day."

Taelia's face eased. "You don't cause trouble, and nor does Birlerion. There is much yet to happen. Keep Birlerion by your side, Jerrol; you need him." She patted his arm and began walking towards the Chapterhouse.

"What do you mean, Taelia? What's going to happen?" Torsion asked, flapping around her.

Taelia ignored him as if he wasn't there, or maybe she wasn't there, and walked through the gates. Jerrol shook his head at the conundrum. When they had time, he'd have to ask her how she kept appearing from nowhere. Accompanied by Parsillion, he set off for the palace.

Palace Archives, Old Vespers

Jerrol returned to the palace archives the next day with a belligerent Tagerill at his shoulder. Even though he had told Tagerill he didn't believe Torsion, Tagerill was fuming at the accusations against his brother. The king had not been impressed by Jerrol's brief escapade with Birlerion, and Jerrol was lying low.

Birlerion was back in the barracks, having spent the night in his tree. He had shown Jerrol his healed hand with a, "See, I told you it was just a scratch. Nothing to worry about," and he took Parsillion off to give him a tour of the palace.

Jerrol collected the folio of papers and climbed out of the musty archives, and he headed for the library which was better lit. Silence fell as they settled and began reading. A sense of expectation permeated the air. Jerrol felt so close to finding out something important, maybe it was just on the next page? The Lady had said to follow the trail. Find the forgotten; help the lost. Who did she mean? The lost Sentinals or the silent descendants?

He was soon deep in the records, cross-checking his references. Tagerill shook his head at his single-mindedness and idly read the name of the books on the bookshelf opposite. A title picked out in gold leaf caught his eye, and he pulled the slender book off the shelf. "*A Treatise on the Origins of Remargaren.*" Tagerill glanced across at Jerrol, deep in his research and oblivious to what Tagerill was doing. He drew back a chair, sat down, and opened the book and began to read.

'It is a commonly held belief by the general populous that the great ancestors of the Lady of the Guardians created the wonderful World of Remargaren. But who was this powerful family? Who had the amazing ability and fortitude to create a world out of nothing? And if they created the World of Remargaren, then where did they originate? These are just a few of the questions this simple treatise seeks to answer.'

Tagerill flipped back to the front plate and checked who wrote the book. The author was a scholar, and Tagerill stilled.

The date of publication was just after the sundering of the Bloodstone. This pamphlet was written almost three thousand years ago. Gingerly, he placed it back on the table and turned the page. Silence fell.

They were disturbed by a clatter of hooves, which slid to a halt in the courtyard outside the library. A spray of gravel clicked against the stone steps, hinting at the urgency of the arrival. Jerrol stirred and looked up as Tagerill peered out of the window. "Courier, by the looks of it," he grunted and left the room. When Jerrol heard Tagerill exclaim, he stood and followed him out of the door.

"Captain, it's Frenerion from Greenswatch," Tagerill said, his face pale. Frenerion was the Grove Sentinal that Jerrol had assigned to support Versillion, the incumbent Greenswatch Sentinal. He was a stockily built older man, dark-haired, and with the inevitable silver eyes.

"You'd better come inside," Jerrol said, a sense of foreboding colouring his voice. "It would be best if we're not overheard." He led the way back inside the library. "What's happened?" he asked once the door was safely shut behind them.

"Lord Aaron has abducted Lady Alyssa," Frenerion reported. "Master Garrick was wounded. He was with the lady when they were attacked by a group of bandits within the grounds of Greenswatch. Versillion says to tell you that the lady is unharmed but restrained in Deepwater. Sentinal Denirion of Deepwater reports that he stands ready for the Captain's orders and watches developments.

"Lord Simeon says he did not feel empowered to attack a neighbouring Watch, even with provocation. Versillion advises to await the king's direction, and although he doesn't say it, it looks like Deepwater has fallen even further into disrepute."

"The king will have to act," Jerrol murmured as he rubbed a hand over his face. Hissing out an impatient breath, he paced back and forth. He should have paid more note to Taelia's warning. "I should have known it would be Aaron causing trouble. Come with me." He led the way out of the archives. They followed him to the king's throne room, Jerrol silently calling King Benedict as he went.

The Oath flared to life as he entered, pulsing before settling into a golden glow. Frenerion's jaw dropped as he followed and saw the brilliantly lit words engraved in the stone wall behind the throne. They were even more surprised when shortly after, King Benedict strode into the throne room unattended, his gaze also drawn to the glowing words over his throne.

He inspected Jerrol, who knelt as soon as he entered, closely followed by the Sentinals.

"What is so urgent?"

Jerrol rose and introduced Frenerion, explaining his sudden arrival from Greenswatch.

The king sighed and sat upon his throne, leaning heavily on the arm. "I assume this location," he said, indicating his throne room, "is to remind me of my oath to protect the Watches?"

"Your Majesty, you have never forgotten your oath. This is the closest location for both of us."

The king raised an eyebrow, but let it pass. "Very well, Sentinal Frenerion," he said formally. "Let's hear it."

Frenerion repeated his report, finishing with Lord Simeon's request and the Sentinals' concerns.

The king's face grew grimmer as he finally came to an end. "Lord Aaron overreaches himself. I think he needs to be reminded of what being a Lord of the Watch means. Jerrol, accompany me to my office. Tagerill, escort Frenerion to the barracks and show him where to freshen up and rest, then join us," the king instructed, rising from his throne. He turned at the door and glanced back at the glowing Oath. "I never tire of it," he said.

Jerrol grinned. "Which is fortunate, as I understand it's not something I can turn off."

"True," the king replied, leading the way out of the throne room, collecting Fonorion, who was lurking outside the door having tracked the king after he had suddenly upped and left his chambers without a word.

Birlerion slid in behind Jerrol's shoulder.

10

KING'S PALACE, OLD VESPERS

Lady Miranda hovered on the staircase, torn between needing to know and being beholden to a Sentinal. She almost hesitated too long. Tagerill strode down the corridor towards the door that led into the depths of the palace. He would be out of earshot soon.

"Sentinal Tagerillion," she called.

Tagerill spun at the sound of her voice, stopping in surprise. "Lady Miranda!"

"Is it true?" she asked, hovering in the shadows.

"Is what true?" Tagerill peered up at her, trying to see her in the dim light.

"That Aaron has kidnapped Alyssa; stolen her away from Greenswatch."

Tagerill mounted the stairs to grasp her hands. "How did you—"

"Servant chatter," she said, clinging to him. "Is it true?"

Tagerill nodded. "I am afraid so."

"To what end?"

"Because he wanted to. I think he grows arrogant."

"What will the king do?"

"Deal with Deepwater once and for all, no doubt."

"But what of Alyssa?" Lady Miranda's hands spasmed in his.

Tagerill drew her down the stairs and into a nearby chamber; a glance confirmed it was empty. He closed the door. "What do you know, Lady Miranda? What is scaring you?"

Lady Miranda pulled her hands out of his grasp and turned her face away. "I—I heard," she began with difficulty.

"What did you hear?" he prompted.

"That the brothers were casting spells that undermine a person's will; that they trample through memories and make a person into someone who will only do their bidding without question."

"The brothers?"

"Yes, the brotherhood of the Ascendants." Lady Miranda began pacing, unable to keep still. "I can't tell you anymore."

"Why not? If it will help save your child?"

"Do you think they would do that to Alyssa?"

"She seems a strong-willed young lady, much like her mother. And they tried once before. We interrupted Mer'iteras trying to enspell her during Simeon's confirmation. If they tried once, there is no reason they won't try again."

Lady Miranda wrung her hands together. "I can't betray them. I owe everything to the princess; she has supported me throughout. I can't betray her trust." Lady Miranda looked at Tagerill earnestly. "They are not bad people. They are just trying to right a wrong. Why shouldn't the Ascendants have the right to live their lives here, too?"

Tagerill raised an eyebrow. "I thought they did. No one is stopping them."

"The Lady didn't protect all the people. What about the

Ascendants left behind? Those not practising? They were abandoned, left with nothing."

"They were left to live in peace, the same as everyone else who lived in Vespiri," Tagerill replied, watching her.

"You really don't know, do you?"

"Know what?"

Lady Miranda took a turn around the room, shaking her skirts out in agitation. "They were hunted, targeted, killed for being the children of the Ascendants. Driven underground to save their lives and the lives of their children. The Lady didn't think about that when she cast them out, did she?"

Tagerill stared at her, shocked. "Leyandrii would never cast them out. She was and is only interested in protecting the world for all the people who live in it. I have never seen any sign of this. Do you believe this is prevalent across Vespiri?"

"It's prevalent across Remargaren, not just Vespiri!"

"Says who?"

"So say those who preach for the return of the Ascendants and the saviours of their heritage."

"I need proof. Hearsay and rhetoric will not sway the king."

"You would help the Ascendants' cause?"

"I would help anyone who is unable to live freely. But I do not support the Ascendants right to overthrow the Lady and destroy our world," he said. "If the Lady hadn't brought down the Veil, there wouldn't be a world for us to live in. Look around you. This city is nothing like what it used to be. The old city of Vespers lies under our feet. Only the rooftops of the chapterhouse exist. The Land protected itself against the attacks and rose to block the magical forces that would have destroyed it, and as a result destroyed much of the city as we knew it."

"Maybe the land was rebelling against the rule of the

Lady, not the Ascendants?"

"Do you really believe that?"

Lady Miranda huffed and took another agitated turn around the room. "Look what she did to you; locked away for over three thousand years. What reward was that for your service?"

A small smile hovered over Tagerill's lips as he watched her; she was enchanting and passionate. "Ah, but I get to live now in a world with you in it."

Lady Miranda froze and turned haughty eyes upon him, ready to take offence. Her face softened as she saw his expression. "Oh, Tagerill," she whispered. "What are we going to do?"

Tagerill reached for her and engulfed her in a warm hug. He smiled into her hair as she hugged him back.

"Meet in the middle," he said as he lifted her chin, his silver eyes intent. "Compromise is always possible if both parties want it," he murmured, his head dipping towards her rising face. Their lips touched, and their clutch on each other tightened.

The soft snick of the door opening interrupted them. Jennery peered around the door, eyes lighting as he saw Tagerill. Tagerill spun, biting off a curse before it left his lips. Lady Miranda hid her face in his shoulder.

"Apologies for the intrusion. Tagerill?" Jennery jerked his head out the door.

Tagerill lifted Lady Miranda's face. "Duty calls. We will find Alyssa; try not to worry," he said as he dropped a kiss on her forehead before leaving the room in Jennery's wake.

"You kept that quiet, didn't you?" Jennery asked with a strained grin.

"So will you, if you know what's good for you," Tagerill warned.

Jennery laughed. "Your secret is safe with me. Anyway,

the king wants us. It sounds like we'll get to relieve Deepwater, after all."

"What does the Captain say?"

"He's in with the king. He sent for us," Jennery said as they headed towards the king's chambers.

Tagerill gripped his shoulder. "We will get her back," he promised.

Jennery paused at the door. "We should have seen this coming. We should have known Aaron wouldn't take defeat lying down." Jennery made a fist, his muscles tight. "If I get hold of Aaron's scrawny neck …" he said, his rugged face bleak.

"Hush, remember he is not himself. We may be able to redeem him for his mother's sake, if nothing else. Lady Olivia's already lost her husband, if we can prevent her losing her son as well, that would be a boon, I think."

Jennery exhaled and shook out his hand before tapping on the door. Darris, the king's steward, opened it. Jerrol and the king were poring over the map spread out on the table, watched by a third man dressed in the uniform of the Commander of the King's Justice; the newly appointed Commander Fenton. He was straight-backed and precise, and he stood inspecting his neatly trimmed fingernails as the king and his captain discussed options.

Fonorion, the quiet, dark-haired Sentinal, who was the king's personal guard, stood by the wall talking to Birlerion and Parsillion.

King Benedict straightened and stretched. "We are agreed, then?" he asked, glancing between the fastidious commander and Jerrol. "Captain, please brief your people."

"Yes, sire. Lieutenant Jennery and Sentinal Frenerion will return to Greenswatch to collect a unit to march on Deepwater. They will engage from the south at dawn and draw out as many of Aaron's men as possible. You are the distraction,

Jennery, so be noisy. We are aware of guardhouses here and here," Jerrol said, pointing at marks on the map. "They have at least one garrison of men, all of similar calibre, but don't underestimate them; they may be sloppy, but there are a lot of them. Sentinal Tagerill and I will skirt the Watch and enter from the north with Birlerion and a unit of the King's Rangers. We will awaken Denirion and rescue Lady Alyssa before you strike.

"Birlerion will lead the King's Rangers, who will accompany us and sweep through the house, taking out any remaining men. They'll then come to meet you. Once we have relieved Deepwater of its current inhabitants, we will instigate the king's rule until the Guardian is reinstated and sweep the Watch for any further dissidents. Any questions?"

"Is the objective to capture Lord Aaron, sir?" Jennery asked, his face stiff and unyielding.

"The objective is to save Lady Alyssa and reclaim the Watch for the king. If anyone surrenders and it's safe to take them captive, do so, if not, no quarter. We will not lose any of our own over this. We have larger battles to wage. Take no risks." Jerrol glared at Jennery, who held up his hands in surrender.

Commander Fenton's cold voice interrupted them. "We don't know if this is Lord Aaron's move or if it is driven by the Ascendants, which calls into question whether Aaron is in thrall or whether he has thrown his lot in with them, which would be treason.

"That is not our decision to make. You will have a King's Inquisitor with you to interrogate those you capture. You do not have the right to execute Lord Aaron. The Inquisitor will make that decision. Understood?" Fenton looked around the room. The men nodded, acknowledging his orders. "Good. You move out immediately. By tomorrow, I expect to be advising the king that he has his Watch back."

11

DEEPWATER WATCH

Alyssa awoke to find herself lying on a bed in an unfamiliar room. She felt distinctly queasy, and as she opened her eyes, the room spun. She shut them again, shuddering as an unladylike burp escaped her lips. Her tummy was definitely unhappy.

Sitting up, she swung her legs over the bed, pausing for a moment to hold herself upright. She heaved and frantically cast about for something to throw up in; a basin, a bucket, anything. She saw nothing useful except a vase of flowers; she emptied it on the floor and repeatedly threw up in the vase.

Drained, she sat on the bed, wiping her mouth with her sleeve. Her throat burned. She still wore her riding habit. Yes, that was right; she had been out riding with Garrick. Her lips tightened. The similarities of the ambush with her father to the attack on herself and Garrick were frighteningly clear. She hoped Garrick was alright; he had gone down under the bandit's rush. They should have been safe enough within the grounds of Greenswatch. Those were no bandits.

Alyssa put the vase down on the floor and tottered over

to the window. She reached for the cord and pulled the heavy blue curtains open. Shading her eyes against the brilliant glare of an orange sunset, she realised she had been unconscious for most of the day and that she was no longer in Greenswatch. She recognised the view. A tall sentinal tree graced the grassy slope next to the lake.

"Deepwater?" she uttered out loud in surprise as the door to her room opened.

The young lord of Deepwater, whom she had once thought so handsome, with his blond hair and pretty looks, hovered on the threshold. "You're awake at last. The fools gave you too much." He wrinkled his nose at the unpleasant smell. "You are unwell?" he asked, his gaze skimming her pale face.

"Something disagreed with me. I don't feel well at all."

"Let me find you some help." He turned and spoke to someone hovering behind him.

"What am I doing here? How did I get to Deepwater?" Alyssa demanded, gripping the curtain.

"We'll deal with that later," Aaron promised. "Let's make you comfortable first. Your maid will assist you."

"My maid?" Alyssa repeated, confused. "Is Millie here, too?"

"I procured a new maid for your use. Just tell her what you need. She is here to serve you as the new mistress of Deepwater," Aaron said as he backed out the door and ushered a young girl into the room. He shut the door behind her. The lock clicked shut.

Alyssa stared at the girl. She was very young, dressed in a shapeless shift, and nervously fidgeting under Alyssa's glare. "And you are?" she asked, holding a hand to her head, which thumped painfully. She let go of the curtains, allowing them to block the brilliant sun.

The child dipped her knees in a travesty of a curtsey and

spoke. "Please, miss, if you tell me what you need, I'll help get it for you. I am to do whatever you tell me to."

"If I tell you to unlock the door, will you?"

"Miss?" The child stared at her, confused.

Alyssa held her head. This didn't make any sense. "Go fetch some hot water and towels. I need to freshen up, and I need some mint tea to settle my stomach. Oh, and take that vase away and empty it," she said, pointing at the vase; the smell made her nauseous. She waited to see if the child would be able to leave the room, but the door opened at her soft tap, and she slipped out the gap before the door closed again and locked behind her.

Alyssa closed her eyes and lay back on the bed. Her head thumped. She really didn't feel well.

Aaron paced in his study. "They gave her a whole vial of the poppy syrup. She is puking up all over the place. We'll have to delay the ceremony until she is better."

"She was unreasonable, headstrong. You'll need to let For'teras spend time with her before the ceremony," Peverill murmured. "She should be fine tomorrow."

"She'd better be," Aaron warned. "Nothing else happens in this Watch until she is my wife. No dredging, no nothing. Not until I get what was promised to me."

Greenswatch

The king's men arrived in Greenswatch in the middle of the night. Jennery threw Jerrol a salute as he and Frenerion peeled off towards Lord Simeon's manor house, leaving Jerrol and his men to continue down the road and disappear into the gloom. They would travel deeper into Deepwater and skirt the Upper Lake to approach from the north.

Jennery took a deep breath of the scented night air before sliding off his horse and handing the reins to a sleepy stable boy. He looked up at Alyssa's home and his face tightened, his eyes hardening. His stomach churned at the thought of Alyssa in Aaron's power.

Frenerion left to search for Versillion and rouse the men.

As Jennery climbed the steps, a manservant met him and led him deeper into the building until they arrived at what had been Lord Hugh's study and was now Simeon's. Sentinal Versillion stood on duty outside. Jennery saluted the Sentinal. "Frenerion is looking for you, but first, you'd better hear what's happening," Jennery said as Versillion opened the door. Simeon looked up as Jennery entered, followed by the Sentinal.

"Lieutenant Jennery, what brings you here at this time of night?" he asked in surprise as he rose.

Jennery forced a grin. "The Captain moves fast."

Simeon brightened. "You bring the king's word? I didn't expect a response until tomorrow. Frenerion must have made excellent time."

"Waystones; they make all the difference," Versillion murmured.

"He's off rousing your men. We need a unit to take with us to Deepwater," Jennery said. "The king expects us to reclaim both Lady Alyssa and the Watch by tomorrow."

Simeon gaped at him, whilst Versillion grinned with relief. "I'll go help Frenerion select the right men."

"By all means." Simeon waved him away. "What's the plan?" he asked, indicating the chair opposite his desk.

Jennery sat and explained what had been decided. "With your men, we'll have Aaron contained, and by tomorrow, we will return with Alyssa."

"I will lead my men. I should deal with Deepwater and Aaron," Simeon protested.

"Jerrol will have liberated Alyssa by the time you arrive, and it's best it is seen that the king deals with traitors."

"What will he do with Aaron?"

"Depends on whether he is in thrall or if he is committing treason. I fear he won't be holding the Watch by the end of the day, either way." At least Jennery hoped not. If he had his way, the man would be suffering exquisite agony and he would be causing it.

"What about Lady Olivia? She still resides here with us. She will be most distressed if her son is injured or, Lady forbid, killed. Especially so soon after losing her husband."

Jennery shrugged, his face bleak. "As the Lady wills. Jerrol has an Inquisitor with him, Peppins, I believe, who is to judge what happens to Aaron once we relieve the Watch. But seriously, you should stay here. We can't have both you and Alyssa at risk in Deepwater. Versillion will remain with you. Frenerion will come with me." Jennery paused, remembering the steward. Alyssa would be worried. "How goes Garrick? I heard he was badly hurt in the attack?"

"Thank the Lady he will recover. He took multiple wounds, but fortunately, none were life-threatening; the challenge will be to keep him in bed while he heals, but that is the healer's job."

"That is good news." Jennery turned as Frenerion appeared in the door.

"We're ready," the Sentinal said.

Jennery stood as Simeon walked around his desk and offered his hand. "Lady protect you all," he said.

The courtyard was full of men and horses. Hooves clattered against the cobbles, loud in the night air. Simeon introduced his captain. "Jennery, this is Landis. Landis, you are seconded to Captain Haven for this mission and Lieutenant Jennery in his stead."

"Yes, my lord." Landis, a thin-faced young man, snapped

a smart salute and, at his signal, his men mounted and organised themselves into two columns and followed Jennery and Frenerion out of the courtyard. The courtyard was eerily silent as the last echo of the horses' hooves faded on the night air.

Simeon remained on the steps, listening, but the night was still. Versillion hovered behind him. "You should sleep my lord. Tomorrow looks to be a busy day."

"I don't think I could, knowing that they are going into battle while we sleep."

Versillion shrugged. "It will make no difference if you stay awake all night. It will only make you less effective tomorrow."

Simeon grimaced in acknowledgement of his Sentinal's words and, with a sigh, re-entered the building. "Very well. Lock up. Place double guards on the perimeter. I want to be informed the instant we get word."

"Very good, my lord."

Simeon climbed the stairs, relieved to be spared having to explain what was happening to Aaron's mother, Lady Olivia. That would be something he would have to face on the morrow.

12

DEEPWATER WATCH

Jerrol crept through the dripping undergrowth, Tagerill at his side. Birlerion ghosted behind him, and the King's Rangers were spread out behind in a thin perimeter, silently getting soaked in the dew. They reached the Upper Lake in the early hours of the morning and skirted around it, crossing over the land bridge between the Upper and Middle Lake, which led to the largest lake, the Home lake, with the lone sentinal standing tall and isolated behind the Deepwater mansion.

There were four guards patrolling the grounds, and they were silently overpowered. With a flick of his fingers, Jerrol directed a couple of scouts to check the garrisons. Leaving Tagerill and the others hugging the ground, he rose and walked up to the sentinal tree. The air shimmered around him as he placed his hand on the trunk, and he entered the tree where Denirion appeared out of the swirling mist. He was tall, broad-shouldered, with a thatch of blond hair and sparkling, silvery blue eyes, pale as the waters of the Watch he protected.

"Denirion, I am so pleased to meet you. Birlerion has

told me all about you."

Denirion smiled. "Birlerion? Is he here?"

"Yes, I'll take you to him, but first I need to explain what's happened." Denirion took a step back in shock as Jerrol explained he had been asleep for three thousand years. He frowned as Jerrol recapped recent events, and his eyes grew distant as he reached out into the Watch he had protected.

Jerrol waited as Denirion searched. The interior of the sentinal came into focus as the mist dissipated. Smooth silver wood surrounded them, and a low hum filled the air. Jerrol smiled and returned the sentinal's greeting. A flush of warmth spread through him and he flexed his shoulders.

"Captain," Denirion said with relief. "I can lead you to the Guardian; she is sleeping in one of the upper rooms. She is uninjured though suffering from the side effects of a drug they induced her to take."

"Do you know which drug it was?" Jerrol asked.

"It made her sleep a long time. The young lord was quite angry at the delay. I believe they overdosed her."

"Do you know where Aaron and his henchmen sleep?"

"Unfortunately not. I can only sense the Guardian."

"The Guardian? You speak of her as if she is *your* Guardian," Jerrol said.

"I believe she is. She can hear me. Lady Alyssa is the intended Guardian of Deepwater. She will return, and this Watch will thrive again," the Sentinal predicted.

"We had better go and rescue her, then. I suggest we bring her back here. She will be safe in your sentinal while we clean out those who should not be here. I assume, if she is your Guardian, she should be permitted entry?"

"It would be our honour," Denirion said, his eyes lighting up with pleasure.

"That's what we'll do, then. We need to get in and out

before dawn. Lieutenant Jennery and the men from Greenswatch will attack then, and the rangers will sweep in from the north."

"Good. It will be a relief to regain the Watch. Aaron is not the true lord of Deepwater. He is only interested in raping the land. There is a distressing lack of duty or concern for anyone other than himself. A true Guardian would know better."

Jerrol was surprised at the intensity of Denirion's words, but not the message.

The mist swirled and coalesced, a frisson of cool air across his skin, and then they were standing outside the sentinal tree, the bark subtly glowing in the dark. With a gesture from Denirion, the glow dimmed and disappeared, a little petulantly, Jerrol thought.

"You can celebrate later," he thought and grinned as a cheerful thrill touched his mind. He felt Denirion's grin in response.

"Don't encourage him," Denirion whispered. "Follow me."

Jerrol followed Denirion towards the house. "The Guardian is awake. I fear she may have taken things into her own hands. She says she is locked in," Denirion said, peering around him in the gloom.

"Just get us there. I'll open the door," Jerrol promised as they skirted the building.

The guard at the front door folded as the Sentinal dealt with him. Trussing him up and gagging him, Denirion left him in the shadows and hesitated at a soft whump behind him.

They spun, searching for the threat, and then at the sound of scrabbling above them, they looked up. Someone was climbing out of the window using a rope of knotted sheets, and they didn't look very secure.

Jerrol's stomach dropped as he realised who it was. Thank the Lady that Jennery wasn't around. "Alyssa!" Jerrol hissed. "Are you mad?"

Alyssa clung to the twisted sheets. Her foot slipped, and she dangled precariously as she thumped against the wall. Her bare feet scrabbled for purchase, and she peered down.

"Captain Jerrol? I couldn't unlock the door." She jerked and looked up in horror as her knotted sheets began to slip, her makeshift knots unravelling.

Jerrol glanced around him. He was surprised they hadn't been discovered yet, with the noise they were making. "Climb back up, Alyssa. We'll come and get you."

"No, no, I'll be fine." Alyssa began climbing down again. Jerrol frowned up at her. What was she wearing? Was she in her underclothes? Where were her skirts and shoes?

Alyssa almost made it down, but her weight on the sheets was too much and the knots slipped. She fell into the waiting arms of Sentinal Denirion.

Her auburn curls were a jumbled mess, but a wide smile spread across her pale face as she realised who it was. "Denirion. What are you doing here? I was escaping."

Denirion grinned. "Rescue party. There was no need for you to escape."

"Well, I didn't know that, did I? I wasn't going to wait for Aaron and his buddies to return. I had enough of them last time."

Denirion set her on her feet, surprising a small squeak out of her.

"Sorry," he breathed in her ear.

Alyssa picked up a bundle of dark cloth and shook it out. She stepped back into her skirts and fastened them under her jacket, and then she tugged on her boots. She grinned at the men. "I didn't think I could climb in them."

"We need to get you safely in Denirion's sentinal. We're about to attack," Jerrol said as he signalled Tagerill.

Alyssa straightened her shoulders. "I'm not hiding in the sentinal, even though I would be honoured to meet him. I want to help save my Watch. I am perfectly capable of protecting myself, as long as I am not outnumbered ten to one."

"Alyssa, you will be safer in the tree. You could rest. We have to journey back to Greenswatch after. Until then, Denirion's sentinal will look after you."

Alyssa shook her head. "I'm coming with you. Deepwater is mine. Stop wasting time, Captain. Make your signal."

"I will protect the Guardian," Denirion said.

Jerrol glared at him. "You'd better. Jennery will be having words when he finds out."

"He'd better get used to it if he intends on helping me," Alyssa said, a determined gleam in her eye. She grinned at Jerrol. "And I very much expect he will. So get on with it, Captain. Retrieve my Watch."

"Denirion, make the signal," Jerrol said, surrendering. "Stay behind Denirion, Alyssa. We have no idea what we are going to meet." He crouched by the entrance to the building, waiting for his support. The repercussions of Alyssa becoming Guardian of Deepwater was a problem for later. Having Jennery as the Lord of Deepwater was not such a farfetched idea, especially as it seemed Denirion had already accepted him.

Jerrol shook the riveting thought away and concentrated on the matter in hand; the reclaiming of Deepwater. There would be no new lord and lady if they didn't recover it first. He couldn't help his lips twitching at the thought, though.

The unit of King's Rangers advanced towards the house. Birlerion led half into the house, and the other half split off to the garrison with Parsillion. The scouts reported that the sentry and the off duty guards were all asleep. It looked like the Watch was going to be reclaimed with minimal resistance.

As the rangers cleared the ground floor, Alyssa followed, peering into doorways. "Ha," she said in satisfaction as she found the study. She sat in the leather-upholstered chair and began rifling through the papers on the desk. She looked up. "Denirion, I promise I'll remain here. Place a guard on the door and go help."

Denirion handed her a dagger. "Don't trust anyone until we give the all-clear. We could still flush out some of Aaron's men."

Alyssa nodded. "Don't worry. I won't." She hefted the dagger. "Nice," she murmured as she placed it on the desk beside her and started reading.

Jerrol followed the rangers up the stairs with Tagerill close behind him, searching for Aaron and his steward, Peverill. Birlerion found a guard with a little more conviction and drawing his sword forced him back down the corridor as Tagerill and Jerrol continued deeper into the house.

Another guard stood foursquare in the hallway, his sword raised in defiance, and although he flinched at the sound of Tagerill's broadsword leaving its sheath, he stood his ground.

"A worthy foe," Tagerill muttered as he advanced.

Jerrol spent the time studying the corridor. Who was significant enough to warrant a guard that was motivated to do his job? This must be where Aaron slept, and he must have been awoken by the racket that Tagerill and the guard were making.

Jerrol managed to slip past when Tagerill had the guard pinned up against the wall and opened the door. His brows rose as he saw a tall, dark-haired man, half-dressed and frantically stuffing papers into a case. The man froze as he saw Jerrol framed in the door, sword in hand.

"You!" he spat.

"Councillor Fortes, I believe," Jerrol said, advancing into the room. "What brings you to Deepwater? Velmouth no longer safe for you? Though you are no longer their councillor, are you? Is your name even Fortes?"

"It's near enough," the man growled.

"Sure you want to die under a false name?" Jerrol asked, raising his sword. He gripped it tightly. It almost jumped out of his hand; it was so eager to taste the Ascendant's blood.

Fortes scowled. "You'll regret this." He grabbed his sword and waved it in front of him.

"Not as much as you will," Jerrol replied. "Did you come here to enspell Lord Aaron?"

Fortes laughed. "Why waste our time? He was already supportive of our goals; there is nothing stronger than innate belief, and, of course, a belief that is fueled by a love of money." He circled the room, his eyes focused on Jerrol's sword. It vibrated in Jerrol's hand.

"He planned the downfall of his father with your help, then?" Jerrol said as he launched his attack, his sword flicking across Fortes' face.

Fortes grunted and felt his chin, wincing at the sight of blood. He counterattacked, spitting out his words as he tried to force Jerrol into the corner. "He came up with it himself. He didn't need us. Except to persuade the guards."

Jerrol manoeuvred out of the trap that Fortes tried to set and went on the offensive. He drove Fortes back across the room and the Ascendant retreated under the force of the blade. "Where did you get that sword?" he gasped.

"Why? What do you know of it?" Jerrol asked as he managed to wedge Fortes in a corner.

Fortes' black eyes widened. "It's not possible," he whispered as Jerrol deflected his blade and drove his sword into his chest. Fortes hissed in surprise and blood bubbled out of his mouth as he slid off the blade and down the wall, his eyes glazing as he collapsed to the floor.

The sword vibrated in Jerrol's hand, followed by a haze of smug satisfaction, which filled his mind. Jerrol carefully wiped his blade on the Ascendant's clothes before sheathing it. He scanned the papers on Fortes' bed and his eyebrows rose in surprise at the damming correspondence. Ambassadors from Terolia and Elothia were vying for Deepwater resources. Jerrol frowned. Why would Terolia need timber? There was also a handful of flyers advertising speeches being held in a range of towns across Terolia by the elusive Var'geris. He stashed the case under the bed and returned to the corridor. He would have to come back for the case later. Tagerill had dispatched the guard and was nowhere to be seen. The guard's body had been left lying across the passage.

Jerrol followed the hall around the bend towards the sound of clashing swords, and he quickened his pace. The corridor ended in an open door leading to an opulent bedroom decorated in blues and gold. Aghast, he halted in the doorway as he saw Tagerill fighting with Peverill. Aaron cowered behind him, backed into a corner of the room.

Peverill cursed as Jerrol appeared in the door. He spun and thrust his sword into Aaron's chest before throwing his cloak around himself and bursting out of the second-storey window. He disappeared, leaving his sword behind.

Tagerill lurched as his opponent vanished and stood swaying in front of Aaron in disbelief.

"Tagerill, are you alright?" Jerrol asked as he pushed passed to kneel beside the Lord of Deepwater.

Aaron gasped desperately for air; his brown eyes frantic.

His fingers scrabbled against the plush carpet, but there was no hope for him. The sword thrust had punctured his chest through a lung and out the back. Blood seeped out of him, absorbed by the soft pile of the rug beneath him. His life ebbing away as he struggled.

Jerrol looked down at him. "What didn't they want you to tell us?" But Aaron was beyond speaking. His shaking hand grabbed Jerrol's arm and he deliberately stared over his shoulder. Jerrol spun to see what was in his line of sight—a fireplace with a mantel. He glanced back at Aaron, but the panic had faded from his eyes and his stare was fixed. Jerrol closed his eyelids with a gentle sigh.

"Captain?" The tremor in Tagerill's voice made Jerrol look up. Tagerill collapsed and Jerrol braced as he caught him, easing him to the floor.

"Where are you hurt?" he asked urgently, but Tagerill was unresponsive; his face waxy and pale. Jerrol tugged open Tagerill's jacket as he found blood and winced at the deep slash across his ribs. He ripped the bottom off his shirt and folded it into a pad, which he slapped against the wound. He called Ari.

Grabbing a sheet from the bed, he struggled to tear it up. He knotted the strips together and tied the pad in place. He searched further, knowing that there was another injury and finding it high on his shoulder. A stab wound, deep and dangerous and bleeding freely. His shirt in shreds, he cursed under his breath as he folded up another pad and held it tight against the wound. Then he eased Tagerill into his lap, his head supported against his chest.

Ari blinked into view. "Find Denirion. Call a healer."

Help was coming. His men were methodically searching the manor and they would arrive soon. Jerrol bit his lip as a sense of loss fluttered in his stomach. Which bit of 'no risks' had Tagerill not understood? No, he calmed himself, the

Lady would protect. Tagerill would be fine, and they had a healer here with them. He would be able to heal Tagerill. Birlerion had fully recovered. So would Tagerill.

Jennery and Frenerion arrived south of Deepwater in the pre-dawn. They positioned themselves at the junction of the road, which led up to the mansion by the Lower lake. One of Jerrol's scouts appeared out of the morning mist and confirmed that most of the guards were asleep in the barracks and the roving patrol had been dealt with. They were awaiting the Captain's signal that the lady had been retrieved and they would proceed.

There was a chill in the air and that peculiar stillness just before everything begins to stir and wake up. Landis' men checked their weapons for the final time and waited expectantly. Jennery turned to speak to the Inquisitor, who was hovering by his shoulder. "Not long now," he murmured. "Keep to the rear. Let the men clear the targets before you approach. Healer Clennin, please stay with the Inquisitor until you are called for."

Jennery was relieved that Jerrol had thought to request a healer from the king. It wasn't often you were privileged enough to get one, and although this mission appeared straight forward, you never knew what might happen. Clennin was a newly qualified healer, and his senior had said the experience would be good for him. Experience of battles helped a healer keep his sensitivity to his patient's needs, or so the senior said.

Jennery sent his scouts out and slowly advanced his men until they could see the Deepwater mansion silhouetted against the early streaks of grey stealing across the night sky. The waiting was always the worst. The night was unnaturally silent, waiting patiently with them.

One of his scouts returned, reporting that the signal was imminent, and a blinding flash of light briefly split the air above the lone sentinal tree. Jennery and his men charged up the road, surrounding the garrison. The resistance was non-existent as the men blearily awoke to sword points at their throats. Jennery looked around the barracks in disgust. The reek of alcohol and the sweet tobacco weed that soldiers favoured permeated the air.

He left his men to round them up and scanned the Deep-water grounds. A couple of pockets of fighting had broken out at the two guard posts, where the sentries were putting up a token resistance, but Jerrol had been right; the guards were sloppy and undisciplined.

As he approached the mansion, a strange Sentinal, who he assumed was Denirion came rushing down the steps, sending the call out for the healer. His eyes lit up in relief as he spotted the healer behind Jennery. Clennin darted forward, gripping his bag as Denirion simply said, "Tagerill," before spinning back into the doorway, dragging the healer with him.

Jennery's gut tightened at the sense of urgency driving Denirion, that did not bode well. He joined the men sweeping through the house, pausing at the study door, where a young ranger stood guard.

"Alyssa! What are you doing in here? You should be safe in Denirion's sentinal. That was the plan."

"I'm quite safe here. I have my guard on the door, and Denirion is listening in, just in case. Lea, you would not believe what I have found. Aaron was going to strip this Watch bare. His plans are horrifying."

Jennery grimaced at her persistent use of his first name; he supposed he would have to get used it. His grimace morphed into a grin. He couldn't help it; she looked quite at home. He tilted his head. "It suits you, my dear. I'll leave

Peppins here to help you." Decanting Peppins, the Inquisitor, whose nose twitched in delight at the scattered paperwork across the room, Jennery left. He gave a stern warning to the guard on the door to stay alert, just in case.

The rangers herded the servants—discovered in cramped quarters in the basement—into one of the upper reception rooms until Peppins was ready to start his interrogations. Jennery mounted the stairs with a sense of trepidation, peering down corridors and following the sound of muffled voices until he found a concentration of people at the end of the East wing.

Jerrol, minus his jacket, his shirt grimy and hanging in tatters, peered into the brick fireplace. Jennery briefly found the time to wonder how Jerrol had managed to ruin so many of his clothes before he saw the gory sight of Tagerill laid out on the floor, the healer working frantically over him. Aaron's body was slumped in the corner, ignored.

"Jerrol, what are you doing?" Jennery asked. "How is Tagerill?"

Jerrol grimaced in welcome. "He's in the best hands. The healer will tell us when he has a chance. Thank the Lady we brought him with us." He considered the fireplace and ducked under the mantelpiece, carefully feeling around inside until a muffled exclamation preceded him back out. His clothes were now begrimed in soot, a black smudge on his cheek.

Jennery watched him as he unwrapped a small bundle. "Aaron tried to tell me something before he died. But Peverill turned on him and ran him through; he didn't have a chance. He deliberately stared over at the fireplace. It seems the final betrayal made him want some sort of revenge or something, I guess." Jerrol looked down at the package in his hands; a familiar notebook and a piece of parchment folded over many times to make it the same size as the notebook.

He glanced up at Jennery. “Where did you leave the Inquisitor?”

“With Alyssa. He was rubbing his hands with glee in Aaron’s study. Or I should say in Alyssa’s study. It seems she’s claimed it. I thought the plan was to hide her in Denirion’s sentinal?”

“She wouldn’t go. You know what she’s like; she wanted claim her Watch, and no one was going to stop her.” Jerrol finished with a grin.

Jennery laughed. “Wouldn’t have her any other way.”

“Let’s join her, then,” Jerrol said as he watched Tagerill being lifted onto a stretcher. His face was far too pale. Clennin had connected a leather bag of fluids and was repeatedly telling the guard holding the bag to keep it up high.

The healer looked across at Jerrol. He rubbed a bloody hand across his face, leaving a smear of red in its path. “Sentinal Frenerion found what’s left of the infirmary. We’ll move him there for now. I have him stabilised, but he has lost a lot of blood.”

Jerrol nodded. “Keep me informed if anything changes,” he said, moving out of the way as the stretcher party left the room. Crouching over Aaron’s body, he gently eased him down on the floor. He rifled through his pockets, which, not surprisingly, were empty, as it looked like he had grabbed the nearest clothes when the alarm had been raised. The Watch ring gleamed on Aaron’s finger, and Jerrol pulled it off. Head bowed, he stared at it before pocketing it. Jennery shook out a bloody towel and lay it over Aaron’s face.

“Move him to wherever we’ve set up the mortuary and send one of the maids up here to clean the room,” Jerrol instructed as he led the way out of the room. He stopped at Fortes’ room. The Ascendant’s body was still slumped in the corner, and he made a mental note to send someone up to move it. He rummaged under the bed and pulled the case back out. It was untouched. He checked the room for any further items of interest, but there was nothing else, so he picked up the case and went down to the study to find Alyssa and Peppins, the King's Inquisitor.

Peppins was seated opposite Alyssa, writing out a request for more assistants when Jerrol and Jennery arrived. The pile of correspondence and incriminating evidence was growing. Jerrol grinned. Jennery was right. Alyssa did look at home.

Alyssa looked up as they entered and smiled as Jennery crossed the room to stand beside her. Unconsciously, she patted his arm. "How is Tagerill?"

"He is stable, which is all we can ask for at this stage," Jerrol replied and added to her workload. "I recommend you check out the household staff first; they need to start righting this house as soon as possible. We also have a barrack full of prisoners who need to be fed and watered until we can unspell them."

Jerrol showed the notebook to an aghast Peppins, explaining how the list of names and keywords were connected and how they controlled people under the Ascendants *Mentiserium* spell; the spell that he had discovered in Velmouth during his previous clash with Fortes.

Alyssa waved a hand as Denirion hovered in the doorway. "Peppins is going to remain here with Denirion and restore the Watch as much as possible."

Jerrol nodded. "I understand Clennin will also stay with Tagerill as he is unable to move him yet." He paused, watching Alyssa and Jennery. "We need to return to Greenswatch this afternoon and inform Lady Olivia of what happened to her son, and then I think we should report to the king and, I suggest, petition him to induct you, Alyssa, as the Deepwater Guardian."

Alyssa glanced at Jennery. "Denirion and I were

discussing it earlier. I would need Lea by my side; do you think the king would release him?"

"Well, I suggest you ask him. Jennery reports to the Lady now, so I expect she would approve." It seemed they were already way ahead of him.

"Well, the Lady's word carries all, so that's what we'll propose to the king. Denirion has stated that I am his Guardian. I want Lea. We come as a package," Alyssa said firmly, linking her arm with Jennery's.

Jerrol's lips twitched at Jennery's stoical expression. He hated his name. In fact, he never used Leander, always reverting to Jennery. Alyssa was determined; it was all she would call him. He was fortunate that she had, at least, shortened it.

"Good, that's what we'll do. Denirion, we will return Alyssa and Jennery to you as soon as possible. Peppins, whatever you need as you unravel this mess, just send a runner to the king, understand? I will leave the rangers with you. They can help manage the patrols and the prisoners. Jennery, can you find Birlerion and round up Landis and his men to return with us? We were fortunate." He scowled. "The only serious injury was Tagerill."

"I need some assistance to unravel this mess as you put it. Could you take my request to the King's Justice?" Peppins asked.

Of course." Jerrol pocketed Peppins' request for aid and clasped Denirion's arm in farewell. "We'll see you soon," he promised as he indicated for Alyssa to precede him out of the study.

Jennery met her in the courtyard, leading her horse, Firefly, who was none the worse for her unexpected stay in the strange stables.

Before they left, Jerrol visited the infirmary for a final report on Tagerill. He found Healer Clennin well entrenched. He doubted Clennin would be leaving any time soon.

"How is he?" Jerrol asked as he stood at the end of the bed, observing the injured Sentinal. Tagerill's complexion was still unnaturally pale, though the waxy appearance of his skin had gone, Jerrol was relieved to see.

"No change; early days yet. As long as I can get the fluids into him to replenish his blood loss, I can stabilise him. The shoulder wound is the worst. It's deep, and we'll have to watch for infection. He's lucky it didn't completely slice any of the tendons, though the damage is bad enough. He'll have to do some work to regain the full use of his arm."

Jerrol sucked his breath in, his face scrunching up in sympathy as he nodded. "Do you need me to send anything from Greenswatch?"

Clennin reached for a scrap of paper. "I wrote out a list for you; the top five are the most urgent. There is nothing here, and my field supplies won't last long. I don't know how they treated anyone for anything. If Greenswatch can't supply the rest, I can wait for it to arrive from Old Vespers."

Jerrol folded the paper over and added it to the parchment in his inner pocket, along with the Deepwater Watch ring. "Consider it done," he said as he left. It sounded like Alyssa would be gaining a healer as well as a Watch. Clennin had already identified its deficiencies, which was no bad thing.

He returned to the courtyard, taking Zin'talia's reins from one of the rangers.

"Alyssa will have her work cut out here. The stables are cold and drafty, and the horses are miserable. They haven't looked after them at all." Zin'talia's voice was soft.

Jerrol glanced at the ranger. "The horses need tending. It seems they have been neglected and are in a sorry condition."

"Yes, sir. Much like everything else. I'll be staying with a unit. We'll soon have the stables repaired and the horses looked after."

"Good, carry on."

"*We'll soon be back in Vespers. I am sure the king will have got you some treats,*" he thought as he mounted. Zin'talia ruminated happily on the promise of some of her favourite snack, Baliweed.

Birlerion hurried across the courtyard with Landis. Their uniforms were filthy and streaked with mud, and Jerrol wondered what they could have been doing. "Captain, I just heard. What news of Tagerill?"

"The healer says he's stable. We'll have to leave him here. The healer won't allow him to be moved. If you want to stay with him, you can. You can meet us in Old Vespers in a couple of days."

Birlerion hesitated, his face strained and grubby. "I'll see him if I may. He ought to be transferred to Denirion's sentinal; it would speed his recovery. I'll speak to the healer, but I'll go with you if you can wait." He hurried into the infirmary.

"Where have you been?" Jerrol asked Landis.

"There was a report of a stash of opiates out by the home lake. We've been dragging the waters, and we found quite a supply. Birlerion thought they were manufacturing some of it here; we dismantled a whole distilling system."

"Make sure the rangers check for any further signs. We need to eradicate all illegal drugs from Deepwater."

Landis twisted his lips. There was a lot of land to cover. "Yes, sir."

13

GREENSWATCH

At Jerrol's signal, the cavalcade formed up around him, and Birlerion returned to his position by his shoulder. Jerrol mused over the fact that it had only been a few hours since they had come down this road. He dispatched a rider to Greenswatch and thence on to Old Vespers with the news. He was not looking forward to explaining to Lady Olivia how Aaron had died, though, when it came to it, she surprised him by saying simply: "He lost his way, my poor boy; he is with the Lady now and his transgressions will be forgiven. I think it would have been worse if he had been tried for treason and dragged Stefan's good name through the mire for no purpose." Jerrol thought she had been secretly relieved that the uncertainty was over.

One surprise that met them at Greenswatch was the arrival of Captain Bryce from Stoneford. He clattered into the courtyard not long after they arrived. After a brief greeting to Jerrol and Simeon, he strode up to Lady Olivia and gently gathered her into his arms. She burst into tears and he led her away to the privacy of a seat in a sheltered arbour where he very agreeably continued to soothe her shattered nerves. A rather smug Ari appeared and perched on Jerrol's shoulder, preening himself.

Everyone had a chance to freshen up, even time to shave and change clothes, especially Jerrol who was particularly bedraggled. Some found time to grab a much-needed lunch. Jerrol spent the afternoon closeted with the Healer and Clennin's list before sending a request off to Old Vespers for medical supplies for Deepwater.

Simeon hosted an impromptu gathering, and they spent the evening discussing Deepwater and how to restore it, and then everyone retired, exhausted.

Jerrol rose early the next morning, eager to get on the road. He collected Birlerion from outside his door and descended the stairs.

It was time to report back to the king, but he had one more job to do before he returned to Old Vespers. He sighed as his clothes shimmered in the sunlight. He encouraged them to dampen down. "Do you have this problem?" he asked Birlerion, scowling down at his uniform.

"Not any more, give it a few years and it will settle down," Birlerion replied with a sly grin.

Jerrol caught the glint his eye and huffed, not sure whether to believe him or not as he paused on the steps. Ari appeared, fluttering around his head. Coaxing him down, he stared intently into his emerald green eyes, concentrating on his questions. How are Saerille and Serillion faring with the Veil? Are they safe? Ari meeped and flew out of view.

They walked out into the courtyard, and Jerrol raised a hand in greeting as he saw Versillion.

Versillion veered towards them. "Captain, you're not leaving already?"

"Lots to do. The king will want an update on the

Watches. At least we have good news for him. You need to make sure the Watch is at full strength as I'm sure the Ascendants haven't given up yet. This is just the beginning," Jerrol said, striding towards the stables.

"We'll be ready," vowed Versillion.

"Lieutenant Jennery will escort Lady Alyssa and Lady Olivia to Vespers. Birlerion, Parsillion, and I need to get on the road."

"Yes, sir. And you are going where?" Versillion asked.

"To wake up some more of your brethren."

"That is good to hear. They will be pleased to meet you," Versillion promised as he left the overcrowded stables.

By the time Jerrol had led Zin'talia out into the courtyard, Birlerion and Parsillion were waiting for him, along with Lord Simeon.

"There's another Darian here, Jerrol," Zin'talia murmured.

"Another Darian? Are you sure?"

"Yes, he's not bonded."

"Maybe he's waiting for Simeon. Have you spoken to him?"

"I haven't had a chance. He was out in the field. I didn't realise he was here, and now we're leaving. We ought to make sure he is looked after properly."

Pausing by the steps, Jerrol shielded his eyes from the glare of the early morning sun. "My mare says there's a Darian in your stables."

Simeon chuckled. "I think you must be mistaken. We can't afford a Darian."

"Maybe you ought to check the bloodlines, then. Maybe he has Darian in his history. My mare said he hasn't bonded yet; he must be waiting for his rider. A Darian is a gift from the Lady. He must be here for a reason."

"I'll speak to our horse master. He knows where all our horses are from. I'll be surprised if there is a Darian here; maybe your mare is mistaken."

"Doubt it. She would know." He turned to Jennery, who had a smile on his face. "Jennery, I'll meet you at the palace in a few days."

"One of us could come with you," Jennery offered. "You're still being hunted; it's not safe to travel on your own."

"Birlerion and Parsillion will protect me, and we'll use the waystones if we can find them. We should be fine. The ladies need you to escort them safely to Old Vespers. By the time you get everyone organised, the day will be much advanced. No. We'll travel fast and light, and we'll meet you there." He shook hands with Jennery and Bryce. "Lady protect your travels," he said as he swung up into his saddle and led the way out of the courtyard.

Jerrol heaved a deep sigh as he rode. He resolved one problem, only to find another. Deepwater may be in safe hands now, but what else were the Ascendants up to? The interference from Terolia was concerning and out of character. The Terolians had a deeply ingrained code of honour; to break it was unheard of. If the Ascendants were weaselling their way into the Families, then nothing good would come of it.

He had visited Terolia, once or twice for the king. It was a harsh environment, lacking the plentiful water found in Vespiri. Remembering the extensive grass plains to the east and the scoured desert landscape curving for miles down to the south, he started to sweat just thinking of travelling for endless days across those shifting sands.

The Terolian population was generally nomadic, moving from one location to another, depending on their needs and the time of the year. They rarely visited the villages, which had sprung up around the scarce water holes, though they did camp on the outskirts to trade their horses and goods at the markets. The whole structure was maintained by the

Families—a network of three dominant family lines and three related lines, the Atolea and Solari Families being the most prominent.

As he rode, he worried about the possibility of the Ascendants upsetting such a community-based structure, the whole purpose of which was to look after one other.

It was early evening of the second day of their journey when the landscape around them changed from rolling arable fields to plantings of ash trees. The frothy canopies swished in the breeze, heavy with clumps of seeds, which fluttered in the wind, spiraling loose and shimmering in the air. Jerrol idly observed the erratic path of the seed pods as the wind swirled around them and led them deeper into the Watch. Thick waxy bushes of rhododendrons led the way to Marchwood Manor, Lord William's home. The grey stone manor house appeared out of the woodland, dwarfed by a tall sentinal tree, its silver bark gleaming in the evening sun.

Lord William's steward was waiting on the steps as they pulled up in front of the manor house. "Is Lord William home?" Jerrol asked as he prepared to dismount.

"He's out at the plantation. I can send a runner if you would like to step inside and wait?"

Jerrol handed his reins to Birlerion. "By all means, though first I need to greet Anterion. He has been waiting patiently long enough." Jerrol walked up to the tall tree and lay his hand on the silvery trunk, welcoming the frisson of the Lady's power as it shimmered through him. A broad-shouldered giant of a man approached him. "Captain," Anterion said, striking his chest as his silver eyes twinkled down at Jerrol. He was pure muscle, and he dwarfed the other Sentinals.

"Anterion, it's good to meet you at last," Jerrol said, looking up at him as he gripped his thick forearm.

"Lord William said you were on your way, he has been keeping me informed. He also explained the situation, that it's been three thousand years since we last walked this land. I appreciate his efforts even though he did not know if I would hear him," Anterion said, his voice a deep rumble as he followed Jerrol up the steps to the manor house. He greeted Parsillion as the steward stood gaping at the top of the steps.

Birlerion shook the steward's shoulder. "I believe you were offering us some refreshments?" he prompted him as he in turn, greeted Anterion. Jerrol watched him thoughtfully; Birlerion seemed to know everyone.

"My apologies. This way, please," the man stammered as he led the way into the dim hallway and down the corridor to a small room overlooking the terraced gardens. Jerrol stood staring out of the window as the steward fussed, before turning to Anterion. "Where were the other Sentinals located? I thought there was more than one Sentinal in Marchwood," he said as he accepted a glass of wine.

The steward bowed himself out of the room as Anterion replied. "We numbered four, myself and Laerille here in Marchwood. Tianerille was on the borders to the South and Venterion to the East towards the new forest." Anterion shrugged. "I know there was heavy fighting on the borders. Tianerille and Venterion were under pressure at the end and we lost contact with them. Laerille lies within my sentinal. I have been unable to wake her. I managed to drag her with me at the end, but although her wounds have healed, she has not woken."

"Do you believe Tianerille and Venterion are gone?" Birlerion asked, his voice tentative as he watched his friend.

Anterion shrugged again, speaking with reluctance. "I cannot sense them. I fear they were lost."

"It seems we are missing quite a few Sentinals. I think if we find one, we may find the others. The Ascendants may have found a way to restrain them. Though where and how, I have no idea. We'll await Lord William, and then I will see if I can awake Laerille," Jerrol said.

Anterion stood straighter; his eyes shining in anticipation.

Birlerion and Anterion were engaged in a low-toned conversation when the dapper Lord of the Watch entered the room, extending his hand to Jerrol. "Captain Haven," he grinned, his glance taking in the occupants of the room.

"Lord William," Jerrol replied with a slight bow. "May I introduce Sentinals Anterion of Marchwood, Parsillion of Stoneford, and Birlerion of Greenswatch."

Lord William swung around, his grin widening. "Finally! Anterion, it is an honour to meet you."

"The honour is mine, Guardian," Anterion responded, shaking the proffered hand.

Lord William greeted the other Sentinals before turning to Jerrol. "We've been expecting you. I'm glad you could make it. We've been struggling with an upsurge in Ascendant rhetoric and council irregularities, but we don't know how to combat it."

"There will be one Ascendant controlling everyone else. They are usually tall, dark-haired, hooded, and hovering in the shadows. As there is no one here influencing you, I would imagine they are within the council," Jerrol explained.

"I will find him for you," Anterion said, a sharp grin on his face.

"Look for a notebook. It will have a list of names and keywords. Repeating the keyword will cancel all previous commands and allow you to redirect them. You will need to instruct them to disregard all previous commands and to be impervious to the effect of *Mentiserium*. We need to release them to make their own choices. Be aware that removing the compulsion can cause convulsions; make sure you hold them steady, so they don't injure themselves."

"*Mentiserium*," Anterion hissed.

"It is prevalent in Vespiri," Birlerion said, "and elsewhere, I expect."

Lord William nodded in agreement. "I saw you release Simeon and Reid. We will also perform a rededication to the Lady for those who wish to attend. I think we need to remind the people of the Lady's grace."

"There should be a waystone here. Anterion, you should look for that, too," Birlerion added.

Jerrol rose and placed his glass on the table. "Anterion says there were four Sentinals in the Watch of Marchwood, yet you only have one present. We need to find the others. Just because they are not in a tree does not mean they are not still here. They couldn't cross the Veil, so they have to be here."

Anterion looked up from his glass. He swirled the liquid thoughtfully. "Maybe Laerille can sense them? Wherever she is. If you can contact her and bring her back, then that's a start."

"Laerille?" Lord William asked.

"Your second Sentinal," Jerrol said with a smile. "She resides in Anterion's sentinal tree, but she does not respond. She was wounded in the last battle, and although healed, she is not here."

"You once asked if we could relocate the sentinal trees," Parsillion said, a crease between his eyes as he pursued his thought. "I had thought the sentinals sheltered us, that the Lady created them at that final moment to protect us. But what if they are part of us and we had to be conscious for them to be rooted? We are separate yet connected. I am miles from my tree; but I can feel him. I know he wants me to return soon. If we can plant one for Laerille and the others, maybe they will be able to return?"

Lord William pursed his lips. "We've never seen a sentinal seed; there have been no sucker roots or seed pods. If there was, my nurserymen could help. They have been focused on the new plantations of late, so they have all the tools we need."

"Let's see what Laerille has to say," Jerrol said as he led the way out of the room, closely followed by Anterion.

Lord William paused to speak to his steward before following them down the steps and around to the towering sentinal, inspecting the tree with fresh eyes.

"We will watch carefully," he promised as one of his nurserymen hurried up, eyes alight with interest.

The air around Jerrol and Anterion shimmered as they faded from view. The nurseryman gasped and Lord William gripped his arm to steady him. "Throw all you know out of the window. Watch and learn. There has to be a way to grow sentinal trees; more than one life may depend on it," he said as they circled the tall tree, watching intently.

Inside the sentinal, Anterion led Jerrol to the supine form of Laerille. She was unnaturally pale; her golden hair curling around her hollow face, looked brittle and lifeless. She lay in an alcove protected by a curving shell of bark, extending from the sentinal. It pulsed gently in time with her heartbeat, which gradually grew louder as they approached. The beat reverberated through the trunk to the men waiting outside, who exchanged startled glances and observed warily.

Jerrol dropped to his knees beside Laerille. She was not only pale; her skin was translucent, her veins opaque pale blue lines beneath her papery skin. Silver scars puckered around her right eye, crisscrossed her cheek, and trailed down her throat and across her chest. Jerrol winced at the sight of what usually would have been death scars; few would survive such wounds. He placed a gentle palm against her right temple and the other on her chest over her heart. He closed his eyes and reached out, extending a firm wake up call.

The sustaining link of the sentinal fell away as all sensation disappeared and he was suspended in nothingness. Jerrol controlled his imminent panic and concentrated on listening for the heartbeat. A soft breeze caressed his skin; a sense of welcome and relief amongst soft murmurs. The sound of multiple voices blended into a soft sigh, like sand sifting in the desert. Bird song; the trill of a bird singing his heart out was a counterpoint to the expectant thrum of voices. The scent of freshly turned soil warming in the sun, recently watered, permeated the air. The essence of life.

His chest expanded as his heart swelled, embracing his lost Sentinal and welcoming her home. Her soft tears fell, moistening the soil as his chest clenched, and a seed pod pushed its way out of the sentinal's trunk and fell into the waiting hole—a home for Laerille to return too. The Land took up the seed and embraced them, and Laerille opened her eyes in wonder and then exhaled.

"My Captain," she whispered. "I am so glad to see you." Her silver eyes glistened with tears, and Jerrol gently wiped them away.

"Welcome home," he whispered, in turn, kissing her cheek, and the sound of her heartbeat faded as she disappeared.

Jerrol slumped to the floor, his limbs trembling, an ache in his chest. Anterion braced him, but Jerrol knew he wasn't finished. He took a breath as he held his mind and heart open to the Land, and the sentinal tree trembled as the Land embraced him in full. An ancient feminine presence touched him. A soft welcome was followed by a flurry of images; a young girl with auburn curls running barefoot across a grassy field, grey stone towers rising from Elothian soil, desert sands sifting under a blazing sun, impenetrable rock fissured by cracks; a maelstrom of wind buffeting protective arms that were sheltering Sentinals, trapped outside time and life.

His hands clenched around what he knew were more seed pods. The Land rummaged through his memories and posed a few silent questions in the vault of his mind before subsiding to a gentle vibration in his chest, slowly filling the void left by the seeds with a sustaining flush of energy that dulled the ache. He opened his eyes to the worried face of Anterion hovering above him.

"What did you do?" Anterion whispered, his voice sharp with fear.

"Me?" Jerrol grinned impishly. "I awoke Laerille, as promised. I think you'll find she has her own tree, now."

"At what expense? We only have one Captain; you can't even stand."

"I was greeting the Land."

"You were what?" Anterion's grip tightened.

"The Land will sustain me. Her tears blend with ours. I'll be fine in a moment," Jerrol murmured, closing his eyes. He felt weak, yet exhilarated. "All will be well," he mumbled.

Anterion picked up Jerrol and lay him on the bed vacated by Laerille. The golden tendrils from the sentinal extended. They would soon wrap him and restore what they could. Anterion watched in concern as Jerrol relaxed.

Anterion stepped out of his tree and transitioned into the Watch. A second tall, silver-barked tree visibly grew beside his tree. It expanded as it rose. The broad leaves unfurled into a pointed umbrella and the vivid green leaves reached out towards the leaves of his tree. His sentinal's leaves were rustling in welcome, and a huge smile spread over Anterion's face. Lord William and his nurseryman were standing transfixed, eyes wide, hands grubby from planting the seed pod.

Birlerion came across and slapped his shoulder. "You did it. It *is* possible." He grinned in relief.

"Not without the Captain," Anterion said, watching the tree in awe as it continued to grow.

"Where is the Captain?" Birlerion asked, peering over his shoulder in sudden concern.

"Recovering," Anterion said, his voice clipped.

"What did he do?"

Anterion sighed. "I don't know. He was muttering about the land and tears, and then he collapsed."

"He spoke with Marguerite? Is she here?"

"He never mentioned her. I don't think so."

Lord William waved a hand, his eyes still fixed on the growing sentinal. "The soil; it rose to take the seed pod. It was like it was waiting for it," he said, his voice tinged with awe.

"A miracle," the nurseryman whispered, his voice choking.

"A miracle, indeed," Jerrol said, his voice laced with exhaustion. They all turned at the sound of his voice behind them. "The question is, how do we make it repeatable? We need to save all the Sentinals, and I'm not going to be around to do this every time," he said, indicating the still expanding tree.

The nurseryman shrugged. "You need a seed to grow a tree like this. That one just appeared out of the trunk. Can it produce more? We could plant and nurture them until you need them."

Jerrol held out an unsteady hand. "Will these do?" he asked with a strained smile. A dozen emerald green seed pods lay in his hand.

The nurseryman grinned. "They will do very well."

"Guard them well. They will be needed soon. Be ready." Jerrol felt a physical wrench as he parted with the seeds; the ache in his chest made him draw breath and sway. Birlerion steadied him, his face tight.

Jerrol straightened, flexing aching muscles, and walked over to the new sentinal tree. He lay his palm against the smooth trunk and Laerille walked towards him out of the swirling mist. "Are you ready?" he asked.

Laerille's smile was lopsided but heartfelt. Her silver eyes were bright, and her golden hair vibrant. Her scars glowed in the subdued light. "We will be ready. You will lead the way, and we will be waiting," she promised.

"Good. It will take time to retrieve them, but they will come," Jerrol warned.

Laerille stretched her arms in the air. "The Guardian stands ready. We will protect them all."

Jerrol stepped out of the tree and approached Lord William. "This is Sentinal Laerille. She will help you nurture the new sentinal trees until I can find those who are missing. Laerille, this is Lord William of Marchwood," he said, observing the expression on Anterion's face.

Lord William held out his hand. "Sentinal, welcome home." He blinked as Laerille's joy at being awake embraced them all.

"Guardian, it is good to be home at last." Her eyes drifted over to the Sentinals beside him. "Anterion!" she gasped, dropping William's hand and striding over to the broad-chested Sentinal.

"Laerille." Anterion embraced her.

Lord William cleared his throat. "Ah, shall we give them a moment?" he suggested, indicating that they enter the house. His blue eyes twinkled as he watched the two Sentinals. "I think this must be a much-belated reunion."

Jerrol grinned as he slapped Birlerion on the shoulder.

"We need to get back on the road. I think this Watch will be in safe hands now, and we have much to do."

"It's late. Stay the night and start early tomorrow. My wife and I will be glad of your company. If I may say so, Captain, you look like you need a good night's sleep," Lord William said.

Jerrol allowed Lord William to persuade him. He was bone-tired, and once the Sentinals agreed with him, Jerrol knew he would be travelling no further that day. The newly awoken Sentinals dragged Birlerion and Parsillion off to hear what had been happening, and Jerrol spent a pleasant evening enjoying a good meal and good company.

14

WATCH TOWERS, STONEFORD WATCH

Serillion found Saerille holed up in the mountains that loomed above the Towers. Her camp was basic but well hidden. Her horse was tethered in a patch of grass behind the shallow cave she had found. Only his Sentinal senses led him to her.

At first, he had thought her dead; she was so still and pale. But her chest rose after a moment, and he exhaled in relief. Dropping his saddlebags next to hers, he folded his long legs as he sat beside her, laying his sword by his side.

Closing his eyes, he reached for Saerille, searching for the sensation, the link that said 'Sentinal' to him. He found the thread and followed it up to the Veil, expanding his senses until he reached the open space and the unworldly magic that protected them. His lips twitched at the conundrum; magic reluctantly restraining magic.

The Veil glistened like a spider's web gilded by the morning frost; a delicate sparkle belying its hidden strength. Pale strands entwined into a protective sheath that encompassed the world of Remargaren, yet allowed the light and warmth of the sun and moon to penetrate and the distant stars to twinkle in the night sky.

The Veil snarled in his mind as he approached, searching for signs of Saerille. Serillion found her trying to untangle herself. The Veil had snared her; the broken threads wrapping themselves around her, trying to burrow into her so that they could extract the life that the Veil so desperately craved.

Serillion slashed at the threads and dragged Saerille back down to her body, where she gulped a deep breath and moaned. He opened his eyes and patted her shoulder.

"Relax, Saerille. Just for a moment; catch your breath." Serillion unpacked his water skin and helped her sit up. "You've been spending too long up there," he admonished, as he offered her a drink.

"It won't stay sealed. My repairs are being undone." Her voice was low and strained as if she had just run up the mountainside without stopping.

"Still, getting trapped in the Veil is not going to seal it any quicker."

"It's learning. I'm sure it is. I thought it was inanimate, but it's not." Saerille gulped more water and then rubbed her face with a shaky hand.

"Rest. I'll go and seal it."

"Be careful, Serillion. There are others up there. They are searching for me. The only reason they haven't caught me is because the vibrations in the threads give you a warning."

Serillion hesitated, his face thoughtful. "You think the Ascendants have found the Veil? That they are causing the damage?"

"I don't know. But whoever it is, they are deliberately shredding the Veil; forcing the holes wider. They undo my patching and extend the damage. Be careful of the threads;

they are voracious. It's easy to lose time up there, so don't stay too long."

Nodding, Serillion lay down and closed his eyes, extending his senses up and away. His body relaxed as his mind absorbed the view, assessing the weave of the Veil and its behaviour. Saerille was right. What first seemed acquiescent, was, in reality, belligerent and devious.

The strands coiled coyly, waiting for him to approach—drifting in the airless void. He began stitching the threads together, sealing the breach, alert for the vibrations that would warn him of anyone drawing near.

It was draining work. His hands shook as he concentrated, fending off the threads yet twining them together back into a whole.

A gentle bump reminded him of time, and after a last glance over his repairs, he dived back into his body and shuddered awake to find that night had fallen. He gasped as sensation returned to his limbs, along with the painful prickle of pins and needles. He had been lying in one position far longer than he had realised.

Sitting up with a repressed groan, he muttered, "I see what you mean."

"I told you it was easy to lose track of time. I thought you should come back."

"How did you do it, Saerille? On your own all this time; you should have asked for help sooner."

"There weren't enough of us awake. There are still far too few as it is. But with two of us, it should be easier. We can take turns and keep watch. Here, eat." Saerille handed him some dry travel rations.

"I brought some fresh food with me. Let's eat that first."

Saerille pounced on his bag and rummaged for the food. She inhaled the aroma of fresh bread. "Oh, my, I have so missed this."

Serillion grinned. "I remembered you liked the finer things, so I brought you a bottle of wine, as well."

A sigh of pure pleasure greeted his statement, and Serillion wasted no time opening it, though he had forgotten to pack mugs, so they made do drinking from the bottle. Leaning against a tree trunk, he stared up at the star-swathed sky and the sliver of the new moon. "Difficult to believe there is a Veil up there when it looks like that, isn't it?"

"Probably why it's thought to be a myth. People rarely believe in something they can't see."

"True."

There was a short silence, and then Saerille handed him the wine bottle. "What do you think Leyandrii did, Serillion? To cause such a cataclysmic event to happen. Being up here, seeing the Veil, it brings it home that what she did was outside the realm of what we thought possible."

Serillion took a swig of wine and shrugged as he stared up at the night sky. "She's a god. What's impossible to us is not to her. Maybe it wasn't so impossible. Birlerion said she and Guerlaire fell at the end. He couldn't reach them. It seems Leyandrii made sure we were all as safe as we could be before she called down the Veil, even though she knew she could never cross it."

"How could she think the world would be a better place without her?" Saerille's voice was hushed as if voicing the thoughts were a betrayal.

"She did what she thought was best for us. She protected her people and sacrificed herself."

"And Guerlaire."

"I'm sure he didn't think it was a sacrifice. He wouldn't have let Leyandrii go without him, and you know it."

"I suppose. But still, it seems a bit extreme."

"They were desperate times," Serillion said, his voice soft

as he remembered the chaotic storms, the crumbling palace, and, more recently, Birlerion's anguish. "Desperate times," he repeated.

15

OLD VESPERS

As the sun peeked through the clouds the next morning, Jerrol and the Sentinals stepped through the newly discovered Marchwood waystone and came out beside the Chapterhouse in Old Vespers. They wended their way through the narrow streets of the city, giving the Chapterhouse a wide berth, and headed straight for the palace garrison.

Stable boys rushed up to take their horses as they drew to a halt in the courtyard. Jerrol dismounted and unstrapped his saddlebags before the stable lad led Zin'talia off, happily rubbing her nose in affection. Zin'talia crooned in the back of his mind, and he smiled as her contentment rippled through him, his eyes distant. Birlerion turned away, fumbling with his saddlebags, his shoulders stiff.

Jerrol acknowledged the sentry's salute as he entered the barracks, but he hesitated in the hallway as an adjutant approached. "Birlerion, you and Parsillion go freshen up while you have the chance. I'll be with the commander," he said with a weary grin.

Birlerion nodded and led the way to the Sentinal's barracks.

The man stopped in front of Jerrol. "Commander Fenton is expecting you to report on arrival, sir."

"I need to clean up first."

"Certainly, sir, but, um, I would recommend you report to the commander first." The man gestured down the corridor.

Jerrol paused indecisively; should he go to his rooms and wash or report first? Reluctantly, he turned away from the barracks and headed in the opposite direction towards the commander's office. He tapped on the door and waited before opening the door. His eyes widened as he saw Commander Nikols was in the room. As a ranger, Jerrol reported to Nikols. As the Lady's Captain, he reported to Commander Fenton of the King's Justice. He trod a fine line between the two.

"Sir, Captain Haven reporting."

Commander Fenton stared at him. "And since when has it been the form to report in all your dirt?"

Jerrol stiffened. "My apologies, sir. I came to report as soon as I arrived."

Commander Nikols stood and cleared his throat. "Let's have it, then. Report. What is the situation at Deepwater?"

"Secure sir, but the garrison needs support. I left a unit of rangers to bolster their numbers until the Inquisitor interviews everyone. Did my request for medical supplies arrive? I had to leave Tagerill in the Infirmary, and it was woefully undersupplied."

"Yes, sloppy work that was," Fenton said. "I thought this was supposed to be a routine take out? How did you manage to get a Sentinal wounded? And the Lord Holder killed, as well! This will not look good on your report at all." Fenton was determined to have his say.

"The supplies, sir?"

"They went the same day. One of the assistants from the infirmary went, as well," Nikols confirmed, frowning at Fenton.

"Thank you, sir. Lady Alyssa and Lady Olivia are being escorted here by Captain Landis. They should arrive tomorrow, I think. The Inquisitor, Peppins, was sorting out Deepwater with the help of Sentinal Denirion. Sentinals Anterion and Laerille have also reported for duty in Marchwood." Jerrol looked across at Fenton. "Sir, I came straight here to report. I need to go and change before the king finds out I've returned."

Commander Fenton glared at Jerrol. "I've just this minute arrived," Jerrol protested, interpreting the glare correctly. He knew he looked grubby in comparison to the perfectly turned out commander.

"That doesn't permit you to be out of uniform when you are on the king's business. Is that even a uniform?" Commander Fenton asked, running his fingers down the edge of his own perfectly presented jacket.

Jerrol looked down at his clothes and winced. "We travelled as quick as we could."

"We?" Fenton asked.

"Sentinals Birlerion, Parsillion, and I."

"And what makes you think the king will want to see you?"

"Well, he did send me on this mission. I am sure he'll want the report personally."

Commander Fenton exchanged glances with Nikols. "There is no need for flippancy. I'll tell him you're here. Go get presentable, and be quick about it."

Jerrol saluted and thankfully left the office. The less time he spent around Fenton, the better. Such a cold and rigid man, he knew Fenton would never warm to him. He seemed determined to find fault, warranted or not. He wondered what the two commanders, who controlled the security of all Vespiri between them, were so busy discussing.

Jerrol waited somewhat impatiently in the antechamber to the king's private rooms. Low voices rumbled behind the wooden door. Darris was no doubt briefing the king. There could be no complaint about him dawdling; he had rushed through the bathhouse and now wore his last clean uniform. It had shimmered into the Lady's colours as usual, and, he admitted privately, he preferred the high-necked jacket with the silver buttons, cut to fit him. He smoothed a hand down the shimmering material. The soft linen shirt was a dream against his skin. The narrow-legged trousers were tucked into his grey leather half-boots. It may look archaic, but it was smart and practical.

Darris entered the antechamber. "The king will see you now."

Jerrol paused outside the king's study to straighten out his uniform. He sincerely hoped Fenton wasn't present as he would no doubt complain about his appearance again. But there was nothing he could do about it. Darris ushered him past Fonorion, who was standing on guard, and into the king's presence.

"Captain Haven, Your Majesty," Darris announced before fading back out into the antechamber and closing the door.

"Ah, good. Haven, over here," the king said, bending over a dark brown piece of parchment on the table. "Tell me if this map is correct. I found it in the archives. These are the last known positions of the Sentinals."

Jerrol hastened over to the table. The map was quite small, maybe the length of his forearm, almost a square, and faint blue markings outlined the watches. The borders of the four Kingdoms were inked in red; Elothia to the north, the deserts of Terolia to the east, and the island archipelago of Birtoli to the south. Golden stars were scattered across the Watches, vibrant against the dull parchment. Some of the stars started glowing as Jerrol touched them. Jerrol looked up. "Sire, where did this come from?"

"I was thinking about what you said the other day, about there being more Sentinals, and it struck me as odd that I didn't know how many there were, nor where they were situated. My Sentinals were left to me by the Lady to protect us, and yet I didn't know who they were. I'd never even thought about the fact that each one was once a living person. I instructed my librarian to search for them, and this is what she came back with."

"We have two more now; Anterion and Laerille in Marchwood. I awoke them yesterday," Jerrol said, touching the stars to make them glow. "There are two missing on the borders; Venterion to the east and Tianerille to the south. They do not have trees to sustain them, yet they are marked here on the map." He touched them reverently, but the stars stayed flat and dull. "And look, Vespers should have at least five more. Where did they go?" he whispered to himself.

The king nodded. "I believe these were their final postings. You will find them. In fact, you *must* find them. You are assigned to finding them and only that. As the Lady's Captain, it is your duty, and as my Oath Keeper, you will report directly to me. I had Fenton in here bleating about discipline and your lack of it. I expect you to report to me and only me. Your Sentinals will report to Fenton in your absence but only whilst you are away; they will revert under your command when you return. Understood?"

"Yes, sire."

"Good," the king grunted. "Now, tell me everything," he

said, moving over to his chair. Jerrol cast a longing look at the map before following him. "Don't worry. I'm having a couple of copies made; one for you and one for me to write on as we find them. They won't be forgotten again," the king vowed, and the words resonated through Jerrol's bones as the Lady and the Land accepted his vow. He shivered as he heard the echo of the Lady's words. '*Find the forgotten.*'

Jerrol summarised the action at Deepwater. He relayed Denirion's acceptance of Alyssa as his intended Guardian and the expectation that Jennery would be her Lord, at least that was what he believed they were planning. He argued how important it was to have a strong northern border with Elothia. Jerrol paused in his report to dig in his pocket for the folded parchment he had found in Deepwater.

"I found this, along with a notebook. Aaron had it hidden in his fireplace. I left the notebook with Peppins to deal with, but this," he said as he carefully unfolded the parchment, "looks similar to the map you found. It is part of a larger document. You can see the edges have been torn, but I was trying to figure out what it meant. It's not a map in the traditional sense, but there are marks here and here, and that looks like the border with Elothia. If we assume that this is related to Deepwater, then you could assume that squiggle is the Vesp tributary. But other than that, what it is recording, I don't know."

"Maybe you'll find the other pieces and then it will make more sense," the king suggested, frowning over the paper.

"Sire, I believe finding the Sentinals is only part of the quest. The Lady said: 'Find the forgotten, heal the wounded'. I believe the descendants are the wounded and are also lost." He recapped all that he had learnt about the Ascendants from the Sentinals, from their persecution to the existence of powerful crystals.

"You can sort of see why they would be unhappy with

us," the king said, "but all of this dissent has been going on silently. Why haven't we heard anything before?"

"I can only surmise, but after years of perceived injustice and persecution, there is now a belief that they are and should be the dominant family ascendant over everyone else. I think they want to prove they should be the ruling family in the same way their forefathers did. I think they have been searching for knowledge that would give them power, and that seems to be the crystals. They've found a source for the crystals. They must have found an old mine, and the only place the Sentinals have mentioned in relation to crystals are the Telusion mountains in Terolia, only they are no longer marked on the map."

"Telusion mountains," mused the king. "That's an old name. They were destroyed, weren't they? The volcanoes erupted all along the southern coastline when the Lady sundered the Bloodstone. The Ascendants must have found a new source. More worrying is the fact that they have found someone who can create powerful magical objects."

"We could have them too if we can find the crystals. A Sentinal called Niallerion is familiar with them, so it would be useful if we could find him. We also have one dead communications crystal," he said, producing the cloudy crystal he had brought with him and handing it to the king.

The king turned it over in his hand. "It doesn't look like much."

"It's clear when it's active, cloudy when the power is used up. I understand there is a limit on the distance it will work across, but you can see how useful it would be if you were directing multiple groups at once."

"And something we would find difficult to combat. An Arifel is not particularly reliable," the king said with a short laugh, handing the crystal back. "What other news have you?"

"I restored Sentinal Laerille in Marchwood, but she didn't have a tree. She had been mortally wounded when Anterion dragged her into his sentinal. They healed her wounds, but she wasn't there physically. I had to plant another sentinal for her to be released," Jerrol said, wincing as he heard himself say such words aloud. It all sounded so farfetched.

The king stared at him in wonder. "You can create new sentinals?"

"Not by myself. The Land helped, and between us, we produced twelve more seeds. Lord William and his nurserymen are growing them, so they will be ready for when we find the missing Sentinals, but there are only twelve seeds, and that was draining," Jerrol admitted. "What if we need more?"

"Then I expect the Land will assist you when you need them. Don't borrow trouble, Jerrol. You won't be able to save everyone, so don't expect to. You have to be prepared for losses. None of this is going to be easy."

"I need to go to Terolia," Jerrol said, suddenly standing and walking back over to the map. His eyes wandered over the Sentinal's golden stars spread across the desert kingdom. "Everything leads back to Terolia," he said. "Ascendants, crystals, missing Sentinals. Find one, find them all."

The king rose and joined him at the table. "Very well. Tonight, you rest. Tomorrow, spend some time in the archives. Find out all you can about Telusion mountains, mines, and the Terolian families. I will do the same.

"We will plan your trip to Terolia, but before that, I believe we have visitors. Anders will be home and it's time to celebrate. This next week will be about presentations and dinners, so be warned, I expect your attendance. You are my eyes and ears. I want to know what is being said and by whom. I will grant an audience and speak with Alyssa and

Jennery. You make valid points. Let's see what they have to say for themselves."

Jerrol nodded agreement. "Yes, sire," he said as the door opened and Darris poked his head in.

"Your Majesty, Prince Anders has arrived."

The king's face lit up. "Excellent, send him in." He turned to Jerrol and said as an aside, "I'm appointing him as the new chancellor. Keep it hush, but he needs the experience. I'll announce it later this week."

Jerrol grinned in return. "Excellent move, Your Majesty." He bowed as a wiry, dark-haired young man, the image of the king, entered the room.

"Jerrol!" the prince exclaimed. "It's an age since I last saw you. You must promise to meet me in the ring later, and we can catch up properly," he promised, with a gleam in his eye.

"It would be my pleasure, your highness," Jerrol responded with a grin.

"But not until later in the week," the king interrupted. "Jerrol needs to rest. Starting now, you are off duty. I'll speak to you tomorrow. Anders, my boy, tell me everything," the king said expansively, turning to wrap an arm around his younger son's shoulders.

Jerrol bowed, turned smartly, and left the room. Darris closed the door behind him.

Jerrol found Jennery, Landis, and Bryce in the guest barracks. They had made use of the bathing facilities and were seated on the beds at the end, talking in low voices. Jennery looked up with a grin as he saw Jerrol approach. "You made it back safe, then?"

Jerrol leaned against the post at the end of the bed. "As did you, I see. You made good time."

Jennery laughed. "Alyssa was eager to get here and receive the king's approval for her to take Guardianship of Deepwater so she could return as soon as possible. I think Denirion is pining already."

"Ah, sounds like he's going to be a hard taskmaster," Jerrol grinned, relaxing into the easy banter.

"He needs to be. Lots to put right in that Watch," Jennery said, sobering up.

"True, and tension on the border won't help, either," Jerrol agreed.

"Tension on what border?"

"You need to keep an eye on the politics if you are going to lord it over that Watch." Jerrol grinned wryly. "Especially your soon-to-be northern border with Elothia. If you are defending Deepwater, you need to be aware of who borders your land. The Grand Duke's daughter is currently under house arrest. He is not too happy about that."

Jennery gasped in horror as Jerrol chuckled. "Admittedly, your northern border is shorter than Stoneford's, but yours does have that really flat, inviting river plain, which is much easier to cross than the mountain ranges."

Bryce grinned at Jennery's dismay. "And here you thought you were going to have a nice, cushy life."

Jennery recovered his composure. "Now that would be too boring. A little tension now and then never hurt anyone," he said, comfortably back on balance.

"Well, you need to convince the king first. He is ready to be convinced, so I hope you have your arguments ready," Jerrol said.

"You've spoken to him?" Jennery asked.

"Just now. He is eager to fete his guests; I think he is ready to party. He was talking about presentations and balls and dinners, and Prince Anders is home," Jerrol said as if the last point cinched it, which it did.

Landis laughed as Jennery shuddered in horror. "You'd better get used to escorting your lady to balls and such like events. This will be your new battlefield during peacetime," he said.

Jennery held his head in his hands. "That explains all the luggage Alyssa insisted we bring, even though she kept saying we would only be here a few days."

"A week, at least," Jerrol said.

"I need to buy more clothes," moaned Jennery.

"Well, you could try, but I haven't managed to persuade the Lady to change my uniform for anything else so far."

"But if we explain it's for a ball," Jennery suggested hopefully.

"I'd be careful what you wish for," Jerrol advised, pushing himself off the post. "I'm beat and off duty, so I'm going to have an early night. This week is going to be hectic. I'll be at the Chapterhouse in the morning. I need to speak to Liliian about some additional researchers. You should show Alyssa around while it's quiet. I'm sure she'd love it." He gave them a casual salute as he sauntered out of the room.

16

CHAPTERHOUSE, OLD VESPERS

Taelia was sitting in the garden enjoying the morning sun when she heard voices by the fountain. A smile lit up her face as she recognised Jerrol's voice. He was back; he had been away for far too long. Torsion was right; he was never here when you wanted him, always gallivanting off on errands for the king. She never knew where he was, and he wasn't very good at writing to her. Admittedly, someone would have to read it to her, her lack of sight galling in some ways, but her other senses compensated most of the time. At least it would have shown he was thinking of her.

She was preparing to rise when she heard a woman's voice and paused. The woman's voice was playful as she teased Jerrol, and the undercurrent of amusement in Jerrol's voice in response sent an unexpected flash of jealousy through her.

She could just make out his voice as he spoke to the girl.

"Alyssa, honestly, it was my pleasure. I am glad you are back to full health."

"Thank you, Jerrol. I love it here; the company is so exquisite," Lady Alyssa replied. "So much more considerate than Deepwater. I look forward to improving the welcome next time you visit."

Jerrol chuckled knowingly, and Taelia's stomach twisted. How could he flirt with another woman right in front of her? She simmered silently as the voices finally faded away.

A little while later, she jumped as Jerrol flopped down on the bench beside her. "Taelia, what a week," he murmured. She heard the fatigue in his voice. The sense of his exhaustion tinged her awareness of him. The bench creaked as he dropped his head back against the wood.

Her hand strayed toward him. Just his presence eased her heart. But no, he was paying attention to that other woman. Maybe she assumed too much.

"Been busy?" she asked.

Jerrol stirred at the edge in her voice. "Is everything alright?" he asked, rolling his head to see her face.

"Oh, yes." She tried to smile. "Just working a tricky problem right now."

"Ah, I was hoping to ask for your help on something."

She heard him rub a hand over his face.

"Maybe another time?" Taelia said through her teeth. "I'm busy right now." A sense of loss flooded through her as her awareness of him faded as he unconsciously withdrew whatever it was they shared. He stiffened beside her before the bench creaked as he rose to his feet.

"I apologise for disturbing you," he said, his voice neutral, giving nothing away. His footsteps faded before she could retract her hasty words.

She regretted what she had said straight away. How could she have been so stupid? She had heard his fatigue, and she had sent him away and in a fashion that had made him put up his defences. She hadn't given him a chance to tell her what he had been doing or ease his tension. Restless, she rose, intending to return to her office.

Walking down the corridor, she paused outside a meeting room as she heard Jerrol's voice. He was tired and frustrated, and a young woman's voice interrupted. It was that girl again from the fountain. Taelia's mouth tightened as she listened. And then to her great surprise, she heard something even more galling; the novice, Mary, spoke suggesting a research protocol. He had found another scholar to help him instead of her. How dare he? she thought, forgetting that she had told him she was too busy.

She stomped off, before the rumble of Jennery's voice suggested he escort Alyssa back to the palace before she was missed.

The group broke up, and Jerrol thanked Mary for her help and swore her to secrecy, not that it was needed; the Deane had already told her the project was confidential and she wasn't to speak of it to anyone. "I think we all need a break, me especially. Let's reconvene tomorrow."

Jennery flicked Jerrol a glance but didn't say anything as he offered Alyssa his arm and escorted her out of the room. Jennery glanced back. "Jerrol?" His face mirrored his concern.

"I'm fine." Jerrol sighed, exhaling his breath in a rush. "I'll see you when you return to the palace?"

"We'll be here for the king's ball, and then we leave for Deepwater." Jennery grinned at Alyssa. "I think it's time the new guardian took up residence, don't you?"

Alyssa smiled in return. "Yes, Denirion is not happy. He is anxious without us, and we need to start rebuilding as soon as possible."

"In the morning, then. Keep safe, you two," Jerrol said as

they walked away, their heads together. He sincerely hoped the reclaiming of Deepwater would go smoothly. He wasn't so sure. It wasn't clear to him what the Ascendants were intending, and he had yet to find any reference in the records.

Enough for today. He would spend the afternoon in the king's archives, and then he would get up early tomorrow and start again; maybe he would be in a better frame of mind. First though, he would visit Torsion.

Making his way through the dim corridors, Birlerion a silent shadow at his shoulder, he paused outside Torsion's door. Taking a deep breath to steady himself, he knocked on the door, and opened it as Torsion's voice bade him enter.

"You wanted to see me?" Jerrol said as he moved some papers off a chair and collapsed onto it.

Torsion peered at him. "What's the matter? You look awful."

"Nothing. I'm heading back to the palace, but I got your message, so I thought I'd check to see if you were here."

Torsion straightened. "Where else would I be? I'm not the one jaunting about Vespiri, waking up ancient guards with social problems."

"Enough, Torsion. They are good people. They are still adjusting; give them a chance."

"I am. Most of them are alright, but you place too much trust in that Birlerion. I'm surprised he's let you out of his sight."

Jerrol grinned. "He's outside your door, so be careful what you say."

Torsion strode over to the door and yanked it open. He scowled as Birlerion turned around, raising his eyebrow. He slammed the door shut. "I'm telling you, Jerrol; he is hiding something."

"He is a Lady's guard, and I trust him. Trust me, Torsion."

"Since when did you ignore my advice? Why now? I've got your best interests at heart. Your life has been at risk more times since these guards awoke than ever before."

"That's because there is an Ascendant threat against Vespiri. The guards are waking because of this threat."

"Ascendants? Don't talk rubbish. They were banished with the Lady. There is no threat. They are making it up."

"Torsion, you know more about the history of Vespiri than any of us. You were chasing down history thieves when I was a kid. What was it you said that time in Stoneford when we first met? There is much history we don't yet know; that is the joy of research. I would have thought this would be your dream; to have living history at your fingertips."

"It is, but I am concerned they have affected you somehow. You are different around them."

Jerrol sighed. "I am responsible for them, and they have just been woken after three thousand years of being encased in a tree. It is not surprising I am different around them."

Torsion gripped his shoulder. "Jerrol, I've never steered you wrong before, but I'm telling you; don't trust Birlerion until you know more about him. All I'm asking is that you dig a bit deeper. Even your Darian is suspicious of him."

Jerrol jerked upright. "What?"

"You know it. My Darian, She'vanne said your mare doesn't like him. Don't you trust your Darian?"

"Of course I do."

"Well, why don't you listen to her, if not me?"

Jerrol massaged his temples. "Torsion, the Sentinals are the Lady's Guard. The *Lady's.* They are sworn to her and Remargaren."

"Just because they *were* sworn, doesn't mean they *still* are."

Jerrol rose. "I don't know why you are so determined to think ill of them, but they have sworn allegiance to King Benedict. They revere the Lady, and they will protect her people. They report to me, and I am their Captain, and I am telling you they are loyal and trustworthy."

Torsion stilled. "You are their Captain?"

"Yes."

"It's you? You are the Lady's Captain?"

"Yes."

Torsion burst out laughing and paced around his room. "I don't believe it."

"Why not?"

"You? The Lady chose you? And you are waking the Sentinals?"

"Why is it so difficult to believe?"

"Jerrol, much as I admire your progression through the rangers, even with your recent mishap, you never struck me as a team player. You are always out there on your own, doing your own thing, not listening to anyone else."

"Maybe that is what has changed," Jerrol murmured.

Torsion's eyes narrowed, his gaze drilling into Jerrol. "Maybe you've chosen the wrong time to start listening to others."

"You can't have it both ways. You can't tell me to listen one moment and not the next."

Torsion snorted. "They are deceiving you; that Birlerion is deceiving you. You shouldn't trust a source you haven't verified."

Jerrol gave him a gentle smile. "As always, your advice is solid. I thank you for your concern. But my sources are verified by the Lady, and that is good enough for me." He turned and opened the door, glancing back at Torsion he left a parting remark. "As such, they should be good enough for you. If I hear of you tainting those sources, I will have words. Am I understood?"

Torsion clamped his lips shut and glared past Jerrol's shoulder, as he closed the door.

17

KING'S PALACE, OLD VESPERS

Jerrol sat in the king's library, perusing the catalogue, searching for references of crystals or Telusion mines. His mind drifted to his conversation with Torsion. He'd never been able to get Torsion to tell him how he'd come by She'vanne.

Scowling at his book, he tried to remember what he knew about Darians, but apart from the fact that they gave their true name when they bonded, and on occasion they could be incessant chatterboxes, there wasn't much else he knew. Birlerion had told him not to share his Darian's name, and he hadn't. Interesting then that Torsion had always openly used She'vanne's name and that he would use her to validate his point.

"Zin'talia?"

"Yes?"

"Why don't you like Birlerion?"

There was a short silence. *"It's not that I don't like him. He is uncomfortable around me."*

"Any idea why?"

"No. He usually keeps his distance. What made you ask?"

"She'vanne told Torsion that you don't like Birlerion. Torsion told me not to trust him."

"Pshht! Don't listen to anything Torsion says. He's lying."

"How do you know?"

Zin'talia sighed in his head; a soft ripple of warmth as if she had breathed over him, and he smiled. *"She is not bonded."*

"What?" Jerrol sat up.

"They are not bonded. He can't talk to her."

"But... they've been together for years and he knows her name."

"It's not her true name. I don't know why she is with him. She won't say. In fact, she rarely speaks. I think it's been so long since she's been near another Darian, she's forgotten how."

"Can we do anything to help?"

"I don't know. As I said, she doesn't want anything to do with me. You could stable me closer to her and I can try. But don't expect much. I think they have gotten used to each other despite not bonding."

"Why would he lie?"

"Maybe he doesn't want to admit that he hasn't bonded."

"Maybe. But why lie about Birlerion? Torsion doesn't know him. It doesn't make sense. Jerrol stared at his book, his mind spinning. "*Keep an eye on her. The Lady would expect us to help her, if needed."*

"Of course."

As he refocused on his book and turned the page, he became aware that he was no longer alone. Glancing up, he saw Lady Miranda hesitating in the doorway. He rose and smiled a welcome. "Lady Miranda, were you looking for me?"

She cleared her throat. "I heard Sentinal Tagerillion had been injured at Deepwater. I wanted to ask if there was any news. He will be alright, won't he?" She gripped her hands together so hard her knuckles were white.

Jerrol had forgotten Tagerill had shown an interest, and it seemed it was returned, by the look of concern on her face.

"Please have a seat," he said, leading her into the room. "What did you hear?" he asked, sitting beside her.

She plucked at the folds of the blue silk dress she wore, concentrating on pleating the material. "He was so badly injured that he had to remain in Deepwater, that he hadn't regained consciousness, and he would lose the use of his arm. Tell me it isn't true," she pleaded, suddenly turning her face towards him and gripping his sleeve. Tears were forming in her anxious blue eyes, and she angrily brushed them away.

"It's not true," Jerrol said, handing her a handkerchief.

"Oh," Lady Miranda exhaled with relief. "I-I was so worried," she gulped, trying to regain her composure.

"Hush, all will be well," Jerrol murmured. "I am sorry you have been so distressed. Unfortunately, battles are usually exaggerated. Though I must admit, there is some basis in the truth." He sighed. "I left Tagerill in Deepwater because he was hurt in a fight. He will have to rehabilitate to get back to full fighting strength, but he will recover," Jerrol said firmly as she stilled. "It was better to leave him in the hands of a skilled healer than drag him over bumpy roads for three or four days. When he can travel, he will return to Stoneford to his sentinal, which will speed his healing, and then he will return to duty."

"Oh, thank goodness," she breathed. "Do you think it will be permissible to send him a letter?"

"I would think so." Jerrol leaned forward. "Lady Miranda, what are your intentions here?"

She lifted startled eyes to his face. "W-What do you mean?"

"I mean, are you an Ascendant? Determined to cause the downfall of the Lady and the rule of the king?"

She gasped. "N-No!"

"Then why do you persist in presenting yourself as one?"

"I don't."

"Yes, you do. You place your star firmly in the orbit of Prince Kharel and his wife, yet you hover on the edges of society like an apologetic ghost, not quite one thing or the other. Just because you were the princess' lady in waiting, doesn't mean you have to remain one."

Lady Miranda twisted the handkerchief in her hands. "You don't understand," she said with some bitterness. "When I fled Greenswatch, I fled the terrible mistake I made. I was shunned by society, branded a terrible mother and worse. The princess sheltered me; offered me solace and support, a job, a place to live. I can't betray her trust."

"She gave you a job and encouraged you to sever yourself from your family. That doesn't sound like a good friend to me. She isolated you; made you dependent on her for everything."

"I isolated myself with my behaviour." Lady Miranda's voice was muffled, though Jerrol hoped she was listening.

"That was ten years ago, Lady Miranda. It doesn't have to be a life sentence. The world has moved on. Greenswatch has moved on, and your son is now a lord. You should be proud of him. Your daughter has arrived here in Old Vespers. Are you going to shun her because of old regrets? You have already missed so many years of your children's lives when you didn't have to."

"It's far too late."

"It's never too late," Jerrol reproved her gently. "That is just pride talking. The question is, do you want your family back? I think they would want you back in their lives, Alyssa especially, with all she has gone through. They may be a little angry and upset to begin with, but that is understandable, isn't it? I think Tagerill would love your children if you asked it of him," he suggested.

Lady Miranda stilled; her head bent over her hands. She lifted her face, hope dawning. "Do you really think so?"

"Well, I can't speak for him, but I'm sure you know him well enough to know what he would expect of you."

"Maybe he expects too much," she whispered, flushing.

"Or maybe you expect too little. Lady Miranda, you are only a victim if you let yourself be one. You don't have to do it all by yourself." Jerrol's lips twisted as he echoed Liliian's words. Listen to your own advice! he thought. "There are people around you who would support you if you asked; me being one of them." He prodded his chest with his thumb, grinning at her encouragingly.

She took a deep breath and sat up. "I must look a wreck."

Jerrol laughed. "Nothing that can't be repaired."

"I have no idea how to request a change of room or whether the king will permit it. He has no reason to trust me."

"But I do, and I can set it in motion if you would like me too. You wouldn't have to return to the princess if you didn't want to."

"That would be a cowardly way out. I should thank her for her support and tell her she needs to hire a new lady in waiting."

"I promise I will come and rescue you should there be any difficulty with you leaving her service. Remember, she does not own you."

Lady Miranda stood, determination in every line. "Captain Haven, if you would be so kind, I would like to request the relocation of my room, though how I will pay for it, I don't know as I will have no income."

"Mere details. I am sure the king will provide you with a bed while you figure out your next step. After all, I would think you are trying to figure out how you can visit Tagerill, aren't you?" he suggested, offering her his arm.

Lady Miranda stared at him. "Captain Haven, I think I

may have underestimated you. I came for news but you are about to change my whole life."

Jerrol quirked an eyebrow at her. "Lots of people underestimate me, though this is all your decision. I just helped you reach it."

She gave a watery chuckle as he escorted her out of the library and back to the tower where the King's Guards stood, guarding the door.

"I will return to collect you in one-quarter chime. Will that be sufficient?" Jerrol asked.

Lady Miranda swallowed and nodded. "I would appreciate that very much." She squared her shoulders and opened the door, closing it behind her.

Jerrol hesitated. Should he wait for her? No, he would speak with Darris who could start organising Miranda's move, and when he returned, he would see what would be.

Miranda crossed the antechamber to her room. As she placed her hand on the latch, the princess' voice floated out to her. "Is that you, Miranda? Where have you been?" There was an edge to her voice. The princess was not happy.

"Yes, your highness, I'll be right there," Miranda called as she opened her door and strode over to her mirror. Her face was blotchy. She hurriedly splashed her face with cold water, but it was apparent that she had been crying. She never could cry prettily. She patted her face dry, straightened her gown, and, gathering her courage, left her room.

"You needed me, your highness?" she asked as she entered the princess' parlour.

"Yes, pour me some wine." The princess inspected Miranda, her eyes cold and hard. She lay on a blue and gold upholstered chaise lounge, playing with a fan decorated with pale pink feathers. Scattered around her on the floor were a variety of scarves, combs, and fans. "Where have you been? It is boring here by myself." She yawned delicately, revealing tiny pearl teeth.

"I was arranging the relocation of my room, your highness. I have decided it is time I took some responsibility for my children. They need me. I am sorry, your highness, but I must resign from my position in your service," Miranda said, forcing the words out.

"Don't be so silly," the princess replied. "You can't leave me. I am all you have."

"I am sorry, your highness, but it is time for me to leave," Miranda repeated.

"No, I think not. This is just one of your little wobbles. You know you have to stay with me; it is the only way you can be safe," the princess said, swinging her feet over the side of the settee. "You need to stay with your princess," she repeated as she twirled her fingers. "This situation is only temporary. Kharel will have it all resolved shortly, and then we will be back in power."

Miranda wavered. "I appreciate all you have done for me, your highness, but you can't look after me forever."

"Of course, I can. You belong with me. You don't *want* to leave me, do you?"

"N-No, I don't want to leave you," agreed Miranda. She shook her head. What was she saying? "No, I do want to leave," she mumbled, confused.

"No, you don't. You know you are safe with me. You've always been safe with me; no one else knows how to look after you." The princess flicked her a sharp glance and gentled her voice to a calming murmur as if soothing a frightened animal.

Miranda stared at the tiny woman, frowning as she tried to remember why she had wanted to leave.

A sharp voice sliced through her confusion. "Is this a new

hiring technique? Is it the only way you can get people to work for you, Selvia?" Jerrol stood in the doorway, observing the princess with cold amusement.

"How dare you enter my rooms?" Selvia replied, stiffening with anger.

"How dare you try to keep someone in your employ against their will?" Jerrol replied. His voice dispersed the cloud of confusion in Miranda's head. "How long have you been mesmerizing Lady Miranda? From the very beginning? Did you persuade her to leave her family in the first place? Was it all your idea?" Jerrol asked, his voice bitingly cold.

The princess watched Miranda, her gaze darting about the room. "Of course not, Miranda chose to work for me. I helped her when she was in need, gave her a roof over her head. No one else would, only me. Miranda knows that, don't you? You are safe with me, aren't you? Always safe with me?"

A white-hot rage rushed through Miranda as the implication of Jerrol's words filtered through her confusion. "How dare you?" she cried. "How could you? All these years you said you were my friend." Miranda shook. "You took my children from me." Her eyes widened. "You took my husband from me," she gasped.

"No, No, I didn't. I swear." Selvia held her hands out before her, hesitantly backing away from the incandescent Miranda. "It was Isseran who suggested it first," she blurted, eyeing Miranda. "We got on so well, he suggested you should stay. He planted the discontent with Greenswatch, and once you were here I just, well, encouraged you to stay. It was easy; you wanted to stay."

"Only because I didn't think I had anywhere else to go," Miranda said, rigid with fury.

Selvia stiffened as she bumped into the wall behind her.

She raised her chin, her eyes hard. "I only encouraged your feelings. I'm not an Ascendant like Isseran."

"So, you know that Isseran is an Ascendant?" Jerrol asked with interest.

"Ha!" Selvia snorted. "He hoodwinked you good and proper, didn't he? He almost had you as well, got you reassigned, and managed to sneak his friends in under your nose. Dishonourably discharged; how does that look on your record?"

"Not too bad seeing as I've been reinstated," Jerrol replied. He looked across at Miranda. "Ready to go?"

"Yes," she said. "Please take me away from here. I hope I never see her again." She turned her back on the princess and stalked out of the tower, her back straight.

Jerrol followed her, pausing in the doorway. "I think you'll find it difficult to find any help once people know what you are," he said to the princess.

"You can't leave me. I need you," Selvia's strident voice followed Miranda as she left the room. "No, come back! You want to stay with me; you love me. I keep you safe! You'll regret it. I can keep you safe." Her voice was muffled as Jerrol slammed the wooden door shut and the lock clicked into place.

"Are you alright?" Jerrol asked as he led Miranda out of the tower and back into the main palace. Tremors of shock shuddered through her.

Miranda hugged herself. "Was that the truth? She was controlling me?"

Jerrol sighed. "I'm afraid so. Do you think you could stand to talk about this to the king? We need to tell him what she said."

"What she said? It was all vitriol."

"She said more than she realised," Jerrol said, leading the

way towards the king's chambers. He requested the king's presence as he strode.

"Are you sure we should be here? I mean, won't the king be annoyed at being disturbed?" Miranda asked as she scurried after him through the corridors.

"It will be fine; he is expecting us," Jerrol said, pausing to tap on the antechamber door.

Darris opened it immediately. "The king is waiting for you in his chamber."

Jerrol nodded and led Miranda through the antechamber. She hung back nervously. "All will be well," he murmured, tugging her forward.

"Sire," Jerrol said, dropping to his knee as Miranda dropped into a deep curtsey.

King Benedict looked across at him. "This is becoming a habit," he said wryly, "and I thought I said you were off duty until I called for you."

Jerrol rose with a grin. "I was in the archives starting the research you ordered me to do."

"Ah yes. I did, didn't I?" He looked at Lady Miranda. "Lady Miranda, rise."

"Your Majesty," she said huskily. "I apologise for my appearance; Captain Haven didn't give me a chance to prepare."

"Yes, he can be a bit hasty at times," the king agreed.

Jerrol's grin widened.

"Well, Captain Haven, what is it this time?"

Jerrol recapped what had happened. "Sire, Selvia was adamant that she was the only one who could protect Lady Miranda. She had persuaded Lady Miranda to leave her family, to remain in her employ. She knew that Isseran was an Ascendant, that he had the power to plant suggestions. She confirmed that he had brought his people into the palace and the government."

"Your Majesty," Lady Miranda said. "She also said her husband would have this situation resolved; that he would soon be back in power. She knows something is being planned."

"Had you heard anything of this plan previously?" the king asked.

Lady Miranda shook her head. "Not in such definite terms. She often said her father would not stand for her being imprisoned, for being treated in such a manner. She said her father would act and that Kharel had friends in powerful places. But I heard nothing fixed or prepared. Thinking about it, Prince Kharel has been absent from his rooms more often of late. He is usually up at the top of the tower. The princess complained that he liked fresh air more than her."

The king frowned. "I thought we searched his rooms?"

"Not well enough, it seems," Jerrol said, his face grim. "He must have a crystal. They must be planning another coup."

"At least we are forewarned. Call Darris for me," the king instructed as he walked over to his desk and started making a list. He looked up as his steward entered the room. "Darris, discreetly get Fenton, Nikols, and Prince Anders here now. Jerrol, get your Sentinals roaming the palace. Full alert, and tell Fonorion to come in here."

Jerrol nodded and left the room to be replaced by Fonorion.

"Fonorion, I want you to check everyone who comes into my rooms, and I mean everyone, including Lady Miranda here. Have them each say the Lady's Oath. Some Ascendants have infiltrated the palace, and we need to find them and quickly. Sorry m'dear, but it's better to be sure."

"Of course, Your Majesty. I'll do anything I can to help." Lady Miranda recited the Lady's Oath, feeling every word burn through her as she committed herself to the Lady with all her heart.

> *"Lady protect us, guard our health. From beyond watch o'er our land.*
> *Our Oath to you will bind us all, Lady, Land, and Liege we stand.*
> *Life and death, a Sentinal breathes, a last defence, well done.*
> *Our lives are yours, and ours, and theirs. Joined together as one."*

The king nodded. "Thank you for your assistance, m'dear. Darris will escort you to your new rooms. I believe there is a dinner tonight. I expect to see you there." The king nodded his dismissal and went back to his list.

Jerrol returned with Commander Fenton, interrupting the king's concentration. The king indicated the chairs and returned to his list. He paused as Prince Anders and Commander Nikols were ushered in.

"Good," he said, steepling his fingers in front of him. "We have a situation," he said, staring at the men in front of him one by one. "It seems my son Kharel has been communicating with the Ascendants, and with the help of Elothia, they are planning to either help him escape or overthrow my Crown. I expect neither to happen."

Prince Anders let a soft curse fall. Jerrol grimaced in agreement.

Commander Fenton stared at them. "How can he be communicating with them? He has not left the tower, and no one has been permitted to enter, except that woman; Miranda, isn't it?"

"Lady Miranda is not the culprit," the king said, nodding at Jerrol.

Jerrol displayed the cloudy crystal. "They have found a way to charge these crystals, which enables them to bespeak each other. They work over quite a large distance, across the city of Old Vespers, for sure."

Commander Fenton's eyes bulged as he took the crystal, turning it over in his hands. "What nonsense is this? This is just a stone. It's not possible to use it for the purposes you describe."

The king contradicted him. "Fenton, it *is* possible. Captain Haven has witnessed its use and the Sentinals confirm its purpose. The Ascendants have discovered a way to charge the stones and use them."

"I suggest we move the prince and his wife to a more secure location," Commander Nikols suggested. "Prevent him from using whatever he is communicating with. That will make it more difficult for them co-ordinate his rescue."

"Fenton, see to it; a deep dungeon would be a better location. Haven, assist him. I want to know what he knows, and I want his rooms searched. We need a timeline." King Benedict paused, glancing at Nikols. "Isseran is confirmed as an Ascendant; we need to redouble efforts to find him."

"He could be in Elothia or Terolia by now, sire," Jerrol interjected.

"Indeed, and I want to ensure he can't return. Make sure all the borders have orders to detain him on sight. Nikols, manage that."

"Yes, Your Majesty. We need to strengthen all the border patrols. I'll advise the Watches. What about Deepwater?" Nikols asked.

The king smiled. "Fortunately, I am about to announce the new Lord and Lady. They will be in residence by the end of the week. Advise Captain Landis of your plans in the meantime. I mean to assign him to Deepwater."

"Captain Bryce from Stoneford is here; he could carry word to Lord Jason," Jerrol said.

Nikols nodded in agreement.

The king looked across at Fenton. "You need to secure Old Vespers and the palace. I know it will be difficult with the plans for this week, but the Sentinals will support you. Check all visitors."

"Yes, Your Majesty. I will set up roving patrols through Old Vespers. I'll also work with the officials to check who Isseran brought in, though, Your Majesty, his tenure has been long; who knows how many are loyal to him?"

The king nodded; his face grim. "I know. Do your best. I am keenly aware that I allowed such a man to control so much for so long."

"Commander Nikols, what of those listed in Isseran's notebook? We should have unspelled them all by now," Jerrol asked.

"Prince Kharel took the notebook. We have been unable to find it."

Jerrol frowned. "I gave Healer Francis a list of those I remembered, though it wasn't all of them. We need to find that notebook."

"Make that a priority, Haven. Speak with Kharel, search his rooms, find that notebook."

"Yes, sire."

"I will be announcing tomorrow that Anders will become the new chancellor. Co-ordinate with him, Haven. He has my complete confidence, and he will weed out those who should not be there. Anders, work with the Justice department to create permits. We need to control access to the palace."

"Sire, those warehouses out to the north of the city—what did the report say?" Jerrol asked. "They were built at Isseran's behest, weren't they?"

"Overflow storage, I believe. Why?" the king said, concern in his voice as he considered the implications.

"I just wondered what use they were so far from the port. I mean, the additional cost of transporting the goods there and then transporting them back; it seemed odd to me."

Fenton eyed him with disgust. "I suppose you want me to check them again?"

"Discreetly, sir. Discreetly," Jerrol said.

"Fenton, you've got your hands full with Vespers," the king said. "Nikols, could you spare a ranger to check it out? Discreetly, as Haven suggests."

Nikols bowed. "At once, Your Majesty."

"We reconvene here tomorrow afternoon at fourth chime. Good hunting, gentlemen." The king nodded his dismissal, and the men dispersed.

18

SENTINAL'S BARRACKS, OLD VESPERS

The next day, Birlerion was lying on his bed, relaxing as much as he could whilst staying in a barracks with three other Sentinals. At least half the time, it was empty as Darllion and Fonorion shared the rotation on the king. Birlerion, and now Parsillion, guarded the Captain. Still, four Sentinals was too few, and with Prince Anders now at the palace, he assumed one of them was going to have to guard him as well.

He had a few hours off duty, and he was debating about what to do with them. There was not enough time to visit Tagerill, though he could use the waystone and see Versillion. Or he could go and spend some time with his tree and visit the temple, as well.

Staring at the ceiling, he deliberated. He ought to be out on the training field, and if not training, checking his gear. He didn't move. He felt adrift. Where was home? It was alright for Versillion to say Greens was still his home, but without their parents, it wasn't really. Greens was unrecognizable, and without the family, to Birlerion it was just land.

He didn't have the same connection the Descelles had, no matter what they said.

But then, he had no family in Vespers either, and he didn't know his family name. He had been adopted by Tagerill's family and had taken their name, so he couldn't track his birth family even if he wanted to. He couldn't go to the Chapterhouse; Torsion would be breathing down his neck every minute.

He scowled at the ceiling. Torsion had to be related to the Clary's; he had the same arrogant manner and the family resemblance. Just the sight of Torsion made Birlerion's skin crawl. It was unfortunate that the Captain trusted him so much.

He sighed. Maybe he should honour his promise to Scholar Taelia. He had said he would show her his sentinal. He sat up. Torsion would not keep him away. He could also visit the temple, instead of moping about the barracks.

Decision made, he felt better, and he rose to reach for his jacket. Strapping on his sword, he deliberated about his bow but left it leaning against the wall. He slid home his daggers. He wouldn't put it past Torsion to be difficult. He wouldn't pass up an opportunity to denigrate Birlerion, especially in front of other scholars. Patting himself down, he strode out of the barracks to find a horse.

Birlerion arrived at the Chapterhouse and after stabling his horse, he gazed around the courtyard, once again realising that the only part he recognised was the tower. The rest of it was still lost underground. He was amazed that they had excavated so little; instead, they had built on top.

Rotating his shoulders to relieve the sudden tension, he went to find the duty scholar. At least that practice was still the same. He smiled at the portly scholar at the desk and enquired after Scholar Taelia.

"Her office is in building four, on sub-level one." The scholar pointed out the route and returned to his work.

Birlerion memorised the route and headed off, smiling at the scholar's preoccupation. All scholars were the same; their work was of utmost importance. He knocked on Taelia's office door and waited. There was a slight pause, and then she called for him to enter.

He opened the door and stepped over the threshold. "Scholar Taelia, it's Sentinal Birlerion. I've come to honour my promise to show you inside my tree." He hesitated at the sight of her face; she had been crying. "If this is a good time. I'm sorry. I didn't mean to intrude."

Taelia wiped her face with the back of her hand. "No, no. Please, Birlerion, come in. Shut the door."

Birlerion handed her his handkerchief. "What has happened? Are you alright?"

"Yes, I'm fine. Don't mind me." She took a deep breath and gave him a watery smile. "Please, sit. What was it you wanted?"

"I was on my way to my sentinal and wondered if you'd like to come too. I said I'd introduce you."

Taelia's face eased. "Oh, yes, would you? I'd love to."

"It would be my pleasure. Though, um, maybe you ought to rinse your face first? I'm sorry, but you do look like you've been crying."

Taelia blushed. "Oh dear. It's just, I have a bit of a headache."

"Then visiting my sentinal would be the best medicine, and it would be my honour to escort you."

"Then let us visit. Why we have to be stuffed down here in a hole, I don't know."

Birlerion waited while Taelia disappeared into an adjoining room for a moment and when she returned, tucked her hand under his arm. As they walked, he began to tell her about his sentinal. "I can't tell you much about how the Lady created them, because I didn't even know I was in a sentinal until the Captain woke me. Though I suppose that's not really true. I knew him; we are one, after all, but it was an unconscious knowing, if that makes sense? I suppose there isn't much about this that is going to make any sense."

Taelia chuckled. "Magic never makes any sense; it all sits outside the boundaries of what we know."

"Yes. It's weird not seeing any onoffs. The scholars always used to use them; much safer than candles or lamps."

"Onoffs?"

"Yes, orbs of golden light that were suspended in the air. Leyandrii used to make them. You tap them to turn them on and tap them again to turn them off. Onoffs. They lit up the room and lasted for weeks. Once the magic was drained, they needed recharging. Mind the steps. We are going up."

"Thank you. No one ever mentioned onoffs."

"They were expensive. They took a lot of effort to make, so not many people had them. The scholars saw it as an investment. Leyandrii and Marguerite used them at the palace." Birlerion smiled. "I guess you could say we were spoilt."

"You miss them all, don't you?" Taelia asked.

"Yes," Birlerion said with a sigh.

Taelia squeezed his arm. "I am sorry."

"No need to be. It's not your fault. Ah, sunshine. We'll soon be out." He turned her away as he saw Torsion entering the other end of the hall. "Let's cut through the gardens."

"What's the matter?" Taelia frowned as he tensed.

"Scholar Torsion. He doesn't like me, and I'm not prepared to show him my sentinal. I'm trying to avoid him, though I think he may have spotted us."

"Oh dear," Taelia said with a smile. "Let's avoid him, by all means."

Birlerion hurried her through the gardens. The tinkling fountain faded behind them, and then Birlerion sighed as Torsion appeared, blocking their path.

Taelia gripped his arm. "Let me deal with him," she murmured.

"As the Lady wills," Birlerion replied, releasing her arm, though Taelia held on to him.

"No, stay beside me."

"Unhand her, you filthy grunt. What do you think you are doing? Taelia, where are you going with him?"

Taelia drew herself up, gripping Birlerion's arm tighter as he stiffened at the insult.

"Torsion, don't be so rude. What I do and with whom is none of your business."

"I'm making it my business. You don't know where he's taking you; you can't trust him."

"Yes, I can. Now, if you'll excuse us, we have places to be."

Torsion prodded Birlerion's chest with stiff fingers. "He's not going anywhere with you."

"It is Scholar Taelia's decision, not yours, scholar," Birlerion said, calmly stepping back. "Move out of the way."

Torsion hissed his breath out as he stepped forward. "Make me."

Birlerion burst out laughing at the expression on Torsion's face. If looks could kill, he'd be stone dead. "This is not a pissing contest." He turned to Taelia. "Apologies scholar, excuse my language."

"Not at all," Taelia said agreeably. "I've heard worse. Torsion, stop it. I am going with Birlerion of my own free choice, and it has nothing to do with you. Now move out of the way."

Birlerion saw it coming and rode the blow. Blocking the follow-up, he jabbed hard and low in response, and Torsion dropped to the gravel with a wheezing groan. Birlerion took Taelia's arm and guided her forward. "Apologies, Scholar Taelia. Shall we proceed?"

"Is he alright?"

"He'll be fine; he might not be able to stand up straight for a while, but he'll recover."

"That might not have been wise," Taelia said as they paused for a cart to pass by before they crossed the road and entered the Temple gardens.

"I know, but he wasn't going to give way, and he wanted a fight. I thought it best to stop it fast before he got carried away and one of us got hurt. Anyway, let's not worry about him. Here is my sentinal." He placed her hand on the smooth bark and it warmed beneath her palm in greeting. "Be welcome in my sentinal, Scholar Taelia," Birlerion said, and they shimmered into the tree.

Taelia gasped and staggered as they appeared inside. She clung to Birlerion. "That was the weirdest sensation I've ever experienced. So weird, I can't even describe it," she said, peering around her. She stiffened in surprise. "I can see!" She spun around, her gaze darting around her, and Birlerion grinned, there wasn't that much to see.

"My sentinal is enhancing your sight. He can't restore it, but whilst you're inside, he can assist."

"Oh, my." Taelia memorised his face and ran her fingers over the graze on Birlerion's cheek that was already fading fast. She patted his face and looked around her. "It's an honour to meet you, and I thank you for your care." She smiled at Birlerion. "It is nice to be able to see what you look like."

Birlerion grinned. "If you like, next time, we'll bring the Captain with us. I'm sure you'd rather see him. Please sit."

He hesitated as her face fell and then rattled on to give her time to recover. "As you know, we've been sheltering the temple since Leyandrii sundered the Bloodstone. I've always had an affinity with the temple. Leyandrii said she built it for me; a way to tempt me off the streets," he said with a shy smile. He reached and offered her a glass of water that appeared in his hand. He took one for himself and sat opposite her, relaxing as the soothing embrace from his sentinal washed away his tension. Taelia's eyes widened as she watched him visibly relax.

"Is your sentinal doing something?"

"He says I'm too tense, so he's easing my worries away. Hopefully, yours have eased, too."

Taelia looked at him in surprise and then grinned as she nodded. "He's rather useful, isn't he?" She looked up into the swirling mist and thought about what Birlerion had been saying. "You said the Lady had to tempt you? I thought you've always been the Lady's?"

"Oh, yes, but I must have been about thirteen or fourteen when she completed the temple. I couldn't resist its call. I used to visit often, I couldn't stay away and Guerlaire caught me and enrolled me in the academy."

"When you were fourteen?"

"Yes. I had been sleeping in the oak tree in the temple gardens when, one night, the Father was attacked. I helped him escape and it gave me away. But anyway, that's old history. You don't want to know about me; you want to know about my tree."

"But you are the Sentinal, Birlerion. I am glad the Lady found you; you've been alone for too long. I can see why she would want you with her."

Birlerion smiled. "She treated us like family. We lived and worked in the palace. Though, I must admit, I usually have a good sense of direction, but when I first arrived at the palace, all I did was get lost. Niallerion used to think it was hilarious. I had to use a page boy as a guide."

"You speak of Niallerion often."

"He was a genius, always inventing stuff." Birlerion's smile slipped. "A good friend."

Taelia patted his arm.

Birlerion looked up into the swirling mist. "Sentinals have their own personalities, linked to their guard, I suppose. Most can heal, certainly their own guard, and sometimes others. They link us to the Lady and the Land. Leyandrii and Marguerite."

"Marguerite is the Land?"

"Yes, she bonded a few weeks before the end. The Land was ancient and weary. They never said but I think he was one of the creator's sons, as Leyandrii and Marguerite were the daughters. He couldn't continue any longer; he was worn out. When Marguerite took over, she became one with our world, she became the land. She tried to alleviate some of the worst effects caused by the Ascendant's magic. It was part of Leyandrii's plan to protect this world as best they could."

"Leyandrii's plan? Not your plan?"

Birlerion laughed. "No, it was their plan; we just did what we were told. The power was theirs. They just lent it to us when needed." He tilted his head; his eyes distant. "Torsion is on his way with back up. Before he gets here, I could show you how I see the temple if you'd like?"

"I'd love that, thank you."

"My sentinal will know you now. If you ever have the need, if you need shelter or a quiet place, you are always welcome. He will allow you entry."

Taelia's eyes shone. "You are very generous."

"He gets lonely when we are away. You would be doing me a favour. He's used to having me here."

"Then I would be honoured, thank you."

"Let us visit the Lady. She likes us to visit, as well." Birlerion offered her his arm and led her out of the tree.

Taelia faltered as her gaze swept hungrily around the gardens and over the sentinal before pausing on the white marble temple.

"I can still see!"

"For a little while, though I am afraid your sight will fade soon. But you'll have time to see inside if you wish."

They entered the temple and Taelia gasped. "It's shimmering; the stone is shimmering."

"Leyandrii is always pleased when we visit. The temple reflects her pleasure." Birlerion chuckled as he reached for the smooth white stone and patted it. The white marble settled into a soothing gleam at his touch and his face softened.

Taelia watched him in amazement. "Birlerion! What did you just do? It's stopped shimmering."

Birlerion shrugged, a soft smile on his face. "I have no explanation. The temple always says hello."

Taelia stared at him for a moment as if perplexed and then walked up to the altar. "She was so beautiful," she murmured as she gazed at the statue of a young woman holding an armful of flowers.

"She still is," Birlerion replied as he knelt at the feet of the statue. He relaxed as the welcoming peace of the temple embraced him. A small smile tugged at his lips as the stray thought that he was older than even this temple passed through his mind. Thank goodness he didn't feel that old. He rose and joined Taelia where she sat in the pew observing him. He gave her a self-conscious smile and inhaled the heady scent of roses.

"Roses. They smell beautiful," Taelia said, her voice soft.

"Uplifting," Birlerion murmured.

Taelia jerked around at the strident clatter behind them,

breaking the spell. "Hopefully they soothe as well. Torsion doesn't look pleased. Birlerion, you need to be careful around him. I would never have believed you if you'd told me, but I think he would kill you if he had the chance."

Birlerion sighed, sad to lose the moment. "I know. I seem to rile him for some reason."

"Taelia!" Torsion's voice was like an explosion in the calm temple.

"There is no need to shout," Taelia replied.

"Where have you been?"

"You can see where I am, and where I have been is nothing to you. Now leave me in peace. I have every right to sit in a temple." Torsion flinched as her brilliant eyes bored into his.

"I'll not leave you with him."

"It's probably best if I leave; no point causing a scene," Birlerion murmured. "Remember, you are always welcome, scholar."

"It's Taelia, call me Taelia, and it's not *you* making the scene. Thank you, Birlerion." She offered her hand and Birlerion bent over and kissed it in farewell.

She smiled as he whispered her name, and her sight began to fade as he left.

19

KING'S PALACE, OLD VESPERS

Jerrol was methodically searching the prince's bedchamber when Jennery found him.

"There you are. I've been searching all over. The king has the whole palace buzzing."

"I hope he remembers there are spies in the palace."

"Apparently, it is a celebration for the confirmation of Alyssa as Guardian, and he's decided to have a full-dress ball."

"Ah, your audience with the king went well then?"

"Better than well. He wants us back there as soon as possible to perform the confirmation. I need to start beefing up the garrison, as you said the Elothian border is going to be key. Landis is going to come and help."

"Umm, the confirmation means you too, doesn't it?"

"Well, yes, I suppose, though Alyssa is the Guardian."

"Have you set the date then?"

"Date?"

"For your joining, numbskull."

Jennery stopped pacing in shock. "By the Lady, I haven't asked her yet."

"But you have discussed it, haven't you?"

"Well, of course, but generally, you know, as part of taking on the Watch," Jennery said.

Jerrol grinned at his dazed expression. "Then maybe you had better ask her before the king does it for you. I am sure Alyssa will want to plan it all. Maybe you ought to suggest that her mother helps her; you know, a way for them to bond."

Jennery bit his lip. "Her mother?"

"Haven't you met her mother yet? Lady Miranda will become your mother." Jerrol's lips twitched. Maybe he ought not mention that it looked like Tagerill could end up being his father.

Jennery paled. "Mother?"

"She could go with you to Deepwater; give Alyssa a chance to get to know her again."

"Do you think she would want to?"

"I am positive she would. Get on her good side, go and introduce them. Though I would slip in your proposal first." Jerrol grinned, slapping his friend on the shoulder.

Jennery nodded. "Propose first, then meet the mother," he mumbled as he left the room, bouncing off the door frame as he stumbled away.

Parsillion peered through the door, a grin on his face. He had replaced Birlerion for the day. "Do you need some help?"

Jerrol laughed. "I think I've pretty much searched everywhere." He gestured at the jumbled mess. Prince Kharel was disorganised; books and papers were scattered across the floor, clothes dropped haphazardly or strewn across chairs. Jerrol had been through every piece of clothing, every book and scroll, even to the extent of pulling up rugs and moving furniture, but there was nothing: no incriminating messages; no sign of collusion.

Sitting on the bed, he scanned the room. It was a basic room; the prince had not bothered with any curtains to soften the windows nor requested any furniture or decorations to ease his comfort. It was quite spartan compared to his wife's plush parlour. He sighed and rubbed his face with his hands. *Lady*, he thought, *we are getting nowhere.*

His eye paused on the door to the ramparts. He stood and opened it and followed the stone steps up around the bend and out into the morning sun, Parsillion on his heels.

The crenulated stone led all the way around the tower; a sheer drop all the way around. The silver spire rose to a point above him. There was a wooden chair positioned on the flagstones, facing west towards the city of Old Vespers. Jerrol sat in the chair and inspected the stone walls around him. The northernmost warehouse just behind the Chapterhouse was visible through one of the gaps. What was the purpose of the warehouses?

The fact that the warehouses were visible reinforced his suspicions. Idly, he inspected the stonework around him. The grey stone was weathered and dull, all except for one stone, which seemed to brighten as he stared at it. He eased the block out of the wall with his knife. The stone grated slightly before falling into his hand, and in the cavity behind it was a cloth-wrapped bundle. He replaced the stone and sat back in the chair, unwrapping the small package.

A clear, tubular crystal fell into his hand, along with a black notebook and a folded piece of parchment; the same as the parchment he had found in Deepwater. He unfolded the parchment and examined the unexplained symbols. Sighing, he refolded the paper and flicked through the notebook. It was the one Isseran had dropped, and he had handed to his commander; the one Kharel had confiscated from Nikols. He sat back with a huff as his eye ran down the list of officials.

There were some heavyweight names on the list, which

Jerrol supposed was not surprising considering the positions Isseran and Kharel held. He pondered. Was there an opportunity for him to use this list without knowing what their directives were? Could he feed in bad information, and if so, what?

The bundle in his lap buzzed and he almost dropped it in surprise. As he flipped the cloth open, the crystal glowed a bright white. Tentatively, he picked it up and it vibrated against his palm. He gripped it tighter in case he dropped it.

Parsillion hissed his breath out. "Another communications crystal."

The buzzing grew louder and a subtle vibration grew in his ears; an unnatural sensation that made him shiver. Jerrol flinched as a voice spoke clearly: "*... all associates, calling all associates, check-in time recalibrated to minus two, repeat, check-in time recalibrated to minus two. We rise with the Lady's Moon, repeat, rising with the Lady's Moon. Do not, repeat, do not, get wet. Allow the decs to clear the way. Final check at minus two.*"

Jerrol froze. The full moon was tomorrow, the day of the king's ball. Was that the day they would attack the palace? What did the rest of it mean? He ran back down the stairs, Parsillion at his heels, and went to seek an audience with the king.

Jennery found Alyssa sitting in the small parlour reserved for the ladies. She was staring out of the window.

"Hey, fancy a walk?" Jennery grinned as he stuck his head around the door.

Alyssa leapt to her feet. "Please. Everyone is busy except me." She slipped her hand around his arm and allowed him to escort her out of the palace. They began to walk down through the gardens.

"Where are we going?" Alysa asked.

"I wanted to talk to you privately," Jennery began, gripping her arm tight.

"Oh? What's the matter?"

"Nothing, nothing's the matter," Jennery said. He flicked a glance around them. The gardens were deserted, and he drew Alyssa to the side of a flower bed. "Errm, I was thinking …" He ran his fingers around his shirt collar, which suddenly felt too tight. "I was, um thinking." He stuttered to a halt.

Alyssa cocked her head at him. "Thinking what?" she prompted.

"Well, seeing as the king will be announcing you as Guardian of Deepwater, and we will be running Deepwater together, and seeing as, well, seeing as we like each other … um … a lot. I was thinking, well you know, I was … um … thinking, we should get joined," he said in a rush, looking hopefully at Alyssa.

"What?"

He rolled his eyes and dropped to one knee, holding her hand in a panicky grip. "Alyssa, I love you. Please will you join with me?" he asked, the colour rising in his face as she gasped. A wide smile spread over her face.

"Lea, yes! Of course I will." Alyssa wrapped her arms around his neck and kissed him hard.

"Um, aren't *I* supposed to kiss you?" he asked rather breathlessly when she finally let him go.

"You did the asking. *I'll* do the kissing," Alyssa said and promptly kissed him again.

Jerrol took a detour via the cells on his way to see the king. Maybe the prince would reveal something. The king called the cells 'the dungeons', but the upper level wasn't the dark, dank holes you would expect of true castle dungeons. As he descended the curved stone steps, he remembered his first sight of an Arifel. It was a fortunate distraction at the time, enabling him to escape his death sentence. Birlerion, again.

Kharel's cell was on the upper level and quite light and airy, with a cot bed against the wall. He sat on the edge of the bed; his shoulders slumped in dejection. A King's Guard stood over him.

"Well, you've thrown away everything, and for what?" Jerrol asked as he entered the cell.

Kharel glared at him.

"The Ascendants have left you to swing for treason. What were they offering you that you didn't already have?"

Kharel clamped his lips together and stared at the wall.

"What, you aren't going to say? Do you think they're going to rush to save you? The Grand Duke doesn't want you; you're no longer any use. You've got no power." Jerrol flexed his hand. "He only wants Selvia, his daughter."

"He can have her."

"I'm sure she'll be pleased to hear you say that. You are aware of the penalty for treason? For trying to assassinate the king? Death. Death by public execution, so that all the people can witness your humiliation. Do you think you'll be able to hold your head high? Act brave while inside, your guts are shaking like jelly and all you'll want to do is spew?"

Kharel flicked a nervous glance at Jerrol, his face tight.

"The king ordered it for the day after tomorrow. No point wasting time. It's not as if you can say anything to prove your innocence as you were caught in the act." Jerrol paced around the cell. "Hung, drawn, and quartered. I always thought that was a bit barbaric, but they say they gut you and drag your entrails out while you are still alive. They make sure you suffer before they chop you up."

Kharel paled.

"I heard you live for quite a while; after being gutted, I

mean. All the bits are still connected, aren't they? In theory." Jerrol paused at the door as he considered the king's eldest son. "What could they have possibly offered you that you didn't already have?"

"You don't know what you are dealing with," Kharel spat.

"Why don't you tell me?" Jerrol invited.

"They don't leave loose ends. They have it all planned."

"You mean you are prepared to die just to make sure their plan runs smoothly?"

Kharel smirked. "You will see. You don't know what they are capable of."

"Really?"

"They have powers you have never seen and magics that will overwhelm you. Just wait. You'll see." Kharel's laugh was a little hysterical. "I can't wait for you all to be brought down."

Jerrol held up the clear crystal. "Is this how you all get your instructions? Traitors like you and Fenton?" Jerrol waved the black notebook. "Someone else is telling you what to do. Who is it?"

Kharel's eyes bulged and he clamped his lips tight.

"You've committed treason, on the word of some other person who you are not even willing to name? Ashamed to associate with them now, are you?"

Glaring at Jerrol, Kharel refused to say another word.

The door clanged shut behind Jerrol as he left. He jerked his head at the guard and they made their way up the stairs. "Did he say anything previously?"

The guard shook his head. "He said more to you than he has the whole time he's been in the cell."

Jerrol sighed. "He knows something is going to happen; he's not sure what, though he expects to be rescued. Stay alert."

The guard saluted and headed back down the stairs.

Jerrol deliberated. The king would get annoyed if he kept interrupting him, but this was too important not to raise as an issue. He entered the palace, intent on reaching the king.

Darris opened the door as he approached. King Benedict was expecting him and was standing behind his desk. "What's the matter? I could feel you coming across the parade ground."

"Sire, I found this hidden in the ramparts above your son's room." Jerrol placed the crystal on the desk. "This is a live communication crystal. It buzzed while I was holding it. There was a message. There is a rising planned, which will coincide with the Lady's moon. An associate's check-in has been recalibrated to 'minus two'. I thought maybe the attack was planned for Lady's day, but I think it's tomorrow to coincide with your ball, and I found Commander Fenton in the notebook." Jerrol tossed the notebook on the king's desk. "I mistook the 'f' as an 's' previously." Jerrol exhaled a deep breath. "Prince Kharel knows something's coming."

The king cursed, long and fluently, and massaged his temples before leaning back in his chair staring at Jerrol. "Very well, see if you can find Fenton, and double the guard on my son. The ball continues. I will not be dictated by nameless people."

"Yes, sire," Jerrol said and bowed his way out of the room.

20

KING'S BALL

It was the morning of the king's ball, and Miranda sat waiting in the king's rose arbour, twisting her handkerchief between her fingers. She had agreed to meet her daughter here, and although she was excited to see her, she wasn't sure of the reception she was going to receive. It had been nearly ten years since she had last seen Alyssa. That had been *her* choice, not her daughter's. She could say she had been influenced, but what sort of mother deserted her children and never checked how they were getting on?

She held her head in her hands. Yes, she'd had her reasons; she had been too young, too immature, not understanding the commitment she had made, scared of leaving the city. All excuses, and thin ones at that. She may have been persuaded against her will but she hadn't put up a fight and, instead, had gone with the easy option, allowing someone else to make her decisions for her.

Arguing that Hugh hadn't tried to stop her wouldn't help her. She knew he had. He had tried to meet her halfway. He'd agreed to attend court more often if that was her desire, yet she had allowed herself to be convinced that her family didn't need or want her. Miranda recalled Captain Haven's words; it's never too late. "It's never too late," she repeated to herself. "Give yourself a chance."

Footsteps on the gravel disturbed her, and she looked up. A young couple strolled towards her; they were holding hands, and the girl leaned into the man. As they walked, the man slipped his arm around her and kissed the top of her head. He gave her a brief hug and let go, leaving her to walk on alone, watching her with concern.

Miranda took a deep breath and stood. This beautiful young woman was her daughter? All grown up and courting? She had missed so much of her daughter's life. She suddenly didn't want to miss any more.

Alyssa smiled shyly as she approached. "Mother?"

Miranda opened her arms and Alyssa flew into them, and then they were both hugging and crying. Jennery retreated to balustrades at the end of the terrace.

Alyssa straightened up and wiped her eyes with her handkerchief. "I didn't think you'd want to see me. I asked papa so many times."

"It wasn't his fault. I regret so much. I have no excuse, except to say that I was young and easily influenced by others. Hopefully, we can start again. I would so much like to be a part of yours and Simeon's lives. I am so sorry, Alyssa, for causing you so much pain. Truly, I hope you will believe me." Miranda marvelled at the change in the young woman before her. "Tell me about yourself," Miranda pleaded. "I've missed so much. I know it's my own fault. Why did Lord Aaron try to kidnap you? And how did you end up here?"

Alyssa sighed and leaned back against the bench. "Well, since Papa raised me, it will be no surprise that I know my guardianship lore, and I will tell you now, I follow the Lady, blood and bone. I guess it all started about half a year ago when Simeon brought in a new Seneschal. He changed overnight; became more argumentative, disruptive, was led down a path that didn't include the Lady. He challenged father's rule, though not overtly. It came to a head when Papa was … was killed." Alyssa faltered and Miranda gripped her hands in sympathy.

"We had been to Lord Aaron's confirmation. What a travesty that was. He had been led astray, as well. I was so bowled over by him; tall, handsome, attentive. I thought he liked me too, and his mother was so sweet. We were returning home when we were attacked by bandits, betrayed by Aaron. Captain Haven and his Sentinals turned up and rescued me. It's all they seem to be doing these days." Her gaze wandered down the terraces to where Jennery was leaning against the rails.

Miranda followed her gaze. "And who is that waiting for you?"

"Lieutenant Jennery. I'll introduce you to him in a bit." Alyssa flashed her mother a brilliant smile. "He is very important to me."

Miranda nodded, a smile dawning on her face. "I can't wait to meet the man that makes my daughter so happy."

Alyssa blushed but continued. "The Greenswatch guardianship settled on me, having nowhere else to go. When Simeon took the Watch, he forswore the Lady and didn't pick up the mantle." She paused as Miranda gasped.

"Don't worry." She leaned forward and patted her mother's hands. "He has it safely now. Captain Haven managed to release him from the spell that his Seneschal had him under and he was confirmed recently. I'll let him tell you all about that.

"Unfortunately, Aaron was not so lucky. He abducted me and injured Steward Garrick," she said, her voice hardening, "and then whilst I was being rescued, yet again, by Captain Haven, Sentinal Tagerill was injured and Aaron was killed. We need to go home and see how Tagerill goes on."

"Have you heard how Sentinal Tagerill fares?" Miranda asked.

Alyssa pursed her lips. "Not good. But he's in safe hands, so he'll be on his feet again soon."

"That's a relief to hear. You are going to Deepwater?" Miranda asked, raising her eyebrows. "Are you not staying here in Vespers? Or returning to Greenswatch?"

Alyssa's face softened. "No, Lea and I will become the Guardians of Deepwater. Sentinal Denirion demands it, and the Watch is waiting." A smile glinted in her eye. "The Lady approves and the king has agreed. And we need to care for Tagerill. Captain Haven misses him sorely." Alyssa gripped her mother's hands. "It's all I've ever wanted, to have a mother. But tell me where you've been and why. I want to understand why you did what you did."

Miranda sighed. "Are you sure you want the sordid details? If it hadn't been for Captain Haven, I think I would still have been ensorcelled."

"Captain Haven? It seems he's had to save all our family. The least we can do is return Tagerill to him. Tell me what happened."

Miranda dropped her eyes. "What can I say? I was young and silly; younger than you when I joined with your father. I had only lived in the city, never the country. I hated the country. It was too quiet. No parties, little attention. In truth, I never gave it a chance. Whenever I was at court, I was feted as one of the beauties," Miranda twisted her lips. "I expect it all went to my head, and then the princess took a liking to me. I was flattered, and she started suggesting I move back to court and live with her.

"Then one day, when your father had taken me to court, I refused to come home. Just like that. Overnight, I moved in to wait on the princess and rejected your father." Miranda looked earnestly at her daughter. "I never meant to leave you; it just seemed the right and natural thing to do at the time."

Alyssa leaned forward to take her mother's hands. "If they were playing with your mind, there would be little you could do about it. I know, they tried it on me. Lately, whenever there has been some emergency in my life, it seems that Captain Haven is always there, protecting me, with Lea not far behind."

"Lea?" Miranda asked.

Alyssa stood and waved Jennery over. She reached to take Jennery's hand. "Mother, may I present my intended husband? Lieutenant Leander Jennery of the Captain's Guard. Lea, this is my mother, Miranda."

Miranda stood and looked up into the rugged features and bright blue eyes of her daughter's intended. She took in his archaic uniform, which was the same as Captain Haven's, and reminded her of Tagerill. "Leander, it is a pleasure to meet the man who makes my daughter so very happy."

Jennery cleared his throat. "Call me Lea, please, or Jennery if you prefer."

"He hates his name; he never uses it!" Alyssa laughed, hugging his arm. "But it will be known now, at our joining and the confirmation," she teased, her eyes alight. Jennery made a face, and she turned back to her mother. "You will come with us to Deepwater for our joining, won't you? You are welcome to stay with us as long as you want."

Miranda's face lit up. "I wouldn't miss it for anything, though I must visit Simeon as well."

"Simeon will come for the confirmation. You can make arrangements to stay with him then," Alyssa promised, her eyes sparkling. "I can't believe it! Everything is turning out wonderfully. The king will announce our Guardianship tonight at the ball, and then the day after tomorrow, we will leave for Deepwater. I can't wait to go home." Her eyes twinkled at Jennery and she enthusiastically embraced him.

Miranda smiled at her daughter's obvious delight and Jennery's embarrassed pleasure, though he seemed to be enjoying the open displays of affection.

Alyssa laughed at herself. "Sorry, he only just asked me to join with him. You're the first person we've told. I'm so happy."

Miranda was delighted and opened her arms to embrace them both. "I am honoured that you told me. I wish you all the happiness the Lady can provide," she said.

Jerrol caught sight of the happy group in the arbour as he travelled across the upper gallery. He paused to watch them out of the window. Alyssa must have made an honest man of Jennery. He wished he had seen him proposing, and he laughed at the picture. He was glad to see that Lady Miranda was back in the fold. It would all develop naturally, he was sure. Deepwater was secure.

His thoughts drifted to Taelia. Hopefully, he would have a chance to dance with her at the ball, maybe smooth over their misunderstanding. It didn't feel right to be at odds with her.

Hurrying down the corridor towards the king's chambers, he scowled at the number of servants clogging the passageways, arms full of cloth, flowers, chairs. This was madness. If Fenton had approved all these additional people to work the ball, they were in trouble. He would have filled the palace with his supporters, all enspelled to fight for a cause that still eluded Jerrol. Apart from taking over power, Jerrol couldn't see what the Ascendants were offering that would improve people's lives.

"Darris, what's going on? Who brought these people in?" Jerrol grabbed the steward as he hurried passed.

"Fenton cleared them. They were pre-checked in preparation for the dinner. The fact that it is now a dance has confused them; they are hopeless."

Jerrol pulled Darris against the wall as two large men staggered passed, carrying a long table. "We need to revoke their clearance. Fenton is working with the Ascendants. Anyone Fenton approved is suspect. I'll warn Bryce and Jennery, and get them checking the staff. A quick check is to get each person to swear the Lady's Oath. If they can't say the oath then they've been enspelled." Jerrol hurried Darris down the corridor. "I'll send word to Nikols, but we need to warn the king."

Darris raised an eyebrow. "The king is in his chambers. You're all due there for a debrief in a chime."

"Go warn the king. I'll join you shortly." He ran off down the corridor, but the floor was slick and he skidded around the corner. Jerrol steadied himself against the wall, and crouching, he ran his hand over the floor and brought his fingertips up to his nose. His eyes narrowed and he hurried towards Fenton's office.

He found Bryce arguing with Fenton's aide. Jerrol flipped though the notebook and found the man's name and his keyword. "Redwood," Jerrol snapped and the man collapsed.

Bryce watched aghast. "He was refusing to tell me Fenton's whereabouts," he said.

"Fenton is compromised, and so is everyone he's brought into the palace. Start rounding up as many as you can, and replace them with Landis' men. At least we know we can trust them. I'll send word to Nikols for help." Jerrol called Ari, the little Arifel and continued. "Parsillion, find Birlerion and Darllion, and meet me at the king's chambers. Don't argue, do it," he said, as the Sentinal opened his mouth to protest.

Jerrol left Bryce calling for Landis and hurried to the king's chambers.

"Sire, we've got trouble," Jerrol said as he entered. Ari popped into view and hovered above him. "Ari, ask Jennery to join us." Ari meeped and disappeared. "Fonorion, the palace is infiltrated; protecting the king is your priority. Fenton has been compromised. Don't trust any of his men. Shout the word 'silverwood' at them; that seems to be the most common keyword in this notebook," Jerrol waved it, "and that might stall them long enough for you to deal with them."

The king leapt to his feet. "What about Fenton, have you found him?"

"I'm sorry sire, but Fenton is nowhere to be found. I am assuming the majority of his men will be likewise affected. I have Bryce rounding them up." He paused as Ari popped into view just as the door opened and Jennery, Bryce, and the Sentinals entered. He waited as they settled, and then continued. "We have another problem. Your palace floors are slick with linseed oil."

The king raised his eyebrows, perplexed. "Linseed oil?"

"When it dries out and gets hot, it's combustible." Jerrol grimaced at the king. "And if that's not bad enough your palace is crawling with strange staff with flash Justice permits. Have you had any word from Nikols?" Jerrol asked.

"He's not due here for another chime. Fonorion, stay," the king said as Fonorion made to leave.

"I also found another piece of this parchment in your son's rooms, but it still makes no sense," Jerrol unfolded the square of paper and lay it on the table by the map.

The king moved over to the table with him. "We don't have time for this. We'll review it after you save my palace from being burned to the ground! Jerrol, if Fenton arrives, I'll keep him here." The king indicated the notebook. "But his men will be everywhere."

"We'll manage. We have Landis and your guards, and we can lock as many of the servants into the servant's hall as possible. The question is, when will they attack?"

"Secure the palace," the king said. "The ball continues, but at least we are forewarned. Let's use it to our advantage."

Jerrol nodded. "Yes, sire." Jerrol swept a glance around the Sentinals and began deploying them. They left at his word. "Bryce, tell the ladies what's up, then find Landis and meet me in the commander's office, and Jennery, go warn Nikols about the attack and the warehouse. We need to contain as many of the attackers in the warehouse as possible. Darris, we need to round up the staff, tell them you have an announcement to make in the servant's hall. I'll meet you there. Birlerion, with me," he added as he strode out of the room still issuing instructions. "Birlerion, do a sweep of the palace. Make sure there are no obstacles or things obviously out of place. You know what to look for. I'll be in the commander's office or with Landis."

Heading back to Fenton's office, Jerrol found a palace steward trying to redirect some burly men who were insisting on carrying tables through the palace. "Gentlemen." Jerrol clapped his hands. "If you please, just put down what you are carrying. We need all staff in the servant's hall, downstairs. I have an announcement, and I'd rather say it only once, and then we can all return to our duties. We still have a lot to do, and the king expects perfection tonight."

Jerrol followed, rounding up the staff, telling them to stop whatever they were doing. Captain Landis entered the main entrance hall just as Jerrol opened the baise door to the servant's quarters; he let it swing shut and called the young captain over.

"Landis, I need your men to patrol the palace and grounds. Help Birlerion clear out anything flammable. Some of these imported staff have been mopping the floor with linseed oil. We need to flush it out. Make sure there are no rags stuffed anywhere. It seems there is going to be an attack on the palace tonight, and Fenton's men are the inside job."

"What? Surely, we are cancelling the ball?"

"Impossible. Safer to allow guests to arrive than turn them back into what could be a firefight. The king wants to use the ball as bait to identify as many disaffected courtiers as possible."

Landis narrowed his eyes. "We're going to find it difficult to tell friend from foe once it gets dark."

Jerrol paused hand on the door. "Good point. What do you suggest?"

"Something easily seen. Reflective armbands would be ideal, but we don't have any. I saw some white armbands being used in the training grounds; I'll see if I can find enough. We'll be able to tell if a person is on our side. I saw it work that time the Elothians tangled with the advance guard north of Stoneford; right mess it could've been!"

"Deal with it. Darris will know which of the staff we can trust. Make sure you give him some armbands. We need to take out as many of Fenton's men as we can before the ball starts and replace them with your men. Try to remove them discreetly. We don't want to trigger anything early. We've only got an hour before guests begin to arrive; you'll know when the ball is starting. Lady willing, Nikols will contain the reinforcements."

Landis nodded and headed back out the way he had come. Jerrol pushed open the door to the servant's quarters and descended the stairs. The large room opened before him, and he stood on a chair placed by the door and clapped his hands for silence. Darris flapped his hands and the murmur of voices died away as the staff turned to face him.

"Apologies, folks, I know you are all busy. The king wanted me to convey a message. Tonight, is an important night, and he wants it to be perfect." He dropped his voice and said, "Silverwood." He watched as half of the staff collapsed to the floor convulsing, while the others tried to move around them in confusion. "Those who have collapsed are not the king's staff; tie them with the twine, now," he commanded as Darris passed out rolls of twine and knives to the shocked palace staff, staring wide-eyed at the writhing people on the floor.

"Make sure you tie them tight. Captain Landis has armbands. All staff still standing, make sure you get one before you leave this room. They will denote you as the king's staff. We need to clear the corridors. Guests will start to arrive in one hour. Make sure this hall is locked once we leave. These folks are going to need help later. Be warned. We are expecting further hostilities, and there may be some difficulties."

Jerrol gazed at the remaining staff. "Stay out of the way of the King's Guards as much as possible. I expect you to act in a manner that the king would expect of you. Remember, armbands denote the king's staff; make sure you have one." Jerrol jumped down off the chair and exited the hall, grimacing as he heard Darris repeating his instructions amongst the rising voices. Rumours that would no doubt flood the city by the morning.

Jennery reined in his horse as he dismounted in a flurry in the garrison courtyard.

"Where's Commander Nikols?" he barked as he threw his reins at a stable lad.

"His office, sir," the lad replied, grabbing the reins.

Jennery hurried down the corridor, pausing on the threshold of Commander Nikols' crowded office. Nikols stood behind his desk, tapping points on a map spread out on the surface. His officers were gathered around him, listening intently. Jennery saluted as he approached. "Report from the palace, sir," he said to Nikols. "Captain Haven advises that an attack will happen tonight. Commander Fenton is believed to be compromised."

Nikols cursed. "Fenton? He left not long ago, saying he was on his way back to the palace."

"I didn't pass Commander Fenton on the way here, sir. Are you sure he was going to the palace?" Jennery asked.

"That's what he said."

"Captain Haven and Captain Landis are replacing the perimeter guards as we speak. Captain Haven asks for news of the warehouses. He believes the attackers are all housed there or manoeuvring from there already. He asks that you contain as many as possible, to prevent them from reaching the palace and his depleted forces."

"The scouts sent to check out the warehouses didn't return. We were just discussing sending a follow-up." Nikols said. "That might explain why, I suppose." Nikols stared at Jennery for a moment and then began issuing instructions to his men. "Units two and four surround the warehouses, see if the scouts can tell which ones are in use. Tell them to hold fast until the signal. Make sure they are all dressed in black-outs, let's not warn them. Unit six, set up a silent roving patrol between the town boundary and the palace. Keep them invisible. Let's make sure no one gets through." He turned to Jennery. "Advise Haven that we will contain the warehouses, but who knows what is out there? I'll detain Fenton as well, if I find him."

Jennery saluted. "Sir, in case you are not aware, the ball

is proceeding. The king wouldn't hear of it being cancelled. He wants to make sure we wipe this threat out once and for all. He is fed up of his palace being a battleground."

Nikols grimaced and shook his head. "I pity Haven that job."

Night descended as Jennery returned to the palace. He passed many carriages beginning the ascent up the torchlit rise. The king's ball would be well attended. It would be interesting to see who stayed away, he thought. He beat the carriages to the front entrance and trotted round to the stables. Strolling into the office of the King's Justice, he found Jerrol behind the desk. He wore a gold strip of cloth around his arm that flashed in the lamplight. Jerrol looked up as Jennery approached his desk. "Report," he said, leaning back in his chair.

"Nikols has the warehouses under control. He has also set up a roving patrol up to the palace grounds, both out of sight. He said Fenton had been after more men from him. You'll be glad to hear Nikols refused. Apparently, Fenton was on his way back here, but I didn't pass him on the road." Jennery reported, adding with a grin, "What's with the fancy armband?"

Jerrol shrugged and threw a strip of white cloth at him. "It's so we can tell who's who, seeing as we can't trust any of Fenton's men. Landis suggested it. We ran out of gold cloth, so you get white."

Jennery raised his eyebrows as he tied the cloth around his sleeve. "The guests are beginning to arrive. I passed them on the way up."

"Very well, then, let's get into place. Fonorion and Parsillion have King Benedict and Prince Anders. Darllion is guarding Prince Kharel. Landis has the perimeter. Bryce, the interior. You have the guests. You can practice your charm. Birlerion is with me. So, I guess we'd better go join them."

They left the office, collecting a heavily armed Birlerion from outside the door and headed into the palace. Jennery considered Birlerion. "Um, maybe Birlerion ought to be up in the galleries? He might frighten the guests."

"They won't see him," promised Jerrol as he led the way to the ballroom. He waved Jennery on as he paused to speak to Darris. "All set?"

"Yes, sir. Guests are being checked on entry. Those not prepared to swear the oath are escorted to a side room. Those who do receive an armband. Our guests below stairs are being guarded by one of the footmen; a big lad, sir."

"Good," Jerrol said as he entered the ballroom, scanning the room, which was ablaze with light and crystal. White cloth-covered tables lined the walls and elegantly dressed guests were beginning to circulate, accepting glasses of sparkling wine from waiters bedecked in gold and white. Prince Anders stood by the door, welcoming the guests.

The glass doors, which usually opened out onto the terrace, were shut. The heavy brocade curtains were drawn, providing a vibrant backdrop for the gold chains that criss-crossed them and glittered in the candlelight. A raised dais was swathed in red and gold at the end of the room, currently hosting a quartet who were playing softly in the background. Four trumpeters stood in the gallery above, awaiting the king's arrival. All present were wearing an armband.

Jerrol left Jennery circulating, anticipating the arrival of Alyssa and her mother. He spotted the discreetly positioned Birlerion up above before he left the room and walked towards the king's chambers. Jerrol nodded as he passed arriving guests, murmuring words of encouragement as he acknowledged the salutes from guards unobtrusively watching all exits.

He arrived at the king's chambers as a clock in the

hallway began to chime seven. He tapped on the door and eased through the gap as it opened. The king stood waiting by the fireplace, resplendent in his navy-blue uniform. He wore a red sash diagonally across his chest, and he sparkled with jewels.

"All is in place, sire," Jerrol reported, blinded by the spectacle before him. "Are we making a statement tonight?"

The king nodded. "Absolutely."

21

BALLROOM, KING'S PALACE

The ballroom was abuzz with voices as Jerrol preceded King Benedict through the doors. He nodded at Darris, who signalled the trumpeters, who heralded the king's entrance with a loud fanfare. The voices died down as the guests turned towards the king. A ripple of bows and curtseys preceded the king as he made his way down the ballroom. He turned before the dais and raised his hands, his jewels catching the light.

"Lords and ladies, welcome to my home," he said with a smile. "This is our first celebration of Vespiri since our recent troubles. You may have noticed the catechism you received at the entrance. We are expecting a few minor difficulties this evening, and I would request that you stay within the ballroom for your safety and enjoyment.

"Captain Haven and his guards will ensure our safety." A ripple of apprehension interrupted him. "You do not need to be concerned. I will speak further with you later. Please enjoy." The king moved away from the centre of the room and paused beside Jerrol. "You will be protecting us, won't you?" he asked with a sharp smile.

Jerrol grimaced and escorted him towards his waiting guests. Handing the king to Fonorion, he stood in the shadows, still and silent, watching the room. The ballroom slowly filled with more distinguished guests, bright and colourful.

Jerrol watched Jennery escort Alyssa, draped in a beautiful gown of forest green, to a table, and he wondered where Lady Miranda was. Scholar Dean Liliian and her assistant entered the ballroom, and he eagerly watched the doorway. Torsion entered, escorting Taelia, resplendent in a deep rose-pink gown that hugged her body. Her cloudy brown hair was artfully piled on her head, and his heart stuttered as he gazed at her. He drank in the sight of her, longing to hold her in his arms just for a moment. She turned her head towards him and gave him a beautiful smile that made him catch his breath before she tipped her face back to listen to Torsion.

Lady Miranda entered the ball room and taking a deep breath, he moved towards Prince Anders, still adeptly receiving guests on behalf of his father. "Enjoying the practice, your highness?" Jerrol murmured as he paused beside him.

The prince flicked him a glance. "No more than you, Captain Haven. Though if you have need of practice, I am always available to meet in the ring. I did offer, you have yet to name the time and place."

Jerrol smiled. "I am, of course, available for your entertainment, your highness, though maybe not when we're in the middle of an attempted coup."

Prince Anders choked and cursed Jerrol under his breath. "Go annoy someone else, why don't you?" he muttered before turning to smile at the next guest.

"Your face will get stuck like that," Jerrol promised as he moved forward to take Lady Miranda's arm as she entered the room.

Anders made a very unroyal face at Jerrol before turning

back to the arriving guests. Lady Miranda cast a suspicious glance at Jerrol. "What did you say to him?"

Jerrol laughed. "Got to keep them on their toes, you know," he said as he saluted the prince and moved her further into the room. "I just wanted to say that we received word. Tagerill has regained consciousness and is progressing well. Not happy, but progressing."

"Oh, Captain Jerrol." She stopped walking, taking a deep breath as her eyes filled.

Jerrol glanced around the room and spun her on the dance floor, giving her time to recover. "I'm sorry. I thought you'd want to know."

"Oh, I do. Captain Jerrol, thank you so much. I'm so relieved. I thought…" She faltered.

Jerrol tightened his grip. "Well, don't. He will be fine." He glanced up into the galleries and nodded at Birlerion as he caught the silent message. He spun Lady Miranda towards the table where Jennery hosted Alyssa and Lady Olivia.

"Thank you for the dance," he said, squeezing her fingers. He nodded at Jennery, and with a quick bow, he swiftly moved away and out of the room.

Lady Miranda stood, mouth agape, as she hovered by the table, and Jennery stepped manfully into the gap. "Lady Miranda, you ought to know that he doesn't know how to stand still. He's always leaving beautiful ladies deserted on the dance floor."

Relaxing, Lady Miranda laughed. "I'm sorry. Thank you. He just told me that Sentinal Tagerill is making a good recovery; isn't that a relief?"

"Oh? That is good news," Alyssa said, shyly watching her mother.

The awkward pause lengthened, and Lady Olivia said,

"Miranda, it has been too long since we last spoke. You look ravishing, my dear."

Lady Miranda smiled in return. "Olivia, may I say how sorry I was to hear about Stefan. I regret I was unable to visit you before."

"Thank you, my dear. Let's sit, shall we? We have much to catch up on." Lady Olivia indicated the table.

Jennery slid an arm around Alyssa's waist. "Dance?" he whispered and twirled her onto the floor as she nodded. His arms tightened as she relaxed into his embrace.

"Thank you," she murmured. "I was surprised. I don't know why; I knew she would be here, but I didn't know what to say."

"It's understandable. Yesterday was the first time you've seen her in how long? Ten years? But I wouldn't worry too much. We should insist she comes with us to Deepwater; give you time to get to know each other again," Jennery murmured into her hair.

"Good idea. Who is that dancing with Jerrol? I thought he left. Oh, he is deserting her as well."

"That, my dear, is Scholar Taelia, an old friend of ours. You forget he is on duty, not like me, who gets to enjoy the ball with my beloved," Jennery grinned.

Alyssa laughed up into his face. "Well, I am sorry for him; he's obviously a good dancer. It's not fair on us ladies."

Jennery made a face. "What? You mean I'm not good enough for you?" he asked as his gaze flickered around the ballroom, noting the number of guards out of uniform. He glanced up at the gallery. Birlerion was no longer in sight.

Alyssa stared up at him. "Is something wrong?"

"With you in my arms? Never," Jennery declared as he twirled her back towards the table. "I just need to check on something," he murmured, kissing her hand and settling her in the chair opposite Miranda and Olivia, who were deep in conversation.

Jennery made his way down the room towards Parsillion, who stood beside Prince Anders. "What's up?" he murmured as they observed Fonorion shadowing the king.

"It's started. There is an altercation down near the warehouses. The Captain went to check the perimeter. First contact is imminent."

"It looks like most of the guests turned up. I can't see anyone of note missing," Jennery said.

Parsillion nodded. "The king said the same. I think there was only one or two people who refused to say the oath. The king seemed pleased."

"I think he takes it as a sign of support." Jennery grinned as he began to move away, pausing as a distant rumble penetrated the room. Parsillion froze before moving to flank Fonorion, murmuring in his ear. Fonorion nodded before speaking to the king.

King Benedict nodded in turn and stepped up onto the dais. "Lords, ladies, and distinguished guests," he began. "If I may have your attention, please. As you know, the Watches are of great historical importance to Vespiri. We often forget their beginnings, created as the Lady extended her protection over our great country. What you may not have been aware of is that the Watches were created at a time of instability to segment our country into areas that needed to be defended." He paused. "Defended against those who sought to subsume us under their power, who sought to take away our free will, who sought to ..." The king's voice continued as Jennery reached the double doors at the head of the room.

He placed his hand on the door handle just as an enormous explosion rocked the palace. The sound of shattering glass further down the terrace was interspersed by the clatter of debris rattling against the windows as shocked exclamations rose over the king's voice. A ripple of fear spread through the room.

"Please, ladies and gentlemen, stay calm. We are safe here," the king promised, his face pale. He bent to talk to Fonorion, who responded firmly. The king nodded and continued his speech. "Many of you are aware of the recent return of the Sentinals. Let me introduce them to you ..."

Jennery slipped out of the ballroom, ducked into the antechamber to grab his sword belt, and rushed down the corridor. He skidded to a halt as Bryce erupted into the entrance hall fighting a man dressed all in black. One arm dangled limply, as he defended himself against an onslaught of overhead blows. Jennery unsheathed his sword and entered the fray, taking the pressure off Bryce, who gave way gratefully. The unexpected arrival of another opponent put the man off his stride, and Jennery dispatched him. A second explosion shook the palace and faint shrieks from the ballroom penetrated the entrance hall.

"Check Darllion is alright," Bryce gasped. "They're after the prince."

Jennery dashed out of the palace, across the parade ground, and down the stairs towards the cells. Bodies were strewn across the steps, a testament to the ferocious defence the guards had put up. A gaping hole in the wall still smoked; Jennery passed it, staring in disbelief. He rounded the curve and paused at the bottom of the stairs, trying to decipher the scene in front of him. Princess Selvia seemed to be trying to climb all over Jerrol.

22

PALACE GROUNDS

Jerrol left the ballroom light at heart and with a smile on his face. He had finally managed to dance with Taelia, stealing her away from a glowering Torsion under the benevolent gaze of the Scholar Deane. She had felt so right in his arms. Her face was aglow as she looked up at him. She must have forgiven him.

Smiling down at her, he had known a few moments of sheer bliss, which he squirrelled away. They didn't happen often. At the end of the dance, he reluctantly returned her to Torsion's arm and left.

He met Birlerion in the small ante-chamber beside the ballroom. "Stay and cover the king and Prince Anders. Don't let them out of your sight."

"I won't." Birlerion said, and went to go back up to the gallery. He paused with his foot on the step. "Who's got your back, Captain?" he asked.

"The king is more important. We've invited the wolves into his home; they won't be able to resist. I'm relying on you. Keep him secure."

Jerrol grimaced as Birlerion gave him a keen stare, before

slowly nodding. "Be careful. I don't want to be explaining anything to Tagerill."

Jerrol left before Birlerion could change his mind. He was halfway around the perimeter, murmuring encouragement to the men, when a bright flash lit up the sky, preceding a distant rumble, and then one of the warehouses erupted into flame. Astonished exclamations rose around him; what terrible magic had the descendants discovered?

His stomach dropped as he looked up at the palace. Lady help him; he had no defence against such destructive power. "Hold the perimeter," he yelled at the king's guards as he saw a movement in the line. There was a ripple in the darkness.

He faded into the shadows, working his way back towards the lower terraces. Guards were engaging along the perimeter. Clashing swords vibrated on the night air as he ghosted along the stone balustrades.

A small group detached themselves from the shadows and skirted the terrace. They paused outside the glass doors before moving on. Jerrol followed. Checking the doors, he found a plain sack tucked away in the murky shadows. The rich baritone of the king's voice came from inside the palace, his words a deep rumble. Sucking in his breath, Jerrol muttered a swift prayer before he grabbed the sack and flung it as far from the building as possible.

He was blinded by the intense flash that lit the sky as the sack exploded in mid-air. The blast blew him across the terrace, slamming him hard against the palace wall. Flying debris clattered against the window. Shattered glass from the windows above fell like glinting snowflakes all around him. Stunned, he lay for a moment, his ears ringing. Stirring, he levered himself up and held his thumping head. His hands came away, shaking and bloody.

Taking a deep breath, Jerrol staggered to his feet and checked around him. Thank the Lady the palace doors were still whole. Guards were engaged across the gardens, though it was like he watched from afar; he couldn't hear the clash of swords, even though the fighting was fierce. He stumbled around the terrace. Where had they gone?

Another loud explosion buffeted him and he lost his footing as the ground bucked beneath him. He pushed himself up off the gravel, sharp stones cutting his palms as clods of dirt dropped around him. The dungeon. They were after Prince Kharel.

Circling the edge of the palace, he staggered towards the grey stone building that housed the king's cells. They must have blasted through the back wall; it was the only place he could think of for them to enter from the outside.

The stone wall that edged the cells had a gaping hole in it. The stone smoked, and the stink of fire coals permeated the air. Had they found a way to burn rock? Jerrol jerked, his heart jumping as a hand grabbed his shoulder. He hadn't heard anyone coming up behind him. A frenzied guard shouted at him, but Jerrol couldn't make out what he was saying. The man's eyes were wild and bulging. Jerrol shook him, noting the gold armband. "Stay here," he shouted. "Don't let anyone out." He pointed at the smoking hole.

Jerrol unsheathed his sword and climbed through the hole, watching the stones above him warily; they didn't look too secure. He descended the stone steps, peering around the curve in the corridor. His ears were still ringing; he couldn't hear a thing. He halted at the bottom.

Darllion was pressed up against the rear wall, guarded by a man with a knife at his throat. He was bloodied, but still standing. The bodies of two of the guards were sprawled on the floor, along with a black-clothed figure. Where were the other guards?

Another man, dressed in black from head to foot, unlocked a cell door and pulled a protesting Prince Kharel out. Shoving the prince against the wall, the man opened the second cell and dragged Princess Selvia out. She was trying to claw the man's eyes out. This didn't make sense. Why wouldn't they want to go with them? Wasn't this a rescue?

An expression of horror flashed across the prince's face as the man flipped a knife in his hand suggestively, and Kharel pulled Selvia towards him. Jerrol launched himself across the room, barging the man off balance and into Kharel. Darllion twisted out of his captor's grip and, having disarmed him, planted the knife in the man's side and let him fall to the ground. Jerrol shoved the princess behind him, parrying the oncoming strike. The absent thought that he was glad he was temporarily deaf drifted across his mind.

The black-clothed man recovered and grabbed the prince around the neck as Darllion advanced on him. Jerrol thought he must be cursing from the look on his face. The man in black hissed something and Darllion snarled in response. Jerrol blocked another strike, trying to keep the princess behind him as she tried to climb over him to reach her husband.

Jennery appeared on the steps behind the man, his face a picture. Jerrol grinned. "Give up, you've got nowhere to go," he shouted, hoping he could be heard.

The man twisted towards him and laughed. He shouted in return before checking the stairs behind him. His expression of shock changed to determination as Jennery charged him. He shoved Kharel at Darllion and spun, bringing his sword up to block Jennery's strike.

Darllion fell, struggling to untangle himself from Kharel's heavy and unresponsive body. Jerrol struck the attacker from behind, who dropped to the floor, unconscious. The princess darted around Jerrol and pulled at her husband's body.

Jennery grinned. "Well, at least we don't have to drag him far!" he said, indicating the cells.

Darllion nodded and inspected his dishevelled captain. "Captain? Are you alright?"

Jerrol put his hand up to his ear. "I can't hear you."

"You're shouting Captain," Darllion said.

"There was a huge blast," Jerrol continued loudly. "I can't hear a thing. Darllion, are you hurt? Can you stay here and lock them all up?"

"Yes, Captain." Darllion exaggerated his nod.

Princess Selvia glared at them; her face etched with grief. "You killed him."

Jerrol frowned at her. "What?"

"She said you killed him," Zin'talia said.

"I think you'll find the Ascendants did that." Jerrol looked down at Kharel's body and then back at Selvia. "Why didn't you want to go with them?"

Selvia clamped her lips shut and narrowed her eyes.

Zin'talia murmured in his head. "*Stop shouting. The whole palace can hear you.*"

"*AM I SHOUTING?*" Jerrol asked.

"Yes, stop it. You're giving me a headache."

"Darllion, lock her up." Jerrol tried to moderate his voice. "We'll send you relief as soon as we can." Darllion gave him a grubby grin and a thumbs up, and Jerrol patted him on the shoulder. "Jennery, with me." Jerrol glanced at Jennery. "Watch my back. I'm having trouble with my ears since that blast. Can't tell if someone is coming up behind me."

Jennery nodded. "Where next?" he mouthed.

"Back to the king."

"I don't think we'll be allowed in," he joked.

"What?"

Jennery shook his head. "Doesn't matter."

Jerrol nodded and then wished he hadn't. He rubbed his

temple, but it didn't help. "Let's check the perimeter is holding, then the king." Jerrol led the way back up the stairs; he paused by the gap in the wall. "Tell the guard to hold station," he said, pointing out the hole. Jennery leaned out and instructed the closest guard, who garbled something about exploding dirt and shooting flames. Jennery glibly reassured him everything would be alright before following Jerrol up the stairs. Jerrol stooped over the bodies of his other guards, his face tightening before he moved on.

They met Landis in the gardens. "Sir, we're struggling to hold the northern perimeter; they just keep coming."

Jerrol frowned at him. "Say again," he said. "My hearing was affected by that explosion."

"North perimeter, need help," Landis repeated.

Jerrol nodded in acknowledgement. "Jennery, go see if Nikols can cut them off. They have to be coming from those warehouses. Landis, I'll send you the men from inside the palace. We have to stop them from getting too near. Watch for men carrying sacks; they cause those blasts. We have to prevent any more breaking through."

Landis scowled, his blues eyes bright in his grimy face. "Khasalts, sir, used for mining. But it's scarce, difficult to get hold of."

Jerrol tried to read his lips. "Khasalts? Well, someone found some and plenty of it. Whatever happens, we have to hold the line."

Landis nodded and returned to his men.

Jerrol skirted the terraces and entered the palace by the side entrance. He almost tripped over Bryce, who was lying across the floor. Pressing his fingertips against his neck, he breathed out a sigh of relief as Bryce stirred. Slipping an arm around his shoulders, he levered him up. "Up you get," he muttered. Bryce staggered to his feet, waving his sword in front of him. "Stand down," Jerrol said with a smile, steering him towards the main ballroom. He searched the corridors for the roving patrols.

"Ah, lieutenant, take your men and go help Captain Landis. He needs support at the north perimeter," Jerrol instructed as they passed a guard discreetly positioned in the hallway. The guard saluted and left at a run.

Jerrol almost dropped Bryce as the sound of terrified screams that even he could hear erupted in the ballroom. Jerrol's blood ran cold as he leant Bryce against a wall and dashed down the corridor. He burst into the room, taking in the scene. The guests had drawn back to the side of the room. Horrified faces were staring down at two councillors sprawled on the ground, arrows protruding from their bodies.

Parsillion had disarmed them and now stood over them. King Benedict and Prince Anders stood safely behind Fonorion. Glancing up at the gallery, Jerrol caught Birlerion's eye and he gave him a brief salute. Birlerion nodded his head in acknowledgement before returning to his vigilant watch.

Jerrol knelt by the side of the red-headed man who lay gasping on the floor. An arrow jutted from his chest. Silver feathers formed the fletching and gleamed in the lamplight as if made of precious metal. Birlerion's arrows, unsurprisingly. The memory of him diligently repairing these arrows distracted Jerrol for a moment. The dedicated concentration was another facet of the man he had once thought a cold and silent killer.

Parsillion hovered over the injured man, a sword at his throat. Jerrol smiled grimly. "*Zin'talia, pay attention. Can you listen to what's being said around me? Can you relay it to me? I can't hear a thing.*"

Zin'talia snickered in his head. "*About time. The king is asking people to calm down. Parsillion is asking you what you want to do with the two men.*"

"Depends. Who sent you?" Jerrol asked, inspecting the red headed councillor. Jerrol watched the man's mouth, but he pressed his lips together and just glared up at them both. Jerrol almost laughed out loud. This was not the place for interrogation, and he was running out of men.

"Parsillion, drag them out to the cells. They can join their friend. We'll talk to them later, if they're still alive."

The councillor jerked, pain lining his face. "You can't treat us like that. We have rights." Zin'talia relayed his words to Jerrol. *"King Benedict just said he was a traitor, and traitors don't have rights,"* she reported.

Jerrol nodded at Parsillion. "You heard the king. Take them to the cells. They are spoiling the party."

Parsillion bent down and grabbed them by their collars, and, ignoring their protests, he dragged them out of the room. The guests watched round-eyed and open-mouthed. A maid darted in and mopped the floor clean of blood before retreating, eyes wide.

"Sire, apologies for the interruption. Please, ladies and gentlemen, continue with your entertainment." Jerrol grinned at the king's raised eyebrows. Prince Anders gaped at him in horror as he backed out of the room. Bryce had followed Jerrol into the doorway, but upon observing Bryce's dishevelled state, Jerrol escorted him back out. "I don't think you're dressed appropriately for a party," he said as he shut the door behind him.

"Look who's talking. You look worse than me."

Glancing down at his dusty clothes, Jerrol brushed a hand through his hair and came away with shards of glass and clods of dirt. "Oops," he said. He steered Bryce into the empty antechamber and, easing him to the floor, helped him out of his jacket. Ripping Bryce's shirt sleeve off, he used it to bind the deep cut down his arm.

Bryce glowered at him. "Definitely can't go to the ball

now," he said as he leaned his head back and closed his eyes. Zin'talia faithfully relayed his words. Jerrol patted him over, checking the dampness on his tunic. He ripped it open. Wincing at the sight of more blood, he grabbed some napkins stacked on a trolley by the wall and pressed them against the wound in Bryce's side. "Hold that," he said, pressing Bryce's hand over the napkins before darting up the stairs. "Birlerion, Bryce is downstairs injured; get someone to look at him, will you? I've sent the roving patrols out to the perimeter, and Jennery has gone for reinforcements. You have the king and his guests."

Birlerion nodded. "Yes, sir. Captain, are you alright?" he asked, frowning at the dust-covered apparition before him.

"Fine. I'll be better when my hearing returns." Jerrol waved as he dashed back down the stairs. He patted Bryce on the shoulder. "Help is coming," he said, and then he was gone.

Bryce opened his eyes to an empty room and shut them again, wincing as he eased into a more comfortable position. He opened them again in surprise a few minutes later as a soft gasp preceded the sound of swishing skirts and gentle hands cupping his face. "I was sure it was you," Lady Olivia said. "What have you done to yourself?"

Bryce gripped her hand. "You shouldn't be here. You're safer with the king."

"Nonsense, you need help now," she said as she lifted the napkins and refolded them before pressing down hard against his side.

"Olivia," beseeched Bryce.

Olivia smiled down at him and kissed him on his cold lips. "If you think I am losing you as well, then you are mistaken."

"Then we'd better make sure we fix him up," a breathless voice said behind them. Olivia looked up to see a short man in healer garb enter the room. He dumped his bag next to them and then gently moved Olivia out of the way. "I haven't much time. Let's patch him up for now until we can look at him properly. I'm sure you can make sure he stays here and rests, can't you?" The healer peered at her over his glasses. His bushy eyebrows rose as Olivia blushed.

Bryce gritted his teeth as the healer probed. "Make sure you catch up with Captain Haven," he said between his teeth. "He got caught in that blast; he can't hear a thing."

"That would explain much. I thought he looked a bit off-kilter when he was in the ballroom," Olivia said.

Bryce grinned in sympathy. "How's the king coping?" he asked, more to take his mind off what the healer was doing than from wanting to know. He hissed as a sharp needle jabbed him.

"I think he's frustrated at being cooped up in his ballroom. The Sentinals were having to talk to him quite firmly about staying put. But then he had to set an example for his guests. We were all surprised when we found out there was another Sentinal up in the gallery. Captain Haven wasn't taking any chances, was he? Good thing, too," she finished thoughtfully. "Who would have thought those men would try and kill the king? It just doesn't bear thinking of."

"Right, drink this." The healer handed Bryce a vial before standing up. "Keep him still; this is only a temporary fix. That draught should dull the pain, and he'll probably sleep. I'll get him carried into the infirmary as soon as I know this situation is under control. My aides are scattered right now." He nodded at Olivia, grabbed his bag, and flitted out the door.

Olivia looked down at the man now lying on the floor. His face was pale, his eyes closed. Gathering up his discarded jacket, she draped it across him. Carefully, she lifted his head and rested it in her lap. She stroked his face, soothing the lines of pain away. She was prepared to wait until the healer returned.

Taelia was confused. She had felt so safe and content in Jerrol's arms, and now he had gone off into danger *again* to protect the king and all of them; who protected Jerrol?

She had been in two minds about attending the ball, but Torsion had persuaded her. He said she couldn't miss out on life just because Jerrol was busy elsewhere. She still hadn't forgiven Torsion for the way he had treated Birlerion, but he had been right, as usual. If she hadn't come, she wouldn't have had those few blissful twirls around the dance floor.

She had smiled as Torsion had taken his place, but it hadn't been the same. She had chatted and danced all evening, waiting for Jerrol to return. He hadn't. Torsion had been attentive and entertaining, but he wasn't Jerrol.

Torsion was always there, ready to guide her steps, hold her hand, talk to her about anything, but he never thought she could manage on her own. He seemed to think she needed him to help her with everything, whereas Jerrol believed she could do anything, and he let her get on with it, dropping into her life whenever he was passing. Which wasn't often enough, she admitted to herself.

Then there had been that brief flurry of activity in the ballroom. She had heard the thrum as the arrows split the air, the thud as the bodies hit the ground, the cries of alarmed guests.

Torsion had wrapped his arms around her, shouting that she was safe with him. Of course, she was safe. She had tried to push him away, but he was much stronger than her. He had released her as Jerrol burst into the room and cleaned up the mess and left again. Jerrol hadn't spoken to her, hadn't checked that she was alright. He had just assumed she could cope.

Taelia wasn't sure whether to be pleased or annoyed.

Jerrol spent the night cleaning up. He breathed a sigh of relief as all the guests safely left. All signs of fighting were discreetly hidden; it could have been a typical evening. Landis and his men had excelled themselves and paid the price for it; half his men lay in the extended infirmary. Jerrol thought it was a miracle they hadn't lost any of them, yet.

Darllion had brushed off his injuries as scratches but agreed to head off to bed so he could relieve Parsillion in the morning. Birlerion was also supposed to be off duty but he was guarding the king, giving Fonorion a well-earned respite. Bryce was in the infirmary in the capable hands of Lady Olivia, and it didn't look like she was letting go of him any time soon.

The king had finally retired in the early hours of the morning after instructing Jerrol to provide a full report later. Jennery had confirmed that Nikols had the fires out at the warehouses. Two were destroyed. The roof of the third warehouse had collapsed.

Nikols had sent up two units of men; one to help herd the captives down to the cells in the Justice building, freeing the Palace of the duty of caring for them, and the other to relieve Landis and his men. The staff were busy cleaning up both the damage and the aftermath of the party.

Jerrol was asleep, sprawled across the desk in the commander's office. He didn't remember falling asleep, but the fact that he was disturbed by someone collapsing into the chair opposite him confirmed that he had been sleeping. He opened bleary eyes and stared across at the equally exhausted man seated in the chair opposite. The man spoke.

The buzzing in his ears had eased, and he could tell that the man was talking, but the sounds were all merged like he was underwater.

The man stood and came around to Jerrol and placed his hands either side of his head. He stared deep into his eyes and then his ears. Jerrol's memory clicked into place; Healer Francis had made his way around to him.

"The buzzing's stopped," he said. Francis winced, and Jerrol's lips twitched. "Sorry," he said, lowering his voice. "Can't hear you or me."

Francis nodded and wrote on a piece of paper. "Headache?"

Jerrol gingerly nodded.

Francis wrote: "Blurred vision?"

"Not so much now, was earlier," Jerrol admitted.

Francis wrote: "Had much sleep?"

"You woke me up." Jerrol had no difficulty translating the healer's expression.

Shaking his head, Francis reached into his bag and pulled out a glass bottle. He wrote on the paper, "Go to bed, take draught. ALL OF IT. Sleep. I'll see you when you wake." The healer glared at him, and Jerrol gave in as gracefully as he could and went to find a bed.

23

CHAPTERHOUSE, OLD VESPERS

The next morning, the Deane called Taelia to her office. She stared at her in silence for so long that Taelia shifted uncomfortably in her chair. "Taelia," she finally said. "What is going on?"

"With what, Deane?" Taelia asked in confusion.

"I am not blind," Liliian said with a twitch of her lips, "But you certainly are. And I am not talking about what you can or cannot see with your eyes. If a man looked at me the way he looks at you I would be joined with three children by now, and don't tell me you don't know how he looks at you, because you look back at him in exactly the same way. Don't let him ride off again without clearing the air with him."

Taelia turned her face away. Heat rose across her cheeks as her eyes blurred with tears. "I didn't realise it was so obvious. I didn't mean it. We had a misunderstanding, he caught me at the wrong moment and he just took it to heart."

"He has a lot on his mind. Think of what they have all achieved; with the reinstatement of Greenswatch, reclaiming Deepwater, protecting the king and all of us last night. The man must be exhausted with all the responsibilities on his shoulders. He relies on you. You must know that he shows you so much more of what is happening to him than he does to anyone else. Don't make him bottle it all up."

"He doesn't show me anything. I don't know what the king expects of him," Taelia objected.

"You know more than you think if you spend the time to understand it. You have a part to play in this, if I am not mistaken. Your talents are unique, and Jerrol needs you to help him with his search. He can't do it by himself. Oh, I have assigned Mary," Liliian said as if she expected Taelia to protest, "but she doesn't have your instinct or experience in the catacombs. He needs your support, make it right, Taelia, or you'll regret it forever."

Taelia raised her head in surprise, hearing the sadness in Liliian's voice. "Will you let me help him with his project, if he agrees?"

Liliian leaned forward on her desk. "You should have been leading it from the start. If you are to find what he's searching for, it will take both of you. He was supposed to be down in the small catacomb with Mary this morning, but after last night, he may not be. I suggest you go find him and speak to him."

The walls of the passageway to the new catacombs, which Jerrol had so spectacularly found, were rough under her fingers as she carefully negotiated the steep steps. As she descended, she heard Jennery's voice, a deep rumble coming out of the ground. What was Jennery doing in the catacombs? He didn't even spend time reading books! He was laughing with a young woman. She stilled as she recognised the voice; it was that young woman again.

"Love, we have to go. There's no point delaying here now."

"I know," Jennery agreed. "I just wanted to find out what Jerrol was up to next."

"We'll have more chance of that at the palace," Alyssa replied. Taelia heard them kiss and closed her eyes. How could she have been so blind? Jennery and Alyssa. It was Alyssa she had heard speaking to Jerrol at the Chapterhouse.

She took a deep breath and entered the chamber. "Jerrol, is that you?" she asked with a bright smile.

"Hi Taelia," Jennery responded as he and Alyssa drew apart.

"Oh, hi, Jennery. I need to speak to Jerrol. Do you know where I can find him?"

"I'm sorry, we thought he'd be here. That's why we came."

"I need to speak to him before the king sends him off again. He can't leave thinking I'm angry at him."

"Where's he going?" Jennery asked. "I thought he would come with us to Deepwater for the confirmation."

"Uh, I don't know. I just had a feeling he was leaving." Taelia blushed as she felt Jennery's gaze on her.

"We haven't seen him this morning. If we see him before we leave for Deepwater, we can pass a message."

Taelia floundered. She couldn't say all she wanted to say in a message. "Just tell him I'm sorry. He caught me at a bad moment," she said, blushing a rosy red. Alyssa squeezed her shoulder sympathetically.

"What about his research? Who is continuing that while he's gone?"

"Mary was going to keep it going for us," Jennery admitted.

"The Deane said I could help if Jerrol agreed. Please let me help."

"That would be great; we need all the help we can get. We leave for Deepwater today, and anyway, I am no asset when it comes to research." Taelia heard the relief in his voice.

"Congratulations to both of you. I hope you will be happy in Deepwater," she said and hurried back up the stairs in search of Mary.

Palace Barracks

Jerrol awoke when the sun was high. Whatever Healer Francis had given him had knocked him out. He had fallen into an empty bed in the barracks in all his dirt and slept soundly. Lying still for a moment, Jerrol catalogued his body's woes. He felt refreshed; his head was clear of that awful clogging headache.

Sitting up, he winced as his shoulder twinged. It was sore; must have been when he hit the wall. If that was all he had to show for last night, then he had got off lightly. He suddenly remembered Bryce and Landis' men in the Infirmary, and he was up and off to the baths without a second thought.

As he strode down the corridor, he attracted glances. Jerrol glanced down at his clothes; he wasn't glowing or something, was he? No, the material had shimmered into his usual uniform. He noticed he seemed to have gained an extra button on his shoulder, but apart from that, there was nothing different.

He entered the Infirmary and hesitated. Additional beds had been brought in and lined the walls, each occupied by a soldier in various degrees of distress. He had never seen it so full.

Making his way down the line, he offered words of encouragement or congratulations to those awake as he went, leaving grins on tired faces. Reaching the end, he peered into one of the small rooms. Bryce was asleep, as was Lady Olivia still in her evening gown in the chair next to him, their hands linked.

Jerrol backed out and went in search of Healer Francis. He found him asleep across his desk, much as Jerrol had been earlier. He was about to leave when the healer woke, straightening up his glasses as he peered up at Jerrol.

Jerrol grinned. "Healer it's time to take your own medicine, I think!"

The healer grimaced in return. "It certainly seems to have worked for you."

"I feel much better, and I can hear again. What a relief."

The healer nodded. "Sleep is a great healer; gives the body time to recover from unexpected shocks."

"How is Bryce?"

The healer rotated his stiff shoulders. "He'll be fine; he has someone to make sure he follows orders." He glanced up at Jerrol. "He'll be back on light duties in a few weeks."

"And the men? Anyone we should be concerned about?"

Healer Francis rose and led the way to one of the smaller rooms. He stopped at the foot of the bed of a young lad, his face expressionless. "Private Deron. He's 18. Had to amputate his leg."

Jerrol stopped in shock. His stomach roiled queasily. It was the type of injury a soldier feared most. "Does he know?" he asked, gazing down at the young and vulnerable face. A mess of black hair framed his strained features, tinged with exhaustion and pain; his chest peeked out from under swathes of bandages, and rose and fell in slow breaths.

"Not yet."

"Keep me informed," he said. "May the Lady bless you," he murmured, pausing as the boy smiled in his sleep.

Healer Francis glanced at him. "Certainly, sir," he said, leading the way out. "Otherwise, this ragtag lot will be back in training in a couple of weeks."

"Good, thank you." He gripped the healer's shoulder. "Lady bless you, Francis. Now go and get some sleep."

"Yes, sir," the healer said, turning to his assistant, his exhaustion apparent in the droop of his shoulders. "Let me know if anything changes," he said as he left the infirmary.

The assistant stood. "Thank you, sir. We couldn't get him to go to bed."

"Any chance you could put a lad outside his door to make sure no one disturbs him? Let him sleep himself out, and if he complains, tell him you were just following Captain Haven's orders."

The assistant grinned. "Yes, sir," he said and set about finding someone to guard his master's sleep.

Jerrol left the Infirmary and made his way through the corridors and galleries to the king's private chambers. When he entered the antechamber to the king's rooms, he found it occupied by an elderly man studying the pictures on the wall. The brilliant white tattoo of a four pointed star on his right cheek stood out against his deep brown skin. Wisps of steel grey hair escaped his neat turban.

Before he had a chance to introduce himself, the door opened, and Darris gestured towards the door. "Captain Haven, if you would. The king has been waiting for you to arrive," he warned. Jerrol nodded and stepped through the doorway. King Benedict was seated in a high-backed chair, staring pensively out of the window, but he turned as Jerrol entered.

Jerrol dropped to his knee. "Sire."

"Rise. You never cease to amaze me; you know that, don't you?" King Benedict said.

Jerrol rose and looked quizzically at the king.

"Yesterday, you saved Vespiri again. You co-ordinated the defence of my palace against unprecedented attacks, with short notice and half the forces you should have had. You arrived in my ballroom, just as your men took down two assassins, looking, I must say, rather wild. You cleaned it up as if you do it every day and then proceeded to ensure the palace was back to normal the next morning."

"Sire, I think you'll find that was done by your staff."

"I have never hosted such an event while a mass battle was going on around us and not one of our guests were affected."

"Unfortunately, quite a few of your men were, sire," Jerrol said. "We are currently being bolstered by two of Commander Nikols' ranger units. It will be a couple of weeks before our men are even back in training; a month before they are back to full strength, and Landis was supposed to go and support Deepwater."

"I have spoken to Jennery. We agreed we would send the half unit with Landis now, give them a breather, and send the rest on when they are fit."

"Are you sure Deepwater will be a rest, sire?"

"Maybe not, if getting his daughter back doesn't placate the Grand Duke. I've arranged for Selvia to be escorted back to Elothia. If he decides to take offence, then Deepwater and Stoneford, our two northern Watches, will take the brunt, and we must prepare for that. I'd like to say, commander—" he pierced Jerrol with a stare as Jerrol opened his mouth in protest; he shut it, "—that you should first rebuild my forces here in Vespiri and then commander you will be. Commander of the King's Justice. There is no man more worthy of the title, but first I have another job for you." The king sighed and nodded to Darris, who opened the door.

Darris opened the door wider and stepped back, allowing the Terolian to enter. The man hesitated, his alert gaze observed the room and its occupants as he paused on the threshold and bowed. The king indicated the two chairs to his side. "Please, ambassador, commander, be seated."

The king's eyes paused thoughtfully on the Arifel, which

popped into the room and hovered over Jerrol's shoulder as he sat.

The Terolian bowed again and sat as requested. Ari settled on Jerrol's shoulder and tipped his head, waiting expectantly as he tucked his wings in.

The king's lips twitched, but he addressed the stranger. "Ambassador Nil'ano. I believe you have yet to meet Commander Haven?"

"Indeed, Your Majesty. I have not had the pleasure."

"Commander Haven, this is Ambassador Nil'ano from Terolia. He is here on behalf of the Families to request our assistance."

"Assistance, sire?"

"Yes, it seems that there is dissension in the ranks. Some members of the Families are acting strangely. I am concerned it is a result of further Ascendant incursions; you did say they were active in Terolia. You are to contact the Solari or the Atolea family, whichever is closer; the Mederas are expecting you. Deal with it as you see fit; you act in the king's name," Benedict said, invoking the Oath and holding Jerrol's eyes.

The Oath stirred within him, and Jerrol shivered. "As you command, sire."

Ari meeped in his ear.

Nil'ano's eyes widened. "Your Majesty? Who is this man that you provide him with a free hand?"

The king's smile was fleeting. "Don't worry. Commander Haven will be careful."

"Of course, sire," Jerrol paused. "Who sent the request for help?"

"Nil'ano brought word from Medera Maraine of the Atolea. You need to meet with her in Mistra or Medera Reina of the Solari. The Solari family should be camped south of Ramila until after the Lady's moon. I need you to discover what the Ascendants are planning and stop it." The king gestured at Nil'ano. "Ambassador Nil'ano has provided letters of introduction to the Mederas. You have a month and no longer. Make sure you are back by then." The king stood, signalling that the meeting was at an end. Jerrol and Nil'ano scrambled to their feet.

"Good luck, gentlemen," he said as Darris opened the door for them. "Ah, Jerrol, a moment," the king said as Nil'ano left the room. He reached out a finger to stroke Ari's chest. "I assume you are going too?" he asked the Arifel, who enthusiastically rubbed up against his hand.

"One last thing. I sent reinforcements to Jason for him to use as he saw fit. He was going to send a contingent of rangers on to the Watch Towers. Scholar Deane Liliian offered the services of Scholar Torsion to take over the management of the Watchers. Once you return from Terolia and have reported, you must go back up to the towers and do whatever it is you need to do to the Veil. You need to spend some time at the towers with Torsion and find out what we have forgotten up there."

Jerrol nodded with relief. He had already delayed too long; he ought to have sealed Saerille's work before now. "Yes, sire. There is much there that will keep the scholars occupied. Though are you sure we should send Torsion?"

"Liliian suggested him. He knows the towers best."

"I suppose. Torsion will be in his element."

"Indeed. A month, no later, Jerrol. We don't have a lot of time. I need you back to get my forces organised. In the meantime, I will be concentrating on the Watches."

Jerrol bowed in agreement and Ari, squawking a protest, flew up in the air and popped out of sight. "May I suggest Captain Bryce as interim commander? It will be a couple of weeks before he returns to duty, but Darllion could stand in for him until then. I'm sure if you spoke to them, both Bryce and Lady Olivia would be quite happy to relocate here from Stoneford, and I could use him as my second," Jerrol said, as the king's face lightened at a solution that met his approval.

"Excellent choice. I'll let you inform Bryce before you leave; give him something to look forward to," the king said, and Jerrol left the room.

Collecting Nil'ano in the antechamber, Jerrol extended his hand. "Ambassador, please call me Jerrol."

Nil'ano gripped his hand and nodded in return. "I understand we are to leave immediately. Our horses have been readied for us in the inner courtyard."

"Very well. I will meet you there in half a chime," Jerrol said as he descended the stairs.

Zin'talia's contentment filled his mind. *"At last! Jerrol, it's about time we went to Terolia. It will be so much warmer. You might relax for a change."*

"*It's not that cold here,*" Jerrol thought, glancing out of the window at the brilliant sunshine. "*Thank goodness we're past the heat of mid-year. The temperature should be manageable.*"

"You forget, it is the start of the hot season in Terolia."

Jerrol scrunched up his face. He had forgotten. All of a sudden, his enthusiasm for the trip waned.

"You can stock up on Baliweed." Zin'talia's voice became dreamy, and Jerrol smiled.

"As if you don't get enough already."

"You can never have too much Baliweed. You should try it."

Shaking his head, Jerrol made a detour via the infirmary. He was glad to see that Francis was still absent, his assistant ably covering for him. He dropped into the chair next to Bryce's bed, which had been vacated by Lady Olivia. Inspecting the extent of the bandages, Jerrol grimaced in sympathy. "How do you feel?" he asked.

"Sore," Bryce replied, "but I'll be back on my feet in a week or so. Healer Francis said I'll be fine."

"Good. Because I need your help. How do you feel about relocating here as my second? Second to the Commander of the King's Justice?" Jerrol asked.

Bryce stared at him. "Commander of the King's Justice? Jerrol, congratulations!"

"Yeah, well you haven't heard all of it yet. Are you interested? You are my first choice. The king approved."

"Interested?" Bryce blew his cheeks out. "Of course, I'm interested."

"Do you need to talk it over with Olivia? I know you were intending on moving her to Stoneford."

"She'll go wherever I go, and she knows a soldier's life moves about. We've already discussed it."

"You are only on light duties, and you only return when Healer Francis says so, understand?"

"Yes, sir." Bryce saluted, rolling his eyes.

Jerrol chuckled. "We have to build up from the ground. The men will be demoralised, confused. Landis and his unit will go to Deepwater to shore up their defences." Jerrol rubbed his face. "Which leaves us with a lot of work, and I'm not going to be here for at least a month as the king wants me to go to Terolia. So, you get to be the interim commander. Work with Darllion; he will stand in for me for now. It will give you something to think about while you're lazing about in here." Jerrol grinned. "Just don't get to liking it too much."

"Jerrol, thank you. I mean it," Bryce said, holding out his left hand, his face animated. It seemed to be the right tonic as he looked much brighter.

"Keep an eye on Deron, the private next door. I want him on my staff when I return."

Bryce nodded. "Yes, sir."

. . .

Birlerion arrived in the courtyard as Jerrol tightened Zin'talia's girth straps more comfortably. His saddlebags and travelling gear were strapped in place; the king's men were efficient.

Jerrol glanced at Birlerion's similarly attired horse. "Who said you were coming too?"

"You cannot go alone, and Tagerill is confined to Deepwater."

"You haven't slept; you've just pulled double duty. You should be in bed. I have Ambassador Nil'ano to accompany me."

Casting his Captain a withering glance, Birlerion refrained from answering.

The Ambassador joined them. "Commander Haven, that is *not* your horse," he gasped. "She's a Darian."

"She should be right at home in Terolia, then, shouldn't she?"

"But how did you get a Darian? They are rare in Vespiri."

"Well, it's a long story. I'll tell you on the way. She found me." Jerrol gripped the reins as he mounted and settled in the saddle. He looked down into Birlerion's stubborn face and knew that even if he said no, Birlerion would still follow him. "This is Sentinal Birlerion. He will accompany us."

Nil'ano ducked his head. "Sentinal. It's a pleasure to meet you."

"Elder." Birlerion's face relaxed as he nodded at the Terolian, and he mounted his horse.

Jerrol led the way out of the courtyard and down the switchback, and after a thoughtful glance back at the golden buildings of the Remargaren Chapterhouse, turned his back and set a steady pace down the road towards the port where they would pick up the East Road to the Watches. "So, Ambassador," Jerrol said, "tell me about Terolia."

Chapterhouse, Old Vespers

Mary and Taelia sat on the floor of the stale and musty catacomb that Jerrol had found. Little fresh air found its way down to the depths; another question Taelia filed away for the Sentinals. They must have had some system for clearing the air in the lower levels.

Taelia ran her fingertips over a section of the wall, frowning at the indentations. She and Mary had settled into a comfortable working pattern, both enjoying the other's keen wit and intelligence. They had found that they worked very well together.

"Mary," Taelia said, her voice trembling. "I am positive this says 'The Oath Keeper.'"

Mary sat up in surprise, noting the location of Taelia's hands. "What does it say?"

Taelia began reeling off a litany of verses, translating the whole section of the wall. When Taelia finished, Mary whooped. "That's our key. We can use that to translate the rest. You are brilliant."

"W-What did I say?" Taelia stammered.

"Don't you remember?" Mary asked.

Taelia mutely shook her head. Mary read it back, and they both sat there in silence as they digested the words.

"The Oath Keeper;
A last resort, a Liege may think
Yet consider well, before you speak
Once spoke, invoked, accepted
No recourse to break the link.
Keeper empowered, your Oath
to hold
Access denied no longer
Submit your will and open your heart

Entwined, you will be stronger.
Lady's blessings, her smile aplenty
A trembling Land acknowledges
The Oath twixt Lady, Land, and Liege
A Keeper's pledge bequeathed."

"Do you think the king invoked the Oath?" Mary asked after a short silence.

"Yes," Taelia said, "and Jerrol is his Keeper. No wonder he is so desperate to find out all he can. I knew something had changed. He felt different, but I couldn't put my finger on it. He has this to carry as well," she murmured to herself. "This we tell the Deane and no one else."

"Absolutely," Mary agreed.

They rose and brushed the dust of their robes before Mary led Taelia out of the small catacomb and back up the steep stairs.

24

MISTRA, TEROLIA

Var'geris relaxed into the cushions and watched the squat dark-haired man sitting stiff and uncomfortable opposite him. The man was red-faced and perspiring heavily. He was suffering in the heat of the Terolian desert.

The man ran his fingers around his collar and mopped his face with his handkerchief. "Why don't you have any fans in here? It is insufferably hot," he complained in a thin, reedy voice.

Var'geris raised his eyebrows. "You seem to have forgotten your heritage, Iss'aren. The comforts of the chancellorship have softened you. Maybe you need to stay here for a while and reacclimatise."

"Don't think you are in a position to tell me what to do. I did everything as planned; it was not my fault. You were supposed to have dealt with Haven. I told you he was a threat." Iss'aren squirmed on the cushions, trying to get comfortable.

Var'geris flicked his fingers in disdain. "You were responsible for Vespiri. After all, you had Kharel and power over the king. One ranger shouldn't have upset all your plans. He couldn't be in all places at once. You should have moved quicker."

"Don't underestimate him. He has the king's ear."

"We have Fenton and the King's Justice. He will deal with Haven. And just to be sure, I put the Kirshans onto him. They will have the final say."

Iss'aren paled. "What? Why did you do that? They will leave a trail of bodies that will lead back to us, you fool. I thought the watchword was discretion. Months I spent laying the foundations, leaving the evidence of the Elothian involvement and their machinations. Vespiri's eyes should be firmly fixed on the pontifications of the Duke, whilst we finish off Terolia. But the Kirshans *shout* Terolia. We don't want them paying attention to us here."

"We've wasted too much time. The mines gave us nothing. We need the Lady's Captain; he is the one who will show us the way. I know he's out there; he is waking the Sentinals. He is the cause of all our troubles. We need to stop him before he finds any others."

"And how are we supposed to find out who this mythical saviour is?"

"You'll see. The attack on King Benedict's palace should draw him out. He won't be able to ignore a direct attack on the king."

Iss'aren swallowed. "Are you mad? We weren't supposed to use any of the powder yet. We don't have enough of it."

Var'geris shrugged. "The reports should start coming through shortly. It's done. I have the Families in my hand." He opened his hand out flat. "In two weeks, they will fall. Ensnared and vanquished without a drop of blood being spilt; that should please the fathers." He clenched his fist, his coal-black eyes glittering on his pale face.

25

STONEFORD KEEP, STONEFORD WATCH

Jerrol led Birlerion and Nil'ano under the portcullis and pulled Zin'talia to a halt in the flagged courtyard of Stoneford Keep. He dismounted and rubbed her cheek. She nickered softly and butted him with her head.

"You're tired. Let the stable lads do their work. You should rest, as should Birlerion. He's hardly slept."

"You tell him. He won't listen to me," Jerrol replied wearily.

"I can't fault his diligence. After all, he is keeping you safe, but he looks like he might fall out of the saddle."

They had been travelling for five days, stopping at roadside inns instead of using the waystone, which he would have done if the ambassador had not been with them. He knew Birlerion had barely slept; Jerrol had caught him patrolling during the night, vigilant whilst he and Nil'ano slept. No matter what Jerrol said, Birlerion was determined.

They had made reasonable time as Jerrol pushed them on late into the evening. He looked at his road-begrimed companions. "We'll stop here tonight; Jason will give us a bed. We need to stock up before we go into Terolia. This is the start of the hot season."

Nil'ano grunted in agreement, swinging his leg over as he slid off his horse and stretching thankfully. "I'd like to have a proper bath," he muttered.

Stable lads came running as Jason appeared in the open doorway. "Jerrol, come in. We've been expecting you."

Jerrol strode across the courtyard. "Jason, I'm glad to see you." He embraced the Lord Warden. "May I introduce Ambassador Nil'ano of Terolia. He travels with us to Ramila, and you know Sentinal Birlerion."

"Welcome to Stoneford Watch, Ambassador Nil'ano. Birlerion, it's good to see you again." Jason led the way into the keep. "Let me show you your room, Elder. I am sure a chance to freshen up will be welcome."

"Where's Chryllion?" Jerrol asked.

"He's around somewhere. That man never seems to sleep. Making up for lost time, I suppose." Jason chuckled. "Freshen up, and then we'll eat."

Jerrol glared at Birlerion. Maybe it was a Sentinal thing. "Birlerion, you are off duty. Go and rest. No arguments! Jason's men will keep me safe."

A little later, Jerrol leaned back in his chair, replete. Nil'ano looked like he was about to doze off. "Nil'ano." Jerrol nudged him. "Don't go to sleep at the table."

"I'll show you to your room, Elder," Birlerion offered, rising. He, too, looked like he would fall asleep where he sat.

Nil'ano grunted and stirred. "That would be much appreciated. I am getting too old for these jaunts." He struggled to his feet.

Jason watched them leave. "Come to my study. You can tell me about Deepwater and the king."

The evening passed while Jerrol filled Jason in on the latest happenings at the palace. He leaned back in his chair and said with a tired grin, "I've seconded Bryce as my deputy. I need someone I trust at the palace while I am in Terolia."

"I had a feeling Bryce wouldn't come back," Jason said, frowning out the window. He stared unseeing at the dimly lit courtyard. "You think the substance they used to control the king was found in Terolia?"

Jerrol nodded. "Along with the crystals that the Ascendants are using to communicate. You know, Jason, it surprises me that there is no mention of any of this anywhere."

"Three thousand years is a long time. Many things are forgotten—some deliberately," Jason said. "I'll see if we can find anything in our archives, though, to be honest, the king's archives go back much further."

"He's searching, as is Taelia in the Chapterhouse. We're all searching. Everyone is searching for something," Jerrol said, following Jason's gaze. What were the Ascendants after? He gave a deep sigh as he stood. "I need to speak with the Sentinals before I turn in. I won't be long."

Jerrol wasn't surprised when Birlerion returned to his shoulder as he set off up the road. He was persistent in his duty and stubborn. And if Jerrol was honest, he was glad of it. The night was dark; the clouds thick. The damp air was heavy with promised rain.

The small copse of sentinal trees loomed up in front of him, a darker shadow against the night sky. He veered off the road and followed the track to the grove. The stillness of the evening embraced him as he approached, a palpable sense of welcome in the air. He unerringly stopped in front of Tagerill's tree and laid his hand against the bark.

"*Your Sentinal needs you,*" he thought to the tree. "*We can't bring him here. I wondered whether you could go to him? He is with Denirion in Deepwater."*

Jerrol felt a ripple of assent, and a soft touch embraced him. A fresh zing of green energy flowed through him, and he patted the trunk in thanks. He wasn't sure what the sentinal could do, but as his foster mother used to say, "you don't get if you don't ask."

He pushed himself upright as Chryllion stepped forward.

"Captain, you surely didn't think you could visit without us knowing?" His deep voice rumbled in his chest.

"Chryllion," he gripped his arm in welcome. "How goes it?"

"It is well. We have cleaned out the barracks and are almost back to full strength. We have closed the pass. They won't be getting any more contraband through that route."

"Good work. Keep an eye on the Elothian border; the Duke is getting testy. I'm just passing through on the way to Terolia, but Tagerill needs some help. I left him at Deepwater, and he wasn't in good shape."

Chryllion nodded. "We heard. Jennery has been keeping us informed." He drew his breath in as he caught sight of Birlerion. "Where did you come from? I didn't hear you arrive."

Birlerion embraced the older Sentinal. "Just keeping an eye on the Captain," he began and stopped as the ground began to tremble. Staggering, he gaped in amazement as Tagerill's tall sentinal began to shimmer. The green fronds of the canopy began to shake violently as the ground vibrated around the roots, shaking the dirt loose, and the tall tree faded out of sight, leaving a slight dip in the ground where it had been standing.

Jerrol began to laugh. "Oh my, I can't wait to hear what the new Lord of Deepwater will have to say about this." He laughed harder as he imagined Jennery's shock as a new sentinal appeared overnight.

Sobering up, Jerrol wiped his eyes. "Is there any word from Saerille or Serillion? I'm hoping I'll be able to call in at the Watch Towers on my way back and seal the repairs properly."

"Serillion reported that he had contacted Saerille. She was somewhat drained, and he was taking over the patching. I think the sooner you can seal the repairs, the better, Captain," Chryllion said.

"I know. We'll see you in the morning. We need to get some sleep. We have an early start tomorrow. The sooner I go to Terolia, the sooner I'm back."

"As you command, Captain." Chryllion watched as Jerrol and Birlerion faded into the evening gloom, much like the tree. An icy chill stole down his spine as he stared after them. Chryllion shook off the feeling and stared at the hole left by the tall tree. He was not looking forward to trying to explain that in the morning.

Deepwater Watch

Jennery woke as the building shook, instantly alert. He struggled into his trousers and holding them up, dashed out of his bedchamber. Deepwater did not usually suffer from ground tremors, so what was going on?

He met Peppins on the stairs. "Did you feel it too?" Jennery asked, his gaze darting around the hallway.

"Yes, the whole building shook. Is it one of those Ascendants' attacks? I didn't hear an explosion."

"I'm not sure." Jennery descended the staircase and, not seeing any problems with the building, opened the front door. He met Landis on the steps and relaxed as he saw him was smiling.

"We have a visitor," Landis said with a grin.

"What?"

"A sentinal tree just arrived. Come see." Landis' smile widened as Alyssa appeared behind Jennery, wrapped in a robe. "My lady, it looks like a sentinal tree has just arrived. See for yourself, look!" Landis had led them around the house as he spoke. He flung his hand towards the home lake, where Denirion's sentinal stood. Only there wasn't just the one tree; there was now a second, tall and majestic, standing between Denirion's sentinal and the house. "It just appeared from nowhere. Gave the sentries quite a shock."

"The Captain's work, no doubt," Jennery said.

"Got to be Tagerill's, wouldn't you say?" Alyssa suggested, sneaking an arm around Jennery's waist and resting her cheek on his bare chest. "No reason for any other sentinal to come visiting." She smiled as Jennery hugged her close.

Lady Miranda stood open-mouthed, having followed them around the building. "That is Sentinal Tagerillion's tree? Does he know it's here?" she asked, peering around nervously as if she expected Tagerill to appear out of thin air as well.

"Ah, Denirion." Jennery grinned as the tall blond-haired Sentinal approached. "It seems we have a visitor."

Denirion's silver eyes gleamed. "Yes, my lord. As you have surmised, Tagerill's sentinal tree has travelled. He is exhausted; it takes a lot of effort."

"Is there anything he needs? Can we help at all?" Alyssa asked.

Denirion shrugged. "My lady, I think the only thing he wants is Tagerill. I was just going to get some help to move him. It's probably best for both of them."

"Carry on, then. Everyone who is off duty, back to bed. You can see the sentinal in the morning; he isn't going anywhere." Jennery called over Landis. "Keep an eye on him, just in case there is something he needs."

Landis laughed. "And how would we know?"

Jennery shrugged. "I don't know. Set Denirion on him; he'll know. I'm going back to bed." He herded Alyssa and Lady Miranda back into the house.

The next morning, everyone naturally gravitated to the new sentinal tree. The silver trunk gleamed in the morning sunlight, and the tree seemed to glow. Denirion shimmered out of his sentinal, and Alyssa gave him a quick hug in greeting. "Is Tagerill inside?" she asked.

"Oh, yes. Tagerill knew he was here and insisted on being transferred. He'll recover much faster now that his tree is here. Having sustained us for so many years, our own sentinals have a closer link with us, as they already know us so well."

Jennery looked around them. "Then I suppose we'd better get this Watch back in order. We have a confirmation to prepare for tomorrow. Let's make sure we are ready." Jennery entered his office to find Peppins, the new Watch steward, waiting for him. The reception room next to Alyssa's study had been repurposed for him.

"What a night," Jennery said as he sat behind his desk. "Right, all preparations for the confirmation need to be approved by Alyssa, so make sure they go to her office. Where do you suggest we start?"

"Security, sir, especially on the Elothian border."

Jennery glanced at him sharply. "Has Captain Haven sent word ahead of us already?"

"Yes, sir. Well, it was a Commander Haven, sir, of the King's Justice."

"He kept that quiet! Is there a full report of the attack on the palace included?"

"Yes, sir. Enlightening reading."

"I'm sure it is. I was there and I don't know half of what went on. Let me have it and the report on Elothia. I'll start with those. You can begin to factor in Captain Landis' unit; he has twenty-four men with him and a further twenty to follow once they've recovered. A full battalion." Jennery took the reports and leaned back in his chair. "We need to consider a recruitment drive. Hopefully, our people will be more willing to support us now that we've cleaned house. Landis can set up a training program; the men we've got need to be retrained."

"Yes, sir. We had the barracks prepared for your arrival. It is a relief to have some trained men here. Captain Landis seems to know his stuff, if I may say so. You'll also need these; these are the personnel reports. There is a transcript of each of the interviews I performed and my findings," Peppins replied, stacking his papers in a pile. He left Jennery to pick up the first report and returned to the desk outside Jennery's study.

Having left the maids sorting out her baggage in the pretty room her daughter had escorted her to the previous evening, Lady Miranda descended the stairs and walked out of the house towards the sentinals. She was drawn towards Tagerill's sentinal. She couldn't say why, just that she wanted to inspect it more closely. Standing under the broad canopy, she peered up in awe, reaching for the silver trunk as she overbalanced. She gasped as the air shimmered and twisting around, she heard Tagerill whisper her name.

"Miranda?"

"Tagerill, how are you?" She hurried to his side, hesitating by the golden strands that spun around the bed that Tagerill lay in.

He stared up at her, a slight crease on his brow. His face was pale and wan, his silver eyes dull with pain. "How did you get here?" he asked in bewilderment.

She bent over him, passing through the strands, and gently kissed him. "I came with Alyssa and Jennery."

His uninjured arm snaked around her waist and pulled her closer, and she giggled in relief. "I've been so worried; the reports of your injuries were so terrible."

"I'm sure they were exaggerated," he murmured against her lips. "I'll be up in no time now that my sentinal is here," he reassured her, his eyes brightening as she relaxed against him. His grip tightened. "I thought I was dreaming."

Miranda chuckled. "I expect we're both dreaming," she said, lifting her head off his chest. "I'm not quite sure where I am."

"With me, where you belong," Tagerill said as his eyes closed and his breathing deepened. "Don't go," he said as she stirred.

"I'll be here when you wake up," she promised, smoothing his coppery red hair off his forehead, and Tagerill relaxed into the healing sleep that his tree created for him.

Miranda held his hand as he slept. After a while, she leaned forward and kissed him on the lips before rising and tucking his hand under the light blanket. Reluctantly, she stepped back, watching the golden strands close the gap she had left. "You will tell me when he is due to wake up? I promised I'd be here," she asked, staring around her.

The interior of the sentinal tree was the same silver sheen of bark as the exterior but softened by a swirling mist above, and a golden glow that was emanating from Tagerill. She felt the assent in the air around her. "Thank you. How do I leave?" She had no sooner said the words than she was outside, leaning against the trunk.

The day passed as preparations for the confirmation were completed. Alyssa had ordered a simple ceremony; all they needed was for the local villagers to bear witness before the Lady.

Lady Olivia arrived, escorted by a convalescent Bryce, released by the healer on condition that he didn't do anything energetic. Bryce gritted his teeth and agreed. Their carriage swept up the approach road and disgorged them and their luggage. Jennery nabbed Bryce and herded him into his office before he had finished greeting Alyssa, pelting him with questions about Jerrol and the Justice office.

Olivia was relieved to be passing on the guardianship she had gained when her husband had been killed, and her son had failed to take up the mantle. She was in full agreement to pass it on to Alyssa, and as the two of them strolled around the grounds discussing the Watch, Olivia shared all she knew. Denirion followed close behind, his alert silver gaze observing all.

Bryce watched amused as Jennery and Landis spent their time planning their defences and sending out scouts, taking it in turns to drive their men to distraction. Tagerill slept long and deep, and Miranda visited every few hours to check his progress. The golden strands were beginning to fade, and Miranda hoped it was a sign that Tagerill would soon be well enough to be released.

On the morning of their confirmation, Jennery surprised Alyssa with a bouquet of scented flowers and, taking her hand led her down to the sentinal trees by the lake. Denirion stood by the water's edge. Tagerill was seated to the side, his right arm in a sling, but looking much better. Alyssa's mother stood beside Tagerill, her hand resting on his shoulder.

"I thought we should be joined in the sight of the Lady

before we took on the guardianship; just us and the Lady," Jennery said, staring deep into Alyssa's eyes.

Alyssa leaned against him, lifting her face for a kiss. She whispered a gentle question, her eyes gleaming as she glanced at her mother and Tagerill. Jennery's smile deepened as he followed her gaze. "We'll witness your joining if you'll witness ours," he said with a soft grin.

Miranda gasped as Tagerill awkwardly rose. He held out a trembling hand. "Shall we?" he asked, his heart in his voice.

And so, under a shimmering green canopy of majestic sentinals, amongst an air of celebration and happiness and a moment of shared joy, Alyssa and Jennery and Tagerill and Miranda said their vows under the watchful eye of the Lady.

Later that afternoon, the townspeople began to gather around the home lake, waiting expectantly for the new Lord and Lady of the Watch to be confirmed. Lord Simeon of Greenswatch had arrived, but on such short notice, the other Lords had sent their regrets along with their congratulations. Lady Miranda and her son, Simeon, were reunited, and a general air of expectation pervaded the Watch.

Denirion stood forward and began to recite the service. "It is my honour here today to invest the Guardianship of Deepwater and the future of our land and its people to be held and protected so that we may flourish and prosper. Lady Alyssa, please step forward."

Alyssa stood and strode up to the dais as the townsfolk stirred in surprise. She knelt before Denirion and stared up into his face.

"Alyssa. The Guardians created Remargaren in the hopes of building a peaceful and prosperous world. In their name, do you accept responsibility for the Land that is Deepwater, which extends from the River Vesp in the west to the Stoneford border in the East and is known as Deepwater Watch?"

"I do," Alyssa replied.

"Alyssa, in the name of the Lady, do you swear to honour Deepwater; to protect and nurture its people; to guard their right to live within your Watch?"

"I so swear." Alyssa's voice was firm.

"In sight of the Land, do you swear to nurture and propagate the natural resources given to your care?"

"I so swear."

"Before me, and at the behest of the King and Lady, do you swear to uphold the laws of the land and to join in the protection of Vespiri should it be needed?"

"I so swear."

"As Guardian, do you swear to honour and protect the treaties of Remargaren?"

"Guardians protect and in turn are protected. Keep the line. All honour to the Lady," Alyssa replied, her voice ringing out across the lake. The audience rippled with expectation as Denirion and Tagerill's graceful sentinals began to glow.

"And so, in the presence of your peers and with the blessing of the Guardians who created our world, I declare that Alyssa, daughter of Hugh and Miranda, be known as Lady Alyssa of Deepwater; hers to keep and honour for so long as she shall live; to pass through her descendants in perpetuity. Rise, Lady Alyssa, and accept the Lady's blessing."

The sentinal trees burst into light, a golden glow extending to the pointy ends of their leaves as they lit up the lake. People began cheering as Alyssa rose, stiffening her shoulders as the guardianship settled, and then she hugged Denirion; a huge smile on her face.

Lady Olivia pulled her out of Denirion's embrace and

kissed her on either cheek. "The Lady is pleased, well done," she whispered. As she stepped back, Jennery swooped in to engulf his wife in a huge hug, swinging her around, and then, after setting her back on the ground, to more decorously lead her towards the celebrations.

The villagers crowded around, eager to be part of the birth of a new guardianship, which was clearly blessed by the Lady. Word would soon spread that Deepwater had been redeemed.

26

CHAPTERHOUSE, OLD VESPERS

It was nearly a week since the king's ball. Rumours were flying around Old Vespers regarding what had happened and Commander Jerrol Haven featured prominently in them. Jerrol hadn't been back to the Chapterhouse since. Torsion supposed the king was keeping him busy, along with that Sentinal. Torsion ground his teeth. Birlerion would pay; Torsion would find a way.

The Chapterhouse was quiet. Liliian had worn a trail up to the palace due to the number of meetings she was having. Torsion was leaving for the Watch Towers at Liliian's request. This was his last chance for a while to speak with Taelia.

Torsion stood in the shelter of the Chapterhouse arches as Taelia walked through the gardens to her favourite seat by the fountain. She raised her face to the silvery gleam of the waning moon, which gilded her and everything around her in silver and shadow. Glancing around the courtyard, Torsion smiled. It seemed they had the place to themselves this evening.

He strolled into the gardens and paused at the fountain.

"The sound of water is always so relaxing, isn't it?" he said as he dipped a hand into the cold water.

Taelia turned her head at the sound of his voice. "Yes, can you hear the music too?"

"The music?"

"Yes, the water sings if you listen carefully."

"I've never sat long enough to listen. The sound always makes me want to doze," he admitted.

"Which is good for you, but you should listen too. The water appreciates a good listener."

"I expect it does," he agreed. "I wanted to talk to you. I am being re-assigned to the Watch Towers to go and clean up the mess Jerrol left behind." He frowned as Taelia's lips tightened in response to his comment. "The history hidden in that place will be amazing. It will take more than one scholar to discover it all."

"You've always been drawn to the Towers, haven't you?"

"Yes. I'd love to show them to you, Taelia. We could make wonderful discoveries. You and I work well together. We've had plenty of practice." He sat on the bench next to her. "We make a good team."

Taelia laughed and reached to grip his arm. "That we do," she agreed with a smile.

"Come with me," he urged, thankful that she couldn't see his heightened colour as he took her hand. "I'd look after you. I've always been there for you, you know that!"

"Go with you?" Taelia repeated, withdrawing her hand.

Torsion grabbed her retreating hand. "Yes, come and experience the world with me. There are great things we could do together." His blood stirred at the thought as he pictured what he wanted to do with her. His grip tightened. He'd have her soon.

"No, I have plenty of work to do here."

"Others can do it. Join me and make a difference,"

Torsion said, excitement rushing through him as he searched her shocked face.

"I-I can't. I have important work to do here," Taelia stammered, her cheeks heating.

"You mean searching the archives for Jerrol?" Torsion scowled at her. "I've seen you and Mary scouring that room. There is nothing to find; there is much more at the Towers." *And she would be away from the influence of those Sentinals,* he thought.

Taelia stiffened. "My work is as important as yours, Torsion. You never value what I contribute."

Torsion pulled her into his arms and tried to kiss her. "I have more important work we can do together," he murmured, tightening his embrace.

"Torsion! What do you think you're doing?" Taelia's voice came out as a squeak as she tried to push her hands against his chest, but his grip tightened.

"You know how I feel about you; I've always been here for you, haven't I? Not like some we could mention." Torsion tried to smother her face in kisses, oblivious to her struggles. His heart raced now that he had her in his arms. He had dreamed of it often enough.

Taelia tried to twist out of his grip. Her voice shook as she struggled. "Torsion! No. Let me go."

Torsion stiffened in shock as a hand gripped his shoulder. "Torsion! She said let go."

Torsion jerked away from Taelia in surprise, Jerrol's voice as welcome as a cold rain shower. Taelia slipped out of his loosened grasp and stumbled to Jerrol's side.

"Where did you come from? Always saving the day," Torsion sneered, as he tried to calm his breathing, furious at being interrupted.

"A fleeting visit," Jerrol replied. "What's wrong, Torsion? I thought you were her friend."

"Well, if she will lead a man on, what can she expect?" Torsion said, his face flushed.

"I never did," gasped Taelia. "I thought we were friends."

"Oh, more than a friend, my dear. I'm good enough when *he's* not around. Is that it?"

"Torsion, I never meant to mislead you. I enjoy your company, but as friends! I thought you understood."

"Or is it that Sentinal you prefer? You seemed to enjoy his company the other day." Torsion bit his words off, the anger building within him. He trembled as he tried to contain the emotions that were about to overwhelm him.

Taelia stiffened, her fingers curling into fists. Her face hardened. "Birlerion knows the meaning of courtesy and good manners much better than you do."

Torsion shook as a mask of indifference descended over his face, the harshness fading from his expression. His anger drained away as icy cold calculation replaced it. Straightening, he stiffened his shoulders and stared at Taelia, ignoring Jerrol. "Oh, never mind. Taelia, my lovely, please accept my apologies. I misjudged the situation." And with a sweeping bow, he stalked out of the courtyard.

Jerrol's touch was fleeting. "I can't stay, love. But you can't trust him; promise me you will be careful. Something is not right." Jerrol dropped a kiss on her head. It was as light as a feather, hardly an impression, but such a familiar action that Taelia went to lean into him in response. But he wasn't there.

"Jerrol?" As she reached out in front of her, she realised she was alone. She must have pulled him to her in her need, a blessing from the Lady. She wasn't sure how she had done it. As instinctive as if breathing, she could translocate herself, and it seemed Jerrol as well. She would have to ponder on that. Could she move other things or people? The scholar within her began analysing the possibilities.

A smile dawned on her face. He had called her 'love'! She spun around, treasuring the warm feeling. He had forgiven her. She hugged the word tight inside her.

Deserts of Terolia

"Captain? Wake up!" Birlerion's voice was sharp on the chill night air.

Jerrol opened bleary eyes. "W-What's the matter?" he asked. He had a cracking headache. He looked around the camp, tugging his robe tighter as his breath misted around him. All was quiet, dawn hours away yet. Nil'ano was bundled up in his robes, fast asleep.

"You called out, and then you collapsed. I couldn't wake you." Birlerion sounded on edge.

"I was dreaming," Jerrol paused, trying to remember. "Or, I think I was dreaming. I'm not sure. It all seemed so real. Taelia needed me. Something to do with her and Torsion." He rubbed his temple, trying to remember. Something had been very wrong. He eased back down into his blankets, exhausted and dozed off, leaving Birlerion glancing over at him as he settled back down in his own blankets.

It took five days to reach the town of Ramila; five days of parched grass plains giving way to unrelenting desert; five days of Birlerion watching him with concern. The sun beat down on them from a clear blue sky and the heat reflected up from the golden sun-baked ground, with Jerrol melting in the middle. The excessive layers suffocated him even though they were supposed to help cool the skin and reduce the chance of sunstroke.

Jerrol was not convinced. He was sweating in places he didn't know he could sweat. The only reason his hair wasn't plastered to his face was because it was hidden under the swathes of material that Birlerion had wrapped around his head.

"Where did you learn to do that?" Nil'ano said in surprise as he inspected their turbans.

"It's the only way I know," Birlerion said with a sad smile. "I suppose a lot has changed since I last visited Terolia."

Nil'ano chuckled. "My boy, you will bring about a new style. When the Families see it, they'll fall over themselves to copy it."

Zin'talia spent an inordinate amount of time telling Jerrol about local tradition and drilling home the point that the locals, in general, knew best. Jerrol did his best to pay attention. He did not spurn an expert when one was presented to him for free.

As they approached the town of Ramila, she was still instructing him.

"Listen to Birlerion. He knows what he's talking about. His ideas may be a little antiquated but they worked back then. No reason why they shouldn't work now."

"You're a fan now?"

"I was never not a fan. I like him. He's relaxed a bit. Maybe he's getting used to me."

"It doesn't have anything to do with the fact he found you some Baliweed when we met those traders?"

"I said he was resourceful," Zin'talia replied, and Jerrol smiled at her smug tone.

"You said no such thing." His gaze rested on the back of the Sentinal.

Birlerion had surprised him again. Taking the lead when they passed a caravan of Terolians heading north, Birlerion had hailed the Terolians like they were old friends, and his greetings broke down barriers with ease. It seemed that Birlerion was familiar with the Families. He should have known.

The Terolians set up an impromptu camp, and Jerrol and his companions were invited to sit at their hearth. They also topped up their water, which Birlerion had been most pleased about. Jerrol remembered a conversation with Jennery when they had first met Birlerion. Birlerion had said that he tried to blend in. He did with ease. As Birlerion's silver eyes swept the town square, bustling with a lively market, he seemed as cool and fresh in his robes as Nil'ano did.

Jerrol caught his eye, and he scowled as Birlerion tried not to smile at his discomfort. Birlerion offered the water canteen again, and Jerrol knew better than to refuse.

"I recommend we take rooms at the Oasis," Nil'ano suggested as he scanned the market. "It is the best boarding house in Ramila."

Jerrol nodded. His throat was excruciatingly dry. He tipped the canteen back, and the warm water trickled down his throat and straight out of his pores. He wished he acclimatised as easily as Birlerion. He looked like he belonged.

Gesturing for Nil'ano to lead the way, Jerrol dismounted and led Zin'talia through the busy thoroughfares. The market was in full swing, making the most of the morning hours before the heat of the day closed everything down. They would have to come back out in the evening and find Nil'ano's contacts. He observed the new slave pens in the north-east corner of the square, the sordid stink recognizable even from this distance. The tight family units had previously frowned on slavery.

Jerrol moved up next to Nil'ano. "Since when was slavery a market trade in Terolia?"

Nil'ano shrugged. "Exchanges started about a year or so

ago; youngsters mainly, unwanted kids, orphans, though it wasn't so desperate as this. It was supposed to be a trade of resources from families who had a surplus to families who had suffered losses. But once started, it evolved. It is now just trafficking, no care for the people. The Medera tries to shut them down, but as soon as we move on, they spring back up again. Considering the smell, I shouldn't think anyone in that pen is disease-free." He wrinkled his nose in disgust as they finally passed out of the square.

The Oasis was a large boarding house that proudly owned the southern corner of the town. It was built around a small oasis, which was fed from the central watering hole via underground springs. The open eating area was tastefully situated around the water, the fountains adding moisture to the air, the tang of water mingling with the fresh green aroma of a wiry sentinal towering over the two-storey buildings.

Jerrol let Nil'ano do the talking. He booked them rooms, stalls in the stables, and a table for the evening meal under the sentinal. He flourished a well-filled purse to pay the resulting bill. Jerrol followed a young boy dressed in a flowing white tunic, who led them to their rooms. On the way, the boy indicated the resources available to guests, making sure they were paying attention when he pointed out the door to the communal baths.

Eyeing the entrance to the bathing room, Jerrol followed Birlerion round the curved passage until they reached their rooms. Zin'talia crooned over her haynet, a happy murmur in his head. The net was scattered with stalks of Baliweed, and she was happily occupied picking them out.

Jerrol sighed with relief when the door closed behind him, and he dropped his saddlebags to the floor. His room was lit by subtle lanterns, casting a gentle glow. The curtains gleamed in the soft light, a glimmer of silvery green edging the material. The room was blessedly cool, and he shed his clothes in relief. Leaning his sword against the wall, he could sense its reluctance at being parted from him, but he was eager to shed his sweaty robes. Hanging on the peg on the back of his door was a thin cotton robe, which he wrapped around himself before heading straight for the baths.

The shower was divine. He scrubbed his skin with the scented sands provided for the guests. He slicked his hair back and eased his shoulders as he wrapped the robe around him and headed back to his room, where he began to sweat again.

He dressed in a clean shirt, a light linen vest, which reached his thighs, and loose trousers he had found to be comfortable on previous visits. He had taken the opportunity to stock up. Inevitably, they shimmered into a silvery-green sheen as he slipped on his boots.

The gentle pull of the sentinal tree led him out of the building. The sentinal had been calling ever since they had arrived. He walked around the fountain and paused, peering up at the wiry trunk. It was much thinner than the trees in Vespiri. He could probably reach all the way around the trunk if he tried, but it was the same smooth silver wood with deep emerald green, pointy leaves branching out overhead. He checked the eating area. The open pits were dark and unattended, the candles unlit on the tables. The staff had not yet prepared for the evening business. He placed a hand on the trunk and relaxed into the exuberant welcome.

An insistent voice intruded, repeating his name. "Jerrol! Jerrol, are you alright?"

Jerrol returned to the present, reluctantly releasing the warm embrace of the Sentinal, staring at Birlerion, who had pulled him away from the tree. "Captain? People are staring. Come, we have a table reserved. Let's sit."

Jerrol flushed as he realised the area had come alive

around him without his noticing. Fire pits burned merrily. Lanterns lit the courtyard, the sentinal tree throwing soft shadows across the seating area. Each low table had a glass bowl containing a flickering candle. Taking a deep breath, he followed Birlerion to their seats.

The Sentinal had been so pleased to meet him. Few had visited over the millennia. He had been enthusiastic in the sharing, and Jerrol was still reeling, overwhelmed by Sentinal Tarenion's revelations. The fact that a man existed at the core of the sentinal, poised to act at Jerrol's command, was strangely terrifying. Fortunately, Tarenion had understood the need for discretion and would wait for Jerrol's word before revealing himself.

Jerrol sat where Birlerion pushed him, on a cushion in a shadowed alcove. Birlerion sat opposite him, blocking the view of the other guests. His intent gaze came to rest on Jerrol, having glanced around the open courtyard full of inquisitive guests. Jerrol looked over his shoulder wincing at the number of tables that were still looking in their direction.

A waiter approached their table and bowed. "Your order, sirs?" he asked in a softly sibilant voice.

Birlerion ordered the house special; a platter of assorted dips, pastries, and breads, followed by lemon and herb marinated chicken skewers and flatbreads. He also ordered a light resinous wine to go with the food and a pitcher of water. As the server left, he finally spoke. "You need to be more careful. We are trying to blend in."

Jerrol snorted. "It's not so easy."

"You'd be surprised." Birlerion grinned, reminding Jerrol how young he was. He kept forgetting. The Sentinal always seemed so self-assured.

"How old were you when you joined the rangers, Birlerion?"

Birlerion screwed up his face as he hesitated. "Fourteen?" he said after a moment.

"Fourteen?" Jerrol gaped at him. "You don't sound too sure."

Birlerion tensed, and Jerrol thought he wouldn't answer, but when he did, Jerrol was sure it wasn't what he was originally going to say. "Tagerill and I share a borning day, though he is a year older than me."

"That's right; you are brothers, aren't you?"

"His family adopted me, so we're not true brothers, but Tagerill won't hear it said otherwise." Birlerion's face softened, his features hidden in the shadows. "Guerlaire saved me from the streets; the Lady gave me purpose and the Descelles gave me a home."

Jerrol stared into his glass, trying to hide his shock. "You were living on the streets of Vespers?"

"Yeah. Serill always said that I was dying on the streets, not living. He and Tagerill knocked that chip off my shoulder when we met in the cadets."

"Sounds like you were fortunate."

"Extremely." Birlerion sipped his wine. "Did you wake Tarenion?" His voice grew firm as he changed the subject.

Jerrol put down his glass. "How did you know it was Tarenion?"

"I could sense him."

"Is that normal?"

Birlerion shrugged. "I met him when I was stationed out this way. Maybe it's because we met?"

"He was lonely," Jerrol said, gazing at the distinctive tree. "His Guardian is not aware." He relaxed into the cushions, thinking how much Taelia would enjoy it here. The contented voices carried on the balmy evening air, the scent of roasting meat and spices combining with the sharp tang of water. Taelia would have a sensory overload.

As if his thoughts had conjured her up, Taelia shimmered into sight, seated on the cushions opposite him. She lurched and Birlerion steadied her. She gave him a brilliant smile and turned to Jerrol as he gasped.

"Tali! How did you find us?"

"It doesn't matter. Jerrol, you have to find the slave pens. Someone is calling on the Lady." She leaned across the table and hesitated. "Oh my, what is that wonderful smell?"

Jerrol started to laugh. "I was just thinking about how much you would love this. A balmy evening, exotic scents, delicious food."

Birlerion placed a sticky nut-covered pastry in her hand. "Try it," he said.

Taelia inhaled the rising aroma and took a bite, and she relaxed into the enjoyment of the food, closing her eyes. "Oh mmm, this is delicious."

"I promise, Tali, I'll bring you back here so you can enjoy an evening Terolian style."

"Terolia? You're in Terolia? What are you doing there?" Taelia opened her turquoise eyes wide.

"The Lady's bidding. Just as you are," Jerrol replied.

Taelia straightened. "Take care, Jerrol; there is much uncertainty on the horizon, and that usually means there'll be conflict of some sort. Trouble comes. Please be careful." She reached and gripped Birlerion's hand. "That means you as well, Birlerion, do you hear me?"

"I hear you, Taelia," Birlerion replied, squeezing her hand in return.

"Good. Now give me another one of those things before I have to go."

Jerrol chuckled before selecting another pastry and placing it in her questing hand. "Why don't you try the wine as well?"

"Wine? My, you do live well, don't you?"

Jerrol gave her his glass and watched her expressive face as she sipped. It was like enjoying the wine all over again as her face lit up in appreciation. "How lovely. It's fresh, yet sweet." She then shimmered out of sight, taking his glass of wine with her.

Jerrol stared at the spot where she had been sitting and then released a deep sigh. An evening with her in this exotic location would have been perfect.

He stirred as footsteps approached. Nil'ano arrived, his face wreathed in smiles. "Apologies for my tardiness, gentlemen. The waters seduced me. You have found our local nectar, and here is the food." He folded onto the cushion before descending on the aromatic delights the waiters had brought out. His platitudes prevented any further discussion, and they concentrated on the food instead.

27

MISTRA, TEROLIA

Their pleasant evening was interrupted, as Taelia had foretold, by the arrival of four strident men, who cut through the Oasis' evening calm straight to Jerrol's table.

"You, up," the lead man said, pointing his finger at Birlerion.

Birlerion raised an eyebrow and didn't move. The light pooled around him as he ignored the command.

Jerrol leaned back on his cushion, his face in the shadows. "And who might you be?"

"The people who matter in this town, and I told you to stand up." The man glared at Birlerion.

"Why?" Birlerion asked, shifting his position.

The man snapped his fingers, and his companions grabbed Birlerion and dragged him upright. Birlerion relaxed in their grip at Jerrol's signal.

Nil'ano rose. "Gentlemen, this is quite unnecessary. I am sure there has been some misunderstanding. We have only just arrived."

"You have but to explain why. There is no reason to resort to violence," Jerrol added, keeping his voice calm.

"The Elders want to speak to him."

"By all means, we will gladly speak with the Elders," Jerrol said, observing the visible tension running down the cords of Birlerion's neck. "Tell us where the Elder's offices are and we will attend first thing in the morning."

"The Elders decide when, not you."

Jerrol's eyebrows rose as the man snarled a command and the grip on Birlerion tightened. Birlerion's eyes were narrowed, his face calm, and yet Jerrol sensed the singing tension in the air; the expectant pause before the strike.

"Birlerion, go with them for now. Nil'ano and I will speak to the Elders," Jerrol said, meeting Birlerion's eyes. Birlerion gave him an imperceptible nod and the tension faded as he was dragged out of the eating area.

Jerrol glanced around him. The patrons were studiously avoiding his gaze. "Ni'lano, who are the Elders in Ramila? I think they owe us an explanation."

Nil'ano scowled after the men. "Terolian hospitality has changed in the short space of time I have been absent. I can assure you, I will be making a complaint. They had no right to take Birlerion like that."

"This was not the place to start a fight," Jerrol murmured. "Innocent people could have been hurt. It is better we talk to them first."

Nil'ano snorted, flinging his hands out. "They didn't look like they wanted to talk. Why did you let them take him?"

"Because they might lead us to those we seek."

Once outside the Oasis, the men bound Birlerion's arms behind his back, and hustled him down the street as if aware of the coiled power prepared to obliterate them. They arrived at a two-storey building built out of local stone, situated on the edge of the marketplace. The guards slammed Birlerion against the wall as one of them fumbled with a bunch of keys. He managed to get the door open in time to prevent a tongue-lashing from his boss, and the guards shoved Birlerion onto a chair in the middle of a room, wrenching his arms behind him.

A grey-haired man slowly walked around Birlerion as the lanterns were lit, his brown robes swirling around his ankles. The golden light cast the lines on his scowling face into sharp relief. His black eyes were hard and determined.

"So," the Elder snapped. "You thought you could just waltz into Ramila and tell us what to do?"

"I thought no such thing, I can assure you," Birlerion replied, his gaze flicking around the bare room.

"You expect me to believe that?" The man circled him as his guards chuckled.

"Why should you not? I am but a visitor to your pleasant town, enjoying a meal with my friends. You can't just take me off the street. I have rights!"

"All innocence, I suppose. And yet, you lie. Tell me what is planned and you won't get hurt."

"Planned?"

"Yes, did you not understand the question? Maybe you need some assistance to remember."

Birlerion's head snapped back as one of the men hit him and he hissed out his breath. "I do not need your help to remember anything," he said.

"Tch, tch, you are not listening," the man said from behind him. "I am in charge here. I can do what I like. Tell me, who are you and what are you doing in Ramila?"

"Is this how you greet all visitors to Ramila?" Birlerion asked, gasping as a fist jabbed him in the side.

"Name."

"Who's asking?"

"I ask the questions, not you." The man circled him. "Tell me why you are here and we might go easy on you."

"Elders represent the family and Family Law. You have no family mark; you are no Elder. You have no right to detain me."

"You are in no position to protest. Answer my questions or pay the consequences," the man replied, stepping back and giving his men space.

Birlerion squinted at the Elder and rocked back under another blow. He spat out blood.

"You're the Lady's Captain."

Birlerion laughed. "Me? Sure, I'm the Captain."

"Var'geris is searching for you. You've got the silver eyes. What are you doing in Ramila?"

"Var'geris? Who is he? And what does he want with me?"

The man sighed. "You're not listening to me," he chided. "You should pay attention. You want to answer my questions, truthfully. You *will* answer my questions. Why are you here?"

"We were enjoying the scenery, until you arrived."

"Have you woken the Sentinal?"

Birlerion's laugh was cut off as a fist crunched into his jaw. His lip split, a sudden sting distracting him from the pacing man. The man's attempts at Mentiserium were pathetic. Birlerion hissed his breath out, trying to gauge where the men were. He twisted his wrists, heat tingling his fingertips as he rubbed the rope.

He wondered how long it would take Jerrol to realise these men were no Elders.

The man was speaking again. "We caught you, and we'll pass you up the line. Var'geris will make you speak."

"As you wish." Birlerion cringed back in the chair, trying to protect his ribs from another stunning blow and allowing the momentum to topple him and the chair over onto the floor. The rope parted and he rose with predatory grace as he pounced on the guard nearest him, striking swift and sure. Leaving the man to collapse, he turned to the next. He got in a stinging blow before more guards arrived and he was forced down to the ground under a heaving mass of humanity.

"Enough," the grey-haired man barked, glowering down at Birlerion. "Get him up."

The guards dragged Birlerion upright, and he stood hunched over after another blow.

The man peered at him in sudden doubt. He scowled as he rubbed his mouth. "If you're not the one we want, then tell me where the Captain is and I'll let you live."

"It's me you want," Birlerion whispered after a moment's deliberation. He licked his lip, the metallic taste of blood on his tongue. His lip stung. His body ached. He restrained the need to growl in frustration.

The man frowned at him, tapping his chin. "I think you need a lesson, maybe a night in the pens will make you realise your situation. Come morning, if you do not answer my questions, then you will regret it." At his signal, the guard hit Birlerion behind the ear, and he collapsed to the ground.

Birlerion awoke to the stench of the slave pens. His hands and feet were manacled, and he lay across the legs of two men scrunched up against the bars. His head thumped painfully, and his ribs ached as he tried to sit up. The men had been generous with their boots while he was unconscious, no doubt retaliating against his attack. His feet were bare, and he was only wearing his thin under robe; not much protection against the cool night air.

"Take it easy, lad," a soft voice said in his ear. "There ain't room to swing anything in 'ere."

Birlerion groaned and tried to sit up again. He drew his breath in against the sharp flash of pain. "Done you over good and proper," the soft voice continued as the men around him propped him up.

Birlerion held his head in his hands. The manacles rattled. They were connected to a metal collar around his neck.

"You'll be alright in a moment, lad. It takes you like that when you first wake up."

"Where am I?" he asked, though he had a fair idea. Did they really think a night of discomfort would make him talk?

"Central market slave pens. We'll be sold in the morning. This is the pen for petty thieves and general offences. The Governor likes to have a full pen."

Birlerion's head swam as he tried to focus on his surroundings. The stench turned his stomach, and he swallowed the rising bile; it burned his throat. "Do they not like to sell their slaves in the best possible condition? Surely they would fetch more money?"

"Nah," the man laughed, "why waste the money?" Some of the other slaves grumbled at being disturbed.

"Who's likely to buy? I didn't think slavery was allowed in Terolia."

"There are strangers in town, and they have a trafficking business up north. Most of us go there."

Birlerion squinted at the man. He was filthy. His clothes little more than rags. His eye was purpling beautifully and just below was the family mark, a yellow sun tattooed on his right cheek. Solari. The man bared his stained teeth. "No buyers so far. They toss you back in for the next sale. You'll sell, no problem, 'coz you're educated. You can tell; nice clothes. You'll wash up well, never mind the bruises."

"I'd prefer not to be sold." Birlerion closed his eyes. His head ached. He needed to think. What had Taelia said about the slave pens? He was sure he was meant to be here. Birlerion sighed. He was getting fed up with being a punching bag. Leyandrii could at least have found a less painful way to get him in the pens. Now he was here, what was he supposed to do?

All he had found out was that Var'geris was actively searching for the Captain. What had happened for him to call off his assassins? If he had, that was. In the meantime, being sold as a slave would not be ideal. He needed to escape and find Var'geris and his brothers. Sitting in a stinking pen wasn't going to get him anywhere.

He paid more attention to his surroundings. The guards were clustered around a barrel in the farthest corner of the square, as far from the stench as they could get. They were suspiciously cheerful, and the glint of a bottle being passed around suggested the reason why.

Birlerion studied the locks. They were new and well oiled; they wouldn't be a problem. He stared down at his manacles and flexed his wrists; they were tight and unyielding and were already rubbing his wrist and ankles. His feet were freezing.

"What you thinking, lad?" the voice murmured in his ear. "Them guards'll be asleep within the chime. They spend the evening drinking; only way they'll agree to guard us."

"What makes you think I'm thinking anything?"

The man snorted. "You're the first one to arrive with any gumption. You ain't gonna sit here and rot."

"Well, not by choice." He tensed as the pen's wire gate opened and closed again. "You're early," Birlerion said, closing his eyes against the sight of Jerrol dressed in a grubby guard's uniform. "How can you wear that?" he said wrinkling his nose against the smell of dried sweat.

Jerrol chuckled under his breath. "You can't talk, you smell worse. I had the feeling you might do something stupid if I left you much longer."

"Your faith in my restraint is reassuring."

"Any good at picking locks?" Jerrol said to the man supporting Birlerion.

The Solarian grinned. "Knew you were a rum'en when they tossed you in 'ere. I said, Lady, 'ere's a bloke who'll not be in 'ere long. He's got friends!"

"You follow the Lady then?" Jerrol whispered as he started easing a thin metal pin out of the hem of his shirt.

"Yeah, most of us in here do; that's our offence, usually." The man scowled.

"Do your family not search for you? I thought the Family took care of their own?"

"It's what you hear, but not so much these days. The Families seem to be crumbling from the inside. Children banished, petty arguments. Family Law seems to be only a convenience, used when it suits them."

"I don't believe it," Birlerion said. "The Family would never stray from Family Law."

The man's manacles clanked; a soft echo in the darkness as he shrugged. "There are stranger tales than that. They say there are ghosts in the desert, voices on the wind up past Il Queron. Not that many people venture into the salt flats, if they have sense."

"There's no such thing as ghosts," Jerrol replied as he shuffled around and began to work on Birlerion's collar and then his wrist manacles. He gave Birlerion a pin and Birlerion twisted around, rubbing his wrists, and began on his ankles.

The man shushed the quavering voices as Jerrol continued to release the slaves, pausing only as a guard staggered passed, oblivious to the gleaming eyes watching him.

The others were no longer in sight. As the guard stumbled away, Jerrol swung open the wire gate, the hinges blessedly silent, and melted into the night, followed by Birlerion.

Jerrol navigated the streets, heading northwards as he cut down alleyways and skirted the thoroughfares. *"Zin'talia, I have Birlerion. We're heading north. Meet us on the outskirts."*

"On my way."

A communal well caught his eye and after a quick glance at Birlerion, he cranked the handle to bring the bucket up. Birlerion crouched beside him, and the dim light from the lantern hung over the well revealed the dark bruising on his skin. Another beating Birlerion had taken for him. He offered him the water. "Are you alright?"

"Yeah," Birlerion sighed. "Just bruises." He shivered in the cold night air and sluiced his face and hands, scooping the icy cold water up to drink.

"I packed all our stuff and sent Zee on to wait for us. She'll be here soon," Jerrol said peering around them, they continued walking north.

The outskirts of the town loomed ahead of them and they hunkered down in a quiet alleyway to wait for Zin'talia. Birlerion crouched behind him, shivering, and it was obvious Birlerion was hurting, even though he wouldn't admit it. He scowled down the road. Where was Zin'talia?

Her grumble interrupted his thoughts. *"I'm coming. I'm coming!"* She trotted into view, Birlerion's hack still tied to her saddle. He had hastily packed everything into their saddle bags before leaving to find Birlerion.

Jerrol waited while Birlerion rummaged for some robes and shrugged into them. Birlerion's shivering eased as he found his boots and stamped into them.

Zin'talia rubbed her head against Birlerion's shoulder. *"Tell him I'm glad he's alright."* she murmured to Jerrol.

Jerrol chuckled. "Zee is glad you're ok."

Birlerion froze in surprise and then slowly relaxed and rubbed her nose. "Thank you," he said. Taking a breath, Birlerion mounted his horse, stifling a groan as he settled in the saddle.

Jerrol mounted Zin'talia and headed north out of the town as the morning bells began to clang.

"Is Birlerion really alright? What happened?"

"Birlerion is fine, just a few bruises. He was thrown in the slave pens."

"He does reek a bit. A hazard of the desert. Never enough water for a wash."

"He had no choice; it seems there was someone waiting to give us a message."

"What message was that?" Zin'talia asked.

"We need to divert to Il Queron," he replied before falling silent as he led Birlerion northwards at a steady pace, leaving the town of Ramila behind them. The sound of clanging bells faded as they travelled.

Birlerion jerked out of an exhausted doze as Jerrol called his name. "We're here," he said as they reached a rocky outcrop that would provide some shelter.

"Where's Nil'ano?" Birlerion asked as he slid out of the saddle.

"He said he would return to Mistra and find word of the Atolea. We need to meet him there. There was no point him remaining in Ramila. The Elders were clueless and less than helpful." Jerrol's lip curled. "They wouldn't even listen to our complaints. Nil'ano was not impressed, though it didn't help you much."

Birlerion grunted. "They weren't real Elders, and they were in a hurry. More muscle than brains. Just followers trying to impress the boss."

"Well, assuming Var'geris is the boss. No doubt we'll find him in Mistra."

Jerrol opened the jar of salve he had in his pack. It was suitable for most injuries, and he offered it to Birlerion who took time to dab the salve on his cut lip. It wouldn't do to leave open sores in this climate. Tucking the jar back into Jerrol's pack, Birlerion folded to the sand with an exhausted sigh and rubbing his fingers together lit the small fire Jerrol had built.

"How did you end up in the slave pens?" Jerrol asked as he put a pot of coffee on to heat.

"The fake Elder didn't believe I was who they were looking for. They wanted you."

Jerrol raised an eyebrow. "Me?"

"Yes. Var'geris is searching for you. They thought I needed time to consider my answers before they sent me up the line. And anyway, I think we were supposed to end up in the pens."

Jerrol nodded thoughtfully. "I think you might be right, though I'm sorry you took the brunt of their displeasure."

Birlerion's lips twisted. "It's what I'm here for, to protect you."

"Still, it would have been nice to spend one night at the Oasis." Jerrol handed Birlerion a mug and made himself more comfortable. "Do you think we'll find more Sentinals in the salt flats?"

"Leyandrii went out of her way to make sure we were told to look there. I would assume that's where we'll find them."

"We still need to speak to Medera Maraine. I need to confirm a few things before we head home."

"Fortunate the Solari told me the Atolea are still encamped at Mistra, then, isn't it?" Birlerion said as he inhaled the steam from his coffee.

Jerrol stifled a grunt as he eased back against the rocks and sipped the steaming liquid. "When did you speak with the Solari?"

"Whilst you were chatting with Tarenion. I also heard that a child was recently banished. A girl, the Medera's daughter. The Family are upset about it. Normally, they would have been tightlipped about such a disgrace," Birlerion said, his voice soft as he watched the fire.

"Are they now?" Jerrol murmured. Tell me about Family Law."

Birlerion laughed. "Family Law? That would take weeks."

"A summary then."

"Family Law is the glue that holds the Families together. The rules by which they live. Each child has responsibilities whether they be brother or son. Sister or daughter. Each to care for and protect the other. It's what makes the Families so strong.

"Each Family has a facial tattoo, you've seen the sun of the Solari, and Nil'ano wears the Atolean star. The mark of the Family is sacrosanct and reflects their honour. To have your mark defaced is the ultimate dishonour; it means you are cast out, banished."

"I've never seen anyone with their tattoo defaced."

"That's why it is a last resort, it usually means death. Banishment is extreme; to banish a child is unheard of."

"What did the child do?"

"They wouldn't say, but they were angry, extremely angry. It brings Medera Reina's rule into question as she has no other heir."

Jerrol frowned at the flickering fire. "Do you think she was influenced?"

"It's possible," Birlerion said. "Though she should hold

the Lady the closest. But to banish your only heir? She must not be in her right mind."

"Do they know where the child is?"

"Dead they think. No other Family could offer her aid. It's a slow death, reserved for a blood debt or a life debt usually."

"It sounds brutal."

"It keeps the hotheads under control. It's meant to be a deterrent."

"But not for children," Jerrol said, his voice soft.

"No," Birlerion replied, staring out at the dark sands. They fell silent, each with their own thoughts.

Jerrol watched the sunrise spread across the sky, burning away to a brilliant blue, Birlerion's quiet movements soothing. "We need to leave," he said at last.

Birlerion nodded and loaded up the horses. "It's a three-day ride to Mistra. If we divert via Il Queron, that will add at least another day to our journey." Birlerion stared off into the golden dunes, his brow creased in thought. "There should be an oasis where we can top up our water, and there should also be a Sentinal."

Jerrol raised his eyebrows. It was uncanny how Birlerion knew where places were. "Are you sure? I mean, it might not be there anymore."

Birlerion flushed. "I looked at a map earlier."

Jerrol huffed out breath. "I thought maps were useless in Terolia?"

"They have their uses if you know how to read them."

Shaking his head, Jerrol mounted his horse. "Lead the way then," he said and followed Birlerion down the dusty trail towards Il Queron.

28

IL QUERON, TEROLIA

Late that afternoon, Il Queron shimmered on the horizon, undulating as the heat rose from the sun-hardened rock. The shadows cast by the dunes had begun to lengthen as the sun sank lower and burnished the sky a molten yellow.

Jerrol scanned the village. Maybe two hundred people lived in the collection of small mud-baked huts and buildings. The central square was empty and the aimless breeze swirled the dust in the deserted streets. A temple building presided over the small oasis. A slender sentinal tree arched over both the temple and the water. Its leaves were thinner but just as pointed.

A row of canvas fronted stalls, currently empty, and a cluster of small tables with spindly chairs covered in dust extended out at a right angle from the temple, depicting where the market would be when the heat dissipated. A hanging rug stirred in the still air as they approached the oasis. Someone was watching.

"Water the horses first," Jerrol said through dry lips.

Birlerion led the horses to the water and let them drink

while he refilled all their canteens. He handed over Jerrol's and then sipped some water himself before topping it up and stowing them securely to his horse's gear.

Unravelling the scarf around his head, Birlerion ran his hand through his black hair, leaving it sticking up in tufts. White creases fanned out at the corners of his eyes, where the sun had found a way in and tanned his skin. Leading the horses into the shade of the sentinal tree, he glanced at Jerrol. "Peterion first?" he suggested.

Jerrol stared at him. His bruises had bloomed. His face was a mass of purples and blues, and Jerrol suppressed his wince at the sight of his swollen lip. "I suppose you know Peterion, as well?"

Birlerion's grin was lopsided and he held his mouth for a moment, suppressing an 'ow'. "What can I say? I got about."

Jerrol placed his hand against the trunk and Peterion stepped out. Tall, dark-skinned, and dark-haired, he wore a soft green robe that shimmered in the sunlight.

The two Sentinals embraced. "Peterion," Birlerion murmured in his ear, "you need some sun, my friend."

Peterion gave a puff of laughter. "You can talk. What have you been up to, Birlerion?"

"Same as always. Though I admit, I've had better moments."

Peterion snorted as Jerrol led the way into the temple. He walked up to the altar and knelt with the Sentinals beside him, praying to the Lady for guidance.

Peterion jerked as Leyandrii spoke. *"Peterion, welcome home. Jerrolion, welcome to Terolia."*

"My Lady," Peterion gasped.

"Jerrolion?" Jerrol queried, a little apprehensively.

"Of course, my Captain, you were the one suggesting a disguise. It is always best to hide behind your true name where possible. Dearest Birlerion, hold true. We are not finished yet."

"Yes, my Lady." Birlerion sounded bereft.

"We are close. My children will be returned. My Captain is here." Her voice embraced them. *"Make sure you listen carefully; you mustn't miss them. Bless you all, stand strong and tall. My Sentinals are coming home."* Her blessing shimmered in the air as her voice faded.

Jerrol leaned back on his heels and glanced at Peterion. "Did that make any sense to you?"

Peterion grinned. "Birlerion will translate." Birlerion huffed beside him and Peterion laughed aloud, his silver eyes gleaming in the dim light.

"Is there somewhere we can all rest? It doesn't look like there are many inns here," Jerrol said.

"Hospitality will flow once it is known, you will see," Peterion said.

Jerrol wondered what would be known but followed as Birlerion rose with a stifled groan and led the way out into the sunshine.

A grey-haired woman swathed in amber robes stood in the empty square, waiting. She was tiny. She might reach Jerrol's chest if she was lucky, and he wasn't particularly tall. Jerrol stopped a short distance away.

Her face was creased and lined, weathered by the hot sun to a deep bronze.

"We are searching for one who knows the salt flats," Jerrol said.

The woman nodded. She paused, staring intently at Jerrol, and then her eyes wandered up the lengths of the Sentinals standing beside him. Her eyes widened as she took in their appearance. She gestured off to her left and, turning, led the way to a small mud-baked building behind the temple. "Here," she waved them inside. It was one room, partitioned by a rich red curtain, with soft cushions and rugs scattered across the floor. "Please, be welcome in my home. What I have is yours."

Peterion held his hand against his chest as he inclined his head. "May your home be blessed and the Lady watch over you," he replied, and a glissade of happiness stirred the air.

The woman jerked in surprise, her face transforming into a joyful smile. Her eyes glistened with sudden tears. "It has been too long since I last heard the Lady's greeting. Lady be welcome. Please, enter and be welcome."

Jerrol did as he was told and followed the woman out the back of her home into a small, shaded courtyard. Slats of wood criss-crossed the open space. Greenery curled around the wooden slats, and purple blossoms hung like delicate lanterns, brushing the Sentinal's hair if they didn't duck low enough. A gap was left in the middle over a small fire pit, dug shallowly in the hard ground. More colourful cushions were scattered on the floor.

"Please sit." She swung a pot over the coals and stoked up the fire. The woman moved her gaze to Birlerion. "And what happened to you?"

"A short sojourn in the Ramila slave pen," Birlerion said with a slow smile.

The woman tutted. "I have something for those bruises. That must hurt. I am Erissia, a town Elder and sometime healer." She rummaged in a small box by the wall and almost pounced on Birlerion, as if she expected him to run away. She smeared a salve over his bruises and his lip. "Il Queron has been here since the time of the Lady; an old town forgotten by many; off the beaten track, now. Few visitors stop here, usually only when they're lost or very lucky." She scowled at Birlerion. "Are there more bruises under those robes?"

"The Lady guides our steps. We are on our way to Mistra to hear the Speaker. My name is Jerrolion. This is Peterion, and you're treating Birlerion." Jerrol introduced them, grinning as Birlerion fended her off, insisting he was fine.

"Jerrolion," Erissia repeated, leaving Birlerion be. "Peterion, Birlerion. Ancient names that remind me of the Lady. She has been absent. People haven't paid attention; they've forgotten what they should have remembered." She cocked her head like an inquisitive bird. "And yet here you are, walking the path of the Lady, bringing the wind of change." She poured the hot water into a jug, and the aroma of mint tea filled the air. "To the north of us, there is a place where the land flattens out and the dunes are compacted into hard, solid rock. The air is stifling, enough to persuade most travellers not to venture in that direction.

"It leads to the salt flats. On occasion, I go to collect the salts—they are useful—and we often trade it. But apart from that, the lands are barren, empty, bare." She poured the fragrant liquid into small cups and continued talking as she handed them round. "The heat shimmers in the air, confusing the mind; people think they see things, hear things that aren't there. People get confused and disappear. The area is avoided; no one goes there anymore."

Peterion sipped the refreshing liquid, closing his eyes as he inhaled.

Jerrol watched the woman. "And you are telling us because…?"

"Because, there were once people like you walking these sands, worshipping at this temple, protecting our people. The waters ran and irrigated our fields. People visited to trade and share news. Our oasis has shrunk year on year. This village is dwindling to dust, though no one will listen when you tell them." Erissia snorted. "How righteous are the blind. They root around in the parched land and wonder why nothing grows. They listen to the words of ignorant men and ignore the voices on the wind."

"The voices on the wind?"

"Listen carefully and you will hear them. Early dawn is best, before the distractions of the villagers begin. They are good people, but very loud. They think everyone is deaf and, as the sands are empty, they believe there is no one to disturb."

Peterion spoke, his voice soft as a desert breeze. "The waters are sinking as they wear away the rock. They sink deeper, making it more difficult to reach. The land struggles, too. She tries to amend the flow, but she is thwarted, her attention diverted."

Erissia stared at him in wonder. "How do you know?" she whispered.

"Sentinal Peterion has been watching over you for thousands of years," Jerrol said.

"Sentinal?"

Jerrol grinned. "Yes, I was considering how widely we should share that detail."

Erissia laughed. "It will be across Terolia within a few days. Hot gossip like that? No one would be able to resist. The return of the Sentinals!" She gazed at Peterion, her eyes sparkling. "At last, the Lady is watching."

"I would prefer to keep it quiet for now. Tell me what's happening with the Families," Jerrol asked.

She glanced at him. "You speak for the Sentinal?"

"He speaks for all Sentinals," Birlerion said.

"The Families?" Jerrol prompted as Erissia gasped. She stared at Jerrol as if memorizing his face.

He grinned, and she started, blushing as she realised she had been staring. "The Families are disintegrating. Their children are scattered and their agreements are in tatters. The successions are at risk. Families are arguing over minor infractions and ignoring the larger ones. They trade people for drugs, trinkets, favours. They forget their laws and listen to a stranger who speaks nonsense and follow his teachings without thought."

"And that person is Var'geris?"

"Yes, Var'geris. He did visit here, but he didn't feel it was worth the effort to preach to us. He invited us to Mistra, where we would hear wondrous things and leave enlightened."

"Do you know why he came here?"

"He wanted to see if I was awake," Peterion replied.

"How would he know?" Jerrol asked, surprised.

Peterion shrugged. "He tried to enter; my sentinal denied him. He sent a challenge; flippantly, I think, as if he was still unsure, but I was asleep."

Jerrol turned back to Erissia. "Have you heard him speak?"

"No, only hearsay, but the reports suggest hysteria and adulation."

"Count yourself lucky," Jerrol said. "They are using a mind spell called *Mentiserium*; it removes free thought and will and replaces it with a desire only to do what they tell you."

Erissia sucked in her breath. "That would explain much. It's not only the Families that are suffering; it's the likes of us, as well. I've heard rumours that in the south there are villages that have been deserted. All the people gone; no one knows where. The Families have forgotten their promise. I'd better speak to the Elders; we need to make sure none of our people go to Mistra."

Jerrol laid a hand on her arm. "Are you sure they will believe you?"

"They'd better," she said, rising. "We will eat shortly. Make yourselves comfortable. I won't be long. There's more tea in the pot."

Peterion rose to top up their mugs. He inhaled the aroma deeply. "I missed this," he murmured.

"Addiction is in the air at the moment," Jerrol said, drumming his fingers on his knee. "At least we know Var'geris will be in Mistra when we get there. I want to hear what he has to say."

"Nothing new. They believe they are better than us and should rule; you'll see. I think we need to speak to the Families first; warn them," Birlerion suggested. "The Medera needs to understand what's happening and why."

Jerrol grimaced. "We need proof. Otherwise, they are as likely to believe us as these Elders will. Expect company, gentlemen. I am sure they will want to observe us for themselves."

Erissia returned alone and furious. "They didn't believe me. I told them to pray to the Lady for guidance, because they need it," she said, stomping into her courtyard and thumping down onto a cushion.

Jerrol laughed. "Is it so surprising?"

"I thought better of them. What do you need?"

"A place to sleep tonight and directions to the salt flats early tomorrow morning if possible, then Birlerion and I will visit Mistra. We need a horse for Peterion if there are any for sale."

"No horses, but I expect I can find you a camel. You are all welcome to stay here; it might be a bit crowded, but it's only one night."

"There's room in my sentinal," Peterion offered.

"But you will eat with me first," Erissia said, carefully pulling a long-necked clay container out of the coals of her fire. Elder Erissia dished up her tanjia; a goat stew with spices and fruit which melted in the mouth having been cooked for many hours. It was delicious, and no one wanted to move once they had finished. "Elder Erissia, you have surpassed yourself," Jerrol murmured.

She laughed, handing him a small cup of her astringent coffee. "Here, this will help the digestion."

"Something needs too. I haven't eaten so well since—" he paused. "I can't remember the last time I ate so well."

"Then I am glad you had the chance to eat tonight. You intend to follow the voices tomorrow, don't you?"

"Someone has too. If it is as I suspect, they have been suffering for far too long."

"If you find them, bring them here. We will help them," Erissia promised.

Jerrol nodded. "Depends on what I find."

"What do you intend, my Captain?" Peterion asked.

"I believe some of our missing Sentinals are up past the salt flats. They have been calling, but no one hears them. It's time someone did." Jerrol glanced at Birlerion silently nursing his glass. His eyes were distant and he had said little all evening. Peterion kept trying to include him, but eventually, he gave up. Birlerion knew how to survive in Terolia. He was familiar with the rhythms of the Terolian people. He must have spent time here and had known many people, now all lost. Jerrol hoped a good night's sleep in Peterion's tree would help him lay whatever ghosts were haunting him.

29

SALT FLATS, TEROLIA

They set out early the next morning in the grey pre-dawn. Birlerion had shrugged off their concerns about his health, saying he was fine. His bruises were gone, healed by the sentinal.

When Erissia arrived with a creamy coloured camel Jerrol gave it a wide berth. Its brown, stained teeth tended to snap the air whenever he was near. Peterion laughed and gently cuffed the camel's flank. "Behave," he said, and the camel fluttered its inordinately long eyelashes at him.

After checking their water supplies, Jerrol mounted Zin'talia and led the way out of Il Queron. He turned and stared back at the small village. "Are there any waystones near here, Peterion?"

Peterion stroked his chin as he thought. "There should be one to the west; do you want to circle and find it?"

"I think we should. It may be the only way we will get the Sentinals back here. Are there waystones at each oasis, do you know?"

"Should be. They are usually to the west of the town."

"Very well, let's check." Jerrol headed west to circle the

village. He jerked in the saddle as a chime vibrated through his body. "Was that it?"

Peterion grinned. "What were you expecting? It's a waystone."

"It's not just a waystone. It's a magical portal; a way of travelling instantly between one place and another."

"Yes, though I'm surprised it's still here after all these years."

Jerrol rubbed his face. The sweat was already gathering under his scarves. "Birlerion, tell us what you know about these waystones. Do you think we'll find them across Terolia? It would be much better than riding in this heat."

"Leyandrii sent Guerlaire to make them when the Ascendants began causing so much trouble. A way for us to travel quickly. They should be located across Remargaren. We're bound to find some of them, maybe not all, but you should be able to make them, if needed," Birlerion replied as he led the way out of the village.

"You did it last time." Jerrol scowled up at Peterion. "You've got the bags Erissia wants filling, haven't you?"

"Of course," Peterion huffed from his heights as he urged his camel forward.

Jerrol grinned and moved up beside Birlerion. "So, tell me what you know about the Families. There are six, aren't there? Three greater and three lesser. Why are they separated so?"

Birlerion pursed his lips and then began speaking as his gaze drifted across the sands. "When Terolia was created, there were three prominent Families, who travelled and protected the Land. They were supported by three Families, some of whom settled in the region. I imagine those settlements have grown into villages now. The lesser families created a base to provide support, and they were elevated to the conclave with representation. The conclave is the meeting of all six, but one has never been called. The Families tend to rule their own and leave each Medera or Sodera to get on with things."

"So, the Families never meet to share ideas or information?"

"They never used to, they may do now, though with the rumours we are hearing I doubt it. Meetings only occur if they are in same place at the same time, which doesn't happen as often as you'd think."

"Why not?"

"Although the Families are nomadic, they tend to stick to their own patch. The Solari and Gusarian tended to the north and the grasslands where their herds breed. The Kirshans and Mynerians stay to the south along the Telusion mountains, where they mined for their ores. The Atolea and Kikeran stay to the west of the Kharma ridge around Mistra and down to Livia. I imagine it is much the same today."

"So, if something was happening in one area, the others probably wouldn't know or care. Each Family has become isolated," Jerrol said.

"I don't know. It is possible. Each Family looked after its own and didn't interfere with the others. Ideal situation for someone to drive further division between them, I suppose."

"From what I know, Terolia, Vespiri, Elothia, and Birtoli were once all united under her rule. Her Sentinals were scattered across the lands to represent her, yet they worked together, shared best practices, helped each other so all could reap the benefit. It kept everyone in balance and made sure that no one would benefit more than another. The Families' way seems counter-intuitive. Each family trying to create their own system in isolation, struggling with issues another family may have solved. How would they co-ordinate to protect their borders if necessary?"

They fell silent as the heat intensified. The rolling sand

dunes gave way to flat plains, and as the sun rose, the heat shimmered over the surface, making the land undulate in the distance. Unusual rock formations, sculpted by wind and sand, were scattered across the flat plain, which extended as far as the eye could see. The ground crunched under foot as they crossed salt-encrusted ridges. The silence was interrupted by a growing popping sound, a constant clicking that made Jerrol squint at the empty horizon.

Peterion chuckled. "It's the rocks. The heat makes the water within them expand and the rock pops." He fell silent again and they continued as the sun shone down from a clear blue sky, turning the endless plain into a blinding glare.

Jerrol pulled Zin'talia to a halt and squinted at the horizon. "Did you hear that?"

"What?" Birlerion scanned the empty sands.

"Peterion, head northeast," Jerrol said.

Peterion waved in acknowledgement and his camel veered off to the right.

"What did you hear?" Birlerion asked as he followed.

"I'm not sure," Jerrol replied frowning in concentration. He halted Zin'talia again. *"Did you hear that?"* he asked.

"I don't hear anything," Zin'talia replied.

Jerrol squinted at the horizon. "Is there a ridge up ahead?" he finally asked.

"The central Kharma ridge extends this far. It descends into the salt flats," Birlerion replied as he shaded his eyes.

"That's where we need to go," Jerrol said, leading the way.

As they crossed the flats, the heat became more intense. The Kharma ridge shimmered out of the haze and began to form a more solid horizon, the red stone solidifying along their right flank. As the heat intensified, Jerrol searched for caves that might provide shelter from the midday heat.

Jerrol waved his arm and pointed to the ridge. Peterion

and Birlerion nodded and turned towards the dark opening Jerrol had spotted. They all breathed a sigh of relief as they entered the dim entrance; the temperature dropped sharply as the rock blocked the sun. The cave didn't run very deep, but it was large enough for them all to fit in.

"Rest here," Jerrol croaked, sliding off Zin'talia and unhooking his water bottle and a leather sack. He poured some water in it for Zin'talia and sagged against the rock wall, gulping his tepid water. He revelled in the taste and then leaned back and closed his eyes. Birlerion and Peterion did the same before joining him on the ground. The camel folded its knees and sank to the floor like a swaying barge.

He must have dozed off because he was dreaming. A beautiful woman with rich, brown hair and silver eyes beckoned to him.

"Captain, help us," she whispered. *"We are trapped."*

"Where?"

"In the rock. We were caught in the upheaval of the land. No time to get clear."

"Where? In the ridge?" Jerrol asked.

"The land rose around us. She gave us shelter, but the sands collapsed and buried us. We were trapped and couldn't reach our trees. We have been here too long, and the darkness defeats us. They are going silent."

"Who are going silent?"

"The others. They enter the between, neither here nor there."

"What is your name?"

"Marianille."

"Who?" Jerrol froze in shock.

"Marianille of Greens. You know of me, Captain?"

"I've met your brothers, they search for you. Birlerion is here with me."

Marianille gasped and reached out, tentative but longing. He grabbed her close. *"Marianille, have hope. I am coming and I will find you. I am near; keep calling me, understand? I am following your voice."*

He heard her sharing the news. Other voices joined hers, deeper, slower, more slurred.

Jerrol woke in the dimness of the cave and sat up. Zin'-talia snuffled in the dust and the camel made a spitting noise.

"Birlerion?" he murmured and the Sentinal stirred. He was beside Jerrol before he had a chance to repeat his name.

"Captain? What's the matter?"

"I've found them. Birlerion." Jerrol gripped Birlerion's arm. "I've found your sister, Marianille."

Birlerion stilled and then sighed out a long breath. "Is she alright?"

"Come with me and I'll show you." Jerrol grinned, his eyes bright with excitement. He gripped his sword, and with the Lady's power swirling around him, he reached out with his mind. Birlerion exclaimed beside him and gripped his shoulders.

Jerrol placed his hand on the rock below him and sank his thoughts into it. He struggled to find fissures. He didn't think about what he was doing, he just did it, desperate to find his Sentinals before he lost them. Zig-zagging down below the rock strata and into an open space, he flew through the subterranean cavern and descended further, aware of Birlerion beside him.

"Marianille?"

"Captain?" Her surprise was evident; he was almost on top of her.

"I'm here. How many are you?"

"Eight of us remain, though three are borderline. I'm not sure they will travel."

"Alright, let me think. I have a safe place they can recover. We have trees waiting for them. They will help sustain those who are weak. I just need to get them there."

"Marianille?" Birlerion reached out beside him and Marianille flew into his arms. *"Are you really alright?"* he asked, the concern evident in his voice.

"I'm so glad you're here, Birler. It's been so long. And we've lost so many. Marguerite did what she could, but her presence has faded as we stirred."

Jerrol ignored their reunion as he reached out, thinking of the Sentinal he had rescued and left in Marchwood Watch overseeing the newly planted nursery of sentinal trees.

"Laerille?"

"Captain?" Laerille replied in surprise.

"Are those sentinal seeds we planted ready to receive their companions?"

"Any time. We have twelve saplings ready for you. Lord William's men have been working hard. You should have seen them grow. They truly are a Lady's miracle."

"That is good news. I'm not sure how this is going to work. I have three Sentinals, I think."

Laerille shouted in the distance. "Anterion! Get ready. The Captain is sending us three Sentinals." She came back to him. *"No worries. We're ready."*

"Hold tight. I mean it. I need you to stay connected to me and direct them to the right sapling. I might let go; make sure you don't."

"I've got you, Captain. I won't let go," she said. The confidence in her voice was reassuring.

He left the channel open. *"Marianille?"*

"Captain?"

"Who's first?" he asked.

"The worst off is Tianerille of Marchwood. She is fading fast."

Laerille jerked at the name. She hissed her breath out and called through the link she had with Jerrol. *"Tianer?"*

A small gasp shivered through him, leaving a sense of regret. He latched onto the faint essence, tightened his grip, and pulled. His sword glowed a brilliant blue in the dim cave above the rock strata, casting his empty face into dark shadow.

"Captain? What are you doing?" Birlerion asked as the hum of the sword got louder, vibrating through the rock and him.

Jerrol puffed out a laugh. *"I have no idea. But whatever it is will save my Sentinals."*

"Then whatever you do, do not release your sword. You are pulling an enormous amount of energy, and I would hate for it to be released unexpectedly."

Jerrol laughed out loud at that. *"That's all you're worried about?"*

"Well, I wouldn't like to get stuck down here, either. But in the scheme of things, that doesn't seem important right now."

Jerrol shook with the effort, but Birlerion's calm voice anchored him, and he reached through the Land searching for Laerille. He recognised Marchwood and the pull of one of the sentinal trees drew him up through its roots and he deposited Tianerille into the embrace of the waiting tree. He gasped out loud as he released her, the pain ricocheting through his veins.

"Who's next?"

"Virenion of Marmera."

Virenion reached out, tentative but longing. Jerrol grabbed him close and travelled once more through the Land and pushed the Sentinal into the sapling calling him, cringing as the pain hit him at their separation.

"I need a minute." Jerrol caught his breath as the pain fizzled through his body; he sucked his breath in as his body trembled with the effort. Birlerion gripped his arm and a jolt of energy flushed through him.

"Venterion of Marchwood is next," Marianille called.

Laerille's eagerness was palpable, so he reached one last time. *"Venterion? Laerille is waiting for you."* A wisp of interest stirred the dry air, and he reached, pulling Venterion through and almost shoving him into the humming sapling, which grabbed him from Jerrol. He steeled himself and groaned, releasing the connection to Laerille and folding in on himself. His thoughts pulled back through the rock layers and into his body, severing his contact with Marianille. He slumped on the floor, gasping.

Birlerion groaned beside him. "A bit of warning next time, might be nice," he gasped as he folded over, breathing in deeply against the sudden shock of separation.

"What's happened?" Peterion asked as he hovered over them.

"Just… give me a moment," Jerrol rolled over and stared at the rock ceiling. "What time is it?" he asked as Peterion helped him sit up.

"We've been here for about four chimes, but you've been groaning in your sleep. It sounded like you were in pain."

Jerrol wrapped his arms around his body. "It hurts," he said, closing his eyes as he shuddered. Birlerion wrapped his arms around him, trying to offer comfort. Jerrol relaxed into his embrace and lapsed into an exhausted doze. He was still lying in Birlerion's arms when he awoke. Peterion hovered over them.

Jerrol tried to smile. "I guess Birlerion's told you the news."

"Are they really below us? Trapped under tons of rock?" Peterion asked in disbelief.

"Unfortunately, yes."

"And you have helped three of them travel to Vespiri?"

"As mad as it sounds, yes," Jerrol said with a wry smile.

"Your sword was glowing," Peterion said.

Birlerion smiled. "Leyandrii guides us."

"I transferred the ones in the poorest condition. It was difficult, and I have no idea how to get the others out." Jerrol leaned back against Birlerion and closed his eyes, comforted by his embrace.

"We have enough water for a few more chimes here, then we need to return," Peterion said.

"Then I suppose we'd better get on with it." He frowned at Birlerion. "What did you do down there? I felt a surge from you."

Birlerion grimaced. "I think you'll find it was from your sword."

Jerrol shook his head. "No, it was you, I'm sure of it. Link with me again. I'm tired, and I don't want to get stuck anywhere. Make sure you bring me back."

"Always, Captain."

"Get ready for some surprised visitors," Jerrol said through gritted teeth to Peterion as he sank down through the rock strata taking Birlerion with him.

"Marianille?" he called.

Her relief washed through him as she reached out. *"Captain? Are you alright?"*

"Sorry, it was more difficult than I expected," Jerrol admitted.

"Do we need to do the same thing?"

"Depends on your condition. I know you've only recently awoken, and some of you are in worse condition than others. Although you have been sustained down here, if anyone doesn't have the strength to cope with the desert heat, then, yes. The desert is brutal. You should only come with me if you are strong enough. I could do with some help here in Terolia but not at the expense of a single Sentinal's life. I will not risk it. If you have any doubts, then go to Marchwood and spend some time recuperating. That's an order, if anyone doubted it," he said firmly. Birlerion hovered beside him intent on the conversation.

They heard a quick discussion. The voices were clearer, more alert. *"I think Illiserille should go to Marchwood if the Captain is able. The rest of us can join you,"* Marianille said.

Jerrol called Laerille and she reached out to meet him.

Her weariness tinged his awareness of her. The effort to transfer Sentinals between them was draining all of them. He had no idea how the Lady was helping him, but he was glad she was. *"Last time,"* he murmured.

"We'll take as many Sentinals as you can find," she said brightly, belying her fatigue and embracing Illiserille as Jerrol released her. Jerrol broke the link and gasped as the pain lashed him. Birlerion bolstered him.

"Marianille, I need to talk to all of you. Who's left?"

"Niallerion, Adilion, and Roberion."

"Can everyone hear me?" he asked, spreading his thoughts wide, aware of Birlerion's quiet excitement beside him. His presence was an unseen strength that sustained him.

"Yes, Captain," multiple voices replied.

"Birlerion is with me. He will assist two of you, and I'll take two of you. I can't explain this in words; you'll have to take the thought straight from my mind. You need to latch onto us and not let go. This is what you need to do and this is where you need to arrive." He pushed his instructions to the Sentinals and shared his experience of travelling through the rock.

"I know Leyandrii performed all sorts of miracles, but is that really possible?" A voice sharp with doubt asked.

Birlerion laughed. *"Only you, Niallerion, would question your rescue."*

"Is that you, Birlerion?"

"Yes, it's me. And as I am here with the Captain, it must be possible. I'll help you and Marianille. We'll have plenty of time to talk once we're out of this rock."

"If we must."

Jerrol reached for Adilion and Roberion. *"Ready?"* he asked.

"Ready," their voices overlaid each other.

The Sentinals latched onto him and followed him through the rock strata to their cave. Jerrol and Birlerion awoke, sprawled on the floor and four tall Sentinals appeared before them.

Jerrol levered himself to his feet, smiling in welcome.

"Marianille. Welcome home," he said.

Marianille's silver gaze darted around her as she swirled her thick, brown hair around into a rough knot and held it in place on her head with a slender dagger. "Well, that was an experience," she said as she adjusted her robes, and then she spied Birlerion rising beside Jerrol and she launched herself at him. "Birler, by the Lady, it really is you. You've lost weight," she scolded.

Birlerion hugged her back. "You can't talk, you've lost weight too. I've missed you," he said, his voice thick with emotion.

Marianille wiped away his tears, even as tears streamed down her face. "As I have you. What happened to you?"

Peterion greeted the other Sentinals as Niallerion watched Marianille and Birlerion.

Shrugging, Birlerion hugged her again as if trying to convince himself she was real. "It was chaos at the end. I awoke in my sentinal in Vespers. Versillion is in Greens, and Tagerill in Deepwater. Both are awake and well."

"Thank the Lady. And Ma and Pa and Penner?"

Birlerion hid his face in her neck and rocked her.

"Birlerion? What happened to them?"

"I'm sorry, Marianille," Jerrol began.

"No, I'll tell them." Birlerion took a deep breath. "We were asleep for a long time. Centuries. Leyandrii encased some of us in trees which sustained us in our slumber. Our families are long gone, having lived their lives. We walk in a very different Remargaren." He stared at the other Sentinals, his silver eyes gleaming. "When Leyandrii destroyed the Bloodstone and banished all magic, she banished herself and Guerlaire with it. She no longer walks this land, and I don't think Marguerite is aware we've woken. It's been three thousand years and the world is a very different place."

Jerrol inspected the three men standing opposite him. Although their faces tightened not one of them spoke. They looked tired, jaded even. As if life had been slowly drained out them over the centuries. Two had the deep brown skin of the Terolians, in comparison the third man, was pale and sickly looking. They all wore long, desert robes, shimmering silvery green in the dim light. The swords that hung on their belts were more curved and were much lighter than the broadswords the Vespiri Sentinals carried.

Without their trees to protect and sustain them, he was amazed they had survived as well as they had. Marianille was the most vivacious, but he was sure that was due to the excitement at seeing her brother. She was as thin as Niallerion, who looked like he might fade away. He wondered if he ought to offer to transfer them to Marchwood and the sentinal trees waiting for them.

Jerrol took a deep breath and spoke. "Although the Lady no longer walks in our land, she is still present, and she still has need of us. She has claimed her Captain. I am Jerrolion. Captain of the Lady's Guard."

"I am Adilion of Berbera." The younger dark-skinned man with blue-black curly hair introduced himself. His silver eyes glinted with interest as he looked around the cave.

"Niallerion of Vespers." The youngest Sentinal said. He was thin and gaunt, with busy fingers that flicked the strap holding his sword as if it wasn't quite right.

"Roberion of Selir," the third man said. He was broad-shouldered and slightly shorter than the others. Jerrol thought he was the oldest, though it was just an impression.

"Marianille of Greens." Marianille said from her brother's embrace. She seemed reluctant to let go of him.

"Welcome, please make yourselves comfortable. I'm not

sure where you were expecting to appear, but we are about four chimes ride north of Il Queron."

Peterion handed around the water canteen.

"Considering it seemed like there was little hope of ever coming out, anywhere is good," Roberion said, his voice gruff.

Jerrol smiled in sympathy. "How did you all end up here? I thought Marianille and Niallerion were based in Vespers."

Niallerion grimaced. "As Birlerion said, it was chaos at the end. The Land was folding in on herself. I think this location was the only solid one in the area and she dumped us all together. Easier for her to sustain us, I guess. She was very apologetic."

"Apologetic?"

"Yes, Marguerite was angry. The Ascendants were causing her severe pain. They were messing with her structure, diverting water, digging deep shafts into her rock, changing her landscape. I think she'd had enough. Some of the changes triggered the volcanoes along the Telusion ranges. She was having to deal with all sorts of problems and trying to save as many of her sister's people as she could."

"The Telusion ranges? Birlerion mentioned them as well. I've been searching for them. You'll have to tell me what you know about them."

"Yes, Captain."

"Well, it seems history is trying to repeat itself. The descendants of the Ascendants think they can do it again. They tried to overthrow the King of Vespiri and fortunately failed. They are now trying to destabilise the ruling families in Terolia and have nearly succeeded. We are on a mission to stabilise the region. The Families are under siege, though they don't realise it yet. We are about to go and listen to one of the Ascendants speak in Mistra. It will be interesting to hear what he has to say. Will you accompany us?"

"Captain, you have but to command," Adilion said.

"Are you sure? You don't need time to adjust? Lady Leyandrii encased each of her guards into a sentinal tree. You haven't had that. The Lady's Guardians have sustained them for the last three thousand years. Not all trees survived, so I planted twelve saplings in Marchwood. Four are now populated with your friends. There are trees awaiting you in Marchwood Watch if you need time to recuperate. After all, you have suffered much and a lot has changed in three thousand years. Remargaren will not look as you remembered it."

The Sentinals exchanged serious glances, and then Marianille shrugged. "Birlerion looks the same, so some things haven't changed. We've slept long enough, it's time we lived again." She smiled at Birlerion and he grinned at her in return and Jerrol left them to reacquaint. The Sentinals huddled round, slapping Birlerion on the shoulder, and Birlerion hugged each of them in turn.

Walking over to Zin'talia, Jerrol sagged to the floor. *"Now we have to figure out how to get them back to Il Queron,"* he said.

"Could you not help them walk through rock again and come out at Il Queron?"

"I'm not sure I could take them that far, safely. And they certainly can't walk all the way back to Il Queron in this heat." Jerrol raised his voice. "Roberion, is there a waystone near here, do you know?"

Roberion rose and walked over to Jerrol, shaking his head. "No, Captain. There used to be one in Fuertes, but that is leagues over the other side of the ridge. There is nothing between here and the sea." He faltered. "At least, there wasn't. There were no towns nearby, so no reason for a waystone."

"Can we create one?" Jerrol asked, hopefully. "Niallerion. Can you explain to me how to create a waystone? Birlerion tried, but he couldn't explain it, so I don't know how to create one."

Niallerion considered him. "Captain Guerlaire created the waystones at the Lady's behest. You have the sword, I see. As you are the Captain, in theory, you should be able to make them. Captain Guerlaire would skim the directional particles from the atmosphere and centre them into his chosen beacon."

"He would do what?" Jerrol asked.

"It's not as hard as it sounds. You have his sword so it should be possible. Swing the sword in an arc and the particles will gravitate to the sword. Then, when you thrust the sword into the rock, the particles will coalesce around the point and crystallise in the middle of it." He paused to take a breath, not used to speaking so much. "That becomes the beacon. It is multi-directional, so you can travel in any direction you wish, as long as there is another waystone open at the other end."

"I'll take your word for it," Jerrol said, offering a silent prayer to the Lady.

"Let's try it," Niallerion suggested.

"If this works, I owe you a beer."

"I look forward to collecting it, Captain."

Jerrol strode out of the cave and into the late afternoon sun, followed by his Sentinals. They watched him casting about for a likely rock, and then he unsheathed his sword and waved it above his head before taking a deep breath and plunging the sword point into it.

A blinding flash lit the sky, and a shimmering chime echoed in the scorching air. Jerrol stood before a newly created waystone. He gaped at it in amazement before turning back to the Sentinals, a wide grin on his face. "It worked," he said, the surprise in his voice making the Sentinals smile.

"Of course it worked. You are the Captain." Roberion laughed, thumping Jerrol's shoulder in celebration.

"I suppose I'd better test it," Jerrol said, staring at the rock thoughtfully.

"Maybe one of *us* should test it, Captain. We can't afford to lose you," Marianille suggested, staring at the inoffensive rock.

"I can't afford to lose any of you," Jerrol protested.

"There are more of us and only one of you," Adilion said as he stepped forward. Before Jerrol could protest, he shimmered and disappeared only to return immediately, stepping out of thin air. He grinned. "It worked."

Jerrol breathed out in relief, trying to calm his sudden panic. "Thank goodness. I owe Niallerion a beer. Don't let me forget."

Niallerion laughed. "I won't let you forget, don't worry."

"The way to Il Queron is open," Jerrol said with a smile. "Let's get the horses. Peterion, did you collect the salts for Erissia?"

"Yes, Captain, the sacks are all loaded."

"Ok, let's go, then."

Chapterhouse, Old Vespers

Liliian sat at her desk, reading the message from Torsion and knew that they would have to send more resources up to the Watch Towers. The history that was hidden within those towers would be equivalent to the knowledge lost below them in the catacombs, but now was not the time. She was busy searching for whatever she could find about the guardians to help Jerrol.

She sat back, considering. Jerrol had been concerned about the Watch Towers; worried the King would not protect them fast enough. Maybe it was time—but to send Taelia?

She read over Torsion's message again. He explicitly asked for Taelia and her ability to translate the ancient's texts; it would be best to send her, especially if he had documents that needed explaining, which was more than they had found here in Old Vespers.

She rose and descended the stairs, pausing at her assistant's desk to ask, "Is Taelia down in the new catacomb, do you know?"

"No, I believe she was in her office this morning with Mary. They were talking about excavating the next level down," he replied.

Liliian nodded her thanks as she left his office. She found them in Taelia's office as expected. She tapped lightly on the door as she hovered outside. Mary looked up and whispered, "It's the Deane."

Taelia raised her head. "Deane, please join us. We were discussing the plans to open the room below the one Jerrol found. We've about finished with the upper room."

"Well, it will have to wait, because you've been re-assigned to the Watch Towers. Scholar Torsion has found some texts he needs help translating."

Taelia's face blanked briefly before a look of caution spread over her face. "Scholar Torsion requested me?"

"Yes, he's found some ancient texts similar to those found in the sub-chamber and he needs your help to translate. I think it's important we take the opportunity to find out what we can from the Watch Towers, and Commander Haven was very interested in them."

"True," Taelia considered a moment. "I think, maybe someone else ought to go. I'm not comfortable going up to the towers with only Torsion and soldiers around."

"Torsion won't hurt you. And your status as a scholar would mean you wouldn't mix with the guards at all."

Taelia flushed. "Umm, Torsion misunderstood out relationship, Deane. I don't want to raise his hopes unnecessarily."

"Mary, would you give Taelia and I a moment?" Lillian asked as she observed Taelia's heated face.

"Of course, Deane." Mary bobbed her head and left.

"What happened?" Liliian demanded.

Taelia flapped her hands. "Nothing, he just thought we were closer friends than we are. He wanted me to go with him to the Towers, to be his companion, but I made it clear that's not how I view our friendship. He didn't take it very well."

"Why didn't you tell me?"

"Nothing happened, Jerrol saw to that. Torsion was very apologetic and I didn't want to besmirch his name over a misunderstanding. We *have* been friends for a long time."

"When was Jerrol here?"

"I'm not sure. One minute he was telling Torsion to stop, and the next he was gone. But it was enough. I didn't want to embarrass Torsion further."

"Don't keep things like this to yourself. I can't deal with it, if you don't tell me."

"I'm sorry, Deane."

Liliian sighed. "In light of this maybe it is better you don't go. I'll find someone else."

"It's not fair. I should be able to go. The history in the Towers is important, and I am the right person to send, only I'm not sure I'd be comfortable alone with Torsion."

"I understand. Let me consider what can be done, maybe I'll recall Torsion to explain himself and send someone else with you. We might find a way."

"Thank you, Deane, I would like to help Jerrol, if I can."

30

IL QUERON, TEROLIA

Jerrol stepped into the brilliant sunshine in Il Queron and continued walking, leading Zin'talia away from the waystone. Jerrol turned, and in quick succession, Adilion arrived followed by the other Sentinals, all with broad grins on their faces as they drank in the sights of Il Queron before them.

"We're truly here," Marianille whispered, shading her eyes. Peterion and his camel arrived last.

"Welcome to Il Queron," Jerrol said.

The town was much busier than when he'd last seen it. The evening market stalls were piled with colourful fruits or swathes of material, with people happily haggling. The café was open, the aroma of the thick, rich coffee drifting on the dusty air and teasing Sentinal noses long resigned to the smell of dirt and stone.

Rickety chairs held grey-bearded men arguing amiably over board games or cards. They gradually noticed the newcomers and silence fell over the square as the people gaped at the tall Sentinals striding down the street towards the temple.

Erissia came out of the temple accompanied by an older man dressed in cream robes and stood grinning on the temple steps.

"Captain Jerrol, this is Elder Mal'em. He is the head of our council."

"It's a pleasure to meet you, sir," Jerrol said.

The Elder stared at them wide-eyed as he called for his manservant to take the animals in hand.

"A moment, if you please," Jerrol murmured as he followed the excited Sentinals into the temple. Mal'em nodded and hovered in the doorway.

Jerrol knelt at the altar and gave heartfelt thanks for the Lady's assistance in finding the Sentinals and bringing them here. The Sentinals knelt around him, and they sighed in contentment as happiness filled the air.

"I thank you, my Captain. Well done," her words whispered in his ear. *"Welcome home, my Sentinals."* Leyandrii's voice drifted on the air, casting a benediction individually on each Sentinal.

Jerrol rose and returned to speak to the Elder. "The Lady is waiting for you," he said as he ushered the Elder into the temple. "Go on. Don't keep her waiting."

Mal'em slowly walked up to the altar and knelt. He bent his head and froze at the soft chuckle in his ear. *"Still so stiff, Mal'em? When will you learn to relax in my home?"*

"My Lady?"

"Your vigilance will be rewarded. Stay strong. You will be tested further, but know that I am always with you," and she was gone.

Mal'em rose, breathless. The Sentinals rising beside him wore the same expression of wonder and amazement.

"You were right," Mal'em said as he reached Jerrol. He grinned foolishly.

"Erissia said she has been cooking another tanjia for us. Lamb, I believe; in expectation of our arrival. She has gone ahead to prepare. Let us join her," Jerrol said as he led the way to Erissia's home. They entered her courtyard with the ceiling made of green vines and purple blooms. The sweet aroma from the blossoms perfumed the air.

"What a lovely scent," Marianille exclaimed as she entered the room. "How lovely." She gazed at the colourful rugs and cushions and the green and purple ceiling. "Colour," she said in amazement and collapsed into the pile of cushions with glee.

"Please be welcome in my home. May the Lady bless you all." Erissia said as she arrived behind them. She hurried up to Jerrol and hugged him. "You found them; you are so clever, Captain Jerrolion, and Peterion remembered my salts."

"We would never have found them if you hadn't told us where to look," Jerrol replied with a slight smile.

"Then we are all clever," she said agreeably, tucking her arm in his. "Introduce us, please."

"The young lady sprawled in the cushions is Marianille of Greens."

Marianille laughed and stood. "My apologies. This is such a beautiful room. Elder Erissia, Elder Mal'em. It's a pleasure to meet you."

"A lady of discernment I see. Welcome," Erissia replied.

"This young man is Adilion of Berbera." Adilion bowed, grinning, as Jerrol continued around the group. "Niallerion of Vespers, Roberion of Selir, and Birlerion of Greens."

"Welcome all. You come from far and wide; we must show you a true Terolian evening," Mal'em said with a wide smile.

"Please be seated, relax. You are all so tall, towering over me. Sit," Erissia insisted. She pushed a nervous young woman forward with a tray of glasses. "We have fresh orange or pineapple juice."

"Orange?" Roberion sat up. "Orange?" he repeated, eyes bright.

"No wine tonight. They are going to have a sensory overload as it is," Jerrol murmured for Erissia's ears only.

"I think you may be right," she agreed, smiling. "They are all so happy."

"Wouldn't you be? After being encased in stone for three thousand years with your friends dying around you."

"We don't forget just because we have a moment of happiness. Relax, enjoy their enthusiasm for life, their appreciation of the things we take for granted. Savour it; it is a gift from the Lady."

"Wise as always," Jerrol murmured as he moved to drop onto a bright red cushion next to a grinning Adilion. Erissia left the courtyard, returning with a tray of flatbreads and dips. Jerrol stretched his legs out and sighed in contentment as the Sentinals tried everything.

The evening progressed. The tanjia was exclaimed over, consumed, and left them all full and sleepy. Mal'em and Erissia tactfully retired early, after Peterion assured them his sentinal had room for all. Erissia lit a large lantern, placed it on the table, and left.

Roberion turned to Birlerion. "Tell us what happened. You were there beside the Lady. What did she do?"

Birlerion stared around their intent faces, his face taut. "I don't know what she did," he replied, his voice low. "The Lady called. I responded. But when Guerlaire broke cover, the Ascendants attacked. I only remember falling; I don't remember much else." He stared at them, but Jerrol thought it was as if he didn't see them at all. He was searching his memories; his face paled and his mouth tightened, whatever he remembered didn't reassure him.

"The Lady told you to hold true. She believes in you, trusts you. You did what she asked," Jerrol said, knowing it was true. "Maybe she is protecting you? You keep saying it was chaos at the end. Maybe it is better you don't remember."

Birlerion's face eased at the suggestion, and Marianille gave him a sympathetic hug as the Sentinals nodded in agreement, murmuring words of encouragement. Jerrol watched as they all tried to reassure Birlerion.

"Tell us about yourself, Captain, and how you managed to get a Darian." Roberion's deep voice changed the subject.

Adilion shifted and cast a concerned glance at Birlerion.

"Me? What do you want to know?" Jerrol replied, stirring on his cushions. He had almost been asleep.

"Everything."

Jerrol laughed. "There's not a lot to tell. I grew up in Stoneford. My father was a King's Guard. My mother died when I was born. I never knew her. My father died when I was about six, out on border patrol, so the keep fostered me. You could say I grew up in those stone walls, underfoot most of the time in the stables until a new stablemaster kicked me out." He eased his shoulders slightly in memory and continued.

"Fortunately, a King's Ranger stopped by and reinstated me. He sponsored me into the rangers. My friend Torsion, a scholar, introduced me to the Chapterhouse. I studied for a couple of years until I was old enough to join the rangers, and I've been in the rangers ever since, doing whatever the king needed doing.

"Spent the last few months putting out fires in Vespiri, and met my Darian on the road. I believe the Lady sent her when I was in dire need, and she's stayed ever since. Then the king received a request for help from Terolia, and he sent me over to find out what was going on.

"The Ascendants seem to be set on destabilising Terolia. They have caused dissension in the Families and are enspelling people to do their bidding. And so, we are here to stop them, and that's about it." Jerrol grinned at the listening Sentinals.

"What he didn't say is that he saved the king's life, twice. He put down an attempted coup by the Chancellor of Vespiri and is also the Commander of the King's Justice," Birlerion added, a trace of his usual assurance in his voice.

"It wasn't just me," Jerrol replied.

"Yeah, but you were the catalyst. They would have succeeded if you hadn't been there, and you know it."

"Maybe. I expect the Lady's Captain will always be in the middle of whatever is happening."

"Captain, what do you need of us?" Niallerion asked.

"Enjoy tonight and tomorrow. Acclimatise to the new Terolia. Have a bath. The day after, we leave for Mistra and a confrontation with the Ascendants, I expect."

"As you command Captain. In that case," Roberion levered himself to his feet. "I will claim the bathhouse first." He left the courtyard, eyes gleaming with anticipation.

Marianille laughed. "He has missed the baths. We'll never get him out."

"What have you missed, Marianille? Tell me a little about yourself."

Marianille pouted. "You should be asking Roberion. He asked the question of you."

"Ah, but I know he likes baths." Jerrol smiled lazily. "All I know about you is that you are Birlerion's sister."

"That's more than you know about the others. I'm sure you didn't know that Roberion is a sailor, for example, hence his love of water," she said with a fond smile.

"I didn't. I'll catch up with him tomorrow when he is out of the bath. Ladies first."

"Oh, all right. As you know I'm from Greens and have four brothers." She faltered. "Three brothers, I suppose."

She grabbed Birlerion's arm. "Versill and Tagerill are alright, aren't they?"

"They are fine. I told you, Versill was in Greens all the time and the Captain woke Tagerill in Stoneford, along with Chryllion and Saerille. We found Serillion in the Grove in Greens."

"Thank goodness," she said and after clearing her throat continued. "I was two years ahead of these youngsters." She grinned at the other Sentinals. "You were all in the same year, weren't you? Graduates of '21?"

"1121, she means," Birlerion interjected. "But yes, we were all in the same year with Tagerill and Serillion."

"Thank the Lady I was well out of it before you came through the Academy. I don't think the rangers were ever the same again," she teased.

"They weren't that bad," Niallerion said. "Made it easier for the rest of us. Birler attracted all the trouble. Not through any fault of yours," he was quick to add as if he thought Birlerion would take offence.

"I think you can squarely lay the blame of that with the Clarys," Marianille said with a frown. "Unfortunately, they thought if you didn't have a blood line with a name to back it up, then they wanted to expel you from the cadets. My father soon dealt with them, though." She hesitated. "Greens won't be the same without them," she said.

"Penner's descendant's still hold Greens," Birlerion said trying to comfort her. "Simeon is the current lord. He's a good lad, Penner did well. His sister Alyssa is taking up the guardianship of Deepwater."

"At least Greens is still there," she murmured.

"It's called Greenswatch now."

"Greenswatch," she repeated, concentrating on pleating Birlerion's sleeve.

"Adilion, neither you, Peterion nor Roberion have family

marks. Why not?" Jerrol asked, in an attempt to steer the conversation onto safer ground.

"When we became Sentinals, we gave up the Families and became one with the Lady. We wear her mark now," Adilion said, raising his chin.

Jerrol nodded. "Makes sense. What was it like in Berbera?"

Adilion rolled his eyes, his curls bouncing as he sat up. "Boring. A small place on the border near East Mayer. Nothing ever happened. You couldn't tell where Terolia ended and Vespiri began. It was all the same. Every day was the same. Couldn't wait to leave for Vespers when the call came. I took to the ranger's life, as if I'd always been part of it. Of course, Birlerion brought all the excitement; the trouble he caused when he first came to Berbera."

"I did no such thing," Birlerion exclaimed, sitting up out of his lounge in the cushions.

"Ha!" Adilion snorted. "A right greenhorn, who proceeded to show us all how to manage in the desert. I'll bet Tiv'erna would say differently. He even let you take his Darian; that's unheard of."

Birlerion hugged a cushion tight and rested his chin on it. "He was a good friend."

Adilion's face fell. "I'm sorry, Birlerion. I didn't think. You must miss them."

"It's in the past; we all have someone we miss," Birlerion replied, and he clamped his lips tight.

"I can't wait to see Tagerill and Serill," Adilion said, changing the subject. "Joining the rangers and then becoming a Sentinal was like being part of a family."

Jerrol nodded. "I know what you mean about joining up. I felt the same. Although I enjoyed my time with the scholars and the skills I learnt were useful, I felt right at home in the rangers. I couldn't see myself doing anything else. Peterion, what about you? Are you from Il Quecron?"

"Yes, though it was much smaller then, barely an outpost. We guarded the pass through the Kharma ridge. It was the shortest route cross country. Otherwise, you had to travel all the way south, virtually to Mistra to go around it. Only other alternative was to sail down the coast to Fuertes, but Roberion could tell you more about that, the waters were rough through the straits."

"Something to check, but I believe the pass is still there. Was it marked on your map, Birlerion?" Jerrol asked.

"Not that I remember, we'll have to look, maybe it was lost in the upheaval."

"Maps don't tend to be very accurate in Terolia," Adilion said. "The sands shift all the time."

Jerrol nodded. "Niallerion, your turn."

Niallerion grinned. "Guerlaire called me an artificer because I always wanted to understand how things worked. I like making things."

"Don't leave anything lying around, Niallerion will dismantle it for you," Birlerion warned with a small smile.

"You can tell us how you made Guerlaire's bridge now," Marianille said. "No reason to keep it secret anymore."

Niallerion shrugged. "Guerlaire did most of it. It was his bridge."

"But still, he had you tinkering with stuff, most days. You must know," Marianille insisted.

"It was his gift to Leyandrii. It's not for me to say how it was made," Niallerion replied.

"And nor should he, Marianille. The not knowing is what made it special," Birlerion said pulling Marianille back down on the cushions.

Niallerion flashed him a smile of thanks.

Jerrol hurried to speak before Marianille could insist.

"The Lady amazes us every day. We should enjoy what she offers. Thank you all for sharing, I appreciate it. Tomorrow relax, get your bearings, the day after we leave for Mistra."

"The Atolea are camped to the south of Mistra. We need to warn them about Var'geris' speech," Birlerion added from his cushion.

"Good point. Very well, there's enough for us to think about. We can plan tomorrow. I am going to retire, and I'll see you all in the morning," Jerrol said as he rose. "May the Lady bless your sleep."

The Sentinals rose as well. "I think it's time we followed the Captain's example," Adilion said as he stood. "Lady's blessings, one and all."

Jerrol allowed the Sentinals the day to explore Il Queron, soothe the towns people out of their suspicions, and generally relax. He called them all together as dusk fell, borrowing Erissia's courtyard again. "Right, Peterion will remain here. The rest of us need to be in Mistra within three days. Var'geris is due to speak on Lady's day."

"Could we not use the waystone?" Adilion asked.

"No, because we don't know where it is, and don't you go trying it out. I don't want to lose you again under a hundred feet of sand and rock, understand?" Jerrol said, glaring at him until he nodded. "You can search for it once we arrive and check it's open. It could be anywhere after all these years."

Adilion grimaced in agreement.

"Mal'em is sourcing us some more camels. Make sure you stock up on water. We'll be camping out in the desert for the night unless we can find the transit post. It tends to move, or so I'm told, so if it is too far out of our route, we will have to give it a miss.

"Once we get to Mistra, I need to speak to Medera Maraine. Birlerion and Adilion will accompany me. I want the rest of you to scout the city, check the mood, find out who is in charge. Adilion, you can search for the waystone after we meet with Maraine, in case we need an escape route back to Il Queron. Il Queron is the only waystone we have apart from the one in the salt flats.

"Make sure you keep a low profile. We don't want to alert anyone to the fact that the Sentinals are waking in Terolia," Jerrol said, though he thought it was already too late.

The Sentinals nodded.

"Very well. Once we've spoken to Maraine, we can plan further. The rendezvous point will be the Atolean camp. Get a couple of hours' sleep if you can. We leave at tenth chime. Peterion recommends we sleep at the height of the day and travel through the night, so that is what we'll do."

They left once night descended and the air cooled. The dull tones of the camel bells echoed into the night as Mal'em waved them off.

31

DESERTS OF TEROLIA

The journey took three days, and they ended up camping in the desert as there was no sign of the transit point.

Jerrol listened to the Sentinals chat as the moon rose and the stars came out. Under that sparkling vista he could have imagined he was back with them in their time, in 1124. Especially when Marianille tripped over the end of a rug and Birlerion created an onoff so she could see what she was doing.

Even Marianille had stood shocked, staring at the silver orb suspended in the air, casting a bright glow over their camp. Her voice was dangerously low as she stood over her brother, hands on hips. "Since when have you been able to do that?"

Birlerion grinned up at her, a glint in his silver eyes. "Since Leyandrii taught me how."

Niallerion reached for it, and Marianille slapped his hand away. "Get your own, that one's mine."

Jerrol couldn't help but laugh at the outraged expression on Niallerion's face.

"Don't you want it understand how it works?" Niallerion asked.

"It's magic, we don't need to understand it," Marianille replied, tapping the orb on and off.

Birlerion swirled his wrist and a second orb appeared. He threw it at Niallerion. "I doubt you'll be able to explain it," he said as Niallerion plucked it out of the air and began to examine it.

"Leyandrii never let me have one," he murmured, his attention already intent on the puzzle.

Birlerion grinned. "That should keep him quiet until we get back to Vespiri."

"But what is it made of?" Jerrol asked, mesmerised by the glowing light.

"Pure magical energy. It will drain over time, and then it would have to be recharged. Leyandrii and Marguerite used to make them for the palace, or for the scholars at the Chapterhouse when they had time."

Adilion peered over Niallerion's shoulder. "They are quite rare. I've never seen one."

"Leyandrii's were gold," Niallerion said. "The light was much softer."

"Don't ask me why mine are silver, because I have no idea, they just are," Birlerion said before Niallerion could voice the thought.

Marianille laughed at Niallerion, plucked the orb out of the air and sat next to her brother. He wrapped an arm around her shoulders and she leaned against him. "What were you doing to have so much excess energy, brother mine?"

"Whatever Leyandrii asked of me," he murmured in reply.

"You weren't on the raids with Tage and Serillion," Niallerion said frowning at the onoff. "This thing doesn't have any seams; you can't get in it."

"I told you it's magical energy."

"What was the purpose of the raids?" Jerrol asked, smiling as Niallerion rotated the orb searching for a way in.

"The Ascendants kept building out these crystals arrays, a way of focusing their power," Niallerion explained. "It made them much stronger, able to do a lot damage. Leyandrii could sense where they were by the lack of feedback. She called it dead space, as if it wasn't there. So Guerlaire would take a unit with him and deal with it, take it out. Tagerill and Serillion went on most of them."

"Now both of them have lots of energy," Birlerion said. "You can see it crackle off them, same with Guerlaire, and you Captain. They had to work it off in the sparring ring."

Niallerion tilted his head. "You can see it?" he asked.

Birlerion nodded.

"Interesting," Niallerion mused, staring at the onoff.

"Why is it interesting?" Marianille asked.

Niallerion shrugged, lifting his gaze to rest on Birlerion. "Oh, nothing."

Jerrol grinned as Marianille huffed. "I doubt there is so much energy around now, with the Veil dampening everything."

"You'd be surprised," Birlerion replied, twisting his wrist, and a blue flicker slid over his skin.

Marianille smoothed her hand over his. "It nips," she said in surprise as the flicker faded.

"Mmm, magic always has a bite," Birlerion said. "That's why Leyandrii took care to contain it." After that, Birlerion would say no more and eventually Niallerion went off to relieve Roberion who was on guard and they all gave up badgering him and settled down to rest.

. . .

They arrived in Mistra late the next day, dusty and tired, none of them having slept well in the suffocating heat.

Birlerion lifted his head, sniffing the air, and veered off towards a barren rocky ridge.

"Where are you going, Birlerion? Mistra is over here," Adilion called, waving his arm in the other direction.

The others trailed up next to him as he sat and stared out at the expanse of golden sea, shifting and glinting in brassy yellows and reds under the relentless sinking sun.

"What's wrong?" Jerrol asked, watching the Sentinals in concern. All their faces had paled to a sickly beige under their scarves.

Birlerion just pointed.

"Birlerion, tell me what's wrong."

"The sea," he said, his voice strained.

"What about it?"

"Mistra was not on the coast. It was many miles inland," he managed to whisper.

"Oh," Jerrol uttered, understanding spreading through him. "I'm sorry," he said, not knowing what else to say. He waited as Adilion dismounted and stared both ways up the coast, peering down over the cliff edge.

Adilion gripped Birlerion as he stared blindly at the other Sentinals, a sheen of tears over his silver eyes. "What of Alora and Tinian?"

Roberion cleared his throat. "It seems Mistra is the new coastline."

Although Jerrol was glad of the sea breeze drying his sweat at last, the Sentinal's expressions made his gut tighten. The shock and dismay at such loss and destruction that must have occurred all those centuries ago, and they hadn't been able to stop it.

Jerrol waited until Birlerion turned his horse away. "It is what it is," Birlerion said, his face carefully calm, and he led the way towards the outskirts of the sprawling coastal town of Mistra.

Zin'talia pulled at her reins as the Atolean camp came into sight. They had circled the town of Mistra, giving the Sentinals time to absorb the changed landscape, and approached the Atolean camp from the south. *"Wait,"* Jerrol thought. *"We haven't been invited in yet."*

"They will let us in, though. I am a Darian," Zin'talia said.

"What difference does that make?"

"They have to offer hospitality to a Darian. It is the law of the Families."

"Why didn't you say?"

"I thought you knew; anyway, Birlerion or any of the others could have said," she said smugly.

Jerrol gritted his teeth and urged her to the front of the caravan. As she said, the guard took one look at her and bowed them in, though their companions were held at the gate.

"We are together," Jerrol said.

"I am sorry. I cannot allow them to enter without the Medera's permission."

"Very well. Birlerion, set up camp. I'll be out shortly," Jerrol instructed, turning back to the Atolean camp. He allowed Zin'talia to lead him to the water and dismounted, making sure she didn't drink too much. *"You'll give yourself a tummy ache,"* he said, nudging her away and scooping a handful to rinse his face. He shook his robes out, trying to remove as much sand as possible, before handing the reins over to a wizened man, who reverently stroked Zin'talia's neck. It wouldn't take long for everyone to know that a man not of the Family had ridden in on a Darian.

Zin'talia nudged Jerrol. *"Don't be too long. I'll be listening."*

Jerrol approached the large canvas tent in the centre of

the camp. Two heavily armed Atolean's glared at him as he stopped outside the entrance.

"I am Jerrolion, here at the invitation of Maraine, Medera of Atolea."

"Wait," one of the men said, raking him with a keen inspection before ducking under the tent flap.

He waited patiently, counting the number of weapons the remaining guard had stashed about his person. Jerrol idly wondered how many weapons there were that he couldn't see.

"Leave your weapons outside," the returning guard said. Jerrol handed over his daggers and waited to see if they would comment on his sword, but they didn't. He was escorted into an outer chamber. There, he was told to remove his sandals and, barefoot, he was led into the presence of Medera Maraine.

The Medera was a tiny woman. Tightly coiled brown hair sat on the back of her head and sharp brown eyes inspected him from head to foot. Jerrol thought she found him lacking. His lips twitched as he looked down at her. He felt ungainly and clumsy, knowing that was her intent.

She indicated the cushions beside her. "Please sit, Jerrolion of Vespiri?" Her voice was silky smooth, though raised as a question, and he could hear the hint of steel that underlay it. This was not a woman to underestimate.

"Indeed, I am Jerrolion, Commander of the King's Justice, Captain of the Lady's Guard, here at the request of King Benedict in response to your message to him."

Maraine stared at him. "All those titles must be heavy to bear," she said.

"Some more than others, Medera."

"What makes you think I sent a message to King Benedict?"

"I don't think he would send me here if you hadn't, and I

came by way of Ramila and Il Queron, who confirmed the fact that Atolea is the voice that speaks the loudest. I am accompanied by some people you may be interested in meeting, but they were denied entrance without the Medera's word."

"Who did you bring with you to overpower the reservations of the Medera?"

"As the Lady's Captain, I thought you might like to meet Sentinal Adilion of Berbera or maybe accompany me into Mistra to meet Sentinal Kayerille at her post." Jerrol doubted Birlerion would mislead him as to who was in the Mistra sentinal tree, and he had seemed very eager for her to be awakened.

"Sentinals?"

"Yes, I have a story if you are interested in hearing it."

"I can't just walk through Mistra unnoticed." The Medera ignored his offer.

"I am sure the Medera can do whatever she wants."

Maraine snorted. "As if." She clapped her hands and a small child brought in a tray loaded with a silver jug and three mugs; her arms trembled with the weight. The child clumsily placed her burden on the low table beside the Medera and gave her a worried look. "Perfect," the Medera said, and the child flashed her a brilliant smile, her black eyes sparkling before dashing out of the room. "My youngest. She wanted to serve the water before she went to bed. My husband will join us soon. He went to meet your Darian first."

"I understand she has caused quite a stir."

"I think you'll find it's her rider who will cause a bigger stir," a deep voice said from the tent's entrance.

Jerrol made to stand, but the man waved him back down. "Please sit. You youngsters bouncing up and down exhaust me." He eased himself into the chair next to the Medera.

"My joints won't let me lounge on those lovely cushions anymore. If I sat down there, I wouldn't get back up."

"Now, don't go making the young man feel sorry for you," Maraine said as she passed a glass to Jerrol and then her husband. "My Sodera, Viktor, as I am sure you've surmised."

"A pleasure, sir, Jerrolion."

"Jerrolion; now that's an old name." Viktor inspected him intently. "A Sentinal's name," he continued. "Been long overdue."

"The Lady did tell me I was late," Jerrol admitted.

"I'll bet she did." Viktor laughed. "And gave you a Darian to speed you on your way."

"That she did."

Viktor glanced across at Maraine. "Invite his companions in. They should eat with us."

"We number six in total."

"Then you should definitely come within our perimeter. The sands are not safe anymore, though I expect six Sentinals wouldn't need much protection."

Jerrol grimaced. "Sometimes they get a bit eager, especially the younger ones, the enthusiasts. It has been a long time since they held their swords in their hands, and much has changed. But I would prefer to keep them secret for as long as we can."

"Our secret weapons. I like the sound of that," Viktor grinned.

Maraine rose and went to speak to her guards. "They will join us shortly."

"Are you sure you want all of us in here in our dirt?" Jerrol asked.

"It will be fine. It will give the children something to do tomorrow," Maraine replied. "Before they arrive, though, you were right. I did send a message to King Benedict, a fact

I would prefer wasn't bandied about too much. The other Families wouldn't understand. We are reaching a crisis point.

"My family is reasonably secure, but I watch with horror the dis-integration of the Solari, and the Kirshans hold themselves aloof and stir trouble elsewhere. The lesser Families mirror the greater Families." Maraine paused and looked earnestly at Jerrol. "I don't understand it. Families are ignoring the Family law, abandoning their kin. I tried to call a Master Conclave but they ignored me. If we can't resolve our differences internally, then an external force must be brought to bear. They must see sense before they destroy Terolia."

Jerrol leaned forward. "Have you heard much about the Ascendants? The likes of Var'geris and his brother, Ain'uncer?"

"Apart from the histories, you mean?" Maraine glanced at her husband. "No, nothing recently."

"Var'geris is due to speak tomorrow in the central market square in Mistra; that's why I am here. He is an Ascendant, and they are practising something called *Mentiserium*. It is a way of persuading people to do things they wouldn't normally do. A mind spell, if you like. People are coming from all over the region to hear him speak, and they will all be enspelled if we don't stop him; your family included, if they attend."

Maraine gripped her husband's hand. "Is that the root of all this turmoil? Have our Families been enspelled? But surely the Lady would protect us?"

"She will if you ask her. But if you walk away, then you close the door and she can no longer help. People have forgotten the ways of the Lady; what she did to protect us and why. Three thousand years is a long time, and we have forgotten what we should not have. She does not demand worship or obedience, but she will provide love and shelter to those who ask for it." Jerrol stopped speaking, taking a deep breath as a disturbance at the door heralded the arrival of his Sentinals.

Viktor watched Jerrol closely. "You don't have to convince us, lad. We believe you." He met Maraine's eyes. She nodded in agreement and rose as the Sentinals entered.

Any remaining doubt that Maraine or Viktor may have harboured fled at the sight of the four men and one woman, who entered. Uniformly tall and silver-eyed, their appearance shouted 'Sentinal' to those with the eyes to see. They could see the Lady's mark as clearly as if it had been tattooed on their faces.

"Sentinals, please be welcome in our home. Lady bless all who enter," Maraine said, opening her arms wide.

Marianille smiled. "We thank you for your welcome, Medera. May the Lady bless your Family."

They sat around the low table, and the Medera called for more water and glasses.

"Let me introduce everyone," Jerrol said, and he went around the circle giving their names.

"It is an honour to be in such company," Viktor said, inspecting his guests. "I imagine the Lady has called you forth for a reason, and not just to respond to our request?"

"Unfortunately, there is a threat to all of Remargaren." Jerrol replied. "It just happens that the focus is currently on Terolia. A group calling themselves the Ascendants are trying to bring down the Families, so they can rule Terolia. They intend to enspell all your people to follow their rulings without thought. They want to remove free will and replace it with blind obedience."

"But how?" Viktor frowned. "They will not find it so easy. Our warriors are not to be underestimated."

"It is not through force. They preach in the market

square and enspell your mind. You don't even know you are enspelled."

"We have to stop them!" Maraine said, horrified.

Jerrol grinned wryly. "We have to find them first."

"Stopping Var'geris will be a beginning," she said.

"That it will," agreed Jerrol, and the conversation moved on to how they would stop him.

They finally agreed on a plan of action. They would disrupt the speech. Whenever it seemed that there was a command or people seemed enspelled, they would heckle and disrupt the flow, making them start the spell over. If there were enough of them and they kept moving about, they should be able to prevent the spell from ever being completed. People would start to get restless and hopefully begin to disperse. Maraine had sent out an order that none of her family was to attend the speech unless she told them to, and she explained why in detail so that no one could mistake the order.

Jerrol and Adilion slipped out of camp that evening; Adilion to check out the waystone, Jerrol to wake up Kayerille. Birlerion followed silently, a shadow at Jerrol's shoulder. They split up and went their separate ways, Adilion heading off into the desert and Jerrol soon lost in the swirling mass of people taking advantage of the cooler evening air. Zin'talia contentedly muttered in the back of Jerrol's mind as she picked out stalks of sweet grass, her favourite Baliweed. Her soft contentment infected him, helping him relax.

Birlerion's company was an unexpected comfort, easing tight shoulders tensed against expected attacks as they wound their way through the narrow streets. Their stride quickened as Birlerion took the lead, passing open spaces with buzzing cafés oozing people and enticing aromas. He cut through the streets, interspersed with quieter residential areas, as if he knew where he was going, until they reached a quiet square in the older section of the town.

A small fountain graced the centre, and Birlerion paused by the grey stone statue adorning the top. It was weathered and worn and lacking water; his fingers brushed the stone surface as if he knew it. A sentinal tree dwarfed the stone buildings and the small domed temple beside it. Its canopy provided a filter and bathed everything in soft green light. The temple doors were open, the dim interior inviting. Jerrol glanced in briefly but stopped before the tall tree. He laid his hand on the trunk, and a beautiful woman shimmered out of the mist.

"Kayerille, welcome."

"Captain," her husky voice matched an exquisite golden brown complexion framed with thick, lustrous black hair, which trailed down her back. A wickedly curved blade sat on her hip, ornate daggers in her belt. "I have been waiting for you."

"Come, some of your friends are with me. They are eager to see you again."

Her eyes brightened with interest. "Who?" she asked as she stepped out into the street with him. Breathing in the warm spice-scented air, she veered towards the open door of the temple. She saw Birlerion and pulled him towards her with a rich laugh. "Birlerion, I've missed you. I am so glad you are here." She stood back and stared him in the eyes. "You did fine. I said you would." She chuckled. "Ah, Lady's blessings, I've missed this place. I am glad to see it is still here."

Birlerion gripped her shoulders. "I am so sorry, Kayerille, but there is much else that is different now. Time has passed, and your brother, sisters, and Tiv'erna are all gone now; gone as if they never existed. It has been three thousand years; their memories are lost in time as, eventually, our grief will be too."

Kayerille stilled and then shuddered in his arms. "You know, I thought something wasn't right these last few months; awake but not awake, everything just out of reach." Her voice was low, thick with unshed tears. "I should never have asked Tiv'erna to wait." And then the tears did flow, and Birlerion held her.

Jerrol turned his back and watched the street, shielding their privacy as they grieved for a loss that was beyond his comprehension.

Kayerille finally stirred in Birlerion's arms. She lifted her face. "Captain, who else is awake?"

"Peterion is in Il Queron, Tarenion in Ramila. Here with me in Mistra are Marianille, Adilion, Niallerion, and Roberion," Jerrol said as she approached the temple. He waited for her by the door. Birlerion stood beside him, calm and composed, his face unreadable.

She did not take long in the temple; enough time to give thanks and to commune for a moment before she rose and joined them by the door.

"Everything changes," she murmured. "Show me the new Mistra." She tucked her arm through Birlerion's.

Jerrol led the way back through the quieter streets into the busy squares. Kayerille observed everything and in turn, garnered a lot of attention. She smiled brightly as a young man leered at her, her hand resting on her sword. "You could try," she invited, patting her sword. The man's friends laughed and teased, before turning back to their games.

She went quiet as she observed the sparkling bay and the single-masted fishing boats bobbing at their moorings. Bare chested men, tanned ebony by the sun, worked on the nets and coiled ropes. Their cheerful voices floated on the warm breeze that eddied around them, and Kayerille shook herself and turned away.

Jerrol led her into the Atolean camp and the guards waved them through. Returning from scouting the eastern edges of the town, Adilion grinned widely at Kayerille. "My pretty, awake at last. Give us a hug."

"Adilion," she cried in delight, accepting the hug enthusiastically.

"Captain, the waystone is open. It's actually nearer Kayerille's sentinal, just on the outskirts. To the east."

"Excellent, I'm sure we will need it at some point. Come, let's introduce Kayerille to the Medera," Jerrol said, leading the way to the tent. Kayerille followed, her gaze flickering around the encampment as if searching for something or someone.

Maraine welcomed Kayerille to her tent and watched in delight as the Sentinals were reacquainted. The evening meal served under the clear night sky by the light of many gleaming lamps, was loud as Maraine introduced her family and many Atoleans vied to sit next to a Sentinal, especially Marianille and Kayerille, who fended them off, laughing.

Kayerille breathed a sigh of relief as the meal finished, and they returned to the relative privacy of the Medera's tent. It had been an overwhelming homecoming, one that each Sentinal had braced themselves for in their own way; the rich food, the excitable company, the heady scents. It was the same but different.

Jerrol kept an eye on Birlerion, who seemed to grow quieter as the Atoleans got rowdier, and by the end of the night, he excused himself and disappeared.

32

MISTRA, TEROLIA

Kayerille and Adilion collapsed onto the cushions in the Medera's tent and laughed at themselves. "Who would have thought we'd be spending the evening in the Atolean encampment?"

"Where has everyone else gone?" Jerrol asked.

"Niallerion was trying to persuade Marianille to dance, though he was also eyeing the wagons, so maybe he was angling for an introduction so he could inspect how they worked. Birlerion was trying to teach the youngsters how to make a sling. Did you know he has a wicked aim with a sling?" Adilion asked, suddenly diverted. "Roberion, walked down to the harbour."

Kayerille smiled, her eyes distant. "Birlerion taught my sister to make a sling so she could teach the other children. A way for her to make friends."

"Jerrol?" Zin'talia whispered a catch in her voice, and Jerrol sat up. *"He's crying."*

"Who is?"

"Birlerion. He was visiting the horses when he saw a Darian mare and he just collapsed."

"Leave him be," the Medera said, her voice soft. "He is grieving."

Jerrol glanced at her. Birlerion never cried; even with Kayerille, he had been stony-faced but dry-eyed.

The Medera's eyes widened as her Darian explained. "He grieves the loss of his Darian."

Adilion stiffened. "Ascendants' balls. I never thought."

"Never thought what?" Jerrol asked as Adilion fell silent.

"Kafinee," he said at last. "She was his Darian. They were inseparable. You know what it's like having a Darian, being that close to one another. Imagine having that ripped away? I've been told it's like losing a piece of your soul."

Jerrol's stomach roiled just at the thought of losing Zin'talia.

"I'm here; you won't lose me," she reassured him instantly.

"With so many Darians around, it must be excruciating." Adilion winced in sympathy.

"That explains why he avoids me all the time," Zin'talia murmured.

"Kafinee is an unusual name for a Darian," Maraine said with a sad smile, her eyes distant as she listened to her own Darian.

"He didn't know she was a Darian when he first got her. He named her Kafinee for the colour of her coat. Turned out it was very close to her true name, Kaf'enir. It was our second year at the academy; he and Tagerill arrived with their horses, as all students do. Edril, a cadet from Tesene, over on the east coast, said she must have Darian bloodlines as she understood what Birler wanted before he even asked it of her. Still, it wasn't until Birler was posted to East Mayer on the borders with Terolia that we found out she was a true Darian."

Adilion flicked a careful glance at Kayerille. "Tiv'erna, a

son of the Atolea was out on patrol. They came to check who was riding a Darian."

"Tiv'erna, son of Janis and Arkan," the Medera murmured and happened to look across at Kayerille. "Oh," she said, understanding dawning on her face. "Kayer, oh my dear, I am so sorry," and then she stood, her face paling as her knowledge of the Family history retrieved the name. "And Birler." She looked at her Sodera. "A son of the Atolea."

Kayerille stiffened. "I doubt he believes that anymore."

Maraine stared across the room. "Once a son, always a son. Especially when it is scribed in the book of the Family for all to remember."

"You should tell him," Viktor said.

"Tell him what?" Jerrol asked, worried there was more bad news for Birlerion.

"I think we should tell him first." Maraine patted his knee. "Don't look so worried. For once, it is a little good news." She caught Kayerille's eye. "Why don't you go and find him, my dear. I expect you understand his loss more than most."

Kayerille rose and left the tent.

She found Birlerion surrounded by Darians, his face hidden in the mane of a particularly elegant, creamy brown coloured mare. Kayerille faltered, tears springing into her eyes as her throat tightened, and she swallowed the lump that threatened to take root. He looked so young and vulnerable. The man who had saved her life.

Wordlessly, she pushed the Darians out of the way and pulled him into her arms. She held him just as he had held her, offering comfort when there was little else to offer.

. . .

There was silence in the tent for a moment after Kayerille left, and then Maraine let out a deep sigh. "So sad. You can't imagine what they are going through. Sorry, Adilion, what you are *all* going through. It must be just as difficult for you."

Adilion twisted his lips. "Saw it, lived it, breathed it. Birler took to the Families as if he'd been born here." He frowned. "He is quite restrained now, in comparison. He and Tiv'erna were like brothers. Tiv'erna even lent him Kin'eril when Kafinee was too exhausted to continue.

"We were attacked by the Ascendants outside Melila. They had a crystal array in the mountains, which they used to enhance their powers. Birler went into the Telusions and stole the lodestone, preventing the Ascendants from attacking us again. They had already decimated us once. He led them away from us; the only reason we survived."

"Where are the Telusions?" Jerrol asked, knowing there was much more to the story than Adilion was telling.

"What's left of them are on the southern seaboard. In the end, the fire mountain erupted and blew out the top of the mountain. Left a huge crater and little else," Viktor said in his calm voice. "The sea rushed in. A boiling cauldron it was described as a place to be avoided. The land threw up a new mountain range in its place."

"The Ascendants have found more crystals. Do you think they could still be mining those mountains?"

Adilion shrugged. "It's possible."

"The Kirshans patrol that area. We would have heard if any strangers were taking up residence," Maraine said.

"Not necessarily." Birlerion's quiet voice came from the tent entrance. "They use *Mentiserium*. If they can persuade people to leave their homes, they can certainly persuade people to lie about what is happening. If they were in the mountains, you wouldn't know."

Jerrol inspected him keenly. He was pale but composed.

Only his eyes gave him away; deep pools of despair. Jerrol marvelled at the strength he must have to bury his loss so deep that none of them had even suspected.

It was a window into the complex person that was Birlerion. Jerrol barely knew him; every day, he learnt something new, yet he trusted him with his life, implicitly, no matter what Torsion implied. He had proved that trust many times over.

These Sentinals had already lived full lives, and now he was asking them to live another. Well, the Lady was asking, and they had answered without hesitation. If he had known, he would never have agreed to Birlerion coming to Terolia, but then he hadn't asked him. Birlerion had insisted, and he wondered why.

"Birlerion, please accept our apologies for our lack of welcome. Welcome home, son of Atolea," Maraine declared.

Birlerion flushed. "Please, that was a different lifetime. You owe me nothing."

Viktor snorted. "We owe you two life debts; that is hardly nothing."

"Life debts?" Jerrol asked, uncertain if he should pursue this line of conversation. Birlerion looked distinctly uncomfortable.

"Life debts are very rare. Usually, when someone is attacked by a member of the Family while under our protection, the attacker forfeits their life. That life is in payment of the debt because the Family failed. Birler survived an attempt to poison him and then saved the life of his poisoner. Two lives owed and never repaid," Maraine said, her voice quiet.

"He didn't mean it," Birlerion replied. "He deliberately failed in the attempt. It's the only reason I lived; he fought the spell."

"The debt is written in the book, and it is passed down to each generation to fulfil if possible; a reminder that you are owed and our family is your family. I am sorry we didn't make the connection between Birler and Birlerion. We should have."

"Please, it was a long time ago. And there is no Birler anymore."

Viktor tapped his lip as he watched him. "Tiv'erna went to see your father, Lord Warren of Greens."

Birlerion froze, all remaining colour draining from his face. Jerrol tensed. He thought Birlerion might collapse.

"We don't wish to cause you any further distress, but you need to know. Tiv'erna made an agreement with Lord Warren. Each generation, a Darian is delivered to Greenswatch in your memory for Warren and his descendants to use as they wish; an unspoken hope that you would be found; a way to bind our families.

"Lord Warren found Kaf'enir in Vespers and brought her home to Greens. Tiv'erna recorded that Kin'eril covered her; the first of their line."

Birlerion choked, and Kayerille pulled him down beside her. He dropped his head in his hands, hiding his face and leaned into her embrace as she held him close.

"Your Darian awaits you in Greens; a descendant of Kaf'enir and Kin'eril. We wondered why he hadn't bonded; he is waiting for you."

33

VAR'GERIS' SPEECH, MISTRA

Jerrol eased back into the entrance of a narrow alley, which led off Mistra's central market square. Mistra was a sprawling city pockmarked with market squares, providing small clearings where people could congregate. Market stalls sprung up around them, providing a range of wares and tempting aromas. Rows of terraced homes radiated out until another market square appeared, and the process of expansion started all over again. It gave the city an unstructured feel; the buildings haphazardly jostling with shops, no rhyme or reason to the layout.

It was early morning and the crowd was growing as more and more people arrived. There was a murmur of expectation in the air; people were excited. They had been promised a spectacle. Life was generally repetitive; little happened that hadn't been done before, but the arrival of a new face with exciting news to share—that was an event.

The square was full of colour and noise; splashes of bright robes interspersed with duller hues. They waited in excited anticipation, their voices a growing hum.

A raised platform stood at one end, and a tall dark-haired

man in a black robe fussed with some papers. He began to circulate, handing out the papers, which advertised a speech by Var'geris the following week in Marmera, a village to the East. Jerrol tucked the advert in his robe and continued to observe.

His Sentinals were spread out around the perimeter; even Birlerion, who had managed to retrieve his calm composure after his collapse the previous evening. Jerrol didn't know how he managed it. He knew he wouldn't have been able to. It had been an emotional evening for all, and he had retreated to Zin'talia for comfort.

He shook off the memory as Maraine entered the square accompanied by two of her family; a scarf covering her face. A low buzz began in front of the raised platform. The black-robed man started to chant, waving his hands in time. "Var'geris, bring out Var'geris. Var'geris, bring out Var'geris." The people near him began to pick up the chant, and once they'd got their rhythm, the man began to move further into the crowd, encouraging them to join the chant.

By the time Var'geris reached the platform, the people were enthusiastically chanting, and he grinned at the loud welcome. He flapped his hands, palms down, indicating the need for quiet, waiting for silence and enjoying the attention. The crowd gradually settled down. A sea of flushed faces stared up at him.

Jerrol observed Var'geris with interest. He looked much the same as he had when Jerrol had glimpsed him at the Watch Towers; tall, black-haired, stockier than the other Ascendants Jerrol had met, but he had that same air of arrogance. Var'geris began to speak, his voice quiet. The crowd leaned forward, straining to hear him. "We can't hear him," a voice called from the back. "Can you hear him?"

Var'geris raised his voice, still not particularly loud, and a ripple of information spread as the people at the front passed the message back. He's an Ascendant, descended from the original family, who fell as they protected the people from the excesses of the Guardians. The people nodded in agreement; eyes bright. Var'geris' voice increased in volume as he began to expound the virtues of the Ascendants, how they strived to be the best they could be, to look after those who were less fortunate.

"The fate of the Ascendants is in your hands." Var'geris raised his voice. "A family like yours, persecuted for believing that people are more important than the rulers." A low murmur of sympathy rumbled around the square. "Ascendants can help you. They rise to the top because their fate is tied to yours."

"Rise to the top of what?" a coarse voice called out.

"The family is important. Those of the line carry the blood," Var'geris continued, his voice calm and even. "We carry the fate of all of us, but we need you. We are few; you are many. You can help us succeed where our forefathers failed. Join us and become one with us. You want to. You must support those of the pureblood; those who can guide your steps."

"We've already got a family, thanks. Don't think we need yours," someone nearer the front called out. The helper moved in and hustled the heckler out of the crowd. The gap closed. "It is the duty of the family to sustain those who lead. You must obey those who rule by right. To obey and to work."

"The Lady doesn't demand obedience. Why should you?" Jerrol called out, moving as he spoke to throw the attendant off.

A frown of annoyance flitted across Var'geris' face at the constant interruptions. "You must obey and work to help select those who should rise to the top and weed out those who are not true. You want to work: to never slacken, to listen to my voice, to do as I say, to work hard, to work for the betterment of all."

"You sure it's not just for your benefit? Why should we believe you?" a woman shouted.

"We can help you to be the best you can be; to protect you from those who are not pure, if you work and obey. You have an overwhelming need to obey, to sign up now and join us. Come with us. We expect much of you, and you can meet those expectations by listening to me and by obeying and working." Var'geris' voice dropped to a croon.

"I don't think so." Maraine's shout cut through his voice, and people shook themselves and blinked. "I don't know what you are trying to do, or where you want my people to go, but your *Mentiserium* rubbish doesn't work here." She spoke loud and clear. "My people believe in the freedom of the nomads, the strength of the Families, and the shelter of the Lady. Why would they want to obey you? Work for you? Do you want to go and work for a stranger for nothing?" she asked the crowd. "Become slaves to his voice and do what he says? Well, do you?" Her voice whipped through the people and they began to back away.

Var'geris stood mouth agape on his podium.

"Your mind tricks won't work here," she spat. "And don't bother setting your little man on me," she said as Var'geris' eyes flicked to the right. "He is indisposed. Your words are empty and worthless." She turned to the crowd. "All of you, go home. You ought to be ashamed of yourselves. Pray to the Lady for guidance."

Var'geris raised his voice. "You listen to the words of a woman? Follow me and you will be free."

"You threaten the Medera?" a deep voice asked, and the crowd looked more closely at Maraine and then at Var'geris.

"These people are already free. They don't need you for that," Maraine said as the crowd jostled closer. Var'geris glared at her, his face so rigid the cords stood out on his neck. "You'll regret this, woman," he hissed.

Jerrol stepped forward. "No, you'll regret it. You've threatened the Medera, and word will spread. I recommend you leave before you say something else you regret. If you step foot in Mistra again, you won't leave."

Var'geris scowled at Jerrol. His eyes widened as he saw his silver eyes. "Sentinal, you *do* get around. Your days are numbered." He scanned the square, realizing his situation as he took in the mood of the crowd. He retreated. Jerrol followed him until he entered a large brick building behind the slave pens. By the time Jerrol returned to the square and rejoined the Medera, most people had left.

Her eyes were sparkling with anger. "I've never seen such a thing. You were right. I saw them all glazing over. They would have followed him like they would a trail beaten through the sands."

"The Families should spread the word and hound him out of Terolia, prevent him from causing any further damage. Maraine, you need to close those pens down. They are inhumane," Jerrol said, his gaze distracted by a portly man dragging a small child across the square. A thin man fluttered around him, gesticulating wildly. The child struggled in the portly man's grip, wriggling to get free.

Jerrol cursed under his breath as the man tied the child to the post and ripped the clothes off her back. He struck the cringing child with the stick in his hand, and the child screamed. Jerrol dashed across the square and blocked the man as he raised his arm for another strike. The child cowered, weeping hysterically against the post. Jerrol disarmed him and stood between the child and the man. "You will not harm this child."

The man stared at him in surprise, which quickly turned

to outrage. "She is mine. I will do with her as I wish. Get out of my way."

"She is not yours," Jerrol replied.

"Yes, she is. I bought her. She's mine."

"By Terolian law, there is no slavery allowed. Therefore, you can't have bought her," Jerrol insisted.

"Please, kind sir, he misspoke. He meant that he employs the child. He is reprimanding her for stealing," his companion said, tugging at the big man's arm.

The man inspected Jerrol, and, assessing his size, pushed out his chest. "No, I didn't. She's mine. Move out of the way, before I move you."

Jerrol laughed. "You could try."

The man lunged, and Jerrol spun into motion. He yanked the man's head back, holding his dagger tight under his chin as he pressed his knee into his back. A sluggishly bleeding welt marred the man's face.

"I suggest you go and get your money back as there is no slavery in Terolia," Jerrol repeated. "This child does not belong to you; she belongs with her family." He pushed the man away from him and stooped to untie the weeping child.

The man scrambled in the dust and rose blustering threats as he brushed himself down. He watched Jerrol and his eyes narrowed as a couple of guards approached. "Guards," he called, "this man is stealing my property."

The guards hesitated as they watched Jerrol shrug out of the light outer robe he wore over his clothes. He wrapped the child in it and scooped her up.

"Arrest that man for stealing. Chop off his hand. That will teach him," the portly man shouted.

Maraine and Kayerille approached, horrified expressions on their faces, and Jerrol held his tongue. He murmured to the child trembling in his arms.

Kayerille looked the man up and down in disdain. "The child is not yours. There is no slavery allowed in Terolia."

Maraine glared at the guards, noting the Atolean tattoo on their cheeks. "You know slavery is not allowed by Family law. These pens are to be opened and the people released. I expect you to bring the perpetrators of this slave industry before the Atolean family conclave first thing in the morning. Arrest this man for molesting a defenceless child."

The guards saluted. "Yes, Medera." They latched onto the loudly protesting man and marched him out of the square, followed by the ineffective attendant flapping around him.

Jerrol spoke quietly to Birlerion, who arrived to stand behind him. "Find out who that man is and who his agent is. I want them shut down, and be careful, Var'geris is in the tall, red building, and he knows who I am." Birlerion nodded and, waving for Roberion to join him, the two Sentinals left.

Jerrol strode out of the square carrying the child, Kayerille at his back, Maraine and her men beside him. They arrived at the Atolean camp and entered the Medera's tent.

"Maraine," Jerrol said. "Is there any chance your daughter can join us? I think the child will be more reassured with another girl beside her."

Maraine raised shocked eyes. "A girl? He was whipping a girl?"

Jerrol nodded. "Kayerille, stay. Everyone else, can you give us a moment?" he asked, keeping his voice gentle. Jerrol laid the child on the cushions. He made to rise, but her hand gripped his trousers, and he paused. "Maraine and Kayerille will help you. I'll come back when they have treated your wounds."

Big brown eyes peered up at him, searching his face intently. She didn't ask him to promise, but he could tell it was on the tip of her tongue. "I promise I will return within a half chime," he said. She released his trousers.

He returned as promised. Maraine cuddled the child as they watched her youngest daughter, Mir'elle, sort through a bundle of colourful ribbons. Kayerille sprawled on the cushions, trying not scare to the child, and helping to unravel the tangled mess of ribbons.

Jerrol sat opposite and raised an eyebrow at Maraine. Maraine hugged the little girl. "This is Tris'eril of Melila. She's five. Her family were taken from Melila and sold. She says a lot of families were taken."

"It's the past repeating itself," Kayerille said. "My father was one who went to do their bidding, thinking he could earn good money. He never came home. You should ask Birlerion or Adilion about it. They were involved in stopping the Ascendants building the crystal arrays in the mountains."

Jerrol, casting an eye at the children, changed the subject. "Tris'eril, would you like to go home?"

She nodded back at him shyly. Tris'eril had the Kirshan tattoo of the peaked mountain on her cheek.

"Then we will take you home," he promised as he reached for a tangle of ribbons. "Would you like one for your hair?" he asked with a smile. "Which would you like?"

A small finger pointed at a bright red ribbon. "I agree. Good choice." Jerrol began to untangle the ribbons. Tris slid out of Maraine's arms and came to stand beside him. She leaned against his leg, watching his busy fingers. He finally managed to pull her chosen ribbon free, and he handed it to her. She ran it through her fingers then gave it to him and turned her back so he could tie up her curly brown hair. He scraped her hair together high on her head and tied the ribbon tightly.

She shook her hair to make the pony-tail tickle her neck and smiled. Climbing into his lap, she rested her head against his chest and sucked her thumb, watching Mir'elle playing with the other ribbons. Tris'eril giggled at something that Mir'elle said, and Jerrol smiled, relieved she was relaxed enough to laugh.

Another young girl entered the tent, older than Mir'elle but with enough of a likeness to claim family. Maraine smiled. "Ah, here is my elder daughter, Eli'sande. She will show the children where to sleep. Go with Eli'sande, my pet." Maraine coaxed Tris'eril out of Jerrol's lap. "It's time to go to bed. You can share Mir'elle and Eli'sande's room. She hugged the girls and then shooed them out, smiling at Eli'sande in thanks.

Once the children left, her smile faded. "I'll call another Master Conclave; the Families need to be informed of all of this. Atolea cannot solve this on our own. They need to be warned about what is eating away at them from the inside. We all need to clean house." She bit her lip. "I'm not sure they will listen."

"They will listen to the Lady," Jerrol promised. "Just get them together and I will set them straight. If they want to rule, they will listen."

Maraine nodded thoughtfully, watching him. "You have hidden depths, Captain."

"Find the forgotten. Heal the wounded," he said, glancing at Kayerille. "It's a start."

Birlerion's shout warned him as Jerrol walked back to the guest tent with Kayerille. He deflected an arrow that ricocheted past them and raised his sword to block the downwards strike, which would have decapitated him had it connected. The impact of the blow ran up his arm and jarred his neck as he stepped back, absorbing the shock, and he blocked the following strike. Kayerille engaged behind him as more black shapes detached themselves from the shadows.

Jerrol spared a glance and threw one of his daggers. A muffled grunt and one of the shapes fell back. His sword clashed, sparks flying as he parried another blow. Retreating under the frenzied attack, he ducked, spinning. His sword skittered off the man's blade and screeched up its length. Jerrol pressed his advantage, forcing the man back, another dagger in his hand.

He left the man slumping to the ground, and, gripping his bloody dagger in his left hand, he turned to meet the next attack, his sword flickering blue in the evening sunlight. Grimly advancing, he parried one blade and then the next. His blade flowed between his two opponents.

A soft whir passed his ear and one of his opponents flinched. Jerrol took advantage of the distraction and hooked a foot, managing to trip one of them. His sword sliced the air, gleaming red as he spun into the other man, breaking his rhythm. Jerrol dropped to his knees as he rotated, his sword above his head as he slashed across the man's stomach. The man gasped. His hands instinctively grabbed his stomach and his sword fell to the ground as he collapsed.

Jerrol continued his spin and regained his feet, hands wide as he assessed the threat. Kayerille had been joined by Marianille whose Vespirian tactics forced her opponent back, her movements smooth and efficient as she followed the body down, before spinning alert for the next threat. Another body joined the one on the floor near her. Atoleans spilled out from their tents, responding to the sound of fighting, swords at the ready, but the Sentinals were the only ones left standing.

Jerrol scanned the tents, searching for the archer, but he had slipped away unseen. He prepared to assist Kayerille, but she had her man beaten and the Atolean guards pinned him to the ground. Birlerion appeared by his side, breathing heavily, his sling in hand.

Jerrol exhaled. "Thank you."

"You do attract trouble," Birlerion grinned, his eyes bright as he assessed the situation. "Maybe I'll finally lose the accolade of being the troublemaker," he said, gazing at the captured assassin with calculating eyes.

The assassin glared at Jerrol. He spoke three words and laughed as he started to foam at the mouth. His eyes rolled and he collapsed to the ground.

Jerrol took a deep breath as he wiped his sword and sheathed it. He bent to retrieve his dagger.

"Kayerille?" he asked.

"All good, sir," she said. "You?"

"Fine. Marianille?"

"Fine," she replied, rolling a body over with her foot and crouching to inspect it. Birlerion joined her, pushing up sleeves, searching for marks.

"Kirshan assassins," Viktor's voice cut through the silence. "His last words: 'Death awaits you.' They have an order out on you."

"I know, but they haven't been able to find me until now. I should have taken Var'geris out," Jerrol said suddenly. "He knows who I am. It had to be him arranging such a fast response."

Viktor looked at him in concern. "They don't stop until they succeed."

Jerrol grinned, narrowing his eyes. "Well, it will be their most expensive hit yet, and maybe we can confuse them for a bit longer."

"How?"

"Could you hound Var'geris out of Mistra? He'll want his assassins around him. He doesn't have many of them left.

It will give us long enough for us to leave for Mistra without him seeing us."

"That won't stop them."

"No, a mere decoy. But I now know it's Var'geris sending them. Once I kill him, the hit will be void, the agreement cancelled. If you accidentally manage to kill him, I'm sure the Lady will bless you for protecting her Captain," Jerrol said. "But make sure your people are careful. It's better they keep him running. I'll deal with him."

Viktor grinned in anticipation. "It will be our pleasure," he said, turning to order his people to remove the bodies littering their camp.

34

DESERTS OF TEROLIA

Early the next morning, Jerrol twisted in his saddle and checked his caravan. He had four camels stretched out in a line behind him, each linked to the other by rope to ensure none went astray, but he still worried.

Tris'eril curled inside his robe, laying across his lap, her hand gripping his tunic. Zin'talia crooned in his head, pleased to be out on the road with him again. He faced forward and followed Birlerion, who with his innate sense of direction, led them across the empty sun-baked sands.

They had slipped out of the camp before dawn and made good time crossing the desert to the south towards the mountain range that ran down the coastline. His thoughts drifted as they travelled. His gaze rested on the back of his Sentinal, and Birlerion turned around.

Birlerion's gaze flicked over the line of camels, and then he met Jerrol's eyes for a moment before turning back to the desert. Birlerion was fading into the background as the other Sentinals drew the attention away from him, and Birlerion let them. Was that how he became so unobtrusive? Was that the trick of it?

The previous evening, after they had settled after the attack Birlerion and Roberion had reported that Var'geris had packed in a hurry and moved out. To where was the question.

Birlerion had been in a contemplative mood, lingering beside Jerrol as they stared out towards the burning sunset. He had stirred as the air shimmered and the little Arifel, Lin, appeared before him. He held out his hand and she settled as he accepted the message. Jerrol could still see Birlerion standing, gilded by the sun to burnished gold. What little skin was exposed glimmered as he read the missive. The black and white Arifel rubbing against him.

When Birlerion raised his head, his eyes were liquid gold as if he had absorbed the very sun itself, and then the sun sank below the horizon and he was just a man again. It had been an unnerving moment, and then he spoke and the impression was gone.

"Tagerill and Lady Miranda have joined. I am so glad. His tree must have worked his magic. And the confirmation was successful; Alyssa picked up the guardianship. That's Deepwater in safe hands. I wondered how Tagerill was doing. It's his borning today," he had said with a soft smile. "He finally made twenty-one. Some thought he'd never make it. I'm glad he has someone to celebrate it with."

It wasn't until much later that Jerrol remembered that Tagerill and Birlerion shared a borning day.

As the sun rose higher and became more intense, they circled the camels before encouraging them to fold down onto the sand. The Sentinals rigged an awning, raising the middle of it to a height for at least one person to stand and stretch. They all lay limply on the sand, leaning against the animals as backrests. No one talked; they tried to sleep to save their energy.

Jerrol stirred as the awning began to flap in a strengthening breeze. He stood and peered out at the perfect blue sky. "Adilion, Roberion," he said, kicking their feet to wake them, "make sure the awning is tied down securely. Drop the height. It looks like a sandstorm is coming." He retreated inside, stepping over legs and retrieving Tris'eril.

"*I don't think this is a natural sandstorm*," Zin'talia said.

"*Why not?*"

"*The air is spinning, sucking the sand up. It's scouring the land. This is not right.*" She stirred as the other animals began to shift.

"Hold onto your rides; this is not going to be good," Jerrol said out loud.

The Sentinals gripped the camel's reins as Jerrol tried to soothe Zin'talia. Birlerion held onto his horse.

Zin'talia rolled her eyes. "*He's here. He's going to sweep us all away!*" she shrieked in Jerrol's head. She reared, and Jerrol fought to hold onto her, but her panic affected the others.

The wind whipped and tugged the awning, which stretched in all directions. The slapping noise upset the animals even more and, eventually, it ripped down the middle. It was whisked away into a swirling funnel, sweeping across the desert, sucking in everything around it.

The air roared and bucked and buffeted them, pulling them towards the funnel. Sand swirled around them, blotting out the horizon and each other. Jerrol hung onto Zin'talia grimly as Tris'eril whimpered into his chest. He hunkered down, praying the reins wouldn't snap, trying to shelter the little girl. The camels fled in all directions; Sentinals tried to act as drags, slowing them down.

As quickly as it had started, it ended. The air stilled and silence descended. Jerrol stood. Sand cascaded from his clothes, and he looked around as Zin'talia trembled beside him. He hugged her neck, and realised his hand stung, burnt by the leather reins sliding through his grip.

The horizon had changed. The sand had shifted, scoured back to bare rock in places. He turned in a full circle as two Sentinals led their camels towards him. Another camel lay in the sand, an immobile lump in the distance; it would never stir again. He shielded his eyes. Roberion and Marianille were trying to offload what was left of the equipment.

What they had brought into the shelter with them had gone. Any trace of them had been scoured clean; nothing remained but bare rock. He checked his water supply. He had two full canteens still tied to Zin'talia. He had been rigorous in ensuring they were tied securely. Birlerion came up, fortunately leading his horse, his eyes wide and dazed.

"That was not natural," he said.

"Agreed, but it's gone now, along with tonnes of sand. No wonder they say the desert never looks the same one day to the next," Jerrol said, trying to slow his own beating heart. "How much water do you have?"

"I've got two canteens. But we've lost what was on Marianille's camel. We couldn't hold it. It got dragged into that… that thing," Birlerion replied, twirling his hand in the air.

The other Sentinals arrived. They all had abrasions and burns on their hands and faces. Their eyes were a bit wild. "Birlerion, see if we've got anything for the burns and cuts," Jerrol asked. "We can't leave them unattended in this heat."

Birlerion rummaged in one of the remaining packs. He resurfaced with a pad and a bottle of lotion in his hand. He removed the stopper and thoroughly wet the pad, then peeled off a thin layer of cloth and handed one to each of them.

"Fortunately, Maraine insisted we pack some healing supplies," he murmured as he crouched by Marianille in the sand. She hissed as he dabbed one on her chin. He passed one to Jerrol and as he laid it across his palm, Jerrol sighed in relief as the pain eased. He flinched as Birlerion pressed another pad against his cheek. He hadn't noticed the sting until the cooling pad relieved it.

"Zin'talia, are you hurt anywhere?" he asked, busy checking Tris'eril over. She seemed fine. She had been well sheltered.

"No-o." Zin'talia's voice didn't sound too sure.

Jerrol spun on his heel and walked over to run his hands down her flank. *"What is it?"*

"I'm sorry." She dipped her head. *"I shouldn't have panicked. I made it worse."*

Jerrol hugged her neck. *"You were marvellous. It couldn't be helped; everyone panicked. How did you know it was unnatural?"*

"I heard his voice in the wind. He was angry," Zin'talia said.

"Who's voice?"

"The one who threatened you in Mistra."

"Var'geris?"

"Yes, he was furious."

"Good," he thought as he squinted out across the horizon.

"Birlerion, was that the Ascendants?" Adilion asked, holding his camel tight, his expression tense. "Remember that attack outside Melila that nearly killed us all?"

"Probably," Birlerion said."Though this was different. Last time, they were able to target us specifically. This was more general, drawing from across the desert. But it is worrying that they have similar skills." He scowled. "We had no defence then. We have even less now."

"If they have power, surely the Lady's power should be just as effective?" Jerrol suggested.

"That's the problem. It is *Her* power. She used us as

vessels on occasion, but it was *Her* power, and She isn't physically here anymore. What we had is gone."

Jerrol stared at him. "What power did you have, Birlerion?"

Birlerion shrugged. "Nothing that will help us here."

Jerrol bit his lip. That wasn't quite the answer he was expecting, but this wasn't the time to dig further. The other Sentinals were listening with interest; it was apparent they didn't know what Birlerion could do either, except maybe Niallerion, who had raised his eyebrows as Birlerion spoke.

Regrouping, they checked their supplies and remounted, the Sentinals doubled up on the remaining camels.

They reached a small village later that evening, more by accident than design as it wasn't marked on any map. The Sentinals shrugged when Jerrol asked them its name. They gazed at the burnt-out shells of the buildings as they rode down the main street. The fields were long abandoned and had reverted to shifting mounds of sands encroaching the outer limits of the ruins. The well was fouled, so they couldn't even top up their water. There was no sign of a sentinal tree. Jerrol listened keenly just in case and double-checked with Birlerion, but Birlerion shook his head.

They stopped for the night on the outskirts of the town; the ruins were too depressing. The following evening, they trailed into Melila.

Most of the houses were deserted and falling into disrepair, though a couple were still standing near the well. The Sentinals stared around them as they made their way down the main street. What were once small vegetable patches had been returned to dust. The surrounding fields were empty and abandoned.

They pulled up by the well, scanning the buildings

around them. Jerrol dismounted, holding Tris'eril's hand. Her thumb was firmly stuck in her mouth as she clutched him with her other hand. Roberion let the bucket fall and rewound it, the ratchet clanking in the silence. He dumped the water into the trough and let the horses drink their fill.

"Check the houses. Niallerion, refill the canteens," Jerrol instructed as Roberion dropped the bucket again and repeated the action for the camels. The Sentinals spread out, searching the ruins.

Niallerion gaped around him. "How many people lived here?"

"It was about the same size as Il Queron, I believe. A couple of hundred maybe," Jerrol replied as he squatted down beside the child. "I'm sorry, Tris."

She stared at him for a moment and then turned back to the road. Marianille escorted an elderly couple towards them. They were clutching each other in fear, even though Marianille had her hands spread apart; they weren't reassured. They had learnt not to trust—the hard way.

Tris let out a loud squeal. "Amma!" she called, releasing Jerrol and darting down the road towards the old woman. The woman opened her arms, and Tris threw herself into her embrace and burst into tears. The woman cradled her in amazement, murmuring soft endearments into her curls. She raised her head as Jerrol approached.

"We mean no harm," he said, observing the Kirshan tattoos on their cheeks, the same as Tris.

The man snorted. "Nothing much left to harm."

"Is there anyone else living here?"

"They won't come out. They're too afraid."

"We came from Mistra. No one knows anything about this." Jerrol raised his arm and indicated the ruins.

"They know. They do nothing about it," the man said, his crooked fingers stroking his sparse grey beard.

"Who knows?"

"The Kirshans. They pass by now and then. Make sure we haven't left." The man laughed bitterly. "Where would we go? No livestock. No camels. We wouldn't survive out there. We hardly survive in here."

Jerrol waved the Sentinals closer. "Adilion, you and Roberion find the waystone and go back to Mistra. Bring supplies, new mounts, and help," Jerrol ordered as he turned back to the elderly man. "My name is Jerrol. We came here to help."

The man stared at him in disbelief. "To help *us*?"

"Yes, to help anyone who needs. We expected there to be more people here. What happened?"

"A tall man came, preaching change and a new way of life and swept everyone away with him. Those who wouldn't go were either slaughtered or chained up, anyway. Destroyed our homes too, just to make sure there was nothing to come back to."

"We lost our tent and supplies in the storm; may we shelter in one of these houses?"

"Take your pick. They are all empty; been empty now for over a year."

A year. Anger stirred in his gut as he stared at the man. "You know Tris'eril?" Jerrol asked.

"Our granddaughter," he said, pride in his watery eyes. "We lost her with our daughter, Sher'ille, and her man last year. The Kirshans came through and swept away every able-bodied person. Left us here to die. Haven't died yet! The Lady watches over us."

"That she does," Jerrol agreed.

The woman rocked the child gently, crooning a soft lullaby, soothing the tears away.

"Birlerion, set up camp in whichever house has a roof and build a fire. Make us a drink."

Birlerion dug a shallow pit outside his chosen house and

lined it with the fire rocks. He soon had a small fire burning merrily. Rummaging for a coffee pot, he filled it and placed it over the fire before venturing back into the house to search for mugs.

Niallerion tied the camels to the ring in the wall and went into a house and brought a chair out, placing it in the shade. He went searching through the house next door and returned with some floor cushions, which he repeatedly whacked against the wall. "Please, be seated."

Chatting quietly with the old couple, who relaxed in his soothing company, Birlerion handed around the coffee, grinning as Marianille returned from scouting around the village. "Smelt the coffee, did you?" he said. "This is Terl'ana and Ame'lie," he said, introducing the old couple.

Marianille cupped her coffee and said, "There is another family, but they wouldn't join us. They are in the house to the north of the well."

"Maybe they'll join us later," Ame'lie said, hugging Tris.

Tris' grandfather inhaled the aroma. "Coffee. I haven't had coffee for so long." He sighed with pleasure. He barely flinched when Roberion and Adilion impossibly returned with three camels loaded with sacks of supplies; ground flour, sweetmeats, and fruit. The couple stared at them a little wild-eyed, but Birlerion had calmed them enough to keep them seated. A broad smile grew on Ame'lie's wrinkled face.

Jerrol quirked an eyebrow in question at his returning men.

"Maraine's men decided to come by the traditional route, by horse. They didn't like the sound of the waystone's side-effects." Adilion grinned, glancing around. "Find anyone else?

"Not yet. We'll split the watch between the five of us. Marianille and Roberion, you take the first shift; rotate every six hours. The Atoleans should arrive in a couple of days. Let's make sure no one else surprises us before then."

Marianille rose to her feet and grabbed a water canteen, which she slung over her shoulder, before heading off to patrol the north perimeter. Roberion went south.

Ame'lie handed the sleeping Tris to her husband. "Let me see what you've brought. I'll fix a meal; maybe the others will be coaxed out."

"I brought a few chickens if you want me to prepare one for you," Adilion offered.

"Yes, do. The others we'll keep. We could do with some fresh eggs. I have a coup; empty, but in good condition," Ame'lie said, leading Adilion and the supplies back to her home and hearth.

The evening meal was very make-shift; baked chicken mixed with some chopped vegetables to eke it out and wrapped in freshly cooked flatbreads. The wafting aroma of food attracted a hesitant family, who slowly approached as Ame'lie beckoned them forward. "This is Kier'iam, her son, and her father."

The woman was thin with straggly black hair tied away from her face. She held her baby close and stared at the crowd of tall men gathered outside the house.

Ame'lie gestured to the cushions. "Sit. They bought us some fresh food."

Kier'iam hesitated. "Why?" she asked.

Ame'lie stood. "They come in the Lady's name; to help."

"Why now? What do they want?"

Jerrol rose and bowed in introduction. "Captain Haven of the Lady's Guard, at your service, ma'am. We found young Tris'eril in Mistra and brought her home." He indicated the child still sleeping on the cushions.

"Tris? You found her! Did you find the others, too?" she asked as her desperate gaze flickered around.

"Not yet, but we are searching. Unfortunately, they could be almost anywhere by now," Jerrol admitted.

The woman's shoulders slumped. "Yes, I'm sorry, you're right. They are probably in the mines."

"The mines?" Jerrol asked.

Kier'iam sighed and came to sit with Ame'lie, propping her young son in front of her. Her fingers caressed his soft curls. Jerrol sat back down, not wanting to startle her. She glanced across at him, absently accepting a mug of coffee. She sipped and paused; noticing what was in the mug, she sipped again, savouring the flavour.

Kier'iam relaxed as she began to speak. "The crystal mines in the Telusion range. Everyone pretends they aren't there, but that's where they take people. My husband followed them once. He came back saying there was a regular trade out of the mines to the port and many guards patrolling the area. He wasn't too impressed by them." She gave them a small smile. "After all, he managed to sneak past them, and he wasn't particularly stealthy, if you know what I mean. He said the villages of Marmera and Lez were also deserted. All the people gone. I keep expecting them to come back and take us, too." She stared down at her mug. Jerrol was sure she was remembering other faces.

Niallerion shifted on his cushion, his face tight, but he held his tongue, reluctant to interrupt her.

"Did he tell you whereabouts in the range the mines were located?" Jerrol asked.

"South of the Feril pass." Kier'iam shrugged. "He said you couldn't miss it. I guess he got too close, because one day he never came home."

Jerrol nodded. "We'll wait for the Atoleans to arrive and then we'll head out to the Telusions." He smiled at Kier'iam and Ame'lie. "Why are they called the Falusion Mountains on the maps, yet you call them Telusions?"

Kier'iam's eyes crinkled as she gave a low laugh. "History, I think. Spellings change over time. But if you come from here, then they are the Telusions, and they always will be."

Birlerion shifted on his cushion. "This is nothing like the old town of Melila. We're further from the mountains and there is no temple."

Adilion grimaced. "And no Edrilion."

"No," Birlerion said, concentrating on his flatbread. "He's not here."

Terl'ana raised his voice. "The Guardians rested here when they created Remargaren." Then he flushed when everyone stared at him.

"The Guardians?" Jerrol prompted, glad of the change of subject.

"Leyandrii and her family. It's said that they rested here; creating a world was hard work, you know. That's why it's always hot in Terolia. This is where the hard work was done before they moved up north where it was cooler."

"Where did you hear that?" Jerrol asked.

"Here and there. The father always spoke of the origins on Lady's day."

Jerrol vaguely remembered Tagerill commenting on a book on the origins that he had found in the king's archives. He should have paid more attention to it. "Are there any other places like that, that you know of?"

Terl'ana shrugged. "Not in Terolia."

Jerrol realised there would be a similar location in Elothia, the third kingdom. One crystal for each kingdom, as there was one for the Lady, Land, and Liege. He had found one crystal under the Watch Towers in Vespiri. He knew the second must lie under the Telusions somewhere here in Terolia, and the third, well, apart from being somewhere under

Elothia, he had no idea. He wondered what the island archipelago of Birtoli hid, if not the Bloodstone.

The Atoleans arrived two days later at first light. They rode into the village, staring wide-eyed at the destruction, and Jerrol recognised the leader as one of Maraine's uncles, Yoa'ran. A lean, swarthy-skinned man with sharp black eyes, who looked like he could deal with anything. He nimbly slid off the back of his Darian and strode up to Jerrol.

"What happened?"

"According to the elders, the Ascendants swept everyone away to work in the mines in the Telusion mountains. Slavery. They destroyed the village so that there was nothing they could return to. Remove any hope for escape," Jerrol said, staring at the ruins.

Yoa'ran scanned the village, his face tight. "And the Kirshans let this happen?"

"Looks like it. They patrol regularly, making sure the remaining people haven't left to tell their story."

"What do you plan to do when you find the mines?"

"Bring the people home," Jerrol said.

"In that case, we'd better make sure they have a home to come back to," Yoa'ran said, turning to his men to issue a few clipped instructions.

Jerrol left the Atoleans busy pulling down the ruins and clearing the village, salvaging whatever materials they could use to build new dwellings. He went in search of Roberion, scowling at the derelict buildings as he passed; such a waste. He found Roberion, stripped to the waist, helping to salvage some stone blocks. His bronzed skin gleamed with sweat from the effort. "Be careful you don't burn," Jerrol said. "I want you to stay here. Help the Atoleans rebuild the village. Spend the time getting to know Terl'ana and Kier'iam. You'll need to use the waystone. There are not enough materials here to rebuild the village; you'll have to bring in supplies."

Roberion grimaced in agreement. "As you command, Captain."

Jerrol led his remaining Sentinals out of the village, now remounted on Atolean supplied horses. He studied the blue shadow of the mountains on the shimmering horizon. Somewhere in that long chain was a crystal mine. How they would find it he wasn't sure. His only clue was to start south of the Feril pass and, apparently, they wouldn't miss it. If that was so, he wondered why no one spoke of it.

They travelled long into the evening, making up for their late start. The mountain range filled their view as they drew closer. The rounded peaks formed a long spine, which changed to a deep red as they drew closer; vibrant against the perfect blue skies. The air chilled as the sun set, and they rode late into the night. They stopped, at last, to rest under the starry sky.

They made their make-shift camp at the top of a rocky ridge. They would descend the narrow trail the next day when it was light. Jerrol didn't want any unnecessary accidents. They collapsed on their bedrolls, drained by the heat.

Jerrol jerked out of his exhausted dose when Adilion snapped at Marianille as she clattered the mugs together, the sound loud in the still night air. Birlerion gripped Adilion's shoulder. "It will be alright. They don't know where we are."

Adilion's gaze darted around them, peering into the shadows. "How do you know? They came out of nowhere last time."

"Relax." Birlerion began kneading his shoulders.

"What are you afraid of?" Marianille asked.

Continuing to massage Adilion's shoulders, Birlerion

glanced at his sister. "Something that happened a long time ago. It won't happen again."

"We don't know that," Adilion snapped.

"Relax, Adilion. We'll deal with it if we have to. We did before." Birlerion's voice was calm, though Jerrol noticed his knuckles whiten at the strength of his grip on Adilion's shoulder.

Adilion clamped his lips tight against the retort that Jerrol knew he had been about to snap at Birlerion. Birlerion relaxed his grip and continued kneading. He began speaking, his voice soft. "This mountain range used to be much higher, the peaks honed like the teeth of a wood saw. They always reminded me of those long, two-handed saws the timber cutters in Greens used to use. They are more rounded now, blunted, like the Ascendants' power. They have nothing like the power they used to have."

"How can you be so sure?" Adilion began to relax under his hands and his soothing voice.

Birlerion chuckled. "Because they are few and are relying on some persuasive mind spells and ancient crystals. They are trying to recreate what they had. They have nothing new to add."

"We don't know that for sure, Birlerion," Niallerion said. He was lying on his blanket and resting his head on a hand.

"They do have some different magics, like that fire powder they used at the palace," Jerrol said.

"That was not magic," Niallerion said. "From the description Birlerion gave me, we used to use it back in the day. Guerlaire used it all the time on his raids, as did the Ascendants, unfortunately. Its basis was a fertiliser for the crops. The Kharma Ridge was full of these crystal formations; Khasalts, it was called. It used to be ground into a powder and sprinkled on the fields; a way to make this sand more fertile. Someone, sometime, mixed it with another powder. Belphur, I think, and set it alight, and it exploded." Niallerion chuckled. "Bet that gave them a shock. Separate, they were fine. Mix them and you had to be careful. But the ingredients are reasonably common. If they've been mining the Telusions, I bet they found them there."

Birlerion rolled his eyes. "We'll have to have words with Marguerite… leaving dangerous minerals around for anyone to pick up."

Jerrol spoke up. "I meant to ask about Marguerite. What happened to her?"

Birlerion flexed his hands and buffed Adilion on the shoulder. "Better?" he asked.

"Mmm," Adilion replied as he flopped on his bedroll.

Birlerion grinned and turned back to Jerrol. "A few weeks before the end, Marguerite bonded with the Land. She went to Elothia and never came back." He paused. "You met her in Marchwood, I believe. She came with me to Terolia once, when I collected Kaf'enir and returned Kin'eril. She was already attuned to the land then." Birlerion paused, his eyes distant, remembering.

"Jerrol, you don't have time to be loitering here. You must leave. Time is running out and you must get to the mountains. You have to save them." Taelia approached out of the gloom and Birlerion grabbed Adilion as he lurched to his feet in shock.

"Where did she come from?" Adilion spun, frantic.

Jerrol rose. "Save who, Taelia?" He grabbed her hands.

"The mountains press down. They are weary."

"You're not making sense, Taelia."

"She doesn't have to," Birlerion said, collecting his things. "We need to move. Get your stuff, Adilion; nap time is over."

"Hurry," Taelia said as she faded back into the night.

35

SOUTH OF MELILA, TEROLIA

They worked their way down the ridge, past the sand-scoured rock formations and dried-out channels, once filled with water. Looking back up at the ridge in the grey predawn, the water eroded rock and deep shadows made an eerie shadowfall. Jerrol shivered in the predawn gloom.

They had only been travelling for a few hours when Jerrol first smelt it. The sky lightened as the sun peeped over the mountains and began its fiery ascent, burning away the darkness and baking the golden sands once more.

He reined Zin'talia in and sniffed the air. The taint of death was unmistakable. He exchanged glances with Birlerion, who nodded in agreement. The stench grew as they approached the mountain range, which filled up the horizon. The peaks hung over them, sheer cliff faces rising to bar the way to the sea.

In each direction, steep slopes rose ahead of them. There didn't seem to be a break in the red stone that barred their way. "Ker'iam said to the south of the pass. It must be here somewhere," Jerrol said, waving his arm.

The Sentinals spread out and began searching the base of the cliffs. Birlerion disappeared into a narrow cleft. "The stench is worse in there," he said on his return, pointing to the pass. "That must be a passage off the actual pass."

Jerrol whistled and waved his arm. The Sentinals soon regrouped and followed Birlerion into the passage. The stench made them gag as they made their way through the rocky opening, sheer red walls crowding in on them. The passage opened into a sandy basin. A beaten path wide enough for carts by the shallow grooves in the rock, led out to the other side of the bowl.

"Marianille, go check that the path leads to the port. Make sure nothing is coming in from that direction. The rest of you, come with me," Jerrol commanded as he led the way down the widening passage. The sheer walls rose above them; the red tinge to the rock cast a reddish wash over everything. Jerrol wondered morbidly if the rock was red because so much blood had been spilt mining these mountains.

The passage opened into a broad expanse of sand fronting another cliff face, only this time, there was a cave entrance at the base of the rock. The mountain towered overhead, rising to a peak that reached for the sky and would touch the clouds if there were any. It was the tallest in this range of mountains, its adjacent companions reducing in height as they marched off into the distance on either side.

Apart from the smell, there was no indication of life or death. The air was still and silent; no cries carried on the wind. No echoes of picks hitting rock.

Jerrol motioned Adilion to take the lead, with Niallerion close behind. They entered the cave, peering into the dim interior; alert for any movement and listening intently. The tunnel led down and opened into a vast natural cavern. The ceiling disappeared into the void above. Torches flared against the red stone walls, revealing columns of smooth stone rising into the darkness out of the flame's reach.

The stench hit them in a wave as they entered, making them gag. Jerrol swallowed, trying to prevent the bile from rising. Wrapping their scarves around their faces did little to alleviate the nauseating smell of rotting flesh.

Jerrol inspected the cavern. Across one side, wooden crates were stacked against the wall. A skinny, grey mule drooped in the corral in the corner. To the right, a narrow passage led off into the dark. Further round to the right, roughly hewn steps led up the rock wall to a small entrance above them. Adilion took the steps. Niallerion led the way down the dark passage. As it sloped down, the smell got worse; the stench of unclean bodies, death, and despair.

The tunnel opened into a complex of smaller caves. They looked like they had been hewn out of the rock by the same hand that had created the passage. Nubs of tallow candles were burning in tiny pockets dug into the walls, providing a dim yellow trail. The rooms were empty, but for a few rags piled in the corners. They continued down the passage, remaining vigilant, and at last, they could hear voices.

A sharp voice echoed through the cave. A dull and defeated mutter replied, followed by the sound of a blow and the thud of a body falling. The voice rapped out a command and the sound of shuffling feet faded as they moved down the tunnel. Jerrol peered around a corner. They had reached a large cavern, which split into three passages on the other side. A guard stood in the centre of the cavern, hands on his hips, a man sprawled at his feet.

Jerrol strode up behind him and grabbed him around the neck, his dagger piercing the guard's clothes just above his kidneys. "Not a sound or it'll be the last you ever make," he whispered. "Where are the rest of your colleagues?" He dug his dagger a little deeper. The man gasped and tried to struggle, but Jerrol's grip tightened. "Where?" he repeated.

The man flung his hand out towards the central passage.

"How many?"

"Th-three."

"I don't believe you. How many guards are in this mountain?"

"Just the four of us. The rest left yesterday. Went to Feril; shipping out," the man stuttered. "Nothing left to mine. Just dirt."

"Shipping out to where?" Jerrol asked as he jerked his head at Birlerion to check the man lying at their feet.

Birlerion rose, shaking his head, his face carefully blank.

"E-Elothia."

Jerrol pushed the man ahead of him as they left the cavern by the central passage. "Where do the other passages lead to?"

"S-slave quarters to the left. Storerooms to the right," the man replied, rolling his eyes, trying to see who was behind him.

The sound of metal striking rock penetrated the dim passage.

"Why are you still making these people mine, then?" Jerrol asked, steering the man towards the noise.

"Keeps them busy; no time to think about causing trouble."

"Trouble?"

"Trying to escape. Stuff like that."

"Where would they go?" Jerrol asked. "It's just desert out there."

"Wastes our time. M-means we have to go chase them down."

The passage had been sloping down and finally gave way to a long, thin cave. It was riddled with tunnels leading off in all directions. Piles of red dirt were stacked to one side. A group of emaciated men shovelled dirt into baskets with their hands, their movements slow and sluggish. Once half-filled, they struggled to lift the buckets and staggered off down one of the passages, eyes on the ground, taking no notice of the people standing in front of them.

"Where are they going?"

"To get rid of the dirt. As they tunnel a new mine, they fill a disused one up with the dirt."

"Where are the other guards?"

"Down at the mine face where they use the tools; making sure they don't attack us," the guard said, stiffening as the tall Sentinals moved ahead.

Jerrol stuffed a rag in the guard's mouth as the pitiful sound of metal on stone grew louder. The passage came to a dead end. At the very end, five men struggled to hit the rock face with pickaxes, watched closely by two bored guards, their backs to the passageway. The Sentinals didn't hesitate. The men were disarmed and trussed up before they realised they had company.

"Where's the other one?" Jerrol hissed, removing the rag from the guard's mouth. The man shrugged.

"He should have been down here."

"Stop. You can stop now," Jerrol called to the men still pounding the rock face, the shock of the blows making them stagger. They continued.

Jerrol pushed the guard off onto Birlerion and touched the shoulder of one of the men. The man stopped and turned empty eyes towards Jerrol. He stood, waiting. Jerrol touched the shoulder of each man and told them to stop. They were all emaciated, underfed, dressed in rags that barely covered their filthy skin. They struggled to lift the pickaxes, never mind use them.

Even after they had stopped and stood staring at him

with dead eyes, the sound of striking metal still resonated through the caves.

"I thought you said this was the only working face?" Jerrol asked.

The guard swallowed, watching Jerrol's grim expression. "It's the kids."

"Kids?" Jerrol's voice couldn't get any colder. "Show us."

The guard led the way back along the passageway and veered off down one of the tunnels. "Where there are fissures, we lower a kid down to see what they can find. They stay down there all day until we pull them back up."

"How many children?" Jerrol asked.

The guard shrugged. "Varies; got about a hundred right now."

"How many?" Jerrol jerked the man to a halt.

"About a hundred kids. Probably a thousand adults scattered throughout the mines. They rotate on three shifts, though we've only got one shift working. No point, really. The rest are in their quarters." The man spoke as if what he was saying was commonplace.

Jerrol caught the expression on Birlerion's face and shivered. He was sure it was a reflection of his own. "You are telling me you have about eleven hundred Terolians working in these mines?"

The guard nodded tentatively, realising that his captors weren't taking the information too well.

"Raise the children, now," Jerrol ordered, pushing the man in front of him.

They watched horrified as the guard pulled at a rope knotted against the wall and started hauling. Ropes were knotted at intervals along the passageway. A small wicker basket breached the wall, and the guard lifted it over. With an eye on the forbidding face above him, he gently placed it onto the floor.

Jerrol squatted down and looked inside; a small girl cowered at the bottom. He lifted her out. She weighed nothing, even the bones of her tiny wrists jutted out. She flinched away from him. "Hush," he whispered. "I won't hurt you." But he could see the child didn't believe him.

He stood still, cradling the child. "Get them all up, now!" he said, his face stern and forbidding. Jerrol put the child down, and she crouched beside the wall. Birlerion helped to pull the baskets up, each revealing a cowering child half the size they ought to be; skin so paper-thin, Jerrol could see the blue veins tracing underneath. Each was dressed in filthy rags and staring at the floor with dull, lifeless eyes.

Jerrol clenched his fists as he tried to control his growing anger. Ten terrified children stood trembling in front of him. The guard flinched back from the fury boiling in Jerrol's eyes, shifting from foot to foot in agitation.

Adilion tied the guard's arms behind his back with the rope. The children waited. Jerrol crouched and took the little girl's hand. "My name is Jerrol. What's yours?"

She stared at him, mute.

"How about Leyla? After the Lady?" he suggested. A faint wisp of interest flickered in her eyes. "Can you say it?" Jerrol asked.

She shook her head.

"We'll practice later," he promised. He stood and led her down the corridor. The other children followed. He led them back to the slave quarters and baulked at the entrance. They were overpowered by the stench; the stink of vomit, waste, and death and horrors yet unseen. The children seemed unaffected, used to it. Jerrol swallowed convulsively and entered the cavern. Bodies lay everywhere, covering the floor like a carpet of reeds. It was impossible to tell how many were alive or dead; so many were still with fixed eyes. This was a place where life had given up.

The children scattered, finding parents or friends, who were squatting on the floor and staring at him as he moved further into the cave. Jerrol turned as Adilion paused in the entrance behind him, an expression of absolute horror on his face.

Jerrol turned towards him and spread his hands. "I suggest we move those still alive out of this hole. Use the caverns on the next level up. Did you find the other guard?"

Adilion shook his head. "There was no one in the upper levels. Just empty offices."

"Alright, everyone, we have one guard unaccounted for. Be careful and keep alert. Let's move those we can up a level. Adilion, find us some water. Niallerion, assess those we can move. Birlerion and I will help you." They started the grim job of moving those still alive out of the dire conditions.

36

TELUSION MOUNTAINS, TEROLIA

Jerrol stood in the entrance of the passageway facing the golden desert, staring into the distance; the small camp they had set up in the lee of the rising mountain invisible to his eyes. Anger stirred within him. If he let it, he might self-combust with overwhelming fury. How could they treat their people so? They had devalued human life until it was worthless. If they weren't going to look after their people, then what was the point of taking power?

He thought back to Var'geris' speech in Mistra: *only those who were pure and carried the best blood would rise.* All others had to demonstrate their worth by being obedient and sacrificing themselves in the name of Terolia. He gritted his teeth. No one deserved to be treated like this. And the children; how could they judge them, deny them the opportunity that should be theirs by right? Jerrol's anger deepened.

Jerrol turned as footsteps stopped behind him.

"Captain?"

Jerrol's glare scorched Birlerion, a physical crackle in the air, and Birlerion flinched, taking a step backwards. He kept his face carefully neutral.

Jerrol breathed out and tried to contain his anger to a simmer. "My apologies," he said, trying to soften his voice. His throat was so tight, he was amazed he could get the words out. "I am not angry with you."

Birlerion nodded. "The Ascendants care for no one. If they had their way, only they would exist. Makes you wonder how they think they could survive on their own."

"They don't think enough, it seems."

"No, they always were short-sighted." Birlerion sighed and gestured back down the corridor. "Niallerion needs you. The people want to come out."

Jerrol gazed back out at the shimmering sand. It was early afternoon and the heat was suffocating. He took a deep breath and turned back into the dim passageway. The stench hit his nostrils as soon as they crossed the clearing and entered the large cavern. He breathed shallowly.

"Marianille returned from the port and all was quiet. No ships. She is helping the children wash first, and we found the clothes store. If they wash, we can give them clean clothes; that will make them feel better," Birlerion offered.

On the surface, maybe Jerrol thought grimly. The damage was deeper than that; they would all be affected by this. "Good, well done," he said aloud.

Birlerion led the way out of the main chamber towards the small tunnel to the left that led down to the slave's quarters. They were met by the sight of Niallerion trying to calm a group of agitated people.

"Please," Jerrol's voice carried across the cave. "We are trying to help you. Calm yourselves. Let us help."

"We have the right to go outside. You said we were free," a strained voice called out from the group. The people parted for an old man to step forward. He was skeletal. His shoulders and ribs jutted through the filthy rags he was wearing. His skin hung from his gaunt grey frame. He had maybe enough energy for one last request.

And then Jerrol realised the man before him wasn't that old; the greyness of his skin and hair was misleading. He was old before his time; something else the Ascendants had taken.

"Yes, you are free. But it is the middle of the day and the heat is intense. You will not survive it. Don't let the sun finish what the Ascendants started. Take the time to wash and change into clean clothes."

"A bath won't wash away what they have done to us."

"No, it won't," Jerrol agreed, "but it will help you feel a little better. We are few. We need to identify those who need immediate help. Those of you who are stronger can assist us. Once we help those we can, the sun will have advanced and it will be cooler. Then you can go outside."

The man stared at him and slowly nodded. "You promise?"

"I swear by the Lady," Jerrol replied. "It is a few hours till evening; let us help each other. I know it is a small start, but we have to begin somewhere." He ran a hand through his hair as the small group of people muttered between themselves. He hoped these were not the only people standing. He knew how people who'd held out in terrible conditions could collapse once help arrived.

"All of you, take the time to look after yourselves, then help us to help your families. I promise, once the sun goes down, you can come outside and breathe the fresh air the Lady provides." His eyes shone silver in the dim light as he made the promise again, and the man straightened up before him.

"My name is Mat'iller," the man said, holding his hand out. Jerrol took it gently. "My wife and daughter are in here somewhere, I hope. Some days, I hope they are not because that would mean they lie safely in the Lady's embrace."

Jerrol waved Adilion forward. "Could you start a list? We need to try to bring families back together. Mat'iller will help you, starting with himself. List the details you know of each individual here; let's see who we can reunite. And find some water."

The man's eyes glistened with tears. "Thank you," he whispered.

Jerrol nodded and glanced around the cavern. "Birlerion, check what's in the offices. They must have kept some records of who is here."

"There's a complex of small rooms up there," Birlerion pointed to the ceiling. "We thought helping the people was the priority."

"Well, we have some help now. Niallerion, carry on. Co-opt those with the strength to help the others. Water, wash, clean clothes. Marianille start preparing something these people can eat, gruel or something. They won't be able to eat our travel rations. Go check the rooms, Birlerion. We need to find out the purpose of this place and where all these people came from."

Jerrol walked back out of the caves, leaving Birlerion to climb the crudely cut steps of the upward passage. He paused at the cave entrance and braced himself between the walls. He squeezed his eyes shut as he shuddered, struggling to contain his despair. These poor, poor people. How they had survived as long as they had was beyond him, and he could offer them so little. Well, if they could get them strong enough, he knew a lovely little village waiting for them. The Atoleans should have it spruced up by the time they were ready to return. He breathed in hope and exhaled despair, trying to control the simmering rage bubbling below the surface.

"Captain?"

Jerrol started as Marianille's voice interrupted him. He had almost forgotten where he was. He needed to get a grip.

He took a deep breath and straightened up. "Marianille, what's up?" Jerrol asked.

"What did that woman mean? You called her Taelia. She said we didn't have time."

"What?" Jerrol frowned at her.

"She came from nowhere to warn us; what was she warning us about?"

Jerrol stared at her as icy dread trickled down his spine. Marianille was right. What was the threat that Taelia warned him about? The people were in no immediate danger and most of the guards had left, so why had Taelia hurried them on?

Most of the guards had left.

Jerrol spun and ran back into the cavern. "Niallerion! Where did you put the guards?"

"Down at the mine face. I can tell you, they struggled; they didn't want to go deeper into the mountain."

"Show me. Marianille, get Birlerion for me. He is up there." Jerrol pointed at the ceiling and hurried after Niallerion.

When they arrived, the guards were still struggling to free themselves. Jerrol bent down and removed the gag from one of them. "What are you afraid of?"

The man's eyes rolled as he stared up at the ceiling. "We have to get out. We have to get out, now!"

"Why?" Jerrol's voice cracked through the cave.

"Th-the mountain. It will collapse."

"What?" Niallerion's eyes narrowed.

"They said we have to leave before nightfall. Otherwise, we'll never leave. You have to untie us; you can't leave us here."

"Why should I? You were going to leave those poor people here." Jerrol paced angrily. "Can you stop it?"

The guard shook his head. "I don't know where they rigged it. All I know is that we have to get out before it gets dark."

Jerrol dragged a hand through his hair. "Niallerion, go warn the others. We need to start moving these people out of the mountain."

Birlerion entered the small room that had been carved out of the rock, by hand, probably. He sniffed angrily as he inspected the walls. Two smaller rooms led off it, roughly circular; one was for sleeping, while the other held boxes of paper.

He sat at a crude wooden desk, just a few bits of wood nailed together. Rifling through the papers lying on the surface, he sat back in the chair as he slowly reread the paper at the top of the pile. It was an order to load the remaining crystals in the carts and transport them to the port of Feril, a little further north on the other side of the mountain range. A ship called *Sente Lenz* would be waiting.

A cart full of crystals, Birlerion thought, his stomach clenching. He checked the date and his heart stuttered at the numbers, the year 4123. It should be 1124. He stared at the sheet until the words blurred and his breathing calmed. As the Lady wills, he thought, as he relaxed tense muscles.

The instructions were a year old. Now, that either meant they had a regular shipment or that was the last shipment they had made. But if that was the last shipment, then why was the paper still on the top of the pile? He turned it over and froze. On the other side was a crude map of the mountain. "Lady, save us," he muttered as he lurched to his feet.

Marianille appeared in the doorway. "Birlerion, the Captain wants you."

Birlerion stared at her and then waved the paper he was holding. The map marked several key intersecting points in the mountain. "They are going to blow the mountain. That's why there are so few guards here. They've evacuated."

Marianille's jaw dropped and she looked around wildly. "What? Are you sure?"

"Yes, we have to get out of here." He stuffed the papers in his tunic as he herded Marianille before him. Giving the crude office a last glance, he followed as Niallerion rushed into the cavern below them.

"Mat'iller, we need to get everyone out of the mountain, now!" he shouted as he ran through the cavern.

Jerrol followed him. "Get as many people outside, as you can. The mountain is going to collapse."

Mat'iller stared at him in horror. "Move, now," Jerrol shouted, scooping up two of the children hiding behind him. He hustled them out to the camp Marianille had set up. The children cowered away from the bright light. "Wrap their heads in cloth; the light is too bright for them," he yelled as he ran back into the mountain.

Niallerion herded another group of dismayed people, each desperately clutching a child, down the tunnel. "Cover your eyes. The light is very bright," Jerrol shouted as he ran past. "Mat'iller, you have to leave, now." Jerrol pulled the man away from the bodies lying on the floor.

"I need to find my wife," he mumbled.

Jerrol shook him. "There is no time. Help people out. We have to save as many as we can."

Mat'iller stared at him and gulped, but he nodded and turned away as a deep groan vibrated through the rock. He stared at Jerrol in panic. "Get out now." Jerrol pushed him towards the first cavern they had entered before turning and running deeper into the mountain.

Birlerion and Marianille froze on the crude steps and looked up. "Hurry," Birlerion snapped as they began descending again.

The groan became a rumble and the ground began to vibrate. Grit and sand sifted down from the ceilings. Jerrol skidded to a halt in one of the lower caverns. "Adilion!" he shouted. "We have to leave now." He strained to see in the gloom and then, remembering, he clenched his fist and opened it flat; the silvery light glowed from his hand. "Adilion?"

He had sent Adilion off to find a water source, but surely, he would be back by now? A huge boom rocked the mountain and Jerrol staggered. A second smaller boom followed it. Jerrol hugged the walls as bits of rock fell. He saw a glow ahead and hurried forward, holding his hand up high. "Adilion, we need to leave, now!"

A flash in the wall stopped him. A faceted crystal winked at him in the silvery light. Jerrol hesitated a moment and then unsheathed his dagger and eased the stone out of the rock. It fell into the palm of his left hand and he hissed as the sharp edge bit.

The crystal greedily sucked his blood. The silvery light in his palm was tinged with pink, and then the light vanished as his hand absorbed the crystal. Jerrol gasped as pain flashed through his veins. Groaning, he leaned against the wall for support. His body trembled. The wall trembled as well.

"Captain? Are you alright? We should leave. The mountain is collapsing." Adilion appeared out of the gloom, holding up a torch.

Jerrol glared at him, and Adilion grinned back at him, his eyes gleaming like pools of liquid flame. "I heard you. Let's get out of here. Captain, your hand." Adilion pulled a grubby cloth from his pocket and offered it to Jerrol. He placed an arm under Jerrol's and helped him back down the corridor. Adilion weaved through the stone passages, leading them back up to the lower caverns.

They entered the sleeping cavern as the ground tilted, making them stagger and flail. Many people still lay on the floor, some more alert than others, but all helpless. "Please," they called hopelessly, "help us."

Adilion and Jerrol exchanged glances and staggered over to them. "Can you stand?" Jerrol gasped as another tremor shook the mountain. A low grinding began, filling the cavern with a growing cacophony of vibrations, which resonated through their bodies and hurt their ears.

"We have to get out of here," Adilion said, pulling at a woman's arm, trying to help her rise.

"At least take my daughter," the desperate woman pleaded. Her faded blonde hair straggled around her terrified face.

Jerrol didn't hesitate and stooped to lift the child into his arms. She weighed nothing. "Adilion, help her," he commanded, and they scuttled up the sloping corridor, which led into the vast cavern by the entrance, followed by helpless cries that tore at their hearts.

Large boulders fell, shattering into splinters on impact across the cavern floor. Jerrol and Adilion hugged the walls, watching the ceiling nervously as it creaked and groaned.

Jerrol inhaled in shock as he saw Birlerion grab Marianille as the steps shifted beneath them, and they slid in a jumble down the remainder of the stairs.

"Birlerion, get out!" Jerrol yelled as Birlerion helped his sister to her feet, shielding her from falling debris as they limped after Jerrol.

They exited the chamber as the rock above them emitted a horrendous rumble. The haunting lament of grinding rock and helpless voices was cut off as the mountain crashed down around them. Fragments of rock skittered across the ground. Adilion grunted as one fragment glanced solidly off his shoulder as they stumbled into the desert amidst a blinding dust cloud, choking and coughing.

"Captain? Over here." Jerrol and Adilion turned towards the sound of the voice.

"Niallerion?" Jerrol choked. "Keep talking."

"Over here. We have shelter and water."

Jerrol staggered blindly into the awning. Strong hands reached out to support him, preventing him from collapsing the tent. "Thanks," he grunted, righting himself as he struggled through the suffocating dust. The tent was a blur in front of them, the flap held open by a tall shape.

Eager hands pulled them into the tent, relieving them of their burdens. "Captain, Adilion, sit," Niallerion pushed them down on the floor. "We need to rinse your eyes out before the sand damages them. Lean back."

"Birlerion, are you and Marianille alright?" Jerrol squinted, trying to see them, and he dabbed at his eyes until Niallerion pulled his hands away and forced his head back.

His eyes streamed, the grit irritating the sensitive membranes. The lukewarm water repeatedly rinsed his eyes. "Save the water," he whispered, shaking his head gently as droplets ran down his neck. He peered around the tent. Everything was a blur. The rumble of grinding rocks echoed around their camp, punctuated by sharp cracks as the rocks settled into their new homes.

"Marianille?"

"I'm fine. A few cuts and bruises that's all."

"Situation report," Jerrol said.

Niallerion stiffened. "Forty-two souls saved, including the two you brought out. Eleven children, thirty-one adults. All Sentinals present and accounted for, injuries minor."

"Forty-two," Jerrol whispered.

"Yes, Captain. It is amazing we got so many out in such a short time." Niallerion rinsed Marianille's eyes and then squatted by Birlerion.

Jerrol swallowed, his face bleak. They had done well, considering the conditions, but forty-two out of how many? There had been at least one thousand people in that mountain, though some had already died. The thought made him stagger to his feet and peer out of the tent flap.

Debris covered the sands blocking the entrance. The central peak was missing. It had completely collapsed in on itself. They were lucky it had collapsed inwards, otherwise, they all might have been lost.

All was silent as if the desert itself was listening for survivors. Dust hung in the air, blurring the scene. The occasional sifting of sand disturbed the stillness.

"How are we situated for supplies? Most of it was inside, wasn't it?" Jerrol asked, already thinking about how they were going to keep forty-two people, in poor condition, four Sentinals and himself alive. Forty-seven people in total.

His first thought was: They couldn't.

"We have food and water for about three days," Niallerion said.

"Three days! Melila is only a day away," he said.

"If we all had horses and were in good condition." Niallerion dropped his voice. "These people won't make it on foot."

"How about if we did it in two journeys? We have five horses." *Not enough, even with the horses the Atoleans gave us,* Jerrol thought as Adilion said the same thing out loud.

"I can make a waystone, but the journey can be strenuous for non-Sentinals.

"They have nothing to throw up, anyway." Niallerion shrugged. "I think the waystone would be best." Niallerion knelt beside Adilion, who was struggling to move his right arm. "Let me see it." Adilion reluctantly complied, exposing a brown muscled chest dusted with black hairs, and a massive bruise on the back of his shoulder. He couldn't lift his right arm above his waist without wincing in pain.

"You may have broken your collarbone," Niallerion said as he prodded his back. "I can't tell. You'll have to wait and see what the healer says. We'll strap your arm to your chest, for now. It'll stop you causing yourself further injury." He set to work.

Jerrol drifted about the tent, giving words of encouragement. He stepped over spindly legs and crouched beside a small boy curled in upon himself. The boy snuffled into his robe.

"Hey, are you alright?"

"I-I want my mama," he sniffled, raising a tear-streaked face.

Jerrol's face tightened and he stroked the boy's head. "Why don't you come and sit with me for a while?" he said, holding out his arms. The boy crept into them and tucked his head in his shoulder. Jerrol cradled him and returned to his space near the door of the tent. He rocked the child, murmuring comforting words in his ears. The boy eventually stopped crying and relaxed into sleep. His tiny hand gripped Jerrol's shirt. Jerrol gently kissed the boy's head and closed his eyes. They had a couple of hours before the first journey would begin. It gave people time to recover from the frightening day; time for what had happened to sink in.

At first light the next morning, Jerrol swirled his sword around above his head and created a new waystone, thrusting his sword into a small red rock. The chime rippled through the Sentinals and Jerrol sent Adilion to Mistra. He would arrange help and stay in Mistra to get checked out by Maraine's healer. Niallerion and Marianille would stay behind with Birlerion, while he would travel to Melila and inform them what had happened. He stepped into the waystone and stepped out into the blinding sun on the outskirts of Melila and took a moment to breathe fresh air and steady himself.

Striding up the main street, he admired the new buildings that had appeared; proof that all had been busy. Roberion came to meet him. "What happened?"

"Let's call everyone around. I only want to say this once," Jerrol said with a grim smile.

The Atoleans and the villagers gaped at his return, and silence slowly descended as Jerrol explained what they had found and what the Ascendants had done.

"We have forty-two survivors, all of whom need the help of a healer," Jerrol finished. "I sent Adilion to Mistra to ask for a healer to come here. These people are malnourished and emaciated. They haven't seen sunlight in years. Many are so down-trodden, they won't even look you in the face."

"Are you sure they should come here? Maybe take them straight to Mistra?" Roberion suggested.

Shaking his head, Jerrol explained. "They are frail, scared. I think it will be daunting enough arriving in Melila. Let's ease them back into the world slowly. We could do more damage if we rush them."

Roberion inspected him, and Jerrol wondered what he saw, by the expression on his face it wasn't anything good. Gesturing down the street, Roberion said, "We built a small infirmary, and we have enough dwellings for forty-two people. The Atoleans erected some tents we can use."

"Very well. Come with me, you can help transfer the people. We'll be back in a moment. Be ready." Jerrol led Roberion back towards the waystone. He grabbed his scarves, wrapping himself up against the sun. The Atoleans watched in amazement as they disappeared, leaving a ripple in the air.

Roberion stared around the tent in shock. Jerrol had warned him of what to expect, but he was still horrified. The Sentinals were all strained and exhausted; they hadn't expected to see anything like this, ever. They were all struggling to cope with the sheer lack of hope emanating from the survivors who huddled together in small groups, eyes dead and unseeing.

"Birlerion, who should we take first?" Jerrol's voice was loud in the depressing silence. He smiled encouragingly at the small boy who was curled up in Marianille's lap. It looked like Marianille was getting as much comfort from the child, as the child was from her. She was murmuring into his hair and the boy relaxed back into her embrace.

Mat'iller looked up in surprise. "Captain, we didn't think you would come back."

"Why not? My men are still here. I wouldn't leave them out here, now, would I?" Jerrol asked with a smile, searching Mat'iller's face.

"No one has cared before." Mat'iller shrugged. "The guards weren't treated much better than we were."

"Well, we care, and you will find there are a lot of people who do care and who have missed you," Jerrol said firmly. He could see that mistreatment would be a lesson that would be hard to unlearn. "We'll leave in batches. They won't be able to cope with us all at once." He smiled down at Leyla, glad to see they had managed to save the small child he had lifted out the basket. "Would you like to visit a nice town and leave this place forever?"

She shrank back and hid her face in her hands. Jerrol sighed and scooped her up. "Come on, you are a very brave girl, and I know another little girl called Tris'eril, who would love to be your friend."

"Tris'eril? Did you say Tris?" A faded woman lurched to her feet, staring hopefully at Jerrol.

Jerrol smiled. "Sher'ille?"

She gasped. "You found Tris? She's alive?"

"Yes, I left her with your parents in Melila."

Sher'ille swayed. "My parents?"

Jerrol wrapped an arm around her thin shoulders. "Let me take you home."

She leaned against him for strength and seemed to find some. She nodded and smiled at Leyla. "Let's go home," she said.

Jerrol led her and Leyla towards the waystone. "I am afraid you might feel quite sick when we reach the other side, but it will pass."

Sher'ille shrugged. "What's a little sickness compared to leaving this terrible place?" She straightened her shoulders. "What do we have to do?"

Jerrol took her hand and Leyla's. "Just take a step forward," he said and thought of Melila. They shimmered out into the warm air outside the village.

Sher'ille paled and heaved, but as Niallerion had said, they had nothing much in their stomachs to throw up. Leyla retched noisily, making her eyes water. She hid in Sher'ille's ragged skirts.

"Come," Jerrol said, leading them towards the village.

Sher'ille gasped, swallowing desperately. "It *is* Melila!"

Jerrol led her down the main street towards her parent's house. Tris'eril squealed as she spotted them and came tearing up the road. "Amma, it's Mama!" she shrieked at the top of her lungs.

Sher'ille dropped to the ground and opened her arms. She wrapped them around a wriggling and very much alive

Tris, who wept copiously in her mother's arms. Leyla sidled up beside Jerrol, watching wide-eyed. She gripped his robe. Jerrol smiled down at her and scooped her up in a hug.

Jerrol left them exclaiming over each other as Terl'ana and Ame'lie joined them. He intended on taking Leyla up to the infirmary, but Sher'ille reached for her and pulled her out of Jerrol's arms. "Leyla, meet my daughter, Tris'eril," she said, giving her a loving hug and then pushing the two girls together. Hand-linked, the family walked up the road to their home.

Jerrol smiled as he approached the waystone, but a soft chime warned him someone was arriving so he waited, and soon, Birlerion led two trembling men and a woman into the sunshine. Their faces paled and they swallowed convulsively. One of the men turned away to retch, setting off the others, and they collapsed to the sand, weakly heaving.

"Are we really in Melila?" the man asked, holding his stomach.

"You certainly are," Birlerion said with a grin as people came running to help them.

Jerrol returned to the mine. "Who's next?" he asked gaily. His spirits, revitalised by the reunification of Sher'ille and Tris, plummeted as he saw the despairing humanity before him. He swallowed and knelt beside the young woman and her daughter that they had pulled out at the last minute. "Come," he said, gentling his voice, "let me take you away from this terrible place."

The woman relaxed. "Make it quick," she whispered, the tears sliding down her cheeks.

"No," he whispered, his throat tight. That she would still think there was no hope, that they would kill her instead of saving her, cut him deep. "You have a long life yet to live. I'll show you where you can begin it."

The woman stared at him bleakly, not believing him.

Jerrol scooped her up in his arms. She was so frail it was if she only existed in thought alone. "Think of the Lady," he murmured in her ear. "Just think of the Lady." Her child clung to his robe, frantic at being parted from her mother as he walked towards the waystone. He knelt. "You hold on to me and don't let go, and the Lady will protect you," he promised.

The child stared at him with fearful black eyes and nodded solemnly.

"One step," he said. "Just take one step with me. Together." He and the child stepped forward and came out in the brilliant sunshine in Melila. Birlerion waited at the other end.

"Go, help the others," Jerrol whispered, his face taut.

Birlerion stared at him before he nodded and shimmered out of sight behind them. Jerrol led the child towards the infirmary. Arms were raised to welcome them. The woman wept as Jerrol laid her on a cot, her daughter safe beside her. Jerrol turned away, his face stiff, silver eyes gleaming with tears, only to be caught roughly by the shoulders by Maraine's uncle, Yoa'ran. "What is it?" he asked.

Jerrol struggled to push the words out. "She thought I was going to kill her. When I said I was taking her away, she asked me to make it quick."

"It will not be forgotten," the Terolian swore, his voice gruff. "We will never allow this to happen again."

Finally, Niallerion and Marianille came through the waystone and the transfer was complete. All were safely transferred to the infirmary and a Mistran healer was caring for them all.

37

MISTRA, TEROLIA

A week later, Jerrol entered the Atolean tent in Mistra with his Sentinals at his shoulder and looked around the room. The tent was spacious. The highest point in the centre held a lantern, which was suspended on a silver link chain, casting a gentle golden glow over the occupants. Unusually, there was a wooden table in the middle of the room surrounded by chairs and not a cushion in sight. There were twelve people seated around the oval table. A gap was left at the far end nearest the entrance, for him, he assumed.

He acknowledged Maraine as he saw her and her Sodera halfway down the right-hand side of the table. The Leader of the Solari should be opposite her, then. A beautiful woman with sharp black eyes and long black hair, sat straight-backed and alert. A slender brown finger tapped the table, belying her inner turmoil. She was accompanied by a fierce looking warrior, armed and tense. The leaders of the six families. The Master Conclave, as he had requested. The first in over a hundred years, and the first any of these leaders would have attended. He muttered an aside to Birlerion. "No one enters; no one leaves."

"Yes, Captain." Birlerion ducked back out of the tent and took up position in front of the entrance.

"Ambassador Nil'ano, if you would take notes. A record of the meeting, please. I expect you to pull together the papers for whatever is agreed here. Watertight, understand?"

"Certainly, commander." Nil'ano moved over to the small table to the side of the tent and set up his papers and pen. He leaned back and observed the room; the occupants were noticing the tall Sentinals at the tent entrance.

A woman with a severe face rose to glare at the Sentinals. Deep lines were grooved on her cheeks and forehead as if she perpetually wore a frown. She had a black tattoo on her face, straight lines sloping left and right, meeting at a peak at the top, four of them like a mountain range, an orange flame beneath it—the Medera of Kirsha. "This is a private meeting. You should not be here. Please leave," she demanded.

"Silva, sit," the voice of the Atolean Medera, Maraine, rang out. "All of you, please sit." She looked around the tent; a diminutive woman demanding attention. "Thank you. You were all invited to this Master Conclave, the first of our time, as the voice of your Families. What is discussed here will affect our future. Pay attention, open your eyes; listen with the ears and heart of the Medera. The future of Terolia depends on it."

"What gave you the right to call a Master Conclave?" one of the Mederas from the lesser families asked.

"I called it," Jerrol said, his quiet voice surprising them all.

"This is Captain Jerrolion of the Lady's Guard and these are his Sentinals," Maraine said, indicating the tall men and women standing behind Jerrol.

The Terolian leaders stared at them.

"Sentinals? There are no Sentinals in Terolia. There are none in Remargaren," Reina of Solari said.

The Sentinals stiffened, their eyes glinting dangerously. They had not believed that the Families would doubt their existence. At Jerrol's signal, they spread out around the room; easier for the leaders to appreciate their height, their archaic uniforms, and their glinting silver eyes. The room fell silent, the leaders watching, wide-eyed.

"Medera Reina, of course the Sentinals exist. You know your history. Mederas are famed for their long memories, after all. When the Lady sundered the Bloodstone, she took all magic out of Remargaren and left her Sentinals bound to their trees. To guard and watch; to remind people of the Lady's protection. There is a Sentinal in Ramila named Tarenion. There is a Sentinal here in Mistra; meet Kayerille." Jerrol pointed towards the Mistran Sentinal.

Stepping forward, Kayerille nodded her head, her silver eyes flashing. "Medera, Sodera," she said politely. Her voice was deep and rich and resonated around the room. She stepped back and resumed her stance. The leaders stared, some with jaws dropped, others swallowing nervously.

"Please also meet Roberion of Selir, Adilion of Berbera, Niallerion of Vespers and Marianille of Greens." As Jerrol pointed, each Sentinal stood forward.

"Where did the other one go?" A small fidgety man seated to the right of the Solari Medera asked.

"Birlerion? He guards our privacy." Jerrol took a deep breath. "The Lady expects you to honour your oath and your laws. After all, your ancestors wrote the laws. They were agreed to by all the families, but for some reason, you have forgotten them."

"We have not forgotten our oaths *or* our laws," Medera Silva of Kirsha snapped, glaring at Jerrol.

"I was trying to be polite. I assume you have forgotten

them, otherwise, why would you allow the people of Terolia to suffer? Not deliberately, I hope." His silver eyes flashed in the candlelight.

"We protect our families and the families of Terolia. We do not have to answer to you," Reina said.

"Really? The Lady thinks differently. Have you visited the villages of Marmera or Melila lately?"

The leaders exchanged wary glances. "Why would we?" Reina asked. "They are far to the south, on the borders."

"Why not? They are your people, too. You swore to look after them in the Lady's name. Do you ignore them because they are far away?"

"You forget who you are talking to," the stern-faced Medera of Kirsha rose to her feet.

"No!" Jerrol slammed his hand on the table and Silva sat back down. "You forget your responsibilities. People who you swore on your blood oaths to protect are dying, and you do nothing. Ever heard of the Telusions?" Jerrol paused, glaring around the room. The leaders were all staring at him, stunned. "No one? You surprise me. I'm sure they're listed on your maps. Well, maybe not the mine that the Ascendants made your people dig by hand; the very people you allowed to be sold as slaves and kidnapped from their homes overnight, leaving villages deserted."

Jerrol waited. Silence. "Since when have the Medera supported slavery? Since when have the Medera allowed heathens to make money from your people? Are you all rich now? Is that what you wanted?"

"It's not slavery. We exchange people as agreed in the laws. To balance out the families, so no one grows too big. It is all written in the book." The Gusarian Medera spoke slowly as if hesitant to bring attention to herself.

"Have you looked around Mistra recently? Have you visited the slave pens? Or the pens in Ramila? Stinking holes of death and disease. You can't miss the smell nor the shackles. All spell slavery to me.

"People in despair. Your people locked up because they worship the Lady; locked up and sold because they happened to be in the wrong place at the wrong time. How did that impact their families, do you think? A father or mother who never returns home. They can no longer pay for their dwellings. They get thrown out on the streets and arrested for loitering and end up in the slave pens; whole families split up and sold, shipped out of Terolia or into the mines.

"What about the children? The future of your families, torn from their family's arms or abandoned needlessly." His voice dropped as he stared at Medera Reina of Solari. Her face tensed as she caught his eye and she looked away.

"I'd make you visit the mine, except it's not there anymore, along with over one thousand of *your* people. You let them suffer, you let them die, and you do nothing."

"We didn't let them die. We knew nothing about them," the Solari Medera protested.

"But you should have known, shouldn't you? You cross the Terolian deserts daily. I mean, you are the leaders of the Families; the people ruling Terolia; the inheritors of the Lady's Oath sworn by your ancestors and religiously handed down from generation to generation. It's part of your initiation as Medera, isn't it? It is as important as the Families laws, which, if I remember right, forbids slavery. Doesn't it say that all are family?"

He quoted the words from the Law: "*The Families protect the right of all, whether they be male or female, to move freely as they wish; to welcome nomads joyfully to your hearths; to provide access to water, shelter, and vittles as if they were of your own family and to allow them to go on their way.*"

"Who are you to quote our laws to us?" The Gusarian

Sodera spoke, his tattoo of three yellow concentric circles visible on his cheek in the candlelight.

Jerrol straightened his back and glared at the man. Power ran through his veins and he held it ready. The Gusarian leaned back from him, instinctively.

"I am Jerrolion," he paused before continuing, his voice weighted, deep, and commanding. The air crackled around him. "Captain of the Lady's Guards, Commander of the King's Justice, Keeper of the Oath, and I teach you your laws because you have forgotten the meaning of them. And if I must, I will teach you each and every one of them until you recall why you are the Medera and Sodera of your families, or you will hand over your rule to someone who will listen."

There was a stunned silence as the Jerrol's words resounded in the tent. "Let me introduce you to Mat'iller of Melila. Maybe you will listen to him." Jerrol turned towards the entrance where Birlerion raised the flap and gently ushered Mat'iller inside. Even washed and dressed in clean robes, Mat'iller's gaunt frame, haunted eyes, and general poor condition was obvious. Jerrol led him forward. "Mat'iller, tell the Mederas where we found you."

But Mat'iller stared around the tent and burst into tears, as if overwhelmed by the opulence and comfort. Jerrol patted his back and let Kayerille lead him away. Turning back to the Terolian leaders, he explained. "We found Mat'iller inside that mountain in a warren of caverns that had been hewn by Terolian blood. Never seeing the sun, existing in the dark, starved, dehydrated; worked to the bone until they died and were replaced by other Terolian bodies and the cycle repeated.

"Mat'iller has been enslaved for nearly three years in the Telusion mines. His wife and daughter died, along with over a thousand other Terolians when the Ascendants blew up the mountain with them still in it. It collapsed in on itself. We managed to save forty-two people. Forty-two," Jerrol repeated, his voice like death, "out of over one thousand, and you knew nothing about it. They are your people. You should know where every one of them is. They are your responsibility; your Family."

The tent was silent.

Maraine rose. "I asked for this conclave because our Families are disintegrating around us. We have lost touch with our people, and I don't know why. I know the Lady would be disappointed in all of us. We are failing our people." She looked around her fellow Mederas. "We have stepped away from the Lady's path and suffered for it. Our *people* are suffering for it."

"*You* may have done," the Kirshan Medera said, curling her lip. "But *I* haven't. I honour my vows."

Jerrol pounced on her. "What about the empty villages of Marmera and Lez, the depleted township of Melila? They all died in that Telusion mine. That mine has been worked for years with the blood and sweat of your people and you never noticed. Your outriders never noticed? They must have! What did you do about that? How is that honouring your vows?"

"He's right. We should have known what was going on. They are our people." The voice of the Solari leader broke the silence as she rose from her seat. "This is our country, yet we don't know what is happening inside it. Why is that? When did we lose sight? When did we forget the tight bonds that tie us all together? I am just as guilty. My Family argues, yet I do nothing. Since when do heathens tell us how to live our lives?"

The room broke into a babble of voices as the Mederas and Soderas justified their actions and their leadership.

Birlerion entered the tent and stood behind Jerrol's shoulder, a reassuring presence.

Jerrol caught Maraine's eye and she nodded. He closed his eyes briefly and asked for the Lady's blessing for what he was about to do.

"Enough!" he shouted, his control slipping. "Are you not listening? The Lady stands in judgment and finds you lacking. Your people are dying needlessly. You abandon the helpless and ignore the plight of the less fortunate. And all you do is justify yourselves?" He glared at them as, one by one, they shrank before him. "You will reaffirm your oaths to the Lady, here tonight, or you will no longer be the voice of a ruling Family." The leaders gasped before him but kept silent in the face of his unadulterated fury. He seemed to glow as he spoke, his silver eyes brilliant.

"You will agree to the unification of Terolia and Vespiri under the rule of King Benedict, as it was in the time of the Lady. He will protect your borders and his Sentinals will protect you and your people," Jerrol bit out, restraining the need to pace.

The Sentinals crashed their fists against their chests in a show of strength.

"You will close down the slave trade and you will clean out your towns of those undesirables preying on your people. You will re-instate family law and re-engage with the town councils on a regular basis.

"How you do that is your business, but you will do it." Jerrol stood straighter, his face rigid, his voice low and full of power. "In the name of the Lady and King Benedict, you will do these things. The Sentinals will help you. You will rectify all that has gone wrong in Terolia and you will help those you have failed. And if I *ever* have to come back here and tell you again, you will regret it."

Maraine stood, her face pale and determined. "I, Maraine, Medera of Atolea, swear by the Lady that I will uphold the oaths and the laws of our land. I agree to all demands as stated by the Captain, and those things will be done. In return, I will remain the Medera of Atolea and speak for my Family and accept the protection of King Benedict and his Sentinals." She sat down again, digging her Sodera in the ribs. He struggled to his feet, frowning at her, but he repeated her words firmly before sitting back in his chair, whispering, "That was quite unnecessary. I was going to swear so, anyway."

The Medera of Solari rose and nodded at Maraine. "I am grieved by our failures and our lack of discernment. She repeated the oath and sat down, staring at her hands.

"You would hand Terolia over to a king of another country?" Silva spat. "Without a fight?"

Maraine faced her. "We have already lost it. Our country is not ours. Our words are ignored and our people die needlessly. Do you prefer the Ascendants as masters? Do you prefer their rhetoric? They claim that only the pure of blood lead the people and all others should bow down before their betters and obey. Is that the law you wish to uphold?" she asked, glaring around the table. "Is it? I prefer the Lady's gentle guidance and to remain the voice of my Family."

Silva sat back in her seat, shocked. The Atolean Sodera snorted. "Gentle?" he asked, glancing at Maraine and then at the furious Captain, still glaring at them from the end of the table.

"He hasn't drawn his sword, has he?" she replied.

"There's still time."

Maraine's lips twitched before she straightened her face and glared at each of the remaining leaders until they stood and swore to the Lady. Only the Medera and Sodera of Kirsha remained.

Maraine sighed. "Silva, Ricard. You have led your Family well; why do you not swear your oath to the Lady?"

Silva leaned forward. "I don't need an outsider to tell me how to manage my Family. You are all fools. You say you don't want heathens telling us how to live our lives. What is he, then, but a heathen?"

"No, he isn't. He is the Lady's Captain, come to show us the error of our ways. In Her name, he speaks. In Her voice he demands. Can you not hear?" Maraine asked.

"Hear what?"

"The Lady. Can you not hear Her? Why do you think we swear to him? He is Her vessel, and through him, we are offered a second chance. We will not get another." Maraine drew herself erect. "Kirsha, this is your last chance."

Jerrol stirred at the end of the table. All eyes swivelled to him. "There are some who act out of character; they can't help it because it has been imposed on them. It is called *Mentiserium,* and the Ascendants are expert at it. Those without the defence of the Lady are more susceptible." Jerrol walked around the table until he was opposite the Kirshan Medera. "It is a mind spell, triggered by keywords. Only I don't know the keywords that may have been used here. I can try a few, but they may not be the correct ones." He hesitated and then said, "Silverwood. Blackstone." He thought a moment. "Redstone."

The Kirshan Medera slumped in her chair and her sodera rose to his feet, horrified. "He's killed her!" he shouted. "Call the guards!"

"Silva, tell us what you have been instructed to do," Jerrol said, ignoring her seder.

Silva raised her head and stared before her. "Allow the Ascendants access to the Telusion mountains and the port of Feril. Keep suspicious eyes averted. The pure of blood will rule; all unworthy should bow before them. We must prepare the way for the new leader." She fell silent.

The men and women around the table gaped at her, horrified.

"Who is this new leader?"

"He will be revealed when the time is right."

"Why do the Ascendants need the port of Feril? Who is running it for them?"

"The Portmaster monitors the port. He allows the Ascendants docking for their slave ships and for their cargo ships. They trade people and goods with Birtoli and Elothia."

"Where do the supplies come from?"

"Across Terolia. Every town has a goods store. Once they have a shipment, they tell the Kirshans and we send word to the port. They arrange the transfer."

"What have you been promised for your help?"

"To be the first Family; the family of pure blood. All others will bow before us and do our bidding."

Jerrol ignored the gasps. "Who will be the second Family?"

"There will be no other Families."

"Anything else you want to ask before I wipe this spell away?" Jerrol asked.

Maraine stood, her face paling. "Who arranged this service with you?"

"Var'geris speaks. We listen. He and his brothers see all. They created the network and my Family provide the connections."

"Could you identify the Ascendants to us?"

"Of course."

"Captain, can you make sure she remembers the people and the processes so that we can shut them down?"

Jerrol considered her request and nodded. "No further questions for now?" he asked the hovering leaders. They shook their heads, silenced by the inescapable fact that one of their own had betrayed them. "She will convulse when I release her. Make sure you hold her down, so she doesn't hurt herself."

Jerrol focused on Silva. "Silva. You will remember the agreement you put in place with the Ascendants. You will assist the Medera of Atolea and her colleagues with any questions they ask and you will answer truthfully. You will no longer be subject to the instructions left to you by the Ascendants, and you will not be affected by any future attempts of *Mentiserium*. Redstone."

Silva started to convulse in her chair and reluctant hands eased her to the floor. Her seder backed away until he bumped into the canvas wall. Roberion moved to block his escape, and he stood still, staring at his wife in horror.

Jerrol took a deep, steadying breath and rubbed his face before walking around the table to Nil'ano. "You get all that?"

Nil'ano nodded, dumbfounded. "Do you know what you've done? You've redrawn the map."

Jerrol grinned, his silver eyes a little wild. "Make sure you get each leader to sign against their oath. Once they have all signed, I will sign and you will witness. Understood? For Kirsha, just list them as deposed, position open. We have a majority of five to one, which is sufficient."

"Yes, Commander, um … Captain," Nil'ano stuttered.

Jerrol turned back to the room. "Silva won't remember everything that's happened. She will only remember the agreement, and she may be distressed. She agreed to it because that was what she wanted in her heart. Her husband, I would suggest, is still enspelled and should be restrained for his safety until you find his keywords. When you clear out the Ascendants' offices and the temple leaders' offices, look for small black notebooks. They tend to keep a list of all the people they have enspelled with their keywords. They can't remember them otherwise; there are too many.

"We were lucky here, but you all saw what happened. The first keyword triggers a specific behaviour; repeating the keyword allows you to reset their instructions. I expect all of you to use this knowledge wisely and for the good of your people. Much damage has been done; work with your healers to undo it."

Silva stopped convulsing and was assisted back into her chair. She drooped listlessly before making an effort to straighten up. She swallowed and smiled hesitantly at the cold faces around her. "What's the matter? Why are you all staring at me?"

Maraine glanced around the room. "By Medera's right, I propose that Silva and Ricard be removed from their position of head of their Family. Supported?"

Reina stood. "First support,"

Lila of Gusar stood. "Second support."

"Proposal passed," Maraine said with regret. "The Kirshan family will need to reapply for membership of the Family conclave once new leaders have been appointed. The conclave will need proof that the Family has resolved its differences and returned to the path. The remaining five Families will be available to assist the Kirshans as needed. We will meet tomorrow to discuss further how we can help them and the best way for us to meet the Captain's demands." Maraine clapped her hands. "All will sign the accords before leaving. We will reconvene here at sunrise tomorrow. Agreed?"

The rest of the leaders clapped their hands, signalling agreement, and rose. Roberion and Adilion escorted the Kirshan leaders out of the tent and held them until Maraine came out to instruct where to take them. One by one, the leaders signed the paper that Nil'ano had written. Jerrol waited until all had passed by Nil'ano's table before signing at the bottom.

"Make a copy. I will sign and they can resign tomorrow; a copy for them to keep. Guard the original copy with your life until you hand it to King Benedict. Until he ratifies it, it's just a piece of paper." Jerrol instructed before leaving the tent. Nil'ano sat staring at the papers in front of him and then looked up at the now-empty tent. He had seen history in the making and he had written out the accords. The accords that would change the world they lived in. His smile grew.

Marianille and Birlerion were waiting for him outside the tent. "Marianille, guard Nil'ano. Those accords need to reach the king, and you will travel to Old Vespers with him."

"Yes, Captain. But what about you?"

"I'll travel with you as far as the border, but I need to visit the Watch Tower and seal the Veil before I return to Vespers. Serillion and Saerille are expecting me, and I am long overdue."

Jerrol walked around the tent and stopped facing out across empty golden sands. He expelled his breath. What had he done? Anger ran through his body, entwined with an exhilaration that threatened to overflow. He wanted to laugh out loud; to shout or scream; anything to acknowledge this momentous occasion. He wondered what the king would say when he found out, and he smiled.

Jerrol relaxed on the cushions, sipping the ice-cold water Maraine handed him. His head pounded, a result of exhaustion and stress, leaving him emotionally drained. He rested his head back against the bolster behind him and closed his eyes. The cushions dipped as Maraine sat beside him and he reluctantly opened his eyes. "What's next, Captain?" she asked.

Jerrol grimaced. "Report back to the king. Advise him his kingdom has expanded. Figure out the best way to defend it."

"And then?"

"Follow the trail. Find the Ascendants and stop them for good."

"It's not over, then," Maraine whispered.

"No, I expect there is worse yet to come," Jerrol agreed, though he dreaded to think what could ever be worse than what they had just been through. "I'll dispatch the Sentinals back to their hometowns. They will reinstate the waystones and check their borders. They can report through Kayerille, and she can liaise with me in Old Vespers for now. I'll leave you to clean house. Please don't hide anything. It could help us elsewhere if we know about it."

"Don't worry. You'll probably be getting too much information to begin with."

"Good point. I need to get some scholars on my staff. We need to send more help. Melila will need time to recover, as will Marmera and Lez," he said, thinking about all the things that were awaiting his attention back in Vespiri.

"A piece of well-meant advice," Maraine said. "You can't do everything yourself. You need to take time to build a staff you trust. Let them help you."

"I know. I'm just never in Vespers long enough to do it."

"Make time. Then you can stop worrying about everything else and concentrate on the things *you* need to do."

Jerrol grinned at her. "If there's anyone you would recommend for my staff, let me know."

Maraine pursed her lips and nodded. "Actually, you could do with a liaison for all things Terolia. Nil'ano was ready to retire, though I'm sure he would be willing to travel to Vespers, I think, and train the next ambassador. I trust him with my life, and he is a true believer. In your absence, he could advise your staff and mediate with the families on your behalf. A familiar face may ease some tension to begin with."

"Maraine, I think *you* are the true ambassador."

She laughed and shook her head at him.

38

IL QUERON, TEROLIA

Marianille stopped and turned around, staring at the empty horizon. "We should have reached Il Queron by now," she said, breathless in the heat of the day. She rewrapped the scarf around her face and scowled at the endless sand.

Jerrol squinted in the bright sunshine and shrugged as he stared out at the shapeless terrain around them. "*Zin'talia, weren't you paying attention?*"

"*It should be over there,*" she said, tossing her head. "*But it's not. We are in the right place.*"

"This is the right place," Jerrol said out loud.

"It can't be," Marianille complained.

"It's that way. I can hear Peterion, but he's very muted," Birlerion said, pointing. "Let's go a bit further; maybe there's something over by that dune."

"We would have seen the sentinal by now," Niallerion argued. "Going further only makes the return journey longer. We need to find shelter out of the sun."

"There will be something over here," Jerrol reiterated, following Birlerion. He slid off Zin'talia, laying a gentle hand against her neck as he stood listening. If Birlerion said that Peterion was here, then he was here. Jerrol knelt and placed his hands on the burning sands. The soles of his thin sandals provided scant protection as the fine sand sifted through the straps. He shifted uncomfortably as the distress from the Land shivered through him, images of powerful sandstorms followed by a wiry sentinal tree bowing before the shifting sand.

"They are beneath us," Jerrol murmured.

"Beneath us? That's not possible! The amount of sand that would have needed to shift to cover the whole town and the sentinal is immense," Nil'ano said, staring around him in disbelief.

"There were sandstorms; unnatural storms," Jerrol murmured. "The storms scoured the land for days, moving mountains of sand. The oasis is below us," he said again.

"Peterion is calling. They are here," Birlerion said, dropping to his knees and beginning to scoop the sand away.

Marianille grabbed the back of his robe. "Birlerion stop, it's too hot to dig now."

Nil'ano looked horrified. "But there were hundreds of people living here. Are you saying they were buried alive?"

Jerrol stood up. "Yes," he said as he walked over to the southern point of the crescent dune. He stood, considering what to do.

"We need to dig here?" Niallerion asked watching Birlerion.

"We need to rig some shelter first; we won't last long in this heat. Then yes, we dig here," Jerrol agreed, turning to his saddlebags and rummaging for a sheet of canvas and his rope. He led Zin'talia over to the end of the dune, frowning at the lack of rocks.

Nil'ano knelt and began digging in the sand. "The sand is heavier below. We can tie the sheet to the horse and weight it below the sand. That will shield the worst. We need to rest in the heat of the day and dig when it's cooler," he said, beginning to scoop the shifting sand behind him.

"It's unlikely they can breathe under all that sand," Niallerion said even as he tugged the awning off the back of the pack horse. "There isn't enough water to waste digging. We have to make all haste to Ramila and hope we can conserve enough water to get us there."

Jerrol ignored him. He dropped beside Birlerion and started digging. Marianille cursed under her breath and bent to help Niallerion set up their makeshift shelter. Half a chime later, Jerrol called a halt through parched lips. "Water," he croaked, staggering over to Zin'talia and unhooking the water bottle. "One mouthful, no more," he instructed, handing the canteen to Birlerion.

Niallerion reluctantly took a swig of his own canteen before re-stoppering it. "We won't have enough water to reach Mistra," he said with concern.

"We can refill at the sentinal," Jerrol said through his teeth, clamping his mouth shut. "Now rest," he said, laying back in the shade of the awning. He closed his eyes, trying to still the sense of urgency and listening to the soft sounds of the shifting sand as the others settled.

Peterion thrummed below them, but just scraping the surface had exhausted them. The heat was brutal and would dehydrate them if they were foolish enough to expend all their energy digging now. He told himself to wait and dozed as Zin'talia muttered darkly about being used as a shelter.

Time passed slowly. The unending blue sky deepened as the fiery ball of flame travelled across it, turning golden sands into ochre shadows. The sands shimmered in the heat as the sun beat down and dried it out further. There was no moisture anywhere and little shade deep enough to offer protection.

He must have slept because suddenly he realised he was awake. Zin'talia crooned to herself, and as he sat up, she swished her tail, causing a slight puff of air to waft past his face. Niallerion and Nil'ano snored gently in chorus and Marianille was curled up on her side next to Birlerion.

Birlerion watched the sunset, his face shadowed and still. Jerrol wondered what thoughts churned behind those intelligent eyes. Maraine had made Birlerion promise to return; to acknowledge them as family. Kayerille had been just as insistent, and Birlerion had promised.

Jerrol would have to find time to allow his trusted lieutenant to go and visit. *Not any time soon, though,* he thought. They would stop at Greenswatch on the way home and ensure Birlerion met his Darian. That was a promise Jerrol *did* make to himself.

The temperature began to drop as the sun dipped below the horizon. Jerrol shrugged back into his robe and surveyed the sands around them. He marked out the position of Peterion. They would need to dig him out first. That would be only way they would find out what happened and how they could help.

Jerrol grinned as the Sentinals stirred. "Time to dig," he said firmly, pointing at the ground.

"What, no tea first?" Niallerion complained as he stood, shaking the sand out of his clothes; it seemed to creep in everywhere. He eased his shoulder, wincing, as he watched Nil'ano line the fire pit with some fibrous strands before adding some more rocks. Jerrol paused long enough to dig out his flint and tinder for Nil'ano before returning to the shallow indentation he had begun. Birlerion rubbed his fingers and lit the fire.

Nil'ano stared at him.

"I forgot you could do that," Jerrol said.

"The Lady's magic is growing stronger." Birlerion grimaced. "It means the Veil must be breached."

Marianille pounced on him. "Since when have you been able to do that? Do you mean you could do that before? Did Leyandrii teach you? Is this like those onoffs?"

"I bet it was after Clary attacked you," Niallerion said with a knowing glance. "You spent a lot of time with Leyandrii then."

"That's right," Marianille said, observing her brother. "She wouldn't let you out of her sight."

Birlerion looked everywhere but at Marianille. "Peterion is calling, we need to dig."

"Don't try and slide out of answering. Tell us how you learnt to do that. Can you teach us?" Marianille was insistent.

"I don't know. Can I?" Birlerion said with a twist of his lips.

"It would be a useful skill," Niallerion murmured, and then wilted under Marianille's glare.

"Later Marianille, we have more important matters to deal with. Nil'ano, could you tend the fire and make the tea. We'll dig," Jerrol said.

They persevered into the night by the light of the flickering fire that Nil'ano sporadically fed with the fibrous material he kept finding from somewhere.

Their canteens were getting desperately low when Niallerion gave a muffled shout as he brushed the sand off the green fronds of the Sentinal. Jerrol stood, stretching his aching back. "Thank the Lady," he breathed as they redoubled their efforts. The thin spindly trunk finally came into view, and Jerrol placed his palm against the bark and shimmered into the half-buried tree.

"Peterion," he called. Peterion stepped forward out of the mist, his face lined and strained.

"Captain," he whispered, his voice hoarse, tears welling in his silver eyes. "I-I can't hold it much longer. I thought we were all lost."

Jerrol gripped his arm. "Lady willing, we can hold it together long enough to save them all."

"How?" Peterion asked, his voice a harsh croak. "The air is running out and the sand is so loose that when I tunnel, it all folds in on itself."

Jerrol grinned. "We have help," he pointed upwards. "We need some water, though. We are just about out."

"Water, I have. It's air that we are running out of."

"Then, if you are willing, let's invite my companions within and plan the great escape. Il Queron needs to be reinstated; it's just a wasteland up above. Let's see what we can do."

The air shimmered and Birlerion and Nil'ano appeared in the mists, followed by the other Sentinals. Nil'ano eyes were wide as he held onto Birlerion with a tight grip. Jerrol smiled. "Welcome to Sentinal Peterion," he said as Nil'ano sheepishly let go of Birlerion.

Marianille gripped Peterion's arms, a gentle smile of wonder on her face. "Peterion," she said as they embraced.

Peterion reached forward, his hands full of mugs of water. He held them out and Nil'ano accepted a mug and sidled up beside Jerrol. "Are we really inside the sentinal?" he asked, his eyes darting around as the mists coalesced into a circular room with a wooden table and chairs growing out of the floor in one continuous piece of living furniture in the centre of the room.

Jerrol winced at the rasp in Peterion's voice as he said, "Please be seated. Drink. You are dehydrated." Nil'ano sat, running his hand over the smooth, silvery wood.

Peterion sat and grimaced across the table at Jerrol. "Over two hundred people are sheltering in the temple. It has been four days. They have no food, some water, and a dwindling supply of air. We have managed to keep them safe, but our shields are weakening. The weight is too great and gets heavier every day. We can't keep them up much longer."

Nil'ano gaped at Peterion. "You are protecting how many people?"

"Two hundred and twelve; all those who managed to reach the Lady's temple. The storm came up unexpectedly without warning. The blackout was complete. Those who heard my voice followed it to the temple. That's what happened to my voice," he whispered. "I wore it out leading the people to the temple. They couldn't see a hand span in front of them."

Birlerion knelt in front of him and gripped his arms. "I can help."

"If you're sure," Peterion murmured.

Jerrol's sword vibrated against his hip. When he glanced down, it glowed a faint blue. He snapped his gaze back to the Sentinals, startled, and frowned at the blue sparkle that flickered around Birlerion.

Peterion relaxed in his arms and Birlerion stiffened. Peterion took a deep breath and sat up, flexing his shoulders, and then helped Birlerion into a chair, murmuring his thanks.

"It is fortunate we didn't use the waystone," Niallerion said, observing Birlerion with interest. "We would have ended up under this sand as well."

Jerrol nodded, still watching Birlerion. "It just didn't sound right. Almost muted. Now we know why." He smiled at Nil'ano's expression. "The temple is right there, isn't it?" Jerrol asked, pointing off to his left. "And the river is running below your roots, through a comprehensive network of caverns. Too deep for it to help us."

Nil'ano stared at Jerrol. "How do you know this? How do

you know where we are? How do you even know they are alive? They are buried in masses of sand." He looked up, a faint sheen of sweat on his face. "So are we. This is all so wrong!" He shuddered, and Marianille absent-mindedly patted his arm.

"It is fortunate my brother is with us," she said, glaring at Birlerion. "His hidden skills continue to surprise us all."

Birlerion grimaced, but didn't reply.

"I for one am glad he is here," Peterion said with a strained smile. "I couldn't hold out much longer, and he can only hold it for so long. Captain, how do we save the people?"

"We could lead them out through your sentinal if we can dig you out far enough. But there are no resources or amenities to protect over two hundred people from the desert. We have little food with us," Jerrol said. "I wonder, if we uncover the temple enough to provide light and air, whether they could continue to shelter there as we dig them out further?"

"I have food and water," Peterion replied. "I just can't reach them."

Birlerion stirred, his movements were sluggish. "Have you thought of trying to contact Marguerite?"

"Don't be daft, Birlerion. She went with the Lady; how would you contact her?" Marianille asked, her gaze boring into him. Her lips tightened as she watched him.

"No, she didn't. She is here with us. I think she would hear you, Captain, if you called her."

Jerrol stared at him, trying to understand what Birlerion wasn't saying. He seriously needed to sit down and talk with him. The man knew so much more than he shared. Case in point…what was he doing to help Peterion that was taking so much effort? Whatever it was, he could only do it for so long. He was already showing the strain. "I need to speak to someone. I'll be back in a bit," Jerrol stated.

Jerrol sat cross-legged on the sand under the crescent moon, suspended in the dark blue sky amongst a swathe of sparkling stars. A soft benediction descended around him. He smiled gently and dug his hands into the sand beside him.

The Lady had said, the very first time she had spoken to him, that he should soothe the Land and make her his ally. He hadn't understood what she'd meant at the time, but he had an inkling now. The storms had been unnatural. She must be quite distressed at the pain such a sudden displacement would cause her. He offered her love and support and a way to relieve her pain.

He sank his thoughts down into the ground, through the layers of shifting sand, past the sentinal and the buried village. He avoided what looked like a transparent shield, holding the sand above the temple. Was that what Birlerion was doing? He reached a deep cavern below. He touched the river that thundered through the dark tunnels, weaving his way deeper and deeper until he came to rest and sent out a welcome. He waited patiently, extending tendrils of gentle expectation and suggestions of partnership.

The moon progressed across the sky as he waited. The faintest streaks of grey began to alleviate the darkness and spread across the horizon. A hesitant query intruded on his awareness and he gently responded with a reply: He was Jerrolion, Lady's Captain and Oath Keeper, come to help in her time of need. A stronger response followed, with a snap of anger in its tail. He soothed her. He could only help if she let him; he reminded her of his Oath, which she had accepted.

She hesitated, suspicious, and extended an ancient touch; a soft questioning that struck him to the core and exposed him for who he was. He almost groaned. Why did these powerful deities want to strip him bare? And why was it always him?

"*Because,*" she said, as a soft sigh rippled through his body, rifling through him and exposing every aspect of his soul. She slowed as she reached his memories of the Sentinals. He had the impression that she was searching. She paused on Birlerion but continued so quickly, he may have been mistaken. "*We want to know to whom we are entrusting our possibilities and our children.*"

Her anger and pain washed over him, and then a soft sigh of acceptance. "*We find you worthy. My sister and I rarely agree, but on this occasion, I accept your Oath and your proposal and will do as you suggest. I must admit, I hadn't thought to relocate, but why not? The relief will soothe. And Oath Keeper, more of your forgotten are waiting. It is time; they have suffered enough. The lost weep bitter tears. The debt that was not is paid many times over. Heal them. Release them. For them, I will help you.*"

Jerrol bowed his head in acceptance. "*I will do what is necessary,*" he vowed.

"*I know you will.*" She sighed. "*Know that I stand ready. The road is long and treacherous. Be strong, Oath Keeper; remember you are not alone.*" Her voice faded away and the sense of her all-consuming presence with it. She had sounded tired and weary, worn out from defending against unimaginable incursions and yet at the same time indomitable and unyielding.

Jerrol slumped where he sat, breathing deeply. Her touch had been overpowering. How could anyone overcome her? He stirred as the ground began to shake. Sand drained away like water down a hole. The sentinal tree and the town he protected seemed to rise in its place. The worn bedrock, exposed for the first time in centuries, curved around the houses like a pockmarked windbreak, providing a protective shelter from future storms.

Water seeped into Jerrol's clothes and he began to laugh.

The Land had a sense of humour, it seemed. A spring doused him as it erupted around him, filling the indentation left in the bedrock now exposed to the early morning sun. He reached up as Zin'talia grumbled her way to the water's edge, complaining about being left behind again.

Jerrol stood, dripping in the shallows as the door to the Lady's temple opened and Erissia peered out. Her face was tense, creased with lines and wrinkles, but her beady eyes were sharp. Her piercing black gaze took in the surroundings: the morning sun, the bare rock, and, lastly, the slender man rising from the water being greeted by a pure white Darian mare, and she smiled toothily. This was what legends were made of.

She moved aside to let the others out.

39

STONEFORD WATCH, VESPIRI

A week later, Jerrol reined Zin'talia to a halt as they reached the Stanton pass. The road diverged, one path snaking through the winding pass to Stoneford, the other leading north to Velmouth. He turned to Marianille and Niallerion. They were all dust-ridden and weary. "Chryllion will introduce you to Lord Jason. You can all rest at Stoneford tonight. I need you to escort Nil'ano to King Benedict in Old Vespers. Parsillion and Darllion will be there to make sure you get an audience. It is imperative you get the accords to the king safely.

"Nil'ano, I'll leave you to report to the king if you arrive before me. Marianille, ask Bryce to provide rooms for everyone in the guest barracks."

"Thanks so much." Nil'ano grimaced, gripping Jerrol's arm. "Take care; those assassins are still searching for you."

"The accords are more important. I will be fine. I have Birlerion, and Serillion and Saerille wait for us at the Towers; they should be protection enough," Jerrol reassured him. "Your mission is to make sure those papers reach the king."

"Make sure you get the Captain to Vespers, we'll be expecting you," Marianille said, hugging her brother tight.

"Of course," Birlerion replied, returning the embrace.

Jerrol pulled Zin'talia aside as Marianille led the way down the road. He watched them until they turned the corner before he took the road to Velmouth, Birlerion beside him. Zin'talia pulled at the reins, so he let her stretch her legs for a while, her loping gallop eating the miles towards the towers.

They had rested for a day at Il Queron, helping the people back to their homes, celebrating the Lady and the Land and the miracle of the new oasis. The legend of the Lady's Captain had spread through the village, most of them witnessing the miracle with their own eyes as they tumbled out of the temple. Zin'talia had thoroughly enjoyed all the attention.

It had taken another week to reach the border. Jerrol eased his shoulders. He would be glad to sleep in a proper bed for once. It seemed like he had spent months in the saddle; it would be nice to go home and see Taelia. They needed to talk.

They reached the Watch Towers late that evening. Acknowledging the salutes of the rangers on duty, he unsaddled Zin'talia in the stables, leaving a young lad to rub her down. He rubbed his face against hers and paused to stroke She'vanne's nose in greeting before heading into the main building, carrying his saddlebags.

She'vanne was Torsion's silver-grey Darian mare. She was old, now. She had been with Torsion when Jerrol had first met him, but she was still carrying Torsion around Vespiri. If She'vanne was in the stables, at least Torsion should still be here.

The last time he had visited the Watch Towers, he had ended up setting the place on fire; he hoped this visit wouldn't be so exciting. He entered the vestibule, calling out silently to Saerille and Serillion.

There was no response.

"Hello?" he called, as he continued deeper into the building.

Torsion strode down the hallway to meet them. "Jerrol? By the Lady, what are you doing here?" Torsion's gaze darted around to see who else had arrived with Jerrol and spied the Sentinal behind him.

Jerrol grinned and thumped his arm. "Don't panic, there's only Birlerion and me," he said as he eased his bag off his shoulder. "We're on our way back to Vespers. Thought we'd call in on the way."

"Back to Vespers? Where have you been? Come through, we were just finishing supper when we heard you call."

"We?"

"Yes, Taelia and Mary are here. They've been working on some engravings we found. They seem to date from when the towers were built. The carvings speak to the purpose of the towers and they mention that grid you were talking about.

"I'm glad you came; you must have known. We were trying to figure out what it all meant, but now you can show us. Amazingly, these towers are connected to the Veil that the Lady created," Torsion continued enthusiastically. His eyes glittered with excitement. "Taelia told me more about you being the Lady's Captain; you'll have to tell me what that means, old chap," he said as he led the way into a small dining room. "Taelia, look who's arrived."

Taelia turned her head towards the door and a smile blossomed over her face. "Jerrol, what are you doing here?" Only Birlerion saw the murderous expression that passed over Torsion's face at her delighted greeting.

"Just passing through on the way back to Old Vespers

with Birlerion. I have to report back to the king," Jerrol said, dropping his bag in the corner. "How long have you been here?"

"Birlerion," Taelia greeted the Sentinal with a smile, and then her face creased in thought. "A couple of weeks. Mary and I were sent when Torsion asked the Deane for help to translate these engravings. They are in every tower. We started in the south tower, and we found mention of that grid you saw straight away, did Torsion tell you?"

Torsion laughed. "Give the man a chance. He's exhausted, by the looks of it. Let's give him a drink, and he can tell us what he's been up to."

Jerrol flicked Torsion a glance and sat in the offered chair. "Thanks," he said as he took the glass. "Mary, it's nice to see you again," he said to the young woman sitting next to Taelia.

"She has been a marvel. I am very fortunate she was able to come with me." Taelia smiled as she patted her hand.

Jerrol observed Torsion's scowl with interest.

"I told you I would help you; you didn't need to bring her."

"I don't mind, Scholar Torsion. It has all been good experience," Mary replied, her voice so sweet it made Jerrol's teeth hurt. He hid a smile as Torsion's scowl deepened.

Taelia chuckled. "Now, Torsion you know this experience is invaluable, you wouldn't want to deprive Mary of the opportunity. Anyway, you were supposed to have left for Old Vespers. Didn't the Deane want a report?"

"We have too much to do here," Torsion snapped.

"You shouldn't ignore the Deane's orders," Mary pointed out. "She might not allow you to return."

"More reason not to leave," Torsion growled.

Birlerion shifted in his chair and Torsion transferred his scowl to the Sentinal instead of Mary.

"He's been grumpy all day," Taelia said. "Ignore him. What brings you here Jerrol? We weren't expecting you."

"Just passing through. We've just completed a quick circuit of the Families to make sure all was well. The king wanted to reinstate some contact. It just takes so long to cross that desert. Even Zee was glad to leave. Even though she loves the Baliweed, she was starting to complain."

"I didn't complain that *much,"* Zin'talia complained in his head.

Jerrol stifled a laugh. "Where is the Announcer?"

"I'm not sure who you mean. When I got here with the rangers, there was only the pot boys and a couple of the kitchen staff. No one else was here."

"Not even the Warden?"

"No. No one seems to know where he went." Torsion looked away. "I guess he got fed up with being out here in the back of beyond. It does get a bit lonely."

Jerrol watched him. "We'll probably need to make sure there is a regular rotation to keep the troops alert. How many scholars did you bring with you?"

"How many? There's only Taelia, Mary and me."

"What? Liliian couldn't spare you some journeymen? This place is huge. One person can't possibly investigate it all."

"He's right, Torsion. There should be more scholars here. Even with what we've found already, we can't possibly cope with all the work," Taelia agreed.

An expression of distaste flashed across Torsion's face. Didn't he want more help? Or maybe he didn't. Birlerion shifted in his seat again and smiled blandly at Torsion as his scowl descended on him.

Jerrol knocked his drink back and leaned forward. "Time for a bath and bed, if you could show us where we can sleep. We've been sleeping rough for weeks. We can check out the

Towers in the morning and I'll show you where the grid is." He stood and drifted over to Taelia. "Sleep well," he murmured, leaning down to kiss the top of her head.

She smiled up at him, her hand rising of its own accord, though she altered the move as soon as she realised what she was doing. "Jerrol?"

"Later," he whispered, turning to Torsion with a bright, "Lead on, where do we sleep in this place?"

Torsion tapped his finger on the table before managing a false smile. "This way. I'll be back shortly, Taelia."

Jerrol bathed, feeling much better for being clean, washing off the dust and sweat of Terolia, but not the memories. He returned to the room Torsion had shown him and changed into some clean clothes before lying on the bed. He stared up at the ceiling and concentrated on reaching Serillion. The empty space echoed; the silence daunting. Where were they? He could sense the edges of the Veil, but it was muted; he knew he would have to go to a tower to get a clearer view. The question was, should he go now or tomorrow?

As Jerrol tried to decide, he fell asleep; an exhausted sleep that was disturbed by bad dreams. Pleading eyes drilled into him and he heard falling rocks and the frantic screams of people dying of suffocation. People dying beneath a collapsing mountain.

He sat up, his heart racing and breathing heavily, all thought of sleep lost. The sound of his shouts echoed off the walls. Had anyone heard him? Swinging his legs over the side of the bed, he tried to control his breathing. He stood and rinsed his face and then stared out the window. The Lady's moon was still high in the sky. Everyone would be asleep. He shrugged into his jacket and left the room, his sword belted around his waist.

Jerrol ghosted down the corridors and across the courtyard, easily avoiding the inattentive guards, which made Jerrol frown. King's Rangers should be much better trained and knew how to stay alert on boring watches.

He entered the Watch Tower and made his way up the stairs. Opening the first door, he found it occupied. A man lay in a reclining leather chair. It had been rotated flat to make a bed, but it didn't look like the man had been moved. The Watchers had been sleeping much as the Sentinals had slept for the last three thousand years, atrophied in position, but they were not being cared for. Torsion had not alleviated the situation. Why not?

"Boy, where are you? Take down those co-ordinates, the Veil still hasn't been sealed," a hoarse voice split the silence.

Jerrol shut the door and approached the Watcher. "How do I seal the Veil?"

The Watcher's hand reached for him and gripped Jerrol's wrist in a bony grip, the fingers surprisingly strong. "You are late; your people are struggling." The Watcher's eyes gleamed in the dark. "You need to be quick. You know how to seal the Veil. Do it properly and do it once. They will not be able to penetrate again for years. If you don't, we will all be at risk."

"How long will it take?"

"As long as it needs to. Do it properly." The voice strengthened. "Go now, Captain, before you are too late."

Birlerion stared up at the stone tower, breathing in the moist night air, so different in texture to the dry desert air. It was strange to be back in his uniform and no longer draped in soft robes. It was funny how quickly a person could adapt. He had always liked the desert, adjusting to the slower way of life as naturally as breathing.

The Captain's cries had disturbed him. He had been

unable to sleep himself; the plight of the Terolian people was heavy on his mind. The sight of so many bodies discarded in the tunnels haunted him. He couldn't get rid of the thought that there were many more unseen, buried in the mined-out passages. They weren't even forgotten, because no one knew they were there. Hundreds of them, lost.

He planted his feet at the base of the tower. He would wait for the Captain; give him the time he needed. He watched the faint sliver of the moon. She was waning; she would be lost to the dawn soon. Her peaceful constancy was soothing.

He allowed himself to drift through his memories of people in the past who he had lost. The deserts of Terolia had brought back memories, many of which he had tried to bury. Thinking of them was too painful, but the faces of family and friends resurfaced, nonetheless. His Darian, Kaf'enir; he missed her light voice and her constant companionship. He missed his family, so hard-won and all lost, especially Tagerill's father, Warren, who had stood behind him no matter what. He wondered how the other Sentinals coped when the present reminded them so strongly of the past.

40

WATCH TOWERS, STONEFORD WATCH

Jerrol left the Watcher and continued up the stairs to the empty room at the top of the tower. He perched on the edge of the chair and then laid back. Wriggling into a more comfortable position, he stared up at the ceiling. The gridwork across the ceiling stood out clearly, and as he stared, his mind broke through the stone. Twinkling stars sparkled in an unending panorama in front of him.

Jerrol stiffened in shock, nearly losing the connection. The stone ceiling shimmered before the starry panorama replaced it again.

"Saerille? Serillion?" he called as he searched. He gasped as a sparkling weave of threads stretched out before him, curving around above him, reaching around their world. The Veil.

Hesitantly, he reached for the Veil, testing the fabric, feeling the damage and the attempted repairs. He picked up the threads of the Veil and began stitching, sealing the edges together, instinctively repairing the damage. The more he restored, the more he realised the extent of the damage. As he worked, he recognised the essence of Saerille in the threads. He followed the scent and gently called her name.

Saerille wept.

He found her entangled in the fabric, trapped and exposed. Serillion stood in front of her, trying to defend her, his shimmering essence limned by the crackle of energy flickering around him.

"Saerille, I am ordering you to let go," Jerrol commanded.

"I can't," she moaned.

"I fear she is caught in the Veil," Serillion said, deflecting a sudden thrust. "She has given too much of herself, and she can no longer separate herself."

"What can I do?"

"You can only offer her shelter until she is ready to return," Serillion said, his glance embracing her and then returning to his watch. "You need to be quick; they have found us, I think."

"But she will return?"

"If you can persuade her, then yes."

"Very well." Jerrol expanded his thought to embrace Saerille. He wrapped her in love and safety and carefully drew her essence out of the Veil and into his heart. He offered her shelter and sustenance and Saerille clung to him desperately.

Jerrol expanded his thought further and reached for the edges of the tear. He brought the strands together and began stitching again. Serillion watched his perimeter, guarding against attacks. There were subtle probes against his defences, but nothing he couldn't handle.

Jerrol continued stitching, working his way around the jagged tear in the fabric of the Veil. Carefully, ensuring he left no gaps, he concentrated on sealing the edges, trusting Serillion to protect him as he worked.

It took a lot of effort. The Veil sucked his energy as he worked. His respect for Saerille rose as he realised how much effort it must have taken to hold the Veil together for so long. He'd had no conception of what was involved. He berated himself for leaving her to cope on her own, but there had always seemed to be another emergency to solve.

The wholeness of the Veil was an enormous presence impinging on his senses as he continued to seal it. It drained his strength. It was not only the physical sealing that was exhausting. The Veil constantly tried to entangle him in the threads of the fabric, and he fought to keep himself separate. His understanding of Saerille's predicament grew as he struggled to control the voracious appetite of the Veil.

He touched the essence of Saerille tucked away inside him. She huddled in on herself, and he offered a gentle blessing. All would be well.

The attack came from nowhere. Serillion blocked and instinctively retaliated, but before he could throw up his defences, a second, concerted attack hit at the same time. Serillion expanded to shelter Jerrol, expending energy, which the Veil sucked in at a lethal rate.

"Serillion, no," Jerrol shouted as he frantically sealed the last section, the lines glowing before his eyes.

Serillion continued to expand. Energy pulsed over and over as he linked multiple waves together before, with a gentle sigh, he exploded in a blinding flash that shattered the attack. He sent an energy bolt pulsing back to the source, burning out those who had dared to attack the Captain and the Veil.

Jerrol launched out of the reclining chair, blinded by Serillion's power. He reached for Serillion in the Veil space and staggered against the stone wall in shock, as awareness returned.

The last of his strength drained away, leaving him weak

and shivery. The Veil was sealed, but at what cost? His mind was numb, seared by the sight of Serillion's sacrifice. He could barely sense Saerille curled up in the corner. She wasn't responding to any of his tentative calls. He couldn't blame her. He wanted to curl up and hide as well.

Taking a deep breath, he blearily looked around the stone tower. Ain'uncer stood opposite him, flanked by two of the King's Rangers.

Serillion was lost, his body consumed by his final sacrifice.

"Well, what do we have here? I still can't quite believe that you are the Lady's Captain. You are not what we expected. You couldn't even save one of your own. Where is the power of the Lady now? Do you think you repaired the Veil? You are just going to have to unfix it, now," Ain'uncer crooned. "I'm going to enjoy making you rip the Veil." With a quick hand signal, the guards moved to flank Jerrol, rigidly holding him in place.

Jerrol cringed. Ain'uncer was solid muscle, and by the glitter in his eye, he had revenge in mind.

"Why are you doing this? You can't want to destroy the world we live in," Jerrol said, trying to delay the inevitable. He tested the hold of his captors, but they tightened their grip in response. He had no strength left. He could barely stand up.

Ain'uncer laughed as he crossed the room. He unsheathed his dagger and ran the cold steel down the side of Jerrol's face. Jerrol shivered. "You think I'm going to hurt you? You're probably right," he mused. "You have quite a reputation. The famous man of iron who doesn't feel anything, ruthless in his pursuits. Killer of men. Do you think you can resist me?"

Jerrol stared at him, grappling with a sense of loss and

inevitability. Exhaustion swept through him as he tried to concentrate on what the Ascendant was saying.

"You think you can escape me? Such a clever man; so smart, he lets his people die in his place."

Jerrol tried to contain a flinch, the anguish raw and painful.

"Ah, that hurts, does it?" Ain'uncer said, sheathing the knife. "Maybe you're not made of iron, after all? Let's test the theory, shall we?" He punched Jerrol hard in the stomach, followed by a swift uppercut, which snapped Jerrol's head back against the guard's chest. Ain'uncer reached around and unbuckled Jerrol's sword belt before snapping his fingers. The guards dragged the gasping Jerrol over to the reclining chair, strapping him securely in place.

"You've been hiding artefacts. Does Torsion know?" Ain'uncer inspected Jerrol's sword. "Where did you find your sword, Haven?"

Jerrol gritted his teeth. "You wouldn't believe me if I told you."

"You know I can't resist. Let's try it the easy way, first." Ain'uncer smiled, his eyes bright, almost feverish in expectation.

"What have you done to Torsion?" Jerrol asked, desperately searching the room for inspiration. He flexed his mouth; his jaw was swelling.

"Torsion? Why, nothing. He'll be disappointed in you, though. I heard he tried to warn you; you should have listened. So, just for form's sake, and the sake of your friendship, shred the Veil. Now."

Jerrol stared at him. "Now, why would I want to do that?"

"Because I asked nicely, and it will save so much pain and anguish."

"Why don't you do it yourself?"

Ain'uncer's frown was fleeting. "It is not one of my gifts. Fortunate for you, I have other gifts. You will listen to my voice. That's all you need to do, listen to me. You feel yourself relaxing, the warmth is flowing through your body as your muscles ease, one by one. It is time to rest, all you need to do is listen to my voice."

Jerrol fought the weight dragging at his limbs. Tagerill had said thinking of the Lady protected you. "Lady, help me. I beseech you, help me." He pictured Leyandrii's face, the brilliant green eyes that sparkled with life, the golden tresses of hair that glinted with sunshine. He thought of Birlerion's steadfast love and Serillion's quiet adoration. Both effortlessly embraced her legacy and brought her to life.

Leyandrii's green gaze sharpened and the heaviness dispersed as she wrapped her arms around him.

"You want to shred the Veil; you know it is the right thing to do. Shred it now, Jerrol." Ain'uncer voice crooned above him.

"Never," Jerrol replied.

Ain'uncer broke off his chant and grabbed Jerrol's hair, yanking his head back and exposing his throat. His blade ran across the vulnerable skin. "Are you sure? You are in no position to resist."

Jerrol tried not to swallow against the cold of the blade.

"You must, you know you must. You can't resist my voice; you have to shred the Veil. It is the only thing you need to do. It is your purpose. Reach for the Veil, yes, you know you must, reach now, that's right."

"No," Jerrol whispered, his thoughts skittering in all directions. He latched onto one. Birlerion would save him. He would come to his rescue. He knew he would.

"You must, it's the only way to protect your friends. That is what you do. Protect others. Don't put them at risk. Shred the Veil, now!" Ain'uncer's breath was hot against his clammy cheek.

Jerrol strained against the leather straps.

"Listen to my voice. You must do as I say. It makes you feel good, it makes you feel fulfilled. You are doing what you should. You…" His voice trailed off as the clash of steel echoed up the stairs.

"No," Jerrol said, his voice strengthening.

"See what's happening," Ain'uncer hissed at the guards. He stared down at Jerrol. "There is no escape. You will do what I tell you one way or the other. Why make it difficult? You do not need to suffer, nor does anyone else. If you shred the Veil, all will be safe."

"I can't."

"Of course, you can. If you don't, you'll regret it, I promise you." Ain'uncer's voice hardened. "You will shred the Veil now."

Jerrol's breath whooshed out as Ain'uncer punched him in the side.

"No," he wheezed.

Ain'uncer paced around him. "You are being stubborn for no reason. It won't save anyone." He took a deep breath and began again. "Focus on my voice, Jerrol. It is the only thing you want do. You want to listen to my voice; it is all you want to listen to. It is wrapping you in a feeling of security… the warmth is flushing through your veins… heating your skin… you are floating as you listen to my voice… floating and calm. All you can hear is my voice, all you know is my voice, you must do what my voice tells you to do. You must shred the Veil. Reach, Jerrol, reach for the Veil and rip it apart. You want to destroy it. You have no other purpose."

Jerrol writhed in the chair, trying to resist his voice. It was insidious, and it curled around his mind, suborning his thoughts. A pair of green eyes pierced him and the compulsions dissipated and he clung to the Lady as Ain'uncer cursed.

"You will regret your decision. You are a fool and you will break in the end, and for what? Anguish and despair." Ain'uncer ran his knife down Jerrol's right hand, pausing at the little finger. "Which is it to be? Left or right?"

Jerrol resisted the urge to clench his fingers and began to sweat. He was in no shape for torture; weak, battered, heart-broken. He wasn't sure he had the strength to fight. Jerrol stared up at Ain'uncer, sweat running down his face.

"Worried?" Ain'uncer hovered over him, a dark shadow blocking what dim light there was in the room.

"Why should I be?" Jerrol hissed. "You're a lousy Ascendant."

Ain'uncer's face went blank before an expression of pure rage stiffened him. "I have gifts you've never dreamed of; gifts of persuasion." He paused, frowning at Jerrol before continuing. "Gifts you wouldn't understand." He pressed the blade into Jerrol's skin above the joint of his little finger. "Shred the veil, now!"

Jerrol flinched as the blade bit. A cold shiver trembled through him as he stared at the stranger hovering over him. The face grinned maniacally, and a thought rushed through Jerrol's mind; the man was mad. He was going to do it, and a shaft of scalding hot pain ran up his arm and exploded in his brain.

He groaned in shock as his vision wavered, bright sparks popping in front of his eyes. His stomach cramped as he tried to process the pain. His hand throbbed; he couldn't move it. He tried to calm his ragged breathing. His heartbeat thumped loud in his chest as he tried to control his panic.

"Shred the veil," Ain'uncer whispered close to his ear. Jerrol jerked and the Ascendant smiled, running his tongue over his lips. He moved the knife to the next finger.

Jerrol tried to swallow. His mouth was dry. Sweat ran down his face; he was burning up and yet he was so cold. Bile rose and he swallowed. He strained against the straps, but they were leather and unyielding.

"Is that your answer?" Ain'uncer's voice hissed beside him and the knife bit.

Jerrol screamed in agony and the room wavered.

Jerrol came too, blinking water out of his eyes and gasping for breath. His hand was on fire and the sensation consumed his mind. Ain'uncer gripped his hair and raised his face. He spoke, demanding that he do something, but he couldn't make sense of it. All that rattled around his head was the fact that Serillion had died; a gentle soul with a love of history and the Lady, and he, the Lady's Captain, had not been able to save him. Serillion's sacrifice blended with the fire consuming him. His head lolled as drops of blood splashed on the floor, a red so bright it seemed to glow; the only splash of colour in his greying vision.

A disembodied voice spoke above him and Jerrol frowned, trying to identify it. "What are you doing? Are you crazy? I told you, there's no point torturing him. This isn't working. It's taking too long. You know we have to leave, move on. You! Wrap his hand; we need him alive."

Jerrol concentrated on breathing in and breathing out; just breathing. The simple function of breathing calmed his disjointed thoughts. Pain engulfed him as someone touched his mutilated hand, wrapping it in something; he felt faint, ill. He opened his eyes and stared up at the ceiling. The grid lines engraved in the ceiling began to glow. Jerrol thought about Serillion and the pain of his death shattered his thread of concentration. His heart stuttered. He breathed.

He was still alive and he had murder in his heart.

Torsion spoke above him. "You awake, old man? Here, drink this; it will help with the pain." He forced Jerrol's mouth open and poured in a liquid that Jerrol recognised as a pain-relieving draught. He choked it down, though it would be useless against the pain and the fire consuming him.

"Hold on. I'll get you out. What's going on? The noise that Sentinal is making; he's fighting the King's Rangers. I told you he couldn't be trusted; he's helping them." Torsion fumbled with the straps, stiffening as he heard something behind him.

"Tor'asion, what are you doing here? That Sentinal is causing problems. Deal with him." Ain'uncer's voice cut through Jerrol's confusion.

"Torsion?" The room blurred, and Jerrol struggled to concentrate.

When his vision refocused, Ain'uncer stood over him, watching him with concern. "Why couldn't you just do as you were told? None of this was necessary," he complained. "You made me do it, and now look at you; it's your own fault. You've lost one Sentinal. The rangers are dispatching the other. I know all about Birlerion, much more than you. Such a distinctive name. But you've missed your opportunity, and now he's dead, and I have to do something that will hurt you even more, and it's all your fault."

Birlerion's defence faltered as Jerrol's scream scythed through him. First Serillion; his loss echoed through him, and he pushed it away; he would grieve later. Where there should be a hum of connection there was only emptiness and sorrow and now the Captain. He was failing in his duty. His breath came in gasps as he tried to fend off another charge by the King's Rangers. None had got past him into the Tower and yet the Captain was being attacked. There had to be a better way.

The air pulsed for a moment and, instinctively, he drew it in and then threw it out, knocking the remaining guards to the floor, leaving them as inanimate heaps in the dust. He turned to run up the tower stairs and was confronted by a tall, dark-haired Ascendant, rushing him. He took a step back and gasped as the shock of recognition, along with the Ascendant's strike, travelled up his arm.

"You," Birlerion snarled.

"You will yield," the Ascendant spat, following the strike with another, forcing the exhausted Sentinal out into the courtyard.

"Never," Birlerion gasped, desperately calling Ari.

"Then it's time for you to die." And Torsion attacked.

41

WATCH TOWERS

Ain'uncer stood to his full height, spread his arms and started chanting. Jerrol tried to ignore the words, but they kept caressing his mind, silky soft and beguiling. He stared at the ceiling and rapidly blinked as it began to shimmer; it made him feel queasy. He thought he saw Ari appear then disappear, but he wasn't sure if he was hallucinating. He didn't feel right. Ain'uncer's voice grew firmer, more confident, as the ceiling coalesced into what could have been a mirror; it was so smooth and precise.

Ain'uncer hovered over him. "You will shred the veil now or she will die."

Jerrol gasped and strained at his straps, stoking the simmering fire in his right hand. The mirror shimmered into a dim picture of a young girl in silvery robes stumbling perilously close to a dark river, trembling hands outstretched.

Taelia.

"What have you done to her?"

"Nothing yet, but it's simple. I can lead her out of that dangerous cavern or I can leave her there in the dark to die," Ain'uncer replied.

Jerrol writhed in the chair. "She's a scholar! She wouldn't harm anyone."

"She is indeed a scholar, but also your friend, I believe. Shred the Veil or she dies, along with your Sentinal. I know you like her. Never dared to tell her though, did you? If you don't shred the Veil, then the opportunity is lost." He snapped his fingers. "And the Captain has failed again."

"Please, don't do this. She's not part of this."

"Of course, she is. You have to make sacrifices such as these," Ain'uncer indicated the ceiling and then Jerrol. "For the greater good. If you love her, you will stop me hurting her. All you have to do is shred the Veil." He twisted his hand and the sound of sliding shale and pebbles reverberated through the room, supplemented by a low whimpering.

Taelia's voice echoed around them. "Hello? Anyone there?" She stumbled on the uneven surface and flinched as her foot slipped into the cold, dark water. "Help me, Lady help me." She murmured a litany over and over. Crouching, she balanced against the sliding stones and listened intently. Then she slowly turned her back to the water and, rising, began to claw her way up the slope, stones sliding in a clatter around her, her face pale and her eyes wide.

Jerrol stilled, trying to control his panic. "That is just a suggestion; you're playing mind games."

"You know better than that, Captain. Mind games don't seem to work on you, do they?" Ain'uncer sneered. "I hear she leapt at the chance to come and visit the towers. Liliian sent her up while you were off gallivanting wherever it is you've been. Chasing the chancellor, wasn't it?"

Jerrol tried to think, but his mind skittered off in all directions. *Lady help us*, he prayed, echoing Taelia's litany. Raised voices, sharp with anger, intruded in the silent room. The sound of men fighting was coming closer. Ain'uncer moved out of sight. "I'll leave you to think about it, but don't wait too long. Who knows what could happen to her next? It's so easy to get disorientated and, I don't know, fall into the river and drown."

Jerrol lay staring at the image of Taelia tripping over protrusions, grazing her hands badly enough to bleed. She could walk into one of those low hanging rocks and knock herself out and fall into the water. She hated water; she was afraid of falling in. She had never overcome her fear.

The sound of swords clashing percolated into his brain. Birlerion! He had to escape. A guard shifted behind him. How many guards were left in the room? Just the one? He cleared his throat. "Water," he croaked.

"You don't get nothing," a voice stated from close behind him.

"Please, take pity. I need water," Jerrol whispered.

The guard moved forward to hear him better. "You agreeing to do what he asks?"

"Silverwood."

"What?"

"Redwood," Jerrol paused, racking his memory. "Bluestone, Blackstone." A muffled exclamation preceded the sound of a body falling to the ground. Jerrol stared up at the image of Taelia as she tried to climb a pile of shifting stones, overbalancing as the shale slid beneath her feet and tumbling back down the incline. The image began to fade. Her face was distraught; tears left a track down her grubby cheeks. She was crying.

"You will obey Captain Haven from now on. You will unstrap Captain Haven from the chair and assist him out of the towers without being seen. You will not sound the alarm. You will show him the entrance to the cavern where the image above us is from. Blackstone," Jerrol said breathlessly as the guard's convulsions stilled.

"Captain?" the guard's voice sounded confused.

"Unstrap me," Jerrol commanded.

The guard stood. His footsteps were unsteady as he walked around in front of Jerrol. "Captain Haven," he gasped, his face blanching at the sight of the famous Captain bruised and bloodied. He began undoing the leather straps, his face paling even further as he released Jerrol's blood-soaked right hand. "Sir, I'm so sorry."

"Not now. Help me up; we've got to get out of here," Jerrol said, trying to rise. The guard helped Jerrol stand, gripping his arm as Jerrol swayed, overcome with dizziness. Using his left hand, he tucked his damaged hand inside his tunic. His face paled and he gritted his teeth as he straightened up.

"Check the hallway," Jerrol said, gripping the back of the chair with his good hand as he breathed in deeply. The room steadied. He swallowed against the growing nausea and concentrated on getting out.

"All clear, sir. The big man was arranging to leave. He'll be down in the courtyard."

"Did he say where he was going?"

"No, sir. Somewhere cold. He was complaining." The guard wrapped an arm around Jerrol's waist and steered him out of the room.

"Water, give me some of that water first." Jerrol cleared his throat. His voice was ragged, not working quite right.

The guard scooped a ladle full out of the bucket and offered it to Jerrol. The ghost of a smile passed over Jerrol's face at the sight of the ladle; useful weapons. He drank deeply and gripped the utensil. "Let's go."

They both flinched as a blinding flash lit up the stairway.

"What was that?" Jerrol asked, peering down the stairs. The sound of fighting had stopped.

The guard shrugged. "No idea, sir. We'd better get out

while it's clear." The guard steered him out of the room and down the stairs.

"What's your name?" Jerrol asked as they staggered down the stairs, each step jarring through his aching body. His arm burned and sweat trickled down his back.

"Corporal Jenkins, sir. Second battalion, King's Rangers."

"Well, Jenkins, see if you can find me a dagger or two. Do you know what they did with my sword?"

"Big man took a liking to it, sir."

Jerrol sighed. He didn't seem to be able to hold onto that sword. The Lady would kill him if Guerlaire didn't get to him first. Everyone seemed to take a liking to his sword. "Is there such a place as that cavern in the image?" he asked as they reached the ground floor and Jenkins leant him against the wall. He stayed there, weak and shivery, even though he was burning up. The hottest part of the fire was his hand, which throbbed against his chest in time with his heart.

Jenkins returned. "Yes, sir, the river flows through caverns under the towers and into the lake on the plateau."

"Can you take me there?"

"Are you sure, sir? We ought to get you out of here so that someone can fix up your hand."

"Too late for that. We need to help Taelia."

Jerrol ignored the sigh and the look Jenkins gave him as if he was some crazy feverish man who was delirious. "You can't help yourself, sir, let alone anyone else."

Jerrol gritted his teeth and he pushed himself off the wall. "Take me to the cavern entrance," he commanded.

"Yes, sir," Jenkins slipped his arm back around Jerrol's waist and steered him out of the tower. They hesitated at the sight of the groaning King's Rangers laid out on the ground. Of Birlerion, Ain'uncer, or Torsion, there was no sign.

Jenkins assisted Jerrol out of the courtyard, round the

back of the woodshed, and through a small door set back in the wall. They climbed up the bank into the tree line, Jenkins grunting with the effort of keeping Jerrol upright. "We have to go up to go down," Jenkins said, leading the way through the moss-barked trees and further up the muddy slope until they rounded a rocky overhang that concealed a dark hole, which immediately sloped down underground.

"Is this the only entrance?" Jerrol asked, shivering uncontrollably as they paused in front of the gaping mouth of the cave.

"There are two that I know of; could be more. The caverns go on forever; easy to get lost, sir."

"Should have brought a torch. Not thinking straight. Come on." Jerrol slithered down the slope, balancing his left hand against the ground, gritting his teeth against the spiking pain shooting up his arm. "Listen out for Taelia. They can't have taken her too far in."

"Are you sure, sir? This passage is quite straight. She could easily find her way out again."

"Only if she found the passage," Jerrol said. He led the way, feeling the rock as he passed. A slight vibration trembled though the rock and he quickened his pace.

"Go careful, sir. The ceiling dips and we'll lose the light."

"She's just up ahead," he said to himself, recognising the sharp metallic tang of water. "Taelia?" he called.

Taelia gasped. "Jerrol? Is that you?"

"Stay where you are. We're coming."

"Jerrol? I don't know where I am, and there's a river." Her voice trembled.

"You won't fall in. I'm here now," Jerrol soothed as he skirted the water's edge. "Keep talking," he said, straining to see her in the gloom as the shale shifted under his feet.

"I don't remember how I got here. Torsion escorted me to my room last night after you retired, and then I woke up here, and the stones keep sliding, and I can't find the way out..." she stopped with a gasp as Jerrol's hand gripped her arm. She flung herself at him, though she stopped dead in shock as he flinched back from her. He wrapped his left arm around her shoulders and hugged her tight against his side.

"Jerrol? How did you find me?" she asked, her hands fluttering over his face. "You're feverish, Jerrol. What happened?" He kissed a finger as it passed his mouth.

"I'll tell you later. We have to leave before they find us. Jenkins? I've found her."

"Yes, sir. I still don't see why she couldn't find the way out, sir. We're hardly past the entrance, and you can still see the light from here."

Jerrol stumbled against Taelia and hissed through his teeth.

"Jerrol? What's the matter?" she asked, reaching to help him up. Her hands patted him, hesitating at the heat coming off his body and his arm, which was tucked in his jacket awkwardly.

"Nothing. Let's get out of here."

"This way, miss." Jenkins reached to grab her questing hand and helped her back up the incline, wrapping his arm around both of them to steady Jerrol. "I suggest we move away from the entrance before we rest, sir," Jenkins suggested. "Just in case they come searching."

"Good point. They would have come back for Taelia, wouldn't they?"

Jenkins cleared his throat. "I'm not sure, sir. The big man wasn't too happy; said she could stay there, but that might just have been talk."

"Let's not take the risk. They'll be searching for me, soon, as well."

"That's more likely," owned Jenkins. "Though you screwed up his plans, so he may not search too hard."

"What plans?" Jerrol puffed as they staggered up the hill.

Taelia became more concerned at Jerrol's erratic progress, between them, they stumbled every other step.

Taelia clung to him. "Jerrol, we have to stop. You're not alright. What happened?"

"There's a copse up ahead. It will s-screen us. We'll s-stop there," Jerrol stammered.

Jenkins pulled the tightly packed trees apart and guided Taelia through. Her foot caught on the roots and she fell through the screen of greenery. She scrabbled out of the way as Jenkins gently steered Jerrol in and helped prop him up against a tree trunk. He stood staring down at him in concern.

"I'll find some water," he said. "Miss, maybe you could take a look at his hand?"

"Don't leave the trees," Jerrol slurred over his words and tried again. "The trees will hide us."

"Jerrol?" Taelia tentatively patted him.

"Don't." Jerrol stopped her from pulling out his hand. "Hurts too much."

She leaned over him. His face was feverishly hot, and she smelt blood. "You're bleeding. We need to stop the bleeding. Where are you bleeding from, Jerrol?" She shook him and, as he slid towards her, she realised he had passed out.

42

LADY'S COPSE, WATCH TOWERS

Taelia reached for Jerrol's arm and pulled his hand out of his jacket. It was hot through the material and swollen. The rough wrappings oozed with moisture; the tang of blood strong. He must have been bleeding the whole time. She looked up as she heard the other man returning.

"Tell me, what happened?"

"The Ascendants chopped off two of his fingers."

"What?" she gasped in horror, the blood draining from her face. She swallowed, sick to her stomach.

"Yeah, he wouldn't shred some veil or something. His fingers need cauterising, otherwise the bleeding won't stop," he said wisely.

"Do you know how to do it?" she asked, paling even more.

"Me? Well, I could, but I'll have to hold him down; right painful. You'll have to do it," he said, holding out the hollow piece of bark he had filled with water.

She appeared to ignore him and stared down at Jerrol in horror.

"You'll need the water."

"Oh," she exclaimed, turning her face towards him. "Did you manage to find some?"

"Yeah," he proffered the water. "Here it is."

She reached out, her hand questing the air a few inches to the right of it. He moved the bark closer to her hand as her face heated. "I can't see. I'm blind." Her blood-smeared fingers knocked the bark.

Jenkins almost dropped the water. "What?"

"I'm blind," she repeated, her questing fingers gripping the bark firmly.

"Well," he gasped, "he never said."

Taelia looked down at Jerrol. "He wouldn't," she said, her hand unerringly brushing his hair off his sweaty forehead.

"You wouldn't know unless you were being handed something. You look like you can see him."

Taelia smiled. "Find some firewood. We're going to need a fire." She began ripping up her petticoat into ragged sections. She folded one piece over into a pad and dipped it into the water before gently wiping Jerrol's face. Jenkins watched her for a moment before turning away to find the makings of a fire.

"I-I c-can't..." Jerrol stuttered as he came too. Taelia's hand fluttered over his face and came to rest on his shoulder. She rubbed it gently.

"Hush," she murmured. "Take a deep breath." She continued to rub his shoulder.

"Tali?" The anguish in Jerrol's voice made her heart clench, and she leaned across to hug him.

"It will be alright," she murmured as he hid his face in her shoulder and took a shuddering breath.

She rocked him as his breathing calmed. He inhaled and relaxed against the tree.

"They only took you because of me," Jerrol said, stiffening beneath her hands. "I'm no good for anyone."

Taelia leaned back on her heels. "What are you talking about?"

"Birlerion, Saerille, Serillion, you. When is enough, enough?"

"Jerrol, it's not your fault. You didn't cause any of this."

"Of course, I did. They wouldn't be dead," he said bitterly, "if they weren't helping me."

"It's not your fault." Taelia wanted to shake him but didn't dare in case she hurt him more. Her stomach stirred queasily at his words. Three Sentinals dead? She caught her breath at the loss of Birlerion; tears welled. To lose such a good person and his poor tree; what would happen to him? And Serillion; she had only just begun to get to know him, but what she knew she had liked. What could have happened? She swallowed; her throat tight. "Look at the people you *have* saved: King Benedict, Alyssa, Simeon, Lady Miranda, me, to name just a few! This is just your fever talking."

"You're better off without me," he whispered, his anguish tangible in the air between them.

She inhaled sharply. "You don't mean that."

"Beautiful Taelia, go back to the Chapterhouse."

"Where it's safe?" she snapped. She gripped his shoulder and gave him a slight shake. "This is not just your burden to bear. We all have a part to play; you can't do this on your own, and nor are you expected too. The Lady wouldn't do that to you." Her face softened. "Jerrol, let us help you; let *me* help you. I lo..." she stopped abruptly as she heard Jenkins return with the firewood.

"Awake again, sir? That's the dandy," he said as he dropped the wood on the ground. "We'll have a nice fire in no time."

"No, the smoke will give us away," Jerrol whispered.

"Your hand," Taelia faltered. "The bleeding won't stop; you're losing too much blood. We have to cauterise the wounds. It's the only way to stop you bleeding out," she continued bravely, reaching for his arm. Jerrol shuddered under her hand, though he didn't say anything.

Jerrol watched Jenkins build the fire. The ranger kept glancing across at him, the concern clear on his face. Jerrol was sure he didn't look too good. He certainly didn't feel well. His gut tightened at the thought of cauterisation and he shuddered as Jenkins lit the fire and shoved the tip of his dagger into the flames.

Taelia had torn up more strips of her petticoat for new bandages and was now unwrapping his bloody hand. He was glad she couldn't see it. It was a bloody mess. He averted his eyes and gritted his teeth against her gentle probing. No matter how you looked at it, this was not going to be pretty. He stiffened as Jenkins unbuckled his belt.

"Captain?"

Jerrol smiled faintly. "Corporal."

Jenkins silently proffered his belt and Jerrol swallowed as he took it and got ready to bite down on it. His hand shook, matching the tremble threatening to incapacitate him. Jerrol tried to ignore the pity in the ranger's eyes and took a deep breath.

Jenkins nodded. "Right. We'll place the Captain's hand on that flat stone. I'll restrain him and you just press the blade across the ends of both those fingers. Feel where they are so you know. Don't flinch and don't stop, no matter what. If you do, we'll only have to do it all over again, and the Captain won't like that," Jenkins said firmly.

Taelia gently checked the position of Jerrol's mutilated fingers. Jerrol couldn't prevent the tremble under her touch. Taking another deep, steadying breath, he bit down hard on the belt as Jenkins firmly wrapped his arms around his chest, pinning Jerrol's arms to his sides.

"Quickly now, lass," Jenkins said, and immediately the air smelt of burning flesh and Jerrol convulsed in agony. White hot pain seared through him and a heart-rending groan escaped his mouth as he bit the leather. He gasped for breath as sweat drenched him and he shuddered violently. Jenkins fought to keep him still as he writhed until his body went limp as he slipped into blessed pain-free darkness.

Jenkins exhaled a deep breath and cleared his throat. "That's it. I'll stick the blade back in the fire. Let me check you got it all." Jenkins laid Jerrol's limp body on the grass and moved over to check Taelia's work.

"Is he alright?" Taelia asked, her face pale. She swallowed, obviously trying not to throw up. Her hand shook, white-knuckled around the blade, as Jenkins eased it out of her grip. It had taken all her determination to continue, knowing that stopping would have been worse.

"Unconscious," Jenkins grinned in relief, "best way. We got one bit left and then job done." There was a short sizzle, and Taelia shuddered.

"I don't think I'll be able to listen to meat roasting on a spit ever again," she said, her voice trembling.

"You did well. He won't forget it; you saved his life tonight." Jenkins wrapped Jerrol's hand in the strips of cloth.

"So did you, Corporal Jenkins. I couldn't have done it without you. Thank you."

"Least I could do," he said, his voice gruff as he tied off the material and folded the arm across Jerrol's blood-stained jacket. "Any chance you got a larger square of material I could use as a sling? Probably best to tie his arm out of the way so he doesn't try to use it. These feisty captains sometimes don't know what's good for them."

Taelia laughed shakily and stood up. She stepped out of the remains of her petticoat. "Is this large enough?"

"That should do the trick," he said, taking the cloth. He took the knife and split the seam of Jerrol's sleeve. The swollen arm strained the material. He didn't mention it as he concentrated on tying the cloth around Jerrol's neck and strapping his arm across his chest so he couldn't move it. He propped Jerrol more comfortably against the tree and heaved a sigh.

"That's him sorted, for now. Best put the fire out." He scattered the embers and tossed the last of the blood-tinged water on to them.

Taelia felt her way over to Jerrol and snuggled up to his left-hand side and faced Jenkins. She listened to Jerrol's slow breathing. His body was relaxed. There was no longer the awful rigidity she had felt when she had first pressed the blade against his skin. "Where did you meet Jerrol?"

"I came with Scholar Torsion to relieve the Tower. King's Rangers, Second Battalion. Corporal Jenkins."

"Well, you are seconded to the Captain's Guard, now. He doesn't tend to let his men get away." Her voice faltered as she remembered what Jerrol had said earlier. There were not going to be any good memories from this day.

"Best we try to sleep. Be a long day tomorrow."

Jerrol opened his eyes and looked up at the underside of the Lady's chin. He lay in her arms under a very tall tree. "My Lady?"

"Finally!" she snapped. "Captain, you have to stop all this melodrama. I can't be rescuing you all the time."

"I'd prefer it if you rescued those in need, my Lady."

"Everyone has their part to play. Don't you listen to your

young lady? Some don't have the endings you want. Doesn't mean they aren't right all the same."

Jerrol inhaled sharply and Leyandrii's face softened. "I picked you because of who you are and for the greatness of your heart, but that doesn't mean you're not dense on occasion." She stood up and dumped him on the ground.

Jerrol rolled to his feet and flexed his mangled hand. The pain was a mere echo. Leyandrii smoothed her hand over it. "It will take time to heal, but it won't hinder you if you don't let it," she promised.

"I lost Serillion," Jerrol faltered, his voice breaking. "And Birlerion."

"I know. Serillion will be safe with me. He performed magnificently, didn't he? You should be so proud."

"Proud?" Jerrol gasped, aghast.

"Of course," the Lady said. "You sealed the Veil. Very well done, by the way. Remargaren is safe for a bit longer. It was what Serillion was born for. Don't take away his greatest triumph; celebrate it."

"Are they here? With You?" Jerrol searched the glade frantically.

"Don't be silly. This is the betwixt space. Serillion is on the other side. Know that he reveres you. Birlerion overdid it a bit. I think he panicked. You would think he'd get better with practice. I'll have words with him. Maybe next time he'll be more careful."

"Next time?"

The Lady shrugged. "There are limits to what I can do. You will heal quickly and cleanly; the infection will clear in a few days. You could have lost your arm. You must be more careful," she chided. "Make sure you wrap up warm."

"Why?" he asked, but the glade shimmered around him and he jerked back to awareness in the darkened camp, conscious of Taelia tucked up against him, fast asleep. He went to smooth her hair out of her face, but he couldn't move his arm. It was strapped against his chest, and she had his other arm pinned under her body. The familiar weight of his sword at his waist made him relax, and he held her more tightly. Taelia smiled in her sleep and sighed. His hand throbbed painfully, reminding him that he hadn't dreamt any of it.

He looked across the glade and saw Jenkins on guard.

"Corporal, rest. We are safe enough here. No one will find us."

Jenkins jerked round. "Captain," he whispered, not wanting to wake the girl. "I heard them searching earlier. Best not to take any risks."

"I understand. The Lady watches for us tonight; get some sleep. We'll talk about it in the morning. That's an order, Corporal."

"Yes, sir." Jenkins snapped a salute and searched for a soft tree root to lay against.

43

WATCH TOWERS

The next morning, Jerrol awoke to the aroma of coffee. He lay adjusting to the burning sensation in his hand, the flush of heat running through his body, and the overwhelming sense of loss and exhaustion. He opened bleary eyes, frowning in surprise as he saw Tagerill standing over him, watching him with concern.

"Tagerill," he croaked, his mouth dry. "When did you arrive? How did you find us?"

Tagerill crouched down and helped him sit up. His face tightened and Jerrol tried to reassure him. He was sure he looked a mess. He certainly felt like one.

Tagerill beat him to it. "Birlerion completely freaked Ari out. He arrived in Deepwater frantic, so I hot-footed it down here." He held out a mug of water and Jerrol took it, his hand trembling. Gratefully, he gulped it down and leaned back against the tree, staring in front of him.

"I lost Serillion," he said. "You should have seen him. He was magnificent."

"I know. We felt him go," Tagerill said as an expression of intense grief flashed across his face. He paused, watching Jerrol. "What happened to Saerille? Do you know?"

"She's safe. She won't come out, but she is recovering. We need to go to Stoneford."

"Where's Birlerion?"

Jerrol shuddered. "I lost him too," he whispered.

Tagerill stilled. "When?"

"Last night." Jerrol closed his eyes.

Tagerill glanced across at Jenkins. "You didn't see a Sentinal amongst the bodies at the Towers, did you?"

"There was no one there except the Watchers, a young girl, a couple of young lads, and quite a few injured rangers. It looks like the big man took the rest of the rangers with him. Well, the ones who could stand. Someone disabled most of 'em," Jenkins said.

"Did you find Torsion?" Jerrol asked.

Jenkins frowned at him. "Scholar Torsion? No, he weren't there either."

"I thought I saw him." Jerrol rubbed his eyes. "I don't remember. I think I saw him. He tried to help me." He dropped his hand and stared at Tagerill. "We need to go to Stoneford, speak to Jason. Get him to send some help up here; the Watchers need to be protected."

Tagerill nodded. "I had intended going straight to Deepwater, but Stoneford will do. Healer Tyrone will help you. We nearly lost you, Captain. You must be more careful."

Jerrol grimaced. "I try, but my life just doesn't seem to find 'careful' very often." He tried to rise, and Tagerill cupped a hand under his arm and helped him up. He swayed dizzily. Tagerill helped him over to the ditch to relieve himself before escorting him back to his tree, where he sagged, exhausted and shivery.

"I think we should go straight to Deepwater. You can recuperate there."

"I must go to Stoneford first," Jerrol insisted. He suddenly sat up as he realised he couldn't feel Zin'talia's soft touch. "Where is Zin'talia?" He reached out in a panic, but there was only silence; she wasn't there. Swallowing a curse, he tried to stand. "We have to find her."

Tagerill restrained him easily. "We will find her," he soothed.

Taelia hovered over him. "Coffee?" She held out a mug above his head. Tagerill took the mug and passed it to Jerrol.

"Are you alright?" Jerrol asked, watching her face hungrily.

"Me?" she exclaimed, reaching for him. "I'm fine. You are the one we need to be worrying about."

"I'll be alright. I'm assured the infection will go down in a couple of days."

"Well, you will be careful for the next month or so whilst you recuperate or I'll be having words with the king," Taelia said, offering him another cup.

"What's that?" he asked, eyeing her with some suspicion as he placed his mug on the ground.

"Pain relief; enough to get you onto a horse and back to Stoneford, anyway. Drink it."

Jerrol drank it under her beady eye, exhausted enough to accept being told what to do. She stood over him, waiting, he realised, for the draught concealed in the drink and now lingering on his tongue to take effect. She had laced it with enough poppy juice, which Tagerill must have had the forethought to bring with him, to knock him out.

Jerrol's eyes drooped, the strain easing, and he tried to grimace as he heard the concern in Tagerill's voice, but everything faded. "Masterfully done, my lady. It's not often you see the Captain bettered."

Taelia snorted. "Make the most of it. It'll probably be the only time."

"This last month has taken its toll. He looks as if he'll smash into pieces if he falls over."

"He is exhausted and hurting." Taelia crouched to cup Jerrol's face. "Do you think we will reach Stoneford before he wakes up?"

"Of course, we could take him to Deepwater. My Sentinal is waiting for him. The Captain opened up the waystones. It will shorten the journey significantly." Tagerill grinned.

"A waystone?" Taelia asked, wrinkling her nose.

"That's how I got here so fast. I found the one in Deepwater; I heard the chime. I warned them at Stoneford about what has happened. I have a troop waiting for us at the Towers."

"Heard the what?" Taelia asked, confused.

"The waystone. When you cross the line, it chimes so that you know it's available. Almost fell off my horse. Haven't heard that sound in years; gave me a shock, you know?"

"How would he know how to open a waystone?"

"The Captain amazes me every day," Tagerill said, observing the sleeping man. A sheen of sweat coated Jerrol's face. "Just by him being present, things happen that wouldn't normally occur. The Lady watches. All we can do is support him."

Taelia stirred. "He blamed himself for Serillion and Birlerion, for your injury. He seemed to think he had caused it all."

"There is no getting away from it. Life is interesting around the Captain. He is a catalyst. The Lady drives him, and we are here to help him, but he carries the burden. If we can help balance out that burden just a little, then we can make his job easier. He is Captain for a reason. We have to sustain him so he can complete whatever the Lady is asking of him."

"What more can she want of him? He is just a man. He can only take so much. You can see he is at his limit."

"I am sure she knows what we are all capable of." Tagerill looked around the small camp. "Stay here. I need to find Birlerion. I'm not leaving him here."

Tagerill walked down to the towers. A quick sortie confirmed that only injured rangers remained; they had broken bones and concussion, nothing that would kill.

"What happened?" he asked a groaning sergeant, who was trying to help his men back to their barracks.

The sergeant scowled at him. "One of your types took us all out. Can't believe it. Single-handed, he did it. And do you know what? He didn't kill a single one of us. Then one of them Ascendants took him out. He retaliated, hit us with something. It was a blinding flash, knocked us flat, when we woke up, they were all gone. It was like waking from a dream."

"Be thankful you are not dead," Tagerill growled. "Where is the Sentinal now?"

The sergeant shrugged and then held his head. "The Ascendants took the Sentinal with them, it took two of them to overpower him."

Tagerill's stomach clenched.

"What about the scholar?"

"Dunno. If he's not here, they must have taken him too." The sergeant dropped his head in his hands and groaned in pain. "I have the worst headache."

"It will pass. It's the after effect of Mentiserium. They had you enspelled to do their bidding. Birlerion was protecting the Captain against you. You were lucky he didn't kill you." Tagerill was amazed Birlerion hadn't injured them worse, and he had broken the spell, how had he done that?

Tagerill walked back out of the gates. A flash in the road caught his eye and he hurried towards it, slowing as he saw a sword. Birlerion's sword stuck point-down in the dirt. He pulled it out and looked around him. Birlerion was still alive; he knew it. There wasn't the same aching emptiness he felt when he thought of Serillion.

He rotated, senses impossibly questing, but there was no sign of Birlerion.

They slowly made their way out of the trees. Taelia clung on to Tagerill's horse as it picked its way down to the road, and Tagerill and Jenkins lifted their makeshift drag over the uneven terrain. Once they reached the road, Tagerill took the reins and strode down towards the Towers, casting frequent glances at his semi-conscious friend. Jenkins trotted behind, making sure Jerrol didn't fall off.

At the Towers, the healer's assistant took one look at Jerrol and said there was nothing he could do. They needed to get him to Healer Tyrone as quickly as possible, though he did redress Jerrol's hand and strap it against his chest more firmly. They picked up the Stoneford guards, leaving half to help the healer with the injured rangers.

Mary reassured Taelia that she was fine, having slept through everything, and set to convincing Taelia to let her stay. "I was only here as a chaperone, and you don't need that now Torsion has gone. The work still needs doing, and if I'm here it will be easier to keep it going. You can ask the Deane to send some more help."

Taelia allowed herself to be persuaded. More concerned about Jerrol than translating old text. She chivied Tagerill to get moving, not that he needed any encouragement and they left the Towers in Mary's capable hands.

It took them two days. They skirted the town of Velmouth and headed straight for Stoneford, arriving as the sun set behind the crenulated stone keep that rose behind the small grove of Sentinals. Tagerill breathed a sigh of relief as the building came into sight. Jerrol had become restless over the last few miles, muttering in his sleep, calling out and flinging his arm out. Jenkins had to tuck him back in, repeatedly.

Tyrone hurried across the courtyard as they arrived, word having been passed down by the sentries on the wall. He took one look at the feverish man and took the end of the drag carrying Jerrol as Tagerill released it and helped hustle them inside.

He took them straight through to the back room where they gently transferred Jerrol onto the table.

"What happened?" Tyrone asked, his mouth tightening as he took in Jerrol's tumultuous pulse and soaring temperature, instructing his assistant to set up a drip.

Taelia paled as she explained that a man called Ain'uncer had chopped off two of Jerrol's fingers, how they had cauterised the wounds as they wouldn't stop bleeding, and that she had drugged him to get him here because he was in some sort of shock.

Tyrone peered at her from under his bushy eyebrows. "I think you need to go and eat something. All of you, go freshen up and find some food. I'm sure Jason will want a report on what's happened."

"I don't think I could face any food," Taelia said with revulsion.

"You'll find you will want it when the food's in front of you," Tyrone said. "Off you go."

He waited until Tagerill had escorted her out of his infirmary before turning back to Jerrol. He began unwrapping Jerrol's hand, hissing at the sight of the jagged bones sticking out the ends of two of his fingers. No wonder the poor man was in shock. Cauterizing them wouldn't stop the pain.

He exchanged bleak glances with his assistant. "Add

some more Opii tincture. We don't want him waking up," he said as he began the gruesome job of cleaning up the damage.

King's Palace, Old Vespers

"He did what?" King Benedict exploded, aghast.

"Um, he annexed Terolia for Vespiri, Your Majesty. Here are the accords." Marianille encouraged Nil'ano forward, who placed the papers on the table. Her gaze darted around the room. The new Chancellor, Prince Anders, and Scholar-Deane Liliian were also present.

"And you thought this was a good idea?" King Benedict said, coldly calm. Prince Anders covered his mouth with his hand, trying not to laugh.

Marianille stiffened. "The Captain made the decision, Your Majesty. I didn't have any say in it. The Captain was, let us say, angry with the Families…" Her voice was firm. "He thought that if they couldn't look after their people, then they didn't deserve to rule."

"And they agreed?" the king asked more moderately.

"Yes, Your Majesty. It's all in there." Nil'ano indicated the papers again. "The Captain left the Sentinals to watch over them. He committed Vespiri to ensure their security, allowing the Families to manage the internal government on condition that they submitted to your rule, Your Majesty. I captured it all as it was agreed."

"And what did the commander threaten if they refused?"

Niallerion swallowed, running a finger around his collar. "Um, he didn't say, but with the Sentinals standing behind him, I don't think anyone dared to ask. They knew what had happened at the Telusions and they knew he was very upset."

"Upset?"

"I would recommend you never see the Captain upset.

It's frightening." Marianille gave a faint smile. "It was all according to law. The accords are watertight, Your Majesty. You, ah, now rule Terolia, as well."

"What happened at the Telusions to make Commander Haven so angry that he would annex a whole country? That's the mountain range, isn't it? The one we couldn't find on the map?" the king asked, his eyes glinting dangerously.

Niallerion blanched. "Um, a lot of innocent people died, Your Majesty. We found the crystal mines; a lot of starving people and no crystals left. Mined out long ago, yet they still had hundreds of people, slaves, working the mines. They were starving and ill-kept, digging for dirt. Such a waste." Niallerion shook himself. "The Captain kept them inside the mountain. They were dehydrated, starving, in poor shape. The heat would have done for them. We were trying to alleviate the worst of the conditions when the mountain blew up, caved in on itself, buried them alive." Niallerion stopped, his eyes wide. "There was nothing we could do; it was a whole mountain that collapsed. The Captain didn't take it well."

"I imagine not," Prince Anders choked.

"We saved forty-two people. Took them back to Melila for help," Marianille said. "Then the Captain took us back to Mistra and called a Master Conclave. Don't know how he did it, but he got representatives from all six of the Families together, and that is the result," she finished, nodding at the accords on the king's desk.

"Where is the commander?"

"He went to the Watch Towers with Birlerion, Your Majesty. Something about a veil?" Nil'ano replied.

The king closed his eyes.

Prince Anders leaned forward. "Sentinal Marianille, Niallerion, we thank you for you assistance and welcome you back to Vespers. Ambassador Nil'ano, that will be all for now.

We will read the accords. The king will call you if he needs to speak to you further."

The Sentinals left the room as fast as they could; eager to avoid any further awkward questions. The king's voice rose behind them.

"He annexed a whole country!"

"He must have had good reason, and by the sounds of it, he did," Liliian responded, trying to sound reasonable.

"And now he's gone to the Towers to seal the Veil."

"He will return soon, and he will tell you about it himself," Liliian said soothingly.

"He is the Lady's Captain, after all," Anders said, reaching for the papers.

"That may be so, but to annex a whole country!" King Benedict snagged another paper and collapsed into his chair to read it.

44

STONEFORD KEEP, STONEFORD WATCH

Many hours later, Tyrone entered Lord Jason's study. Jason raised his head from the papers littered over his desk and Tyrone internally winced at the sight of his face. New lines of worry creased his skin, adding to the wrinkles. He had visibly aged overnight.

Taelia was curled up in a chair in the corner, dozing against the arm. She jerked upright as the door clicked. Jason stopped working and leaned back in his chair. "Well?" he asked as Tyrone flopped into the chair opposite.

Tyrone's face tightened in anger. "If I ever get my hands on whoever attacked Jerrol, he will regret it."

"Join the queue," Jason said. "Will Jerrol be alright?"

"He's tough. I will say that for him." He glanced across at Taelia and shrugged. "I had to amputate the damaged fingers; it was the only way to get them to a state for them to cleanly heal. As long as no infection sets into the bone, we should be able to save the hand." He paused as Taelia gasped. "Sorry, m'dear, but it is a risk. Generally, he's stable.

We've got the fever under control and he is much more comfortable."

He didn't mention the delirium or the distress that kept dragging Jerrol out of the induced sleep he was trying to keep him in. "We'll observe him tonight. He should be recovered enough for you to visit him tomorrow afternoon," he said, as he levered himself out of the chair. "You should go to bed too, both of you." He nodded at Jason and left the room.

Jason rose. "He's right, Taelia. You need some sleep. You'll see...be with him tomorrow." Taelia reluctantly stood. "Come, let me show you to your room," Jason said as he steered her out of his office.

Jason tapped on the door of the guest room assigned to Tagerill, opening the door at his acknowledgement. Tagerill looked up as he entered. He lay the sword he was sharpening across his lap as Jason shut the door behind him and briefly closed his eyes.

"Tyrone had to amputate the damaged fingers. He says they'll heal cleanly. Jerrol is comfortable now, not so distressed. We can visit him tomorrow afternoon."

"Good," Tagerill said with relief, some of his tension easing. "He was determined to come back here. He wanted to do something for Saerille, I think. I don't think he could face losing a second Sentinal."

"What's this? Who was lost? What happened?"

Tagerill hunched his shoulders, keeping his face carefully blank. The horrendous loss ripping through him was not for public viewing. "We lost Serillion. Saerille and Birlerion are missing. I don't know what happened. The Captain wouldn't say, though I think he blames himself. What I got from Taelia and Jenkins was that the Captain had been in Terolia for over a month with Birlerion. They were on their way back and stopped in to see Torsion. There's some confusion over Torsion, as well. It seems he's missing, too."

"Now you mention it, I remember him passing through. That's right," Jason paused, his brow wrinkling. "He spoke to your sentinal and it upped and left. Stoneford not good enough for you?" he teased.

Tagerill's face eased. "That was such a shock. I felt him arrive. They couldn't keep me in the infirmary after that. Certain sentinal trees can speed up the healing process. That's why I was going to take the Captain straight to Deepwater. My sentinal is prepared to heal him."

"How are Jennery and Alyssa doing?"

"Loving life and each other at the moment. It was a shame you missed the joining. It was special."

"I'm glad all is well with them and you too, I hear."

Tagerill blushed. "Indeed, I am fortunate. I've been training with their troops; undisciplined lot. It has been good rehabilitation for me," Tagerill said, flexing his arm. "But now I think it's time to return to the Captain and Vespers. He is not safe out on his own."

"Safe for whom?" Jason laughed. "We'll see how he is tomorrow. Sleep well, Tagerill."

"Lady's blessings," Tagerill replied, returning to his sword and sliding the whetstone down the edge.

When Jerrol awoke, he lay still, listening. He wasn't sure where he was. He had a cacophony of images in his head and he wasn't sure which ones were real. He remembered speaking with Serillion, but that wasn't possible. He was dead. His stomach fluttered at the memory. Ain'uncer had attacked him and he had stolen Zin'talia, as well. Why? He missed her touch, her soft crooning, and her complaints. His head echoed emptily.

Images of Taelia and Tagerill were mixed in with a ranger he had never met before, and he had lost Birlerion, as well. His breath caught. He had been searching for him, desperately. He would no longer have the reassurance of him behind his shoulder. He opened his eyes, trying to ease the growing tightness in his chest, and breathed a small sigh of relief as he recognised his surroundings. Stoneford infirmary.

His stomach clenched in panic. He couldn't feel his hand; had Ain'uncer chopped it off? He tried to lift it but couldn't. He attempted to sit up but hands pressed him back down. "Oh no, you don't. You stay right where you are."

Jerrol stared up into the healer's face, and fear lurked in his eyes. "Tyrone, my hand."

"Your hand will be fine if you do as you are told. Yes, you've lost two fingers, but you've still got the other three," Tyrone replied, seeing the need for reassurance as Jerrol relaxed back against the pillows.

Jerrol's brows contracted. "I don't remember how I got here. I'm not sure what was real and what wasn't."

"I expect most of what you remember was hallucinations as we've been dosing you to keep you under whilst we tidied up the mess you made of your hand. But Tagerill and Taelia brought you here with a King's Ranger yesterday. They'll be in to visit you later when you've eaten and had another nap."

"I can't sleep my life away. I have to return to Vespers and report to the king."

"He can wait another day or two. You sent Marianille and Niallerion on ahead, didn't you? He can make do with that report for now. Here comes your breakfast; some nice scrambled eggs. Make sure you eat them all." Tyrone eased Jerrol upright and stacked another pillow behind him. "Take it slow," he advised, "you're not going anywhere today."

Jerrol stared at the plate in front of him, forgetting as he tried to lift his right hand. It was splinted and heavy. He fumbled for the fork with his left hand and began clumsily eating. He was suddenly famished.

Tyrone observed him from his desk. Time was what Jerrol needed; time to adjust, time to cope, and he knew he wouldn't get it. He would give him what he could. A day or two maybe. Even that would not be long enough. Tyrone shook his head and returned to writing up his notes.

Jerrol did doze once he had chased his eggs around the plate for a while. Giving up, he had let the assistant take the plate away and had accepted his help to lay back down. He dozed some more, listening to the gentle sounds of people moving about the infirmary or talking in low tones. It was soothing.

After a bowl of soup for lunch—he was much more successful with the spoon than the fork—he lay propped up by pillows, ruminating over the events at the Watch Towers. He flinched away from thinking about the people he had lost, squirming against his pillows. He thought of Terolia. He hoped the king had approved of his decisions. Well, it was too late now.

"They were the right decisions," a soft voice said in the back of his mind.

He relaxed. *"Saerille, how are you?"*

"Better than you, I fear. I am sorry, Captain."

"For what?"

"For not being there to help. I failed Serillion, not you."

Jerrol rubbed his face. "*We did our best, and no one can ask for more. We didn't fail; we sealed the Veil. You managed to hold the defences for far longer than you should have had to, and Serillion gave me the time to repair it properly. Both of those events occurred because someone else was trying to stop us. It is their fault, not ours. I was the one who put you in danger; all of you. You did what I asked of you, and I couldn't expect more. Thank you, Saerille; thank you for holding on.*"

Saerille was silent for a moment. "*Thank you, Captain; and thank you for the shelter. But I think it is time I returned to my sentinal. He is calling, and I can see the path. I will assist Chryllion and we will await your orders. I recommend you stay within Chryllion's Sentinal for at least a day; he will speed your recovery, and the waystones will cut your journey, so the king will never have to know.*" Jerrol felt her smile grow. "*Oh, and for goodness sake, tell Taelia you love her and put us all out of our misery. The poor girl deserves better from you.*"

Jerrol winced. The downside of sharing your head with someone else was that they knew what you were thinking. He would have held his hands up in surrender if he could, but instead, he wished her a fond farewell and a small weight lifted and disappeared. His head was getting emptier and very lonely.

Worrying about Zin'talia, he tentatively reached out again, pushing as far as he could, extending what, he wasn't sure, but he concentrated on calling her. Silence. He almost laughed out loud at the thought that hearing Zin'talia complain all the time was normal and that he missed it. He led a strange life. Would Taelia really want to share it?

"*You won't know unless you ask her.*" Saerille's gentle thought intruded.

He brightened. "*Hey,*" he thought, "*does this mean we can still talk? Across distance?*"

"*Seems like it,*" she thought in return, and he smiled in response.

"Well, someone is in a better mood this afternoon." Tyrone's voice cut across his reflections.

"I feel much better. As I said, I wasn't sure what was real and what was not. Things don't seem so out of control now."

"Good. In that case, you can have visitors. Jason and Tagerill are waiting outside; you can have fifteen minutes with them and then you can see Taelia."

Jason and Tagerill entered his room, relief on their faces

as they saw a clear-eyed and centred man in place of the feverish wreck they had seen the previous day.

"Well, Tyrone works wonders," Jason said. "You don't look the same person."

Jerrol grinned. "That he does. I'd shake your hands and say thank you, but it's all a bit awkward now. I'll figure it out."

"I think Jenkins is the one to thank. He got you out and stopped you bleeding to death," Tagerill's deep voice corrected him.

"Ah, yes, he must feel a bit displaced with the rest of his unit missing."

Lord Jason chuckled. "He seems to think he's been reassigned to the Captain's Guard, so he isn't too worried."

"Good. I need all the help I can get."

"Nikols will be complaining soon. We keep stealing his men," Tagerill said.

"I'll send him some of my apprentices. They need to widen their experience," Jason said with a laugh.

Jerrol looked at him. "I think that is a great idea. We should rotate the men, so they meet more of their counterparts and understand how they work. Makes it easier when we need to co-ordinate across the Watches. If the rumbles from Elothia continue, we could have an all-out war. Having consistent working practices will make all the difference. Once I am back in the Justice's office, I'll suggest we get our captains together for discussion and agree on how it could work."

Jason stared at him. "You really are going to take over the Justice's Office?"

"Didn't the king announce it? Haven't you had any dispatches from them?"

"Nothing for at least a month."

"Well, I'll fix that for sure, and if you don't hear anything from me for a week, then send a runner and ask why."

"Yes, commander," Jason replied, and they all broke out into laughter.

The laughter faded, and Jerrol looked up at them. "What news of Birlerion?"

Tagerill's face tightened. "There was no sign of him, but he's alive, Captain. The Ascendants must have taken him."

Jerrol closed his eyes. "I shouldn't have taken him up there. I led him into an ambush."

"Well, it was a good job you did or you wouldn't be here now. From what I hear he took out your ambush and the Ascendants," Jason said.

Jerrol rolled his head on his pillow. "Tagerill?"

"He is resilient. They won't find it easy to break him down." Tagerill was silent a moment and then he asked, "Do you have any idea where the Ascendants were going? Did Ain'uncer say anything?"

Jerrol tried to remember. "It's all a blur. Jenkins said something about him planning a trip. Ask him." He relaxed back on his pillows, exhausted. He raised his arm off the bed. "I'll be rehabilitating for a while."

"Chryllion's sentinal has offered to help with that," Tagerill said.

"I'll accept his offer gladly," Jerrol said with a washed-out smile. "Oh, and visit Saerille before we leave. She is back in her tree. Jason, she will be ready to support Chryllion in a couple of days. She just needs a little time to readjust."

Jerrol tried to keep his face straight as she made a rude noise in his head. *"Stop eavesdropping,"* he thought to her.

"Yes, sir," she thought back, laughing.

A smile blossomed on Tagerill's face. "Saerille is alright? That is great news. Wait till I tell Chryllion!"

They were interrupted by Tyrone. "Time, gentlemen. We don't want to exhaust our Captain in one go."

"He's a commander now," Jason said, eyes twinkling. "Commander of the King's Justice."

"Is he, now? Then it's time for the commander to rest before his next visitor."

"Jason, I'll send a report to you on Vespers and Terolia. I need to arrange a scribe. There is no way I can write it all left-handed. Tagerill, come back in the morning. We need to talk about waystones."

"Yes, Captain," Tagerill said as he rose under Tyrone's glare.

Jason corrected him as they left the room. "He's a commander now."

"He will always be the Captain, being a commander doesn't change that," Tagerill replied. They continued to argue as they left the infirmary.

Jerrol scowled at Tyrone. "How long will it be before fifteen minutes of talking doesn't exhaust me?"

Tyrone smiled and patted his shoulder. "Longer than you'll like, but if you build up gradually, you'll regain your strength. I think your activities over the last month in Terolia have contributed to your general debilitation. This is not just a result of your hand. However, it is a contributing factor."

"Not surprising, I suppose. A chance to sit behind a desk for a while, then, and have a rest," Jerrol murmured, closing his eyes. Exhaustion ambushed him and he drifted off to sleep.

She sat next to him when he woke. A smile spread across his face as he opened his eyes. Taelia held his left hand, stroking it gently. The impression from her kiss was still warm on his skin. He basked in the glow that warmed his heart whenever she was near. "Tali," he said.

She turned her face towards him and smiled the smile

that was just for him. He was a fool; how could he live another day without her?

"Jerrol, how are you?"

"Much better for seeing you."

"Truly, Jerrol? You're not just saying that?"

"I wouldn't lie to you, Tali. You'd know, anyway." He laughed. "You can always see straight through me."

"Not always."

"I'm sorry," he said, watching her face.

"What for?"

He had surprised her. She didn't realise how much of what she thought she expressed on her face.

"For not being there. For not writing. For not saying I love you often enough." Jerrol gripped her hand.

Taelia hesitated a heartbeat, her face an open book. Her beautiful eyes shone with tears. "Oh, Jerrol, I love you too. Anyway, I'm the one who should be saying sorry." Her tears fell on his hand.

"Don't cry," he said, trying to disentangle his hand long enough to wipe her tears away. "This is going to be a darned inconvenience."

"What is?"

"Only having one useful hand!"

Her face screwed up in distress.

"Hey, don't be upset; it will heal. I'll get used it. My writing may be atrocious for a while, but things will improve."

"Jerrol, do you forgive me? For pushing you away that day in Vespers, for hurting you the other day."

"Sweetheart, you've never pushed me away, and if you hadn't cauterised my fingers, I probably wouldn't be here today. You didn't hurt me, Ain'uncer did."

Her face tightened again, displacing that beautiful glow. "I don't understand why he would do such a thing."

"Let's not talk about him. We have more interesting things to talk about." Jerrol pulled her nearer.

"Like what?" she asked, a smile lighting up her face.

"Like this," he said as he kissed her.

Checking in on Jerrol a little while later, Tyrone smiled to himself. The healing was progressing nicely.

Two days later, Tagerill escorted Jerrol and Taelia to Old Vespers. Jerrol argued that only his hand was injured; the rest of him was alright, especially since Chryllion's sentinal had helped speed his healing.

Jason and Tyrone helped Jerrol into his clothes, the shirt and jacket a larger size than normal to get over the splint, but both Jason and Tyrone watched in awe as Jerrol's borrowed clothes shimmered into his usual uniform. The larger size made no difference in the end. Tyrone strapped his arm up, making sure he wouldn't be able to use it. Jerrol finally laughed. "Peace, Tyrone. I'll never get out of it on my own. You don't have to truss me up."

Jerrol agreed to Tagerill's escort on condition that he returned to guard Alyssa and Jennery in Deepwater and stayed with Lady Miranda. Jennery would need all the help he could get to whip his forces into shape, and anyway, Jerrol would have Marianille and Niallerion to keep an eye on him in Vespers.

They stepped out of the waystone behind the Chapterhouse, and Taelia bent over, hugging her stomach. "I don't think speed compensates for the discomfort," she gasped, her face pale and sweating. Jerrol rubbed her back and offered the canteen. Jenkins fared no better, and he groaned into the ground as Tagerill stood over him until they had recovered enough to mount their horses.

They clattered into the palace courtyard, and Jerrol

handed off the reins of his borrowed horse as Darris appeared at the top of the steps to take him to the king. Jerrol stopped just over the threshold as he was pierced by the glaring blue eyes of the king, though the king's expression softened as he took in the state of his commander.

"Jerrol," the king said mildly. "You'd better sit down before you fall over."

Bowing briefly, Jerrol walked over to the chair that the king indicated. If he knelt, he didn't think he would be able to stand again, and it seemed the king had some inkling of his exhaustion as he sat in his chair.

"I think you have a lot of explaining to do. But first, you're hurt. Do you need a healer?"

"Thank you, sire. No. It's been treated. It will heal in time," Jerrol replied with a slight smile.

"You'd better tell me what you've been up to," Benedict said.

"Didn't Marianille or Niallerion report what happened in Terolia?"

The king snorted. "Marianille presented me with the papers and Niallerion was too terrified to be coherent. He just about managed to get out that I now rule Terolia and that you would explain before he bolted."

"I suppose it was a bit unfair, expecting them to carry the news."

"A bit. Why don't you start at the beginning?"

The only time the king interrupted was to ask, "What made you think you could annex a whole country for me?"

"I was so overwhelmed by the enormity of the Ascendant's network. The fact that all the Families must have been involved in some way or another; that they had let go of the fundamental principles upholding their society and weren't falling over themselves to reinstate them. I thought they didn't deserve to be in power."

"Simple as that?"

"Well, not at the time. I think having had time to think about it on the way home has clarified my reasoning. They need someone overseeing them; someone who can keep an eye on the bigger picture and not become so insulated as they had done. I think they will do a better job of managing internal politics now. And I was furious about what happened at the Telusion mine," Jerrol admitted.

"So I heard. Your anger was … frightening was the word used; I believe."

Jerrol reddened. "It was the only way to break through their shell of self-interest."

"Well, it worked. And may I say, the accords are a masterpiece. We have much to discuss, but not right now." The king looked at him, keenly. "And after all that, you went to the Watch Towers?" The king's face was grim as Jerrol finished his report.

Jerrol shrugged. "It'll heal," he said wryly. "If it hadn't been for Birlerion, I wouldn't be here at all. We have to find him."

"We will. But first you need to look to yourself." Rising, the king pressed a button on his desk and met Darris at the door. He spoke softly and returned to Jerrol. Jerrol waited, content to drift. Exhaustion hovered, waiting to ambush him again.

Darris entered the room with another glass on a small silver tray; the glass was filled with amber liquid. The king passed the glass to Jerrol. "Drink it."

The king watched as Jerrol drank. The brandy eased the tension in his body, and Jerrol relaxed against the back of his chair.

"I think they'll find that the price to pay for all their actions will be too high when it comes time for them to account for it," the king said. "Right. You are off duty and on convalescence leave until I say otherwise. I will work with Anders and Ambassador Nil'ano to make the accords work.

"You will rest and spend some time with your young lady. When you've recovered, we'll speak again. Bryce and your Sentinals can hold the fort for a while longer. Darris will show you to your room. Healer Francis will be up to see you shortly. Don't argue, do as you're told," King Benedict said sternly as Jerrol opened his mouth to protest.

"Yes, sire," Jerrol said, placing the empty glass on the table. He rose, his exhaustion visible.

"And Jerrol? Thank you. I am honoured to have you as my commander and Oath Keeper," the king said formally before he dismissed him into the healer's care.

Jenkins ended up helping him into the bath. He had appointed himself as Jerrol's aide, and he helped Jerrol undress and get into the water. Jerrol awkwardly held his hand up as he was sluiced down and then wrapped in warm towels. Jenkins helped him into his nightclothes and into bed. He obviously wasn't going anywhere tonight. A light tap on the door heralded the arrival of Healer Francis.

Francis looked at him from under grey, bushy eyebrows. "Well, looks like you've been busy, then."

Jerrol scowled, feeling somewhat disadvantaged. "I'm already in bed, and I'll have no trouble sleeping."

"I think we'll make sure of that," the healer said, sitting on the side of the bed. "Drink that." He handed over a vial as he began to unwrap the bandages on Jerrol's right hand. Jerrol sighed and drank the vile liquid, knowing that he was not going to have a choice. His eyelids drooped almost immediately. The Healer distantly tutted before rewrapping Jerrol's hand in clean bandages.

Whilst Jerrol slept, King Benedict interrogated everyone

he could find, and that evening, he sat discussing Jerrol with Healer Francis.

Francis shrugged. "Traumatic experiences affect people in different ways. We'll have to keep an eye on him, and, to be honest, keeping him away from his work too long could be just as detrimental. It's fortunate his young lady is here to distract him for a while." He knew the king wanted him to tell him exactly when Jerrol would be fit for duty, but it was too early to commit to anything. "We'll have a better idea in a week. Let's see how he copes."

Jerrol awoke the next morning, still tired even after a good night's sleep. The exhaustion crept through his body and he deliberated about not getting up. He lay in bed, worrying about Birlerion. Everyone kept saying that Birlerion was strong, but their expressions were bleak as they said it; more hope than conviction. Jerrol knew Birlerion was more vulnerable than they had realised, his experiences piling up like Jerrol's and just as overwhelming.

As his mind drifted towards memories he didn't want to think about, he made an effort to get up. He began to dress before he could be stopped, deliberately concentrating on fastening the buttons with his left hand. He was sure they were all askew. Leaving his room, he found Taelia seated at a table, eating breakfast. She raised her face and smiled at him. "Good morning."

"Good morning. We are to be spoilt, are we? Breakfast delivered to our rooms?"

"And so, they should. You are to be cosseted."

"As long as you are doing the cosseting, I'll be happy."

"Deal," she said with a coy smile that he couldn't resist. He bent and kissed her. Taelia leaned into the kiss, her arms reaching for him, and then he embraced her, their bodies pressed tight together.

"You need to eat some breakfast," Taelia murmured against his lips.

"In a minute," Jerrol replied as they tottered over to the settee.

Jerrol was stretched out on the settee, Taelia hovering above him, redoing his buttons by touch, when the door to their sitting-room opened and Jenkins arrived with a fresh pot of coffee.

"Miss, he's supposed to be resting. Healer's orders," Jenkins said, trying to keep a straight face as he placed the pot on the table.

"He's horizontal, isn't he?" Taelia said with a laugh. "Count that as a win!"

"Yes, miss, if you say so." Jenkins backed out of the room with alacrity.

"Oh dear." Taelia smiled down at Jerrol. "He thinks we are depraved."

"He wouldn't dare," Jerrol said, pulling her towards him.

45

SOMEWHERE OFF THE COAST OF ELOTHIA

Torsion stared out across the choppy grey water to the passing Elothian coastline, a frown on his face. He leaned against the boat's wooden rail and inhaled the moist sea air; a blessing after the dry, dusty stone of the Watch Towers. He had let Jerrol escape. Jerrol! The Lady's Captain. Who would have believed it?

His brothers were not going to be amused when he finally arrived. He idly wondered where Var'geris was as he stared out across the sea. Var'geris had not been at the meeting point, and they had set sail without him. Ain'uncer was already upset with him for detouring into Terolia to find out what Jerrol had been up to. He should have known better, but to have discovered what Jerrol was doing in Terolia might have mitigated the disastrous news he was bringing home to his brother Ascendants.

Well, he had a Sentinal to tell him everything now. The Sentinal would be a mine of useful information, if only they could get it out of him. Torsion flexed his bruised hands; his knuckles were raw and sore. Shrugging his shoulders, he tried to ease the tension. He admitted to himself that he had got a little carried away, taking his frustration out on the man who had spoiled their plans. It was fortunate that the sailors had interfered, preventing him from pulverizing that stubborn Sentinal; otherwise, he would have lost the Sentinal as well as Jerrol.

He scowled as he thought of Jerrol again; everything was always so easy for him. Everyone liked him, including Taelia. He would not give up on her. She was his. She would see sense in the end.

Torsion tried to relax. He had tensed up again and his back ached, along with his hands. He closed his eyes and listened to the seagulls wheeling overhead, letting the scent of the sea erase the memories of the Watch Towers.

A seaman hovered behind him and he stiffened, pushing himself off the railing.

"Uh, Mr. Tor'asion, sir. The captain says we'll be docking in one hour, sir. And, uh, your prisoner is conscious." Duty done; the seaman retreated.

Tor'asion straightened, his shoulders squaring, his face firming. The hot anger transformed into cold calculation. He blamed Ain'uncer. He shouldn't have left Jerrol. Instead, that Sentinal, Birlerion, had drawn them both in and it had taken both of them to overpower him and carry him away, and in so doing, they had let Jerrol escape. He should have let Ain'uncer die, he thought. He flexed his fist again. Well, the Sentinal would pay.

It was soothing to hear his real name: Tor'asion. It was like relaxing into a familiar set of clothes that fit for once. He had been hiding beneath Torsion for too many years. He needed to survive just a little bit longer. He needed to come up with a good story to explain what had happened; one that would gain him sympathy.

And then there was the Veil. It was well and truly sealed now. They hadn't been able to find any points of weakness.

All those centuries of gradually breaching it, wasted. They had charged a few crystals but nowhere near enough

He thought about the Grand Duke of Elothia, his face grim. Their final chance. Sul'enne had been preparing him. Maybe this was the plan they should have followed first. Smash Vespiri with force instead of allowing them to awaken to the threat.

They had lost the element of surprise, but Iss'aren had been persuasive. A peaceful coup would reap them many more rewards than violence. Well, the ex-chancellor would have as much to explain as he would. Iss'aren had failed at 'peaceful'; let's see what they could do with violence. Tor'a-sion clenched his fist and slammed it against the rail. They would prevail.

THE END

The adventure continues in Book Three:
Sentinals Justice. Available September 7th, 2021.

Sign up to my newsletter via: linktr.ee/helengarraway to find out first when it is available and to download a free novella in the same world. Book 0.5: *Sentinals Stirring*

If you have a moment and you enjoyed reading *Sentinals Rising*, then please do leave a review and tell other fantasy readers what you enjoyed.

Reviews are so important to independent authors to drive visibility and to help us to continue publishing our books.

Thank you for your support.
Helen Garraway
March 2021

Other books in the series:
Novella 0.5 Sentinals Stirring
Book One: Sentinals Awaken
Book Two: Sentinals Rising
Book Three: Sentinals Justice

ACKNOWLEDGMENTS

I am so excited to have finished my second novel in the Sentinal series. An accomplishment I wouldn't have achieved without the support of some very special people.

First, my thanks go to my wonderful daughter, Jennifer, who has supported all my dreams to write and publish my novels. This one is for you!

My very good friend, Kaye Adams, who is my sounding board, and keeps me sane when I go off track.

Michael Strick, my ever faithful beta reader and Jill Wells who helped hunt down those darned typos. If you find any lurking, the fault is mine.

Jeff Brown of Jeff Brown Graphics (jeffbrowngraphics.-com) designed my gorgeous cover and Tom from Fictive Designs (https://fictive-designs.com/maps) drew the wonderful map of Terolia.

And finally, thank you to my street team: Sloane, Eva, David, Rosalyn, Andrew, Jami, Carmen, Patty and Stephanie.

Thank you for all your support! This book wouldn't be the wonderful story it is without you.

Printed in Great Britain
by Amazon